CHARLES BAYFIELD

Charles Bayfield grew up on the north coast of Cornwall, attended the local comprehensive school and studied German literature in Birmingham. After a string of dead end jobs in Hamburg and London, he found work as an advertising copywriter.

Having spent most of his adult life in the down at heel London suburb of Cricklewood, he has encountered plenty of characters whose stories furnish this book.

He currently lives with his family in Tasmania.

Charles Bayfield

CLOWNBURN

Based on a hundred true stories and a lie

For Kevin Hassett, who also
walked these roads

A traveller was walking along a beach whose sand was littered with starfish. In the distance, he noticed a lone figure. As he drew nearer, he saw that it was an old man. The old man bent down, picked up a starfish and threw it into the sea.

"Why are you doing this?" the traveller asked. "The starfish are food for the birds, nature has provided them a feast."

"I don't like birds," the old man said, and taking another starfish which was probably dead anyway and casting it back into the sea, he threw his head back and laughed.

Kilburn, 26 March 2016

Hussein Hassan runs down twelve half flights of stairs pushing on a metal handrail laminated in chipped, black plastic and, using Newtonian laws to propel his eight-year-old body swiftly to the ground, hurls himself at the heavy dark blue fire door with its oblong panels of unbreakable mesh glass. Once it has swung open the requisite inches, Hassan squeezes his bony brown body through the gap and runs along uncut spring grass, past towering Falkirk and Edinburgh Houses and out onto the main A5 trunk road, heading north towards Kilburn, Edgware and St. Albans. To the east, the last remaining terraces of old Kilburn, to the west, the brownbrick wall of the school where bespectacled head teacher, Philip Lawrence was felled by the blade of Woo Sang Wu gangster, Learco Chindamo, a grey stone plaque mourning his passing. Hassan's grey Asda George trainers pound cracked precast concrete slabs as he runs towards Carlton Vale; Edwardian mansion blocks and the old people's home to his right, the high, brutal brick of Dibdin House with its twin crests to his left. Just a few blocks behind Dibdin, another survivor from an earlier time; St Augustine's, the great ecclesiastical palace founded and led for thirty seven years by white-bearded Tractarian, Richard Carr Kirkpatrick, bath stone with red brick dressing, its foundation slab laid by Bishop Charles James Blomfield in 1879.

It is the month of blossoms when every tree from Kilburn north to Cricklewood, east to Hampstead, and west to Willesden shimmers in its bridal bloom. And today, Saturday, is the day when the delicate arboreal mantle is at its pinkest and whitest, when petals float to the ground like April snow to lie in small drifts where eddies have gathered them on the concrete paving, yet to rot or be shovelled away by a council sweeper. A convoy of three red double decker buses pass on their journey north where the wide and straight carriageway known as Maida Vale becomes Kilburn High Road. Once, it was Watling Street, a path hacked through the Forest of Middlesex, a vast tract of ancient oaks stretching north from the city wall at Houndsditch as far as the Harrow Weald.

In one hand, Hussein Hassan swings a blue plastic bag containing two samosas for his uncle's lunch, and a prepaid envelope to the Brent Council Housing Department in which scanned and printed documentation proves his family have been granted asylum under Immigration Rule 334. Thirty metres beneath the boy's feet, a southbound Bakerloo Line train races through a tunnel, dragging among its human cargo twenty-three-year-old Emily Whitehorn, still dressed for Friday. Whitehorn stares at an overhead advertisement for a hair loss clinic on Harley Street, wondering what the 'tricho' means in the word 'trichology'. Her head hurts from yesterday's wine. "It is what it is," she tells herself, resolving not to reply to the two texts which the newly lovelorn Gavin Finney has already sent her. She only slept with him to forget. Delete. Delete contact. Done

Hussein Hassan runs past the Queens Arms pub, built, bombed and rebuilt. Today a mess of shops line the western edge of the wide blacktop where a tollhouse charged two shillings for a six-horse coach and a pair of pennies for a horse or mule. Eight-year-old Hussein Hassan, born in Las Khorey, Somali city of legend where, while rebels attacked his father's fort in 1492, watchful servants hid the infant prince, Gerad Ali Doble in the stinking hold of a dhow bound for Aden. The same year the pirate Colón wrought evil on the land he named Hispaniola. Ali Doble 'the fire bringer', for once he had attained his majority, it was he who brought back gunpowder and cannon from his exile among the Yemeni caliphs. Ali Doble, Warsangali chieftain whose ruined redstone citadel bakes beneath Somali skies on the edge of the city where Darod factory workers fleeing civil war cradled the new born Hussein Hassan, eight years, three months and seventeen days before he sprints past Raina Bechara and her sister-in-law Carla Taha as they walk past a Ladbrokes bookmaker's with Carla's eleven year old daughter, Fatima. Raina wearing a peach-coloured silk headscarf and black Dior sunglasses that make her resemble a fat, startled insect. She talks loudly in Arabic, angry that her uncle has overlooked her husband for promotion, choosing instead her brother, useless Khalil with his flat feet and lazy eye and God knows what else he forgot to give him. Carla nodding but not listening, her mind on her sick mother; an irregular heartbeat and water retention that makes her feet swell. A waft of Raina's perfume bringing her back, so aggressive on the nose and she always wears so much of it. Fatima neither caring nor listening to brash, old fashioned Auntie Ray; watching instead the skinny boy running towards them.

Past the nineteen sixties telephone exchange on the eastern side of the street that was once a fire station, past the Islamic Centre that was once a picture palace, Hussein Hassan runs, bag swinging, his ten pound blue jeans from Peacock a blur, across the junction where the road named Kilburn Priory hooks behind the glass and steel Marriott Hotel. Here he runs full pelt into a stationary clown, an awful green-haired, white-faced clown who breaks from whatever reverie he was caught in, sneers down at the child through face paint and kohl, and the boy shits himself.

A thousand years before, a swineherd walked these roads, hollow eyed and expressionless, shambling over the mud and shit, the street a mess of cart ruts and pocked with animal hooves. Once, the paved slabs of the Roman via had formed a smooth white strip from Verulamium to Londinium then south to Durovernum Cantiacorum. When Rome retreated, it became a highway for cows and sheep and the occasional foot traveller. Here, Saxon soldiers ankle deep in ooze stepped over fallen trees as they marched north to battle the Danish prince, Cnut. Not even a hut on either side of the track then, nor any village. The boy pulls away, and runs on past the clown, tears of shame welling, to his uncle's shop, to the toilet at the back, to clean the micturate from his legs.

There was once a bridge across the stream here. Stone with a Gothic arch, a single span built eight centuries ago by Prior Paul. Ironstone blocks, each precisely cut to form a voussoir and laid one atop the other, supported by a wooden centring. Once the keystone bore the weight, the centring was struck away with great ceremony to reveal the pointed bow, Paul himself wielding the great hammer and landing the first blow. The bridge replaced the thick logs with rough planks nailed crossways that had carried the lane across the burn for centuries. Tall elms and ashes leaned in on either side, clumps of hazel and holly and the occasional cherry, plumes of grey smoke climbing the quiet sky from distant cottages. The race known as the Cunebourne ran south across the centuries to the Serpentine pool until the city buried it and Bazalgette paved it over to form the Ranelagh sewer, a roaring culvert of shit and piss gunnelling into the Thames and rolling with bloated rats away to the cold brown sea. It was on the banks of this sacred brook that the saintly Godwyn fished for pike, turbot, and trout with barely a single passer-by on the road and none who would step off it to disturb her prayers. The river now invisible, though an ear placed to a grating outside a boarded up pub on West End Lane after a few days' rain will hear its undead spirit roar.

The clown is in no hurry and stands looking up at the great glass hotel. Before the Marriott dominated Kilburn's southern gateway, it was called the Plaza. Before it was a hotel, the corner was home to a venue where excited children dashed around in darkness shooting one another with lasers. The building was formerly the Essoldo cinema but before it screened its first matinee, it had been the Empire Theatre, designed by W G R Sprague and opening in 1908 with a performance by the Arthur Lloyd Trio. The Empire replaced a row of nondescript nineteenth century terracing built on what was once southern part of the pleasure gardens adjoining the nearby Bell public house. Prior to that, it was pasture and before they cleared the woods to make land for grazing, a stand of oaks in a vast and ancient forest. The clown knows this because he was there.

Two hundred years ago, he watched as the first houses rose up along Abbey Road and West End Lane, scarring a landscape that had been his for centuries; obscuring his view of the sacred fields. When the London and North Eastern Railway carved through what had once been priory lands, he loitered at the coins, tessellated tiles, ornately patterned keys, and the clapper of a bell that had been arranged with human bones on a rough blanket at the road's edge, awaiting a delegation from the British Museum. He picked up a rough piece of pottery and touched it to his lips until a foreman ordered him to drop it and hop it.

Two weeks before, a motorcyclist bled out here. Three police cars and an ambulance, blue light adding a chill to the already cold predawn. The rider died as soon as the Toyota Land cruiser rolled over his head, but at least it was a bit of theatre. A nearby Ford Transit T350 Luton van blocks the bus lane while its driver brings freshly laundered sheets to the hotel, leaving a southbound 98 bus unable to pass. As the clown watches the van driver who seems impervious to the obstruction, a small brown boy carrying a blue plastic bag runs into him, then races away as if he has just seen a ghost.

On the western side of the road opposite the hotel towers gaunt Tollgate House, a nineteen sixties high rise built on the ruins of a bombed-out bus depot, its name anchored to a past the city has destroyed. Marion Stringer hurries under its shadow on her way to holy Rosary at St Augustine's. Stringer running late and texting as she walks, reminding Denis that the man is coming around at 11.30 to buy the gym ball. Denis pronounced in the French way, from St Denis, the Christian mystic who carried his head a mile after he had been martyred, his mouth still uttering hallelujahs and which gifted Australians the city of Sydney. Stupid thing takes up so much space and it's such a palaver to inflate. Eyes down, Stringer narrowly avoids the bulky form of Bertram Bancroft on his way to a shift at Chaïwalla, the Indian restaurant at the boutique Maitrise Hotel where the wine importer, Harris Pechard lived in a fine townhouse with his wife, four sons, a maid and three staff, and beat them all.

The clown had no intention to scare the child, but Hassan is not the first. He may, however be the last. As all good things come to an end, so too do the bad and, before the day is out if he so wishes, the child can enjoy a ringside seat at a final performance beyond any that ever graced the stage of the Essoldo. The Marriott consumes an entire block and at its far corner, where Greville Road meets the High Road, a plane tree casts confetti like an ebullient wedding guest on the grey slabs. As the boy runs off to clean himself, the man in the greatcoat and greasepaint walks slowly north. He glances up narrow Greville Road where distant trees also bloom. Greville after the childless nineteenth century politician and soldier whose relatives divvied up his estate, amassing gold from developers whose rapacious streets and railway lines gobbled up Kilburn's tranquil Victorian parkland. A she wolf rested here once, so close to him that he could see her grey-blue eyes, licking her paws for a few moments before disappearing back into the birchwood. It was November and he had been gathering leaf litter to make winter beds for cattle, one of the many chores they had given him, and he pulled his load on a two handled wooden sledge. The wolf was his animal, he was named after it but they were far from kindred. The beast stared at him, tongue lolling. He was alone and a good hour from the village. If he ran, the wolf would give chase and he had no weapon save a short knife in his belt. He waited as she turned. Perhaps she had already feasted on pig. United in name only, he watched with dry mouth and beating heart as the animal padded away into the trees. What he would give for there to be woods today, even those where wolves roam.

Dieter Thiesman, fifty seven, short grey hair and wearing a maroon hoodie under his dark blue gilet warms his hands with a takeout coffee as he waits at the automatic doors of the library centre facing the hotel across Greville Road. Thiesman staring at glass that doesn't slide open and which

17

won't spring into action until 11am on Tuesday, the German not realising that it is a bank holiday weekend in England. Not that he is here to read books. The coffee too is just a screen. Since the accident, every hour is a happy hour apart from the one where he's just woken. At least the library is a change of scene and it's warm. An Evian bottle full of gin and a pack of Tramadol. Thiesman checks the opening hours on the sign. Disappointment turns to action. The Bell should open soon, and he looks around for someone to ponce a cigarette.

The clown has cigarettes but steps around the corner into Greville Road before Thiesman can spot him. He looks across to the west side of the High Road at a print shop, the curry house and an Italian chicken bar and tries to picture a red roofed farmhouse with ivy thick to the gables, an elm tree, two thatched barns and a lane stretching across the meadows to Willesden where the old manor house sat in over one hundred and sixty acres of pasture. He sees jackdaws on chimney pots, hawthorn hedges in bloom and an anxious wagtail hurrying to feed her infant cuckoo. A mare and her foal in the next field as a distant dog barked before everything properly broke. With Thiesman gone, he walks back onto the trunk road classified in 1922 by the Ministry of Transport as the A5. At the time Harris Pechard took a leather strap from a packing case and whipped his wife Catherine in the nearby town house that is now a hotel, the ground on which he is standing was a woodman's yard adjoining the stables of the Old Red Lion. Now it's the library and an upmarket apartment block. Unless foul weather prevents him, the clown passes here every other morning on his journey north, and every second afternoon as he travels south. No purpose other than to see and to be, to feed on the fallenness, to inhale the decay, to witness the cancer metastasise around the pristine heart of a glade which, to him, once seemed like Eden.

A Belisha beacon blinks outside the library where twenty-seven-year old Tarik Majid crosses on his way to meet his cousin brother Malik. Perhaps the crossing is a tribute to Belisha himself who lived in a street behind the Marriott, one of a maze of lanes built over the ancient priory lands where eminent Georgians, Victorians and Edwardians composed librettos, penned plays, sculpted, painted portraits, danced and wrote poetry. Belisha counted among his neighbours statesmen, sea captains and impresarios. The draper, Dickins who with his partner John Prichard Jones opened a department store on Regent Street. John Spedan Lewis who opened his own on nearby Oxford Street. Samuel Chappell, the music publisher and Charles Douglas Home, editor of *The Times*. Here was Sarah Garrard, widow of the jeweller, Robert. Here Henry Vesting Jones, Captain of the Naiad which towed the stricken Belleisle back to Gibraltar in the fury of the storm that followed Trafalgar. John Gutzon Mothe Borglum whose dynamite chiselled faces of four presidents from the rock of Mount Rushmore lived on Mortimer Place. Orwell was a boy here, H.G. Wells taught in a school on Mortimer Crescent and the barrister, Leslie Isaac Hore-Belisha who became Minister of Transport walked these roads. The clown passed them all on his north and southward travels; some he recognised. Once while he rested on his haunches outside the Westminster Bank, Spedan Lewis handed him sixpence, thinking him a vagrant, and he played checkers in the Old Black Lion with Captain Jones who had no teeth and whose hand shook.

Majid walks past the Starbucks beneath the apartments next to the library. Wearing a grey hoodie and grey sweatpants, without the black sleeveless puffer he might be an inmate of Wormwood Scrubs or Pentonville. He glances up at pouting lingerie models pasted to the boarded up pub next to the café. Two half-naked women side by side, staring confidently across the thoroughfare where children can see, their immaculate skin, ripped abdomens and full lips a siren song. He tries to fight the impulse but looks anyway. One woman standing, one reclining, breasts balled into bra cups, one in a corset, one in a two piece, images burned into his retinas in the split second in which he glanced, and logged in his hippocampus. Yet another transgression for which to beg forgiveness from Allah, who sees everything.

The plywood boards replace the glass of what, until recently, was a pub called the Westbury known for six centuries before that as the Red Lion. As Tarik Majid walks on towards the nearby Tesco Express supermarket, the clown looks up at the building, one of the few constants beyond autumn leaf fall, winter frosts and the bloom of spring trees. Above the fly posted boards, an impressive moulded lion surveys the street from beneath a plasterwork arch, attitude statant to sinister gardant. Tincture; body and face sanguine with mane argent; the grandiose folly of fin de siècle master builder, Hieronymus Oldney. The original tavern had been a freestanding wood and wattle affair, thrown up in the early 1600s by the sons of a Willesden farmer. Trade was steady and the road led all the way to Canterbury, bringing with it many thirsty pilgrims. The clown remembers when the pub was a hostium, a guesthouse for the nearby priory whose crumbling ruins stood surrounded by meadow, until it finally tumbled down during the reign of mad King George. Pilgrims on their way north to the shrine at Willesden and who lodged with the priory nuns drank here or at the Cock, the street a near constant stream of penitents seeking the blessings of the black Madonna. The clown holed up here for three days during one of the great frosts, when those who could reach the Thames played ninepins, ate beef from an ox roasted by the cripple Atkins, and drank ale poured by the monks of Greyfriars on the river's frozen crust. A good fire kept him and his fellow travellers warm and the innkeeper poured mugs of hot, honeyed wine, set a table with victuals and prepared him a bed, the first he had slept in for over a century. And now it's gone to shit like everything else.

The clown hovers at the entrance to the Tesco Metro and watches Dinesh Galogre slip a bar of Cadbury's Dairy Milk into his pocket while pretending to survey the miniature spirits on the high shelf behind cashier, Amrit Kaur. Kaur turning to reach a bottle of Glen's vodka, Galogre snatching a handful of Twirls and punching them into his open bag. Kaur scanning the bottle and turning the screen bearing the price towards his customer. Six pounds thirty nine.

"Is too much."

Galogre turning and leaving Kaur with the bottle in his hand, Danila Ramos with her back to him, stacking shelves with Hobnobs and chocolate digestives, paid too little to keep an eye on stock that walks out of the store in the pockets of Georgian day labourers. Or to care.

Galogre exits the store and crosses the road to the junction of Cambridge Avenue where he jiggles a bike leaning against a lamp post, checking whether it is chained. The clown looks up the avenue. Along its northern edge, the guts of Cambridge and Wells Court stand wrapped in scaffolding and polythene; Wells Court after the healing wells behind the Old Bell, a derelict sixties low rise where nineties ganglords peddled smack, hid guns under their mothers' beds and injected poison into the necrotic veins of the city. Let it rot. What comes around goes around. We rise and we fail and we fall again; Kilburn a wound that no drug can numb, no restorative waters can heal.

These precious roads. He breathes in. No beech mast or birch sap, just diesel, the tang of chicken shops and curry. A repulsive stench that overcomes him whenever he passes, knowing that he is the reason Galogre steals, that Thiesman is a drunk and that Danila Ramos is paid seven pounds twenty an hour working for a company whose annual profits total more than a billion. He has stood by, powerless as it fell, a firestarter doomed to watch the horror of his handiwork for an eternity, each new catastrophe another faggot on the fire. Why won't it die? Maybe today they'll all go out in a blaze of glory.

The clown looks to his right. Springfield Road. Street names all that is left to describe the paradise he knew. Where today's wanderer is afforded excellent views of the gaunt, grey towers of distant Abbey Estate, the pleasure gardens began. Elegant willows and manicured lawns stretching out behind the Old Bell; spreading north beyond the present railway lines. A fenced off glade where stockinged and bewigged players coaxed allegros, adagios and largos from viol, lute and harpsichord. Kilburn Wells, where gentlefolk from the city came to hear Vivaldi, Scarlatti and Handel, and taste reviving waters from a spring that bubbled up beneath a brick arch beside the pub. Inside, a great room filled with the elegant and the mannered, Handel himself once visiting with his niece, a wan girl with dark curls and a slight limp who the clown waylaid on the pretence of asking the name of an air by Rameau. The two walked between twin oaks, conversation polite but intention clear, he admiring her for her boldness; she thrilled by the sin of it, finding a rough stone shed where tools were kept, the clown bending her over a wooden sawhorse, hitching up her skirts and enjoying amorous and consensual congress with her.

In later years, the musicians packed away their instruments and the great room at the Bell gave way to bar stools and tables for loo, crib and dice. Sometimes, they cleared the floor, scattered sawdust and marked out a rough square. He fought a butcher here, a lumpen man with a lazy eye and breastettes, more flab than heft, an easy contest when you know you cannot lose. The clown barely landed a punch; only when it bored him not to capitalise on the lurching anger and brawn trying to pummel him did he crack the man in the teeth. The cheers of the crowd, the explosion of sweat when the giant's fist smashed into the clown's face, the blood, his head under the man's arm, thumbs in his eye sockets for there were few rules and none to keep them. The righteous pain, his foot in the brute's groin, the man's howl, a raised barstool, then blackness. Waking where he had been thrown on the floor of an anteroom, a rough cloth over him and a wooden beaker for water. The crack of bones reordering, sinews mending, flesh healing. Running his tongue across his teeth and finding them all intact. He stepped back into the bar and seated himself next to the triumphant butcher who, terrified at what he was seeing, spilled grog over his bruised belly. Stumbling away, the man gaped at the clown who now danced around the room collecting money in a cap, for this was the show they had all come to see. He walks past the old pleasure house now, long since rebuilt, brown

Edwardian polished tiles cladding the lower walls. Like the old broom that outlasts new heads and handles, yet remains the old broom, a building has been sloshing ale into mugs hereabouts under the name of Old Bell for four centuries. Before the creep of the city, before the pleasure gardens, before they rediscovered the well then lost it again, in the time before the Conqueror, a woman bathed his wounds in its waters, and he kissed her.

Even if he wanted to drink, the pub is not yet open. The clown steps out into the road, forcing a Red Ford Focus CL to brake sharply, Mario Forzello hitting the horn. Bowing graciously, he continues across to the west side of the street as Forzello swears at him from the safety of his aluminium and steel monocoque. Here, where Cambridge Avenue and Coventry Close converge to spill onto the High Road, a moneylender's where the needy borrow coin until cunning, fortune or hard work place gold in their palms again. Inside, Usman Yiğit stares at the watch that Emmanuel Gbeho has laid on the counter, a gift from his ex-wife. Yiğit naming his best price, even writing it in pencil on a yellow chitty. Gbeho shaking his head. Or there's the jacket. The jacket he wore in a bar in Abuja when Guy Warren had been there, and he bought the man a daiquiri. Warren commenting on the tan jacket with the wide collars and belt that he had bought himself in Accra. It has to be the watch. His knuckles clench by his side.

"Thirty pounds."

Yiğit, hands on the counter shakes his head and stares at the timepiece.

"No thirty pound. Is cheap watch, twenty is good money."

Gbeho looking at the watch and seeing the harridan Vida became, chain smoking and wired to the TV, shouting so hard that she coughed until she retched and blamed him for making her ill. A lifetime away from the day they arrived in Camden, opening the door of their bedsit on Royal College Street, together in London; finally in the real world and him singing an old show tune, dancing and laughing and whooping so loudly that the Russian hit the wall with a shoe. The glow on her face when Kwesi was born, Kwesi who went to America and never came back. Gbeho Amoah who missed his son's birth, too busy meeting Femi in Forest Gate to collect some fake Calvin Klein jeans from the man in China, hurrying to the recovery room on the fifth floor of the Royal Free and Vida, touching the immaculate mocha skin of his son's cheek with a finger.

"Twenty pound, boss."

Yiğit bored already. Gbeho still finding defiance but nothing mattering to Usman Yiğit, only cash.

"It's Rolex".

The corner of Yiğit's mouth twitches.

"Is not Rolex boss."

Gbeho hearing the derision.

"See, no serial number here. Just name."

The watch now a base object, valueless, stripped of meaning in a moneylender's paw, Yiğit reaching into a black leather wallet, taking out a twenty pound note and laying it on the counter.

'Twenty is good money for cheap fake."

The clown presses his forehead against the glass of the moneylender's. Always a good show in here. He watches Gbeho take the purple note with its silver band, ornate swirls, guilloche patterns and Queen's face. Gbeho owes the Afghan, fifty. Hamid's sons, Ibrahim and Ali, meat faced and boneheaded will knock on his door at five and demand the money made from hawking his history. Something

25

delicate and unseeable breaks inside Gbeho who pockets the purple banknote and goes home to fetch the jacket.

The clown pulls back from the window and continues north, crossing Coventry Close. He passes a chicken shop and grabs a plum from the abundant trays of fruit outside an Asian supermarket. The place is riddled with them. He wonders who buys all these apples? The mangos are half rotten. Inventory, money in and money out, food run through the tills then tipped into giant bins at the back of the store; money in the register but not from selling ghee or cans of lychees. Not that he judges; he's as damned as they are, and if they offered him a toot on whatever it is they're really selling, he'd take it. He throws the plum into the air, then another. While the fruit is still airborne, he takes another two pieces and casts them up, catching the first two effortlessly before throwing them up again. He snatches more, the bluish-purple balls rising and falling like a graceful fountain in his hands. Passers-by stop and look over, as do a couple of passengers atop a southbound 332. The fruit change direction and speed as the clown performs his impromptu aerial ballet outside a nondescript convenience store on a trash filled street in northwest London. He's had time to perfect the routine, and as a tossed pound coin drops and spins at his feet followed by the clatter of other loose change, he gathers in his balls, bows, places the fruit back in its punnet and collects his take. He could be wrong about the shop, but conjecture helps kill time.

As he replaces the plums, Doreen Brown rummages nearby among the avocados but they are too soft. Brown in the same woollen hat and pink coat that she's worn every winter and spring since 1980, her face pinched, in a hurry to get back to her invalid son, Rudy. Rudy Brown whose body is too whacked from booze and ketamine to leave the house, a slow bodily disintegration since he went cold turkey, the man now diabetic, blind and toothless, his heart barely pulsing through the last infarction, only tramadol and codeine to numb his cortexes. Doreen Brown's only child, a ball of bloated biomass squinting through cataracts at conspiracy pedlars on the Discovery Channel while his mother fusses around him. None of the avocados are good and Brown shuffles off to see if Tesco have any.

A swineherd stood at the back of St. Mary's church at Michaelmas, a woman at his side, her belly swollen. Compacted mud underfoot, no pews or other seats in those days and walls daubed with bright scenes from the Testaments. Babies cried and children ran as a psalm was chanted poorly and acapella in the Latin language to the beat of a goatskin drum. He did not sing, nor did the woman at his side. They clasped hands as voices lifted in atonal doggerel, for none had been trained in the art of singing as they had at St. Albans or Barking. The priest, Cynefrith reciting Scripture, "Create in me a clean heart, O God, and renew a right spirit within me," continuing with a homily extolling the virtues of purity, the sin of lust, the punishments which await those who take a carnal path and give in to the weakness of the flesh. The woman squeezing the swineherd's hand, the only solace in a universe in which they span, rootless, far from the light, a loose thread cut off from the skein, only their skin pressed against one another keeping them from the abyss. Cynefrith's voice rising and falling for effect, painting pictures with words, the swineherd certain of his own damnation, gripped with an image not depicted on the chapel walls; a tear-streaked, snot-caked couple fleeing furious Cherubim from a garden after the fall.

On the eastern side of the High Road, forty-three-year-old Carl McAlister from Drogheda, flush with cash from Soft Touch Ollie heads towards the amusement arcade between the Bell and the Overland railway station. It's either there or the William Hill bookmaker's next door; plenty of places to burn the one hundred and twenty pounds he made from stripping the paint on the fireplace, cutting back the tree and mounting a TV in the bedroom. Ollie North, a kindhearted IT trainer who pities McAlister and provides him with chores, and who McAlister refers to privately as a golden fucking goose. North with no idea that McAlister spent six years in Portlaoise for helping kidnap a loyalist priest, and is now unemployable, hustling where he can for money to gamble, snort and pay the hundred pounds a week for a room on Dyne Road. Carl McAlister hands the cashier three twenties to change, scoops coins in both hands, shovels them into his pockets and positions himself in front of a slot machine decorated with a green hatted leprechaun playing a fiddle beneath a rainbow. Centuries earlier, a Benedictine monk and a hermit girl lit a fire here and roasted a hare, feeding each other as a robin looked on, the flickering glow of the flames adding new colour and beauty to Godwyn's blessed and radiant face.

Beneath McAlister's stool, a train from Queen's Park to Euston slows on its approach to Kilburn High Road Station. Ramon Poyet, Portuguese from Coimbra, tight curled black hair and eighteen stone four in his vest, sits back in his sideways facing train seat, both hands resting on his great belly. A life's work. Last night, he ate the whole thing and both the sides. By himself. They should have taken his picture and put it on the wall like they do in Texas. Unbelievable, even for him. Poyet shaking his head, pleased beyond measure at this latest gastronomic exploit. A belch inflates his cheeks and he taps his lips gently with his fist. Opposite him, Bengt Ole Thorsen, thirty eight, athletic with wispy receding blonde hair. Thorsen who represented his country at junior level in the pole vault, his mother welling up in the crowd even though he only made seventh. Now a data analyst for a city bank, the Swede marvels at the bliss on Poyet's closed eyed and goateed moonface. Poyet, who works as a receptionist in a hotel in St Pancras rubs his teeth with a finger as Thorsen glances down at the headline on the paper in the fat man's lap. They are no closer to finding the missing plane. Poyet yawns, covering his mouth and glancing at his watch, an analogue Seiko with a metal strap buried in his wrist, then closing his eyes again. Thorsen fixes his gaze at Poyet's belly and his brown, moccasinned feet. How does the fat man put his shoes on? When did he last see his penis? The train jerks to a stop, and on the street above, while Thorsen stands, stooping so as not to crack his head on the train ceiling, Nicolay Vidinov accompanied by the idiot, Krastev passes a green haired clown where Cambridge Avenue meets the High Road. Vidinov with a bush of wire wool bursting either side of his black baseball cap, like giant ears made of hair so that he too resembles a clown. He carries two full bags from the nearby Iceland supermarket; cigarettes, milk, bacon, white bread, oatmeal and soap. Appliqued to the back of his oversized pale blue denim jacket is a large man's shoe. Krastev is shorter; clean shaven and stocky with a grey buzzcut. A man who would never have found his way to Britain without Vidinov, the immigration procedure too complex, his English too poor, his understanding of the world to unformed and uninformed. But Vidinov had promised the man's mother, saw the idiot as a loyal dog and treated him no better. A bed, food and morning walks. Vidinov stops to light a King cigarette, cupping the flame from a translucent plastic lighter and cursing the Rosicrucians.

"They're the ones still guarding Nazi gold in Swiss bank vaults," click click, "Everyone knows. They don't want to give it back to the Jews," click, "because they need it to stabilise the EU." Click click, a spark, a flame, a glowing tip of tobacco and an adrenalin shot to the lungs of Nicolay Vidinov. "Eh?"

Krastev grins.

"Car truck car car bus truck car."

Vidinov shakes his head at the idiot.

"No, Dimitar, they don't want to give any back to the Jews."

A cloud of smoke and the two men turn into Coventry Close.

The clown glances over to the east side of the street. Here, a corroded green cupola crowns the old bank building at the junction of Belsize Road, its deep Edwardian walls slicing into ground once blessed by Benedictine nuns. Here, where the ribbon straight Wæcling Strete met a rattling watercourse known as the cow's stream, the Cuneburna, the Counebourne, the Keeleburne, the Coldburne, the Caleburn, the Kilburn; the blessed hermit Godwyn walked in agonies of devotion, her lips never ceasing, *Noli aemulari in malignantibus. Perfecto odio oderam ilios* in endless paternoster and amen. Blessed Godwyn, child of God, berating her own worthless heart, her sacred brook now barrelling through sewer pipes deep beneath the asphalt. He looks at the bookmaker's where Carl McAlister is already down to twenty eight pounds and at the entrance to the Overground, a stone parapet still bearing the words "KILBURN AND"; the "MAIDA VALE STATION" buried behind the sign for a kebab shop. It's like a tombstone he thinks, and what the place deserves.

The swineherd raced along the field track that connected Willesden Lane to Wæcling Strete. Breathless, he looked up and down the road and saw three men approaching on horseback from the north. All three were dressed for battle and he ran to them, begging them to carry him on a fast horse to Hampstead, or his wife might die before their child was born. One of the men peered at him.

"It's the monk!"

The swineherd's throat became dry. It was him. Of all the people to meet in his hour of need, the man who had lost him everything. Running was futile. Fighting too was destined to fail.

"Forgive me sire, my wife is in great need."

The pain sudden and burning. He fell to his knees as whipcord cracked around his torso a second time. Comfortable that a man who had once bettered him was suitably restrained, his attacker dismounted and locked eyes with him, his breath reeking of sour ale.

"This for the man who denied Athelstan Dunheld a woman."

With that, he thrust his seax into the swineherd's belly and pulled it out, still staring into his victim's wide, horrified eyes.

"Die, shithead."

The swineherd fell sideways onto the dirt.

"And so we will kill our Vikings!"

Dunheld wiping the blade on his tunic and sheathing it in its scabbard, his two companions hanging back, their faces drained of blood, staring at the corpse on the road as Dunheld mounted his horse and kicked it into action.

"Let the pigs eat him."

A hawk alighted on his shoulder and he rode away to fall in with Ironside's army as it marched south to defend the city.

It is the penultimate day of Lententide and cloudless. Sharp shadows carve patterns on the pavement and air that has yet to lose its winter teeth bites at any metal, stone and skin that cannot see the sun. The brakes of a 16 bus bound for Victoria hiss above the grove where yellowhammers nested in blackthorn hedges, where psalms of penitence and praise mingled with the music of birdsong. At the entrance to the former London and South West Bank building are Brendan MacAuley, 'Dublin' John Forrest and O'Dwyer's boy. The ground floor has been gutted and new concrete laid. The clown was in the bank when Terrence Fleahy and Jack Cooper pointed a wartime Luger 9mm at a twenty-one-year-old cashier, demanding that she fill a brown leather Gladstone with the savings of good, upright people in denominations of five and ten. He watched from a corner as fumbling hands stuffed banknotes into the bag, Fleahy barking at him to get on the ground with the others, the clown reaching instead for a harmonica =and playing *Home on the Range*. Fleahy red faced with rage, his hand shaking as he gripped the pistol, screaming at him to comply. Forty-nine-year-old Latin teacher, Donald Cohen looking up from the carpet and yelling at the clown to drop to the floor or they'll all die. Fleahy, snot rolling over his lips pulling the trigger and sending a bullet through the clown's chest and into the wall behind him. A shriek from the cashier who ran in terror towards a fire door. The bullet winded him and he dropped to his knees. Fleahy shot again, Cooper grabbed the bag and the men fled. An ambulance and panda cars, the clown strapped to a gurney and taken at speed to St. Mary's Paddington. Blue lights and an urgent two-tone siren, the doors to the ambulance opening and a white faced paramedic unable to speak, the gurney empty and the victim nowhere to be seen. He crosses over to the former bank in time to hear that MacAuley's boys have done a good job for the money.

"It's always tight, sure boy," says Dublin John, tall and thickset, his nose broken in Trainor's pub Armagh in 1981, John too many sheets to the wind to land a punch.

"Thank fuck for the Poles" says MacAuley. "Cunts know what they're doing."

O'Dwyer's boy pointing out that the labourers on this job are Romanian.

"That so, boy?" says Dublin John. "Romanian."

O'Dwyer's boy, tall with a rock for an Adam's apple, ears like stopcocks and limbs too long for his clothes. MacAuley glances at the young man who O'Dwyer paid to send to college and sneers inwardly. Boy may have A levels but he's still the same pig ugly bogtrotter his old man was.

"Romanians was it?" MacAuley lights a cigarette from a case and they step inside.

The clown follows, casting a long shadow as he stands in the doorway. Dublin John turns, Brendan Macauley and O'Dwyer's boy looking around too. Macauley, whose dosshouses in the streets off Cricklewood Broadway he neither heats nor cleans; rooms infested with creeping things and rodent nests, with toilets that no longer flush, because the families have neither paperwork nor power. King Brendan, expanding his empire, buying premises like this for cash, hiring boys who wait outside Matalan at six in the morning, don't speak a word of English and work like blacks for half the money. Yes boy, cash at the end of the day, and I don't care how much you put away in a night, who you wire it to or what bench you sleep on, as long as you're back with your shovel in the morning. The clown moves on, Macauley finding himself involuntarily mumbling words of Latin whipped into him by the Christian Brothers in Letterkenny: *"Confiteor Deo omnipotenti, quia peccavi in cogitatione, in locutione, in opere."* I confess to the Lord Almighty that I have sinned in word, in thought, in deed.

Ten centuries after a swineherd fell to his knees, dying, the clown steps back out into the sunlight where a 332 grumbles past Belsize Road on its way to Paddington. Upstairs, Vincent Lassalle stares at Veronica Sleeman carrying three heavy Tesco bags on the street below, her frizzed hair greying out, waddling so wide along the pavement that the two women walking behind her are unable to pass. Vincent Lassalle, hands gloved, awake since six, washing for an hour, scrubbing until the skin is red, always a clean towel which is flung in the corner for washing like a hotel. Lassalle who has three locks on his door to turn and unturn, turn and unturn, turn and unturn, who jumps to the jerks of the devil's paddle, his marionette hands hurting from touching the yellow grab rails of the bus even through the gloves, staring out of the window at the woman with her bags. WHY WON'T SHE LET THEM PASS?

Had Lassalle looked out of the other window, he might have seen Malcolm Shriever and Marco Race walking shoulder to shoulder around the old bank, past the green-haired man in a trench coat on the corner and into Belsize Road. Two estate agents in blue suits and brown shoes on a recce to a flat on Priory Terrace. Race shares his plans for the afternoon; a visit to his friend Damon who is about to go into a hospice. Shriever jumping in that he had a mate with pancreatic cancer, regaling Race of how the two of them once jumped off a bridge in Mostar, such a blast, and on to more stories involving the man whose name is Harald and who beat his cancer. The clown has never been to the flat on Priory Terrace, condemned as he is to patrol the High Road ad infinitum, but he was there when it was hazel thicket, when pine martens built dens among the roots of ancient trees. And he was on the High Road when four sixty-pound shells dropped from a Luftstreitkräfte Gotha GV biplane a thousand feet above the city. It was well into the evening and snow had made his southward journey slow, Westminster still many hours away, the ominous drone of the Mercedes D.VIa engines drowning out the whistle as their bombs fell. A crack of light and fire, the thud as the earth bent and rebounded and masonry, wood and glass shot skyward, falling back into a crater where seconds earlier, landlord Robert Hill had been drawing ale, porter and spirits for his handful of clientele in the Princess of Wales pub on Abbey Road. The second bomb destroying three villas commissioned by the landowner, Fulk Greville Howard at the southwestern end of Priory Terrace. The Greggs, the Inneses and the McHenry's, one dead four injured. Seconds later a flash of light on Mortimer Crescent, close to where V-1 doodlebugs would send George Orwell running from his blasted home in a future conflict.

The lightshow continuing; a fourth shell smashing into a home on Greville Road owned by the Kleinberg family, killing a maid. Two dead, two injured and one hundred and eighteen houses damaged beyond repair. A Sopwith Camel scrambled at Hendon Aerodrome, a pursuit, the Gotha's Parabellum MG14 machine gun flashing seconds ahead of its ratatatt, gunner Walther Heiden gripping the handle and unloading at the approaching enemy. The Sopwith piloted by George Hackwith, his gunner, Lieutenant Charles "Sandy" Banks looking for his first kill. Hackwith climbing out of range of the larger warplane, then swooping within twenty feet of the cockpit, so close that Banks could see three heads beneath the wide upper wing, there Heiden, there Commander Friedrich von Thomsen and there, pilot Karl Ziegler fighting at the controls, trying to pull the Gotha sideways and down. Banks unloading his Vickers into the balsawood and paper fuselage, tearing it; another volley and Ziegler was hit, his head slumping forwards, the plane burning, veering suddenly left and down, spinning; a dropping torch, a yellow ball of flame and a crater in a field near a farmhouse in the Essex village of Wickham Bishops. Silence in the Sopwith, two men looking down, exhilarated at the kill. Two new widows and a mother grieving her youngest son. Military Crosses for Hackwith and Banks; the three Germans scooped up and afforded a miliary burial at St. Peter's church, close to where they fell. Momentarily free of buildings again, Priory Terrace soon returned; red brick homes with flat, white-framed windows contrasting the villas' stucco and bays. Shriever and Race now on their way to a stunning three bedroom, two bathroom garden flat with a private side entrance and lovely southwest facing rear garden, unaware of the tragedy that landed here almost a century earlier, the heroics that followed, or the three coffins lowered into graves among the sycamores behind a church deconsecrated in 1970.

It was somewhere around here, though it's hard to tell now with all the buildings and the roads. When it was still farmland he had his bearings, but since the fields became criss-crossed with streets and the village exploded into a great sprawling suburb, his memory of how it once looked has faded. It was a few hundred yards before the brook passed under the plank bridge that had already been carrying Wæcling Strete across it for centuries. The morning was quiet and a Benedictine far from home was carrying Augustine's great Bible from St. Albans to the monks of St. Peter's, keeping it beyond the reach of the Danes whose invasion was imminent. A courier in need of a piss, but not here on the road; a drover and his herd ambled slowly towards him and so he slipped into a lush thicket of hazel that dropped down to the river, the water truckling over rocks adding to the urgency in his swollen bladder. The relief as the jet burst from him and spattered over the reedmace at the water's edge. And then a sudden movement out of the corner of his eye; a figure rocking near a large willow, a hood shading him from the sun, for the June was hotter than most. Dropping the skirts of his cloak and washing his hands in the river's edge, the Benedictine ventured towards the man, calling out a greeting.

"Hail!"

No answer. Instead, the figure flinched and retreated. He made to follow, his sandalled feet cracking the dry grass. A defensive hand, an averted face – and a woman's voice.

"Please, come no further."

He stopped, contemplating the stranger. From the distant road, the bleating of sheep and the occasional shout of the drover. Nearby, a shrill sparrow and the shallow brook; otherwise, silence.

"What is your business here, sister?"

The woman still looking away.

"None but my own."

The grass by the river was flat, like a lawn and he could see a small plot where beets, turnip and cabbage grew.

"It is a lovely spot."

He stepped towards the water to see if he there were any trout.

"It is God's Creation," she replied, "how could it not be so." A statement, not a question. "For me to take pleasure in it would be selfish; it would be to gratify my desire, and would distract me from my meditation."

Not welcoming, but not running, nor asking him to leave. If only he could see her face.

"Who feeds you?"

"A miller leaves flour and milk. I make fire and bake loaves. I trap animals and fish. The trees bear berries and I grow what I can.

"And where is your shelter, sister?"

"Do not call me sister." Then, "A cell on the riverbank."

In the distance near a tall oak, he could make out a lean-to made from rough stones and branches. Beneath her hood, two downturned eyes and a pleasant face the colour of sandalwood. A bird chirruped three times quickly.

"Sparrows," she told him. "The female telling the male she's tired of sitting on the nest."

"It's dreary for her being in one place day after day," he suggested. She said nothing. "Will you eat some victuals with me?" he asked. "I am hungry and have plenty."

"That would not be proper."

"A man and woman who have taken holy orders cannot break bread together? Of what Scripture are you thinking?"

"My own orders carry their own rules."

He had no idea of her orders nor her rules, but the company was welcome.

"At least allow me to eat."

Dusting dead leaves from a thick log, he seated himself on it, pulling bread and cheese from his knapsack and drinking from a small flask of ale which he blessed, The woman remained a short way off, watching him. He bit into the loaf, the crust cracking.

"You are a Benedictine."

Mouth full, he nodded assent.

"Where is your house?"

Swallowing:

"The great abbey of St. Alban, at Wæclingacaester, half a day's journey north."

"And your business?"

"To Westminster. More I cannot say. Cheese?" He offered some to her but she remained where she was, looking down at her clasped hands.

"Godspeed you on your journey, Benedictine, I shall pray for your safe arrival."

With that, she turned and walked back along the stream, the sun throwing her shadow upon the water. His repast over, the Benedictine's journey south to Westminster continued without incident.

On the pavement outside the old bank, a slab tells passers-by that the Kilburn Spring could once be found here. A plaque affixed to the wall tells the same story. Before the publican of the Old Bell discovered the fount in 1714, it lay beneath a tangle of thorns, a rude pond that never drained. The oak whose hollow trunk formed part of Godwyn's shelter had long since been felled to make tool handles and brooms, consumed by the voracious city, the city that eats everything but is never satiated.

It is the Paschal month and a gust of chill April air kicks up a dervish of blossom on the paving. On the day after the Messiah was nailed to a tree outside a city wall in Palestine, the clown stops at the carcass of a shoe shop next to the old bank, a place lately given over to hawkers of the contraband and the counterfeit. A man holds up a box that once contained a Morphy Richards toaster. A huckster cheating his fellow men out of money for which they have either toiled, robbed or signed DSS forms. Bennett, or Bonnett, or Parrot, or Price, who knows his actual name? Father drowned, mother at the end of a bottle, rocking backwards and forwards as the demons dictate while her son packs the van with whatever's in the lock-up and drives to wherever he can hoodwink the gullible and the weak.

"Forget about forty nine ninety nine. Forget thirty nine ninety nine. I'm not even asking twenty nine ninety nine. This is yours for nine ninety nine."

Ten people standing around him waving banknotes, half of them the band of robbers who took him in, the rest credulous fools. Five people believing that the cheaply assembled mess of plastic and wire in the box will make toast, who wholly trust that this brazen street barker will eventually sell one of them an iPad 4 for the one hundred and fifty pounds advertised in yellow dayglo in the window of the abandoned store. Among them, the Brazilian, Rosalie de Moraes whose family in São Gabriel da Cachoeira still talk about an uncle from a previous century, Ramon the priest who flew thirty metres, maybe fifty on the mass of St Irene in front of the whole town, which even then must have been two thousand people. They would have made him a saint, everybody knows they would, only he left the priesthood in disgrace; Ramon dying penniless, still owing José Jorge Pereira the money he lost in craps, municipal cleaners shovelling up his diseased bones and shit encrusted clothing and carrying him in a wheelbarrow to the morgue. Some are born to believe and de Moraes digs fingers into her purse for a ten pound note before the others can beat her to the toaster.

On the west side of the High Road opposite Bonnett's pop up electrical store, an estate agents, a dry cleaners and an opticians. Resting with his back to the glass of the optician, Earl Graham; long hair in a ponytail, grey handlebar moustache, blue boating shoes and denim.

Graham looking over at the building which Brendan Macaulay will eventually rent out to a pizza chain, and at the Nationwide building society next door to it, figuring out what to do. Graham smokes a menthol roll-up as a bus rolls past bearing a movie advertisement for *Eddie the Eagle*. Graham who was in Calgary back in the day can't see what the fuss is about. Kid didn't even win a medal. Fucking Brits and their love of lost causes. Earl Graham more loved and lost than most, running on vapours and skinnier than he should be. Poorer, greyer and smoking more. If you can't change it, change yourself, he thinks, and wonders how he will tell Roseanne the news.

The clown is not one you might encounter at a circus nor a child's party. Clad in a trench coat and army boots, his cleanshaven face is smeared in white stage paint. His lips are black and turned down in an expression of permanent derision, and hair that was once brown is now a brilliant green. Kohl encircling his eyes adds to a sense of menace and despair. He is tall, over six feet and imposing, a presence whose mask allows him to look as ugly as he feels. He pops a Hubba Bubba into his mouth and chews, waiting for the gum to elasticise as Eyvind Ålstrom looks over from the cab of a Veolia refuse truck heading south towards Maida Vale. A pink bubble inflates slowly as the clown pinches the remaining gum with his tongue, seals the gossamer balloon and blows another bubble into it. Now a third which inflates until the ball is the size of his head, fragile and delicate, dependent on the breath which fills it. Ålstrom watching as Alun Campbell in the cab next to him talks about a broken boiler, and how the company are trying to wriggle out of the warranty. Beauty among the greys, a strange flower that blooms for a few moments and which perhaps only he sees, and then is gone.

Needing an escape route should Forkbeard and his Danes attack, Æthelred set his engineers to work on a bridge that linked Lundenwic to Southwark. The men followed the line of the original Roman structure, placing stone slabs in the river at low tide to create pontoons on which ten arches could be built. Once the bridge had opened, traffic was plentiful and many hawkers, hustlers and street entertainers set up their stalls here. The girl was among them, skinny; a child barely into her teens, the dark complexion inherited from her mother, the daughter of a captured Barbary slave, making her an exotic curiosity. The woman died as the child was born, her father dead by the time she was seven; an orphan taken in by an uncle and passed around the men he drank and gambled with like a plaything long before she bled. Fleeing from there, she worked the alleyways close to the tower where soldiers slept, or the wharves where trade ships arrived from the continent laden with wine, furs, slaves, and sailors hungry for women. It was early November and chilly and she pulled her shawl tightly around her. Among the crowds passing to and from the bridge, a group of boorish Flemings warmed by too much beer. One saw her and stepped towards her. She pulled her shoulders back, jutting out her chin, and tried not to flinch from the reek of the man's breath as he teased the dark coils of her hair between his fingers.

"Well here's a novelty" he shouted in his own tongue, and they half dragged, half carried the child towards an inn by the river where a couple of pennies would buy a room, a filthy bedspread stained with semen and blood where bugs hopped, but it would be over soon. Men too drunk or too excited, rushing to the end before it had properly begun. She knew how to make that happen, what to do with her fingers and her tongue, the words she could whisper in their ear as they tore at her clothing.

"Godwyn."

She did not recognise the voice, nor the name, but something in the man's tone made her turn around.

"Let her go."

The men looking round too, releasing the girl as the stranger stepped forward.

"Your mother and I miss you terribly. Come, let us go home."

He held out a hand. Unsure if this was just a ruse to steal her from the others, she remained where she was, but the merchants seemed chastened. Giving the girl a name dampened their ardour. She was a lost and missed daughter, and they fell away quietly into the night, leaving her as penniless and hungry as when they found her.

"What do want from me?" She asked the man.

"Now," he said, stepping towards her and bending so that he could look her clearly in the face. "That is the question."

As this is his last day, the clown is in no particular hurry and zigzags across the High Road many times on his journey north. Navigating a gap in traffic, he reaches the opticians where Earl Graham tosses his half-finished cigarette and turns towards Coventry Close. The clown passes an Italian restaurant and stops outside the cafe next to it where there is hubbub on the street. Adrian Balaci suffering a diabetic crash and in desperate need of insulin, the Romanian slumped against the café wall as Cynthia Morris and her daughter Jade comfort him. Morris has called the emergency number, an operator dictating instructions from a call centre in Park Royal. The manager of the café hovers, unhappy that this is happening on his turf, asking Morris if they can possibly move Balaci somewhere else. Jade Morris holding Balaci's hand, appalled at the manager, telling him loudly that she will never visit his café, and that she'll be giving him one star on Trip Advisor. Cynthia Morris looks up from the phone:

"They're sending an ambulance."

Others who have stopped to help look at the manager who shakes his head, as if Balaci meant to collapse here, meant to harm his business. The clown walks past the mêlée into the café, pushes the swing door at the back that leads to the rest rooms, unfastens the buttons to his trousers, yanks them down and lays a shit on the toilet floor.

Two hundred years ago, this was marsh and waste ground. Trees had been felled but the land proved too wet to farm. Rakes from the city came here to duel; it was less than an hour's ride from Marble Arch and the bleakness made any combat all the more sombre. The clown remembers the battle between Lauderdale and the traitor, Arnold. Arnold who fought under George Washington, became colonel then commander of the city of Philadelphia; a great man who lived beyond his greatness, squirrelling away government supplies for his own pot until he was felled by court martial and disgrace. Arnold who slunk at night to the British bastion, turned on his new country, lined his palm with silver for the secrets he shared then fled to London with a bride half his age. The duel the result of a slight from the Lauderdale earl in the House of Lords, the bewigged gentlemen standing at twenty paces, Arnold shooting but his bullet missing its mark, the pop sending a murder of crows flapping away. Lauderdale laughing in derision and failing to return the shot, as if the man before him did not dignify the loss of a musket ball. The clown watched at a distance as seconds were summoned,

Lauderdale announcing via his wing that he had no desire to see Arnold dead, that his comments still stood, and that Arnold should shoot again if he had the brio. Arnold declining and tranquillity returning. Back then, you could still hear the rush of the river.

Refreshed, the clown exits the café, Balaci now with his bag as a pillow and a coat thrown over as a blanket to keep him warm. Passing a nail bar and a chicken shop, the clown dawdles outside another café to see if any half full cups have been left on its tables. Miley Warren sits on her own, grieving. Two days since they vacuumed life from her womb. Relief turning to a sadness hanging over her like fog that hasn't lifted. At least she doesn't have to work for a few days, so no fake smiles needed. She's not even wearing any make-up. It had to be done. Had to be done. Warren taps her cup on the table, then gets up and heads over the road to find temporary joy in chocolate from the M&S Foodhall. Even though the three quarter filled americano she leaves behind is cold, the clown grabs it and takes a long draught. Caffeine is caffeine.

The pain. Spasms of fire in his belly. Wave after wave. All he could see was blank, white sky. His eyes closed but the whiteness remained. A voice.

"Wake up Benedictine. Wake up."

A presence leaning over him. Indistinct. The sky a halo; he unable to determine if the words were in or outside him, if it were real or unreal.

"Wulfstan."

Life draining out of him, the voice his only focus, breath on his face, warming him, a single thread holding him to everything that had ever mattered. He needed to know it was real, reached out and touched a cold skin the texture of parchment. He flinched, pulling his hand back.

"Who are you?"

"It's not who I am Wulfstan, it's what I offer."

He saw no one, only the light. The voice seemed to be rising from the belly of the ancient earth.

"Death now, or a thousand years of life."

Next to the café, the restaurant on the corner of Brondesbury Villas was once the Rifle Volunteer; a high ceilinged gin palace with a billiard table where he drank porter and chose whores. His palate long since bored of anything that passed his lips, and the morning after pain of brandy no longer worth the joy, a courtesan was one of the few pleasures left. He remained a frequent visitor here until the Ripper ravaged Shoreditch and London's mollies fled to safer towns. Even then, he was often bored, as were they. Few chose the profession because they had a passion for it; few were game or had any energy or intent beyond grabbing a few fast coins, and the hour was often over long before the one he paid for. A cottar lived here when it was forest, his single storey homestead fenced around with wooden palings to keep the boars and wild bulls away. An illiterate who carried out useful jobs at the priory. Once, the wheel of his cart had broken and the man needed help to raise the wagon. The clown had already passed by and, cursed as he is, could not backtrack to offer assistance, nor would he; kindness brought no reward and only wasted time. The man stared at him blankly, not understanding while the traveller continued on his journey.

At the junction with Brondesbury Villas, the clown glances quickly westwards at smart, stucco fronted town houses with steps leading up to front doors past which he has never walked, the street a forbidden country to one doomed to keep to the path. Alice Gould, late again, brown coat and grey hair in a messy bun walks towards the High Road eating the remains of a yoghurt with a small spoon. She looks for a bin to throw the pot, but that leaves the spoon which will become a sticky mess of crumbs and hair in her pocket. Sucking it clean, she grabs a tissue from her bag, wraps the thing up and pops it in to join her purse, nail scissors, keys, library book and other chattels. Not that it matters if she's late. Clarence will be putting stock on the shelves and Dawn will want to chat for ages. Books and games to price up, but no rush for that either; they're all fifty pence unless the thing is obviously brand new, and the good stuff always goes under the counter. Finders keepers. The coat is Laura Ashley and Grey has two better ones back at the flat. Plus she needed the extra sleep; transcribing diaries from her schooldays at Burgess Hill ate into the night, adding girls to Facebook who she hadn't thought about for twenty five years. Victoria Lyons has got so fat. Gould turns into the High Road as the clown saunters across the junction towards Greggs the Bakers.

Over on the east side of the street, Lana Toohey pushes her double buggy into the Primark clothing store. She hasn't told Lex about the babies, despite chatting to him for four hours last night. Hasn't told him about Rico who she met last week in Costa's café when Dylan and Eloise were at nursery; Rico who roughhoused her in the café toilets like she asked him to, the sleaze thrilling her and only the fug of his BO ruining the moment. She doesn't know that Lex is catfishing her with a photo he found of a graphic designer from Ontario. He wants another picture. She parks the buggy by a rack of long sleeved jumpers, flicks through her photo feed and sends a pair of photogenic breasts belonging to a Russian porn star culled from a website hosted in Lviv. Her phone buzzes. Rico. An aubergine emoji. She giggles and replies with a bath and some soap, then pushes the buggy to the back of the store to buy coats for the twins. The clown looks up at the elegant art deco façade of the building, announcing the date of its construction on a parapet. 1930. An upmarket drapers and a Lyon's corner house filling the original floorspace. At the turn of the century, this was a simple terrace of shop fronts, one of them a post office, with flats above. Before the terrace, a scattering of freestanding workers' cottages with small gardens on the edge of the Fulk Greville Howard estate. Centuries of bucolic tranquillity until carts loaded with barrows, shovels and sledgehammers arrived to flatten, clear, dig and build. Numberless lives lived in these long vanished homes, people he saw but never knew, whose comings and goings he witnessed. Men and women who met and fell in love, who screwed in overcrowded bedrooms and created life; straw-haired girls in grey-white smocks running barefoot along the street, boys throwing coins at the wall of the bank on Belsize Road while women laundered sheets and mended stockings. People who died of tuberculosis, cholera and the pox. No tombstones legible enough to read their names anymore and no one alive to grieve them; few left who realise they ever lived. He tries to recall a face, anything to remind him of the families whose lives played out before they raised an emporium, clad it with white tiles and lit it with great lead glass windows. He stares at the building as if trying to peer into a pictogram. A father and his boy. Sweeps. The two of them returning home in the early evening, ragged and dirty, the man in a tall hat always carrying the child who was aged around six, too exhausted from his labours to walk. He'd seen the man when he was young, less lucky with his own father who beat him for dallying. They all die, he thinks, and tonight it'll be his turn. No quiet creeping to the grave for him; he'll make damn sure this is a night that no one forgets.

As the merchants staggered off into the Southwark gloom, her new acquaintance remained, considering his latest find. She wondered where he would take her, whether he would beat her, or worse, weep when it was over. The man seemed wealthy; his black robes woven with gold thread.

"Come."

They boarded a boat rowed by a woman who said nothing, her skirts hitched to her knees, wheezing slightly from the effort needed to pull them along. They travelled east, less than a mile to where the city of Lundenwic spread north from the river's bank. She knew its streets, its yards and market squares but at this late hour, only the alehouses were lit. Stepping out of the boat at one of the many wharves, they walked together into the warren of unlit roads. She felt no fear, as if she were being guided, that this man might be some kind of angel. They passed a servant wrestling a stubborn goat while another gathered up a bundle of kindling and turned off the street towards a building and into a room grander than any she had seen. The hall was lit by tallow candles, and two young girls played with a small, short-haired dog. The walls were lined with round wood and metal shields and hung with tapestries whose design she could not make out in the gloom. Along the side of the single long room, people were already asleep in their cots and it seemed a strangely public place for a tryst that might normally be transacted quickly in a doorway, or a stable, or the cheapest room above an inn. In the middle of the floor, embers glowed in a square pit surrounded by a low stone wall. Above this was a large cauldron hooked to a metal chain anchored into a ceiling beam, warming water for the morning. From the high rafters hung the body of a pig, slowly curing in the smoke.

Beyond the fire were a wooden table and some stools. The man led her here, ordering her to sit. A woman brought cups which she filled from a jug, wine that had been mixed with well water. The woman placed a small board with meat and cheese on the table and pushed them gently towards her. Suddenly panicked that these people thought she was someone who she was not, the girl spoke:

"I am not Godwyn."

The man smiled.

"I find it is not who we are that matters. It's what we become."

Hungry, she began eating, two handed, in case the food might be taken away.

"How many summers are you?"

She couldn't count, so had no answer. Nor had she any idea where she lived. Her father's name had been Odred and she was born, she believed in the hundred of Ossulston. She was small, her face and hands dirty, her clothes ragged. A body that survived how it could, went where it needed and had asked few questions of the world that birthed it.

The man didn't eat but watched quietly as she fed. Grabbing the cup, the girl drank, then wiped her hands on her skirts.

"Child," he said when she was settled, and thus began her first conversation with a man who was sober and didn't want to beat her or bed her.

"I see you have little money or bread to eat, and that which comes to you is not without struggle."

At the far end of the hall, behind a low partition, a cow exhaled noisily in its sleep and the embers crackled. The man spoke in a low tone about the harlot Rahab who aided

Joshua's spies, the sinful woman who anointed Christ's feet with perfume, wiping them with her hair, and the woman caught in the act of adultery and humiliated in the marketplace in the Gospel of John. He spoke of the whore, Mary of Egypt, her love of the carnal act so strong that she refused any payment, travelling to the feasts in Jerusalem not to pray but to work the crowds. Mary who found God, went into the desert to pray and remained there for such a time that her clothes wore out. By then, her hair had grown long enough to cover her modesty. The man spoke of the Alexandrian courtesan Thais who also converted, and Pelagia who rode proudly on horseback, her diaphanous cloak barely shrouding a naked body draped from head to toe in jewels; riches which she gave to the widows and the poor once she too had confessed her sins. The girl had heard of none of these women, but knew there was no hope for her. Still, her belly full, she listened.

"How much do they pay you?" the man asked.

"Threepence, maybe."

That's what she asked for. Many paid less, a few tipped. She kept her voice low, it seemed strange to be talking business with children nearby.

"How many in a day?"

She was pretty, and darker skin would draw attention, and he felt certain that the men he had interrupted weren't her first of the evening.

"If they pay me, one or two, sometimes three. If not, I go again. If they're generous, I don't work for a day."

The man got up and walked over to a large wooden chest which he opened. She drank some of the wine. Nearer the fire, the woman darned a smock, watching her, keenly. She seemed kind. They all seemed kind and the house calmed her. The man returned with a leather pouch, placing it on the table in front of her. It chinked.

"In here is three years' wages."

She stared at the bag, unable to form words.

"The abbess at Barking has a room for you. If after three years you wish to return to this life, the choice is yours. Or you can leave now. The door is open."

Now the woman spoke.

"We have prepared a bed for you here tonight. Sleep, and tomorrow you can give your answer."

The girl looked at the woman, then to the man and back to the money bag. Taking her hand, the woman led her to a cot in the corner of the room. The sheets beneath the embroidered coverlet were clean and cool. Who were these strangers? And why were they doing this? She felt she should pray, but did not know how, nor could she believe that any God could forgive someone who had lived as she had. The sound of the cows' slumbering lulled her into her own deep sleep.

Alphonse Lamb also sleeps, lying comatose on a sheet of cardboard on the hard tiles near the automatic door of a pharmacy a couple of stores down from Primark. The shop is clad in scaffolding and planks above Lamb's head offer shelter from spring rains. On this drag of suburban northwest London, no one even stops to check the man's pulse. Unshaven, a woollen hat is pulled over Lamb's brow and a stained sleeping bag keeps out the worst of the chill. Half a bottle of whisky from Aldi do the rest, insulating him from gusts that periodically bite any exposed skin. Not for Lamb the charity night shelters; he rejects the life he had. Rejects keys and bills and National Insurance numbers, rejects relationships, responsibility and rules. It comes at a price, but so does anything worth working for. The clown looks over at him. A little beyond where Lamb is lying, there was a clearing. A huntsman crouched, not moving, waiting.

Little foot traffic and no wind made the crash of the beast through the bracken unmistakable. His bow creaked and as the hog blinked in the daylight afforded by the trackway he released. A squeal as the animal spun round, not knowing what had stuck him. The hunter drawing again and a second bolt flying into its haunches, an axe blow, another, a third and the boar lay dead. The hunter fell to his knees. He could sell the meat or salt it for the winter, not that he would eat any himself; he could neither starve nor die, not at least until the appointed time. A kill like this was rare. Mostly, he only took fowl from the king's woods; trespass here was now a capital crime and though no noose could kill him, being known as an outlaw was an inconvenience he preferred not to suffer. Wiping his blooded hands on his leggings, he grabbed the beast by the tusks and tried to drag it to the track's edge. It was too heavy. Rooks called an alarm and he retreated behind a tree. When no one came, he took his knife, hacked off the animal's head and tossed it, a heavy ball that rolled lopsidedly into the bushes. Then a butchered hind leg and another. These he hid in a thicket before returning to the carcass which, by now he was able to heave onto his shoulder and throw down next to the head. Lighting a fire and smoking the meat was out of the question, wood stealing as forbidden in these woods as poaching. Further along the track, a cottar knew to turn a blind eye should the dice roll to his advantage. The hunter brought him the head, telling him to fetch salt and a barrow if he wanted the rest of the pig, his payment a fat bag of copper coins and a fine buckskin coat that reached his ankles and replaced the sheepskin he had worn for the last four centuries.

Today, the clown wears an army greatcoat brought home from Passchendaele in 1917, where it had kept the worst of the wind from sergeant Alec Cleverley until a German bayonet drove through his stomach, piercing the fabric as it exited with his spleen and part of his small bowel. Cleverley's widow laundering it and mending it lovingly before answering an appeal by St. Peter's during the Depression, donating her dead husband's coat and good trousers, three shirts, a suit and two pairs of shoes; the clown receiving it gratefully and pulling it over his skinny bones where it hung, the tails flapping as he walked, hands thrust deep in the pockets, an immortal nobody marching in the clothes of the heroic dead.

Carla Simoes leans on the railings outside the chemist on her break from the Marks and Spencer foodhall. Simoes more tired than usual, many of her Saturday staff failing to show because it's Easter and they've left town without telling her. She sucks on an e-cigarette and checks her messages, wondering if she should send another text because all she got from the last one were Ramon, Belle and Jürgen saying they couldn't come. Otherwise it will be just her and Tamara and all that food. No, too needy. She checks her watch. Her stomach grumbles and she sucks in more nicotine as, over on the western side of the road, Maureen Keep wearing a purple beanie pulled down against the chill and a cinched camel coat she bought new in 1982 walks past a phone repair shop and a vape shop on her way to Brondesbury Villas. The clown remembers Keep when she was a dancer, not that she ever looked his way. Blonde beehive, pouting lips and fake lashes. A modelling contract with Mary Quant, a shoot with David Bailey, paparazzi snapping as she left a club with Georgie Best. Assignments dwindling as late nights and opioids robbed freshness from her face, dancing jobs that didn't quite pay for the amphetamines, the fug of hotel parties where the drugs were free. Slim, supple Maureen Keep spending her summers on yachts, partying with Khashoggis, gyrating in a two-piece as billionaires applauded, congratulating one another on putting on such a show for their guests. Scandal with a Saudi prince, a hurried return to London and a glamour shoot to pay her court fees, topless Maureen Keep gracing a thousand bedroom walls. Twenty-year-old Luke Eldad passes Keep on his way into the mobile phone shop next to Greggs and sees an old woman with dyed blonde hair. Momentarily ageless, Keep smiles at him. Eldad nodding back politely, feeling he should know her, ignorant of the calendars that adorned transport cafés and bus drivers' canteens across the country for a decade, Keep coquettish with a finger on her chin, hair in a curled bob, breasts pushed up with invisible tape. Seized by a sudden coughing fit, she leans on the pole of the pedestrian lights, hoping that the good looking young man isn't watching.

Death. He had never contemplated it. He had sinned, he had violated and it was too late for repentance; the Almighty would see any confession as too self-serving. No mercy for the commandment breaker, the one who had made fleshly desire his guiding star. If any one of you cause one of my little ones to stumble, it were better that he were cast into the sea, tied to a great millstone. Death would come with judgement, the eternal fire his inevitable destination. But a thousand years grace before the flames burned? He would outlive Godwyn for many centuries, watch her and their child wither and die. But while he lived, there was hope that he might still save them. Through a mouthful of blood, he spoke.

Decades before Maureen Keep gyrated to grinning mullahs on a yacht moored off Muscat, a man named Phillips built his music emporium on the eastern edge of the

High Road at the corner of West End Lane. Pianos for hire at ten shillings a month and kept in tune for free by the blind man, a black who came over from who knows where to Liverpool, rattle tapping his white cane all the way to Kilburn. Plasterwork composers' faces set into the bricks facing the street, staring out at the human ordure, the base masses they hoped their scribbled dots and slashes might elevate. There the roughneck, Mozart, there the glutton Handel and the choleric Bach. Dark rooms heavy with the scent of beeswax and teak oil, long players on the gramophone, Benny Goodman, Fred Astaire, Tommy Dorsey. Youths gathering at the racks of records, waiting for the next big thing, mothers hustling reluctant Joans and Sallys towards violins, recorders and tin whistles. A place where old men in horn glasses leafed through sheet music; brass rods on the stairs, glass cases and signs warning not to touch. Three floors given up to the arts, flats today on two of them and vintage second-hand clothing hawked for charity at street level. Marie you'll soon be waking to find your heart is aching, and tears will fall as you recall the moon in all its splendor, a kiss so very tender, the words 'will you surrender' to me Marie Marie. Downstairs, the clothing store plays Belle and Sebastien and a blue-haired girl behind the counter bags up a pair of vintage black Levi's 501s. Outside, a green-haired clown stares at busts of composers installed by Alfred William Phillips above his shop windows one hundred and twenty six years earlier.

The nun Æthelburh had been blind from birth and, being a Saxon princess was fed, clothed and washed by her ladies-in-waiting until she reached her majority. It was then that she began to see visions, the archangel himself ordering her to build a house for the Almighty, to dedicate herself to prayer and surround herself with penitents who, like her, would shun their worldly wealth. But it seemed the Godhead had not chosen his daughter to merely lead the simple life of a coenobite. She was to rescue poor girls, particularly those who had thrown away their virtue, and teach them the ways of righteousness. To do this, she would need money and the angel led her to an oak on the banks of the Mayes Brook at Barking. When a hole was dug, gold coins were found among its roots, buried by a Roman who either fled or forgot. The miracle inspired Æthelburh's brother Eorkenwald to join her in the founding of a great religious house which they named Berkyngechirce. Some two hundred years had passed and Æthelburh was long dead, but many of the nuns who spent their days in contemplation behind the abbey walls had once thieved, cheated or whored, yet now lived chaste lives of charity and prayer. The man who had found the brown-skinned waif by the jetties near the bridge was called Albric, a trader in clothing dyes. As the nuns at Barking had vowed to remain recluses, they depended on benefactors such as he to procure oblates. Albric could often be found at the Westminster wharfs where ships unloaded, but though the harvest was plentiful, few were chosen.

Across the junction of West End Lane, Angie Boyle steps out of the bank that used to be Parrs and which was once an endless swathe of forest from Hyde Park to Bushey Park. The road between the clothing store and the bank was an old field lane near the parish boundary that hopped over the Cunebourne before climbing to the village of West End. Until the city grew around them, two piebald horses grazed in acres of green. Before the woodland was cleared to make pasture, only an unbroken cycle of spring rains, summer breezes, autumn leaf falls and winter frosts marked the passing of centuries.

Angie Boyle reaches for the cigarettes in her bag. Lighter click, eyes closed and breathe. There. Now to Argos for something pink for the wee'un's birthday. Angie Boyle who goes to mass when she can, who believes in the triune God and said as much at her confirmation on the day fire broke out on Apollo 13, 321,860km above the church in Shanaglish where the geriatric priest mumbled the Sanctus, his hand shaking so much she thought the wine would spill over the lip of the chalice. Cruel that the old fella should still be working. Boyle looks up as she exhales and her gaze rests on a slim young man with a buzzcut leaning against the wall of the bank, smoking too, a Japanese tattoo emblazoning his neck. Boyle wonders what would induce a man to have his throat tattooed, what she would have to say to a son who came home looking like that. Who'd give the fella a job? And Gabriele Vezzali, an entrepreneur who owns two bars and a barbershop in Exmouth Market feels her eyes upon him.

Where foxes once played in ryegrass at the road's edge, Ahmad Khan, reed thin and bony steps out of the internet café next to the bank carrying three sheets of A4 paper for his daughter, a frail eight year old who seldom speaks, Khan's over large navy suit flapping like a great bird around him. Tall for an Afghan, tall for a man his age, sixty in a year, Khan's otherwise clean shaven face dominated by a bushy moustache and his hair the burgundy hue of one whose eyes have seen the prophet's tomb, peace be upon him. Ahmad Khan walking with small, dainty steps across the road, carrying fifteen pennies worth of photocopies for Sohelia's school project. Now to the market to talk to Ibrahim. This then that then that then this, and so the day is done. Ahmed Khan, glancing at the man with the Japanese tattoo, the defined musculature beneath his tight blue shirt, the line of his jaw and fire detonates deep within the bombproof bunker he has built inside his heart. The aftershock brings a bead of perspiration to his brow, and only his prayers, those frantic paramedics rushing to clear damage caused by yet another blast keep his legs moving and his body upright. Shaking the impulse from his fingers, Khan disappears behind a Waitrose truck heading north as the clown watches. All this scum his magnum opus. A crusted canker on the virtuous green, a suppurating wound that never heals. Crossing the junction, he strides into the chemist's next to the internet café.

The swineherd opened his eyes and looked around. Nothing. The same sparrows singing. The same distant flume of chimney smoke. Trees still in blossom. He felt his chest and looked at his hand. Blood, but no pain. His shirt sodden and red, pierced with five or six slits. He tore the coarse fabric and examined his skin but there were no wounds. Placing his hand to his heart he felt a slow beat. Whatever had happened to him, he was alive. Over there, two miles maybe, his wife lay too weak to even cry out, their unborn child unable to crown. He must reach her before it was too late and made off in the direction of Willesden.

Ten paces away from the road, maybe twenty, lay a felled oak. That was the last he remembered. When he woke, he was kneeling on the road again, exactly where he began. Again, he walked to the tree only to find himself once more waking up on the road. A rider in a hurry to reach the city passed him, mud from the horse's hooves slapping against his side and face. He stood again. This time, he ran at the tree. Darkness. Sparrows singing. He on his knees again in the middle of the track. Barred from the only path he wished to take, the swineherd's face contorted into a cry so terrible and raw that, deep in the oak woods, a wolf sprang to her feet and ushered her cubs further into the forest. Everything he loved was now lost, a husband and father powerless to help the ones who needed him most.

In the chemist, May Wesley waits patiently for the lady in the lab coat to serve the man at the counter in front of her. Wesley with her brown twiglet fingers, the pain so bad that sometimes she doesn't bother getting up from the housing association bed with its three counterpanes, none of which match; her bones crumbling away from the top of her head to the tip of her toes. Eighty six and mad as mercury, eldest of eleven, May Wesley who delivered babies in hospital scrubs for forty years, staring daily at the butchery which nature wreaks on woman, Lord kill her if she ever let a man place any part of his person inside her. Poor, crippled May Wesley, alone in her ramshackle flat, dropping things she can't pick up and always a dry lemon cake in the cupboard for visitors who never come.

She prays while she waits, the same prayer for the Dear Lord to take her away, but he won't. May Wesley in a patterned woollen hat, stooped and frail, leaning on an aluminium crutch, blue canvas shopping trolley by her side, waiting for the lady to give her an ickle bit of codeine. This the third chemist of three; Wesley can't get all she needs from just the one, and it goes down so easy and feels so good. When it's finally her turn, the chemist warns May Wesley of the dosage; Wesley not listening, turning with her trolley to the home in Willesden where she adds herself to the clutter and waits for the beauteous anointing of the opiates to undo her.

On the west side of the street, a Café Nero sits on the corner of Brondesbury Park Road; the park one of two manors built between Kilburn and Willesden when they cleared the forests in the reign of the third Henry. Gone now, just Manor Park Drive to remember it by, the moated medieval house rebuilt in the eighteenth century by a daughter of Admiralty judge Sir Henry Penrice, a woman who in her widowhood entertained the dandy, Brummell in a three storeyed villa with grounds landscaped by Repton. A hundred years ago, long after the house had been demolished and its park given over to developers, a spire towered above the street's residential terraces and evenly spaced lime trees. This too has gone, swept aside like St Paul's and the Baptist chapel to make way for houses, shops and offices; tending to the needs of the living, not wasting space for the souls of the dead.

Next to the chemist is a Sainsbury's supermarket. Three storeys above it in the space beneath the eaves is a room, one of many where migrant workers store their belongings and sleep off cheap vodka. Twenty-four-year-old John Gregg, a wiry Scot who works in the bookmaker's next to the Cock sits on the floor with his eighteen-year-old colleague, Ruby Chan who he lusts after. Their shift over and his room only a short walk from the shop, Gregg invited her up for a coffee. And because he's never come on to her like the other male staff – in fact he seems bored by her, Chan followed him in. There are no chairs, only the bed, and so Gregg and Chan sit on the carpet. While they talk, he moves a few strands of long, black hair away from her face without permission, and wonders what else he might do with her without asking. Ruby Chan who is engaged to Sammy and whose parents speak no English gets up to go to the toilet which Gregg shares with three Irish and four

Poles, and which is blocked with so much wet tissue that the water rises almost to the rim when she flushes. She feels spiteful, the weight of expectation smothering her, wanting to take something pure and break it. When she returns to the room, Gregg is sitting on the bed and she places herself on the floor with her back to him as he continues his annexation. In a room that was once the servant's quarters in a household run by James Wilberforce, an importer of Madeira wine and no relation to the abolitionist, and where *A Fistful of Dollars* plays silently on a small TV, John Gregg presses his thumbs into the flesh either side of Ruby Chan's neck and her head bows involuntarily. He rubs between her shoulders, pressing his palms around her ribs, watching her back arch as he strokes down towards the rise of her buttocks, because he can. They have stopped talking and his fingers slip under her leotard, feeling warm skin, stroking the top of her arms and the front of her shoulders, her head now resting against him, heavy; John Gregg feeling her body give, his hands over her breasts, reaching for them inside the black Lycra, pulling it over her shoulders until she takes her arms out of the sleeves herself and climbs onto the bed next to him where, still fully clothed, he kisses her, Chan's dark eyes wide open, staring at him. John Gregg lays her back on the bed and kisses the Sammy, the engagement and all the wedding plans out of her, wanting to know how much she will let him do before enough's enough. Opportunistic John Gregg, kissing the small bone of Ruby Chan's sternum but thinking about the call he has to make and if it can wait, but it can't and he doesn't want to rush this. Getting up, he covers Ruby Chan with the duvet, tells her not to go anywhere and to lock the door in case the others come in. Gregg runs down the stairs, out of the front door of the flats to the street and wishing he'd put a jumper on.

She woke at first light, the children on her bed shaking her. The unfamiliar surroundings bewildered her for a moment as they chattered, dragging her to the table. The man who had brought her here was not home but a maid fed her bread and honey, the sweetness shocking as she had never tasted it before. When the girl had finished eating, the servant poured water from the iron pot hanging over the fire into a pail and mixed in some lavender and rosemary. A screen was placed around the bucket while the children squealed, then wailed because they weren't allowed to join in. The maid helped her out of her rags, handing her a cloth and a cake of soap made from sheep fat, ash and thyme to wash herself. Lathering away the caked-on grime and revealing the clean skin beneath felt like a baptism, and by the time she was finished, the water had turned deep brown. A linen sheet was brought for her to dry herself, then the maid placed her on a stool by the fire and combed the knots patiently out of her hair. On the table behind them, the cook pounded dough while a large log spat from the fire onto the mud floor. The little girls stared as the comb pulled through the twists of ebony hair, asking to touch it, each with a hand on her back as if she might fall without their support. Taking her hands, the maid clipped the girl's nails with tweezers, then cleaned the dirt away from under them with a sharp wooden pick.

"They'll bathe you again at the abbey," she told her, "but you will be clean enough when you reach there."

In the year Kaiser Wilhelm and the freakish laureate Lear gasped their last breaths, when poor Mary Ann Nicholls and those other Shoreditch doxies were discovered stripped, their throats slit and their bowels arranged with obsessive attention to detail; the same year the Abyssinian duke,

Gobana Dacche and his cohort Moroda Bekere routed the Islamist forces of Khalil al-Khuzani at Guté Dili and, in the small yellow house on 2, Place Lamartine in Arles, the pervert Gaugin grabbed a sword and sliced off part of the right ear of his friend Vincent; in the year that gave the world Irving Berlin and Raymond Chandler, T E Lawrence and Harpo Marx, the J Sainsbury grocery store first opened its doors on the High Road. The first store was a few blocks to the south and the clown stood among the hatted gentlefolk attending the grand opening, a cup of sherry in his hand while trays of madeira cake were passed around and a band played *While the Lindens Bloom*. Today, Balthazar Vikkonnen wanders out of the supermarket and into the fresh morning chill with a reusable plastic bag containing a Monster energy drink, a turkey and cranberry sandwich, and a packet of Walkers prawn cocktail crisps. He waits next to John Gregg for the lights to turn green. Balthazaar Vikkonnen, a musician whose music no one pays to hear, submitting trance beats to online radio stations which few listen to, his phone fat with ideas for songs, all of which might now be lost because the fool at the Samsung store in Westfield said it might be the motherboard, not the battery, and he might lose his data forever. Balthazaar Vikkonnen's heart beating quicker and his throat suddenly dry because he hadn't backed any of his music up. In the end, they couldn't help him as they had no batteries to test their theory, suggesting that he find one on eBay instead. Their flagship store with the giant blue sign, right as you come out of the tube.

"Fucking eBay!"

Vikkonnen shakes his head as the green man beeps and he crosses behind Gregg and the clown to the west side, to the phone repair shop where the Rastafarian behind the counter reaches wordlessly for a battery on a rack on the wall behind him, places it in the phone and the blue light comes on and Vikkonnen is saved. The Finn suddenly so thankful that he wants to kiss the ground but instead he clasps the man's hand and walks back out into a world that will only truly be worth living in once it synchs itself to the beats in his Galaxy GII.

The clown has been watching Vikkonnen but is diverted by the décolletage of Anne-Marie Bennemeier, a South African from Durban, late to view a house on Brondesbury Villas. Tight black top, chocolate brown jacket, blue jeans and high red platform slingbacks that make it hard for her to walk without pushing out her derriere like a low rent Kardashian. He feels a pang of lust, sees for a split millisecond his scrawny bones riding her strong body, her fat breasts clapping beneath him as she swears at him in Afrikaans. Fantasy always better than reality, sex a transaction best completed with a stranger who expects nothing more than money or company; a connection of bodies, a release of fluids, the thrill of an unexpected tryst. He had a relationship, and once that ended, he wanted no new memory to replace it. If nothing else, he was constant, loyal and eternally devoted; an old romantic. His face cracks into a smile as an uber carrying Philippa van Schaar, her seven-year-old son Leo and the child's father Pradeep passes him on its way to the West End. Van Schaar who never meant to have a child with Pradeep, besides, who gets pregnant at thirty-seven? But he was so kind and so desperate to be a father, and promised to look after them which he has, the two of them never together but Pradeep paying for Leo's school and buying them a house, so there's that. A movie in Leicester Square, a meal in the Shard then dessert in Covent Garden even though it's just an ordinary Saturday, but he so rarely sees Leo. Leo who is autistic and easily overwhelmed grips Phillipa Van Schaar's phone and stares at the screen while Pradeep chatters excitedly about *Batman vs Superman*.

Now that he could no longer leave the road and be reunited with his wife, the swineherd rued his decision bitterly, and wept. Not simply tears of grief and regret, but pity and fear; great rivers of saline running down his cheeks to the point of his chin where they fell like rain from the eaves, pooling in the mud and shit that soaked him. It was daytime, long before Willesden became a destination for pilgrims and though he wept for an hour, no other travellers passed him on their north or southbound journey. He stood slowly, his knees sucking at the mud as he rose. There was no other choice; he must cheat the cheater. Staring up and down the long, thin stretch of brown bordered by scrub and trees, he saw no one who might stop him. Only the atonal shriek of a crow broke the silence. Determined, he clambered through the brush to the river beneath the bridge where he stepped into the still, clear water, wading to where some eddies circled in a deep pool. He sank down, the ripples closing over his head, the cold sudden, his body clenching, bracing himself for the final indraught, three, two, one; the water coursing into the buckets of his lungs, and out. He breathed in again, the pain of the cold against his bronchia the sole discomfort. A brown trout swam past, eying the manfish with suspicion, and the swineherd felt an even deeper agony. The demon's curse was truly upon him. As he was propelled out of the water and back onto the road, he realised three things. He was cold. He was wet. And he was eternal.

The amplified sound of gospel music fills an ugly shopping precinct where, eighty years earlier, a church spire dominated the skyline, the first to be built in Kilburn since the priory. Red bricks, a rose window and a grey slated steeple; a white cross atop the tower, a bell and a weather vane. Kilburn then was still a village, and the brook where Godwyn once made devotions still rich with trout, bream and whiting, trickling lazily through birchwood to the east of the unmetalled road. A vaulted stone nave sang to Bach cantatas and Victorian hymnody pumped from the colossal pipe organ played by Henry George Bonavia Hunt. Hunt who later founded the Trinity College of Music, a man whose ghost still walks the corridors of 11-13 Mandeville Place in Marylebone.

As a small group of Pentecostals sing on the edge of what had once been the churchyard, the clown recalls a travel weary day when shops were fewer and the distance between them farther away; a July afternoon when a cruel sun blasted the mud of the High Road until it baked into cracks. On this day, he sought the cool of stone flags and walls too thick to be warmed by the sun. Seating himself on a wood pew at the back of the church, he genuflected as was the custom. The day was a Wednesday; the curate, an effete boy from Peterborough or one of the villages thereabouts reading first the sixteenth chapter of the Second Book of Samuel, followed by the First Epistle of Peter chapter two commencing at verse eleven, his reedy voice concluding at chapter three verse seven, husbands, in the same way be considerate as you live with your wives. Once this was complete, Bonavia Hunt in majesty striking the whalebone keys of the great organ, a suspended C, an A major, E in the seventh, C again and trilling down the scale like water over flat stones. The notes resounded against the tall pillars and mullioned rose of the great church of St Paul that is now a graffiti stained precinct of market stalls and cheap fashion, and a seventeen storey tower owned and managed by Brent Council. It was the last time he attended a church service, and the first he'd been to in a century.

The Benedictine learned to sing early. There was written music, but most hymns were like folk songs, woven into the collective memory of the abbey. Many psalms shared the same melody, perhaps a symptom of too little outside influence and no new ideas reaching Wæclingacaester. Some were call and response; a lone monk singing a musically complex verse with the choir responding more simply. Others were antiphonal, each verse sung alternately by soloist and choir, necessitating a more straightforward melody. Lastly, there were solo pieces which the choir might sing as a single voice, though these melodies were often more intricate and were left to a monk who had a gift in that field. Organum had reached them from France, a plainchant that added a second voice to harmonise with the first, creating a richer, more melodic song. The resulting polyphony resounding from the arched brick ceiling and sarsen stone pillars seemed like a foretaste of the heavenly symphony, a faint echo of the glorious eternity around the shining throne. The tunes stayed with him, flitting in and out of his hippocampus. Occasionally, he had crept into the grand church of St. Paul on Kilburn Square, making sure no other pilgrims loitered there. The stones had a peculiar resonance and had any visitor snuck into the shadows at the back of the nave, they would have heard a green-haired clown singing in vulgate words that passed from regular observance in England's churches sometime in the mid twelfth century.

She was still the child she had been when she arrived the night before, but already, she had begun to change. She felt no hunger and no fear, companions which thus far had followed her through life. Without them, she was unsure of who she was, or what she was supposed to do. Albric arrived an hour or so later and seemed pleased at the transformation. Already, the girl was unrecognisable.

"The abbey is not to everyone's liking, but Wendreda's heart is good," he told her, surveying what she had become, no longer seeing a ragged beggar child but the bride of Christ she might one day be.

"Have you considered our offer?" he asked.

The girl's belly was full and she was well rested. If every day for the next three years would be like this, she would be a fool to turn him down. Godwyn he had called her, Godwyn she would be. The maid had dressed her in a loose linen smock which, as she was little more than bone, hung off her. Albric beckoned to her and though she had no idea of where she was going or what awaited her there, she followed obediently. Whatever lay ahead must be better than the life she had fallen into. She was no saint, nor did she have any expectation of being one, but actual saints appeared to have been placed in her way to rescue her. She knew girls her age who were dead already, pox, drowning, their throats slit; surviving as long as they could until the flame went out, a half-life, and almost all of it a horror.

She had nothing to fetch and left her old rags for the fire. They retraced their steps to the jetties, the streets busier in the late morning; a bustle of horses, dogs, and men pulling carts and carrying packs on their shoulders along gravel lanes. They passed yards where artisans worked metal, wove cloth, carved bones and antlers, and tanned hides. The main road led through East Cheap market where begowned traders from Pavia haggled over spices and ivory, goldwork and precious stones, their cargo arriving from the East at the great tented market by the Ticino River, then hauled on horseback over the Alps and through the Rhineland. Merchants from Normandy, Flanders, Germany and the Baltic ports laid out their stalls next to men from France and the low countries, while locals brought their wares down river on barges. They passed sellers of purple cloth and silks; oil, bronze and copper; tin, glass and brimstone. A crooked beggar hung from a stick, his cupped hand trembling, a dewdrop waiting to fall. Albric nodded at some of the men and women who they passed, but he was neither to be interrupted nor delayed. A boat lay ready, a sturdy waterman at the oars. The man stared the girl as she climbed in, dark skin still an uncommon sight in the city. Not wishing Godwyn to feel uncomfortable, her benefactor ordered the rower to keep his eyes on the river.

The singing that has taken the clown's attention from the great bosom of Anne-Marie Bennemeier is accompanied by a Yamaha PSR S650 electronic keyboard played by a young African man, and he and his accomplices swing, clap and close their eyes, lifting their voices with words that fall like discarded cigarette butts, coffee cups and burger wrappers on the hard stones of the precinct. This blighted square that once resounded to the hammer chords of Bonavia Hunt alive again with sacred song.

"Celebrate Jesus Celebrate!", these brothers and sisters from Senegal or Nigeria or Cote d'Ivoire raising their honeyed song to the Lord God, Creator of heaven and earth, the crucified one, on the last Saturday of Lent.

Maybe these pilgrims truly believe. The clown knows their church and the self-appointed bishop who once spoke there. Two policeman in a jail cell kicking the life out of the brown boy who they found in a white 1997 Hilux in the Shoprite carpark, his lover still running through the Kampala night, shirt ripped off in the fight, face swollen red from the baton, crying. The men who struck him both pillars of the community, one of them an elder in a church whose bishop boarded a British Airways 747 jet to London paid for by these people, stepped into a double breasted suit and alligator skin mules and spouted his poison here in Kilburn. To hell with them and their hate. He'll be there waiting for them.

By the time Kilburn had its own church, the mile that separated the village from Willesden was still parkland planted a century before around the manor houses of Brondesbury and Mapesbury. In those days, anyone travelling a mile north from the end of Oxford Street found themselves among fields and farms, the square and its church the first settlement or any size through which they would pass. Here, the clown watched ragged children chase one another around the yard of a school nestled behind the church. A little to the west, the Rifle Volunteers banded together to face a threat posed by the unhinged megalomaniac, Napoleon III. The pops of their muzzle-loaded Brunswicks firing at cork targets faded once the emperor was captured by Prussians at Sedan, then exiled to the Wilhemlmshöhe fortress where he passed his time designing an energy efficient stove and growing the gallstones that would kill him.

The swineherd raised himself up from the roadside and brushed off thirsty beetles drinking from his sodden clothing. He pinched his arm and felt a surge of pain. He was alive. His belly growled. While Godwyn and her unborn child were left to face their battle alone, angels lifted him to his feet, or were they devils? They ushered him slowly north towards Wæclingacaester as the curse dictated. Away in the

71

woods, a magpie's shriek. Where was she? Did their child live? Did she? If this was a dream, it was one that he would continue to live for a millennium.

The gospel harmonies recede and the clown stops outside a discount shoe store where, on what was once consecrated ground, the eternal destiny of a man's spirit hangs in the balance. Brown men with beards and grey shalwar kemeez have strung green banners between iron bollards declaring "Abraham, Moses, Jesus, Muhammad, peace be upon them" and "Many Prophets, One Message." The men approaching anyone who passes, hoping to engage them in conversation in exchange for a ticket to paradise. Meanwhile, one of the young black men whose church is singing to Jesus hovers, waiting to pounce himself. Archie Hatton, leaning on a wooden walking stick and carrying an Iceland shopping bag has stopped at the banner to pass the time of day with a bearded Egyptian. He wants to tell the man who wears a brown cord jacket and blue jeans with turn-ups and black shoes of his time in Suez. Midshipman Hatton, twenty five, serving on HMS Diana, the one that blew the Egyptian frigate Domiat out of the Red Sea back in '56. Well, to be fair, it was the cruiser Newfoundland that fired the torpedo, he tells the man, but the Diana that finished her off. Mahmoud Ahsrif staring at Archie Hatton's white baseball cap, fawn zip-up cotton jacket and grey scarf, Midshipman Hatton, first class, back on board the Diana, fishing the A-rabs out of the drink. "Over sixty of them, most of them young lads like you who couldn't swim. And this one fella, couldn't have been more than fourteen, thrashing about so much it took four of us to haul him in, shivering in the corner of the deck wrapped in a British ensign."

The bearded man tells Archie Hatton, whose campaign medal sits in a sideboard drawer next to some napkin rings and cake forks, that the half drowned youth whose bulging eyes still stare at Archie Hatton in his dreams was considered a man at that age, would have been proud to defend his country and Allah. Hatton telling him again that the lad was crying and convulsing so much – he puts his hand to his face as if to shield his words from others – they had to give him brandy even though the darkies weren't meant to touch the stuff. Ashrif trying to steer Hatton away from the waters off Ras Ghareb and back to the teachings the prophet, transcriber of the final book of guidance given to man, alayhi as-salām, and Archie Hatton grinning, telling him he likes his bacon too much to go Jewish or Muslim. Mahmoud Ashrif on rails, not deviating, telling Archie Hatton that he himself was a profligate and an abomination before God, who drank and abused his body with pig, hashish and prostitutes until, aged twenty eight, the fruitlessness of his chosen path and the hurtfulness of his actions to Allah, blessed and exalted, visited him in his prison cell in HMP Belmarsh and returned him to the true path. Isaac Leoh now butting in with a Christian tract in his hand, sharks circling, Ashrif politely asking Leoh to back away. Archie Hatton needing to eat before he goes hypoglycaemic, choosing an Iceland ham and mustard sandwich over paradise, slipping away as a debate begins over who owns Easter, cheerio-ing the men, still thinking of Suez. Twelve gates to the eternal city but Hatton in his baggy brown trousers, grey trainers and walking stick will not be passing into the garden.

And the pristine Godwyn whose cell by the Cunebourne stream gave this unremarkable strip of city its name? Not a day went by when he didn't think about her. Of what she

73

was left thinking when he failed to return. What did she tell their child? Did she ever forgave him? He hoped not, for he would never release himself from the burden of guilt hanging over him; it is because of him that streets fan out all around him, tearing into lands that she once walked, lost in prayers for the life of Æthelred, his son Edmund Ironside, and for protection from the Norsemen.

Here on the west side of the great road, stuck between a carpet seller and a fashion boutique, close to where John Gregg slots coins into a payphone beneath a silver maple, a WHSmith stationer's. Not so much as a blue plaque to remember the man who lived in a grand townhouse just a few hundred yards away. A plaque adorns the façade of 12, Hyde Park Street where Smith passed his formative years, but this shabby outlet is his true memorial. Empires fall, nations crumble but it must have been decreed that there will always be a WHSmith at 113 Kilburn High Road. The clown never spoke to Smith but passed him on the road; an elderly gentleman in a bowler hat waiting patiently as children patted his Jack Russell, Scottie; the broadsheets, penny dreadfuls and yellow shilling novels which flew from station newsstands across the country adding a hundred pounds to his coffers every minute.

The journey to Barking took two hours. A late May sun danced on the river and gulls swooped to grasp darting fish in their claws. Reeds grew on the banks and alders and willow branches overhung the water. They passed one or two mills, the wooden machinery creaking, but the land was largely fields and woods, Barking being some twelve miles east of Lundenwic. She trailed a hand in the water. A man and woman in a boat travelling towards the city waved at them. A family of otters swam where the Ravensbourne flowed into the Thames and at Greenwich, the river broadened as it began its final race to the sea. They spoke little, Albric assuring her that she would be well looked after by the sisters, that she might learn the Scriptures and that her prayers for the country were of more value than satisfying the carnal needs of quayside drunks. At Plumstead Marshes, they turned north into the Roding River until they reached the quay which served the town of Barking. Here, Albric shook a silver coin from a leather bag and pressed it into the waterman's palm, thanking him for his silence. As the man roped the boat to a wooden paling, they climbed the steps which led to the abbey.

On the east side of Kilburn High Road, Radovan Blaus walks into the Holland and Barratt health food store and grabs some cans of protein powder, whey and arginine to add ropes to his muscles. Blaus who pops half a tab of MDMA every morning, working out to dynamic trance music in his Maida Vale bedsit; his evenings spent guarding the doors of a club in Kings Cross. A human rock; his arms folded, rarely making eye contact, allowing in girls in but a shake of the head and an outstretched palm for some of the men. Not tonight boss. Checking bags but half-heartedly; anyone who comes here often enough knows that Blaus is the drugs, that he can get you anything, or knows a man who can. They know that he can be paid in kind in the VIP toilets, it's his favourite currency; he just has to keep it low key. You and your friend? She can watch, yes? From across the road, the clown stares at the man's muscles. He's like an ox.

Where Radovan Blaus picks out supplements to further increase his bulk, a dairy farm owned by the Liddell family occupied the land east of the road. After its nuns were relieved of their sacred duties by Henry VIII's commissioners, the priory lands where Godwyn once prayed changed hands frequently. A red-faced merchant who had no use for a Kilburn estate married his daughter to Robert, grandson of Sir Thomas Liddell of Ravensworth Castle, County Durham. The couple made their home here, passing the centuries with only a few modifications to their grand pile until, in 1771, they rebuilt it according to the fashions of the day. A three storied square and brick house with a chimney at either gable and a porticoed entrance. They planted blackthorn and hazel hedges to keep the cattle from the road and raised up tall, stone barns to store winter feed; barns filled generously with hay on which to throw the fat cook Elizabeth who giggled as he pulled off her bloomers, complaining about the straw scratching her back, her hot belly clinging to his as he rode her; a genuine respite on his journeys until she married a baker and moved to Wendover. The replacement cook was skinny and pious and looked down a long nose at the clown, like he were a boil on the tip of it.

The Liddells sold to the hunter, Powell-Cotton who never visited Kilburn, flitting between his seat in Kent and the Veldt, his double-barrelled Holland & Holland decimating more game than any white before him. The plains flashed and cracked as Powell-Cotton's insomniac firearm felled elephant and rhino, antelope and leopard, the Savannah his own personal Eden in which he played in guiltless abandon as giant beast after giant beast reeled and bled out. By then, the Great Middlesex Forest which once formed the Conqueror's hunting grounds had been cleared, ready for Powell-Cotton to butcher land instead of game, erecting dull, terraced streets, schools and churches where William Rufus shot arrows and the clown himself, in the days before he coloured his hair green and smeared white paint on his face, bagged partridges, pigeons and migrating wild geese.

The clown sucks his teeth and looks east, beyond the Iceland supermarket on the corner of Birchington Road, up towards West Hampstead. The spire of St. Mary with All Souls, once the tallest in all London, silhouettes black against cotton wool clouds that will grow until they blot out the afternoon sun. Like Birchington, all streets scarring the Liddell farmland bear the names of towns in Powell-Cotton's beloved Kent – Fordwych, Westbere, Woodchurch – or places where the intrepid traveller hunted – Mutrix, Sumatra, Gondar, Smyrna. Powell-Cotton so driven by wanderlust that, when he fell in love and married in Nairobi, he simply added his young wife to his travel bags, bringing her on a honeymoon which lasted two years. It was during this odyssey that she watched a lion who, refusing to become another trophy hanging above a Quex Park fireplace, mauled her husband; only a rolled up copy of *Punch* employed as a baton saving the hunter from the brute's claws and teeth.

They built the church of St. Mary on Powell-Cotton land in the year the first medals were fashioned from the gun metal of Crimean cannons and stamped with the words: "for valour". Medals handed that year to Hampden Churchill, Alexis Doxat and Donald Farmer who fended off Boers, rescued comrades under heavy fire and captured guns on the Transvaal while, at the top right hand corner of the continent, the great hunter enjoyed the lavish hospitality of Emperor Menelik II, taking aim at nyala and bushbucks who had no idea he was even stalking them.

Unable to go south, and as if thrust by an invisible force,

the swineherd staggered, soaking wet, hauling his bones slowly north, his choice to move anywhere on his own volition sabotaged by the curse. He had a thousand years to make good but was still too young to have any notion of a life beyond thirty, let alone sixty, or ninety. Now he faced what seemed like an eternity adrift. A life bereft of all those he had known, who knew him or his people. Everyone on the road was a stranger; few if any of the men and women who lived in Willesden had any reason to travel these roads. Having failed his family, he now had his own path; the demon had set it out for him and the rules were clear. Life was his even if it had been denied to them. Within an hour, he had reached the village of Hendon, a lurching puppet, staggering where he was led.

On the corner of Birchington Road, bending busily over the apples arranged on a fruit stall in the lea of the supermarket, Harriet Dawe. Busy, busy. This one no, that one yes, too bruised, too – what's that on it? Put it back, put it back. Apples, it has to be, that's what it said, apples it is, green and ripe, one on the windowsill, one by the fire, one by the door and one on the pillow and quick, quick, fruit of the tree, thirteen, fourteen, fifteen, sixteen; apples keep the nightbeasts from the manplace, say it nightly, nightly speak it, darkly, nightly keep the creeppe cripp craw creppie crawthings out of the bedplace; seventeen, eighteen, nineteen, twenty. Harriet Dawe placing the apples in a green plastic carrier bag carefully so as not to bruise them, stooped in a beige mackintosh and towing her pushcart, strawberry blonde hair dye almost grown out, paying in cash for the twenty pieces of fruit she will drag home to the third floor flat on Kingsgate Place which she shares with voices that never rest, a dried lizard and a jar of mouse skulls.

At the doors of the abbey, they waited while a short, stout sister in white surplice walked away slowly to find the abbess. Godwyn said nothing; it didn't seem her place to speak, but she gaped at the great building rising from the river, its scale all the more impressive with no other structure near it. Albric tapped his toe unconsciously, then addressed her.

"I sailed with Wendreda's brother to France," he said, as if justifying bringing her here. Advice followed. "Listen, learn, pray for your soul, those of the lost, and for the safety of our nation. Forkbeard's army has landed in the north, and we must pray for Æthelred and his men that they might repel them. Pray for us, Godwyn."

As the footsteps of the abbess moved along the great hall towards them, the merchant leant in for one final whispered word of counsel:

"There is nothing that cannot be forgiven, no soul that cannot be renewed."

She looked up at him, but his head was turned away, as if he were talking to himself as much as he was to her. He wore sadness like a garment, and Godwyn tried to guess his crime. For the first time in her life, she felt compelled to pray, if only out of gratitude and sympathy.

Wendreda arrived in full sail and grasped her by the shoulders, sizing up her latest project.

"This is Godwyn," Albric told her.

"Oh yes," she said, taking the bag of money which he handed her. "We shall do what we can."

Wendreda smelled of dense, ancient perfumes. Albric bowed graciously and the nun nodded her thanks.

"Come child."

Kilburn Square stretches for an entire block, and were it in Rome, or Florence, or Venice and bordered by handsome, five storey buildings where artisans sell chocolate, bake bread and brew espresso, it might be called a piazza. Instead, it is a drab space bounded by low rise sixties flats, permanent market stalls, a grim tower block and a chain store selling homewares, appliances and electronics. Behind the market where idle stallholders wait for custom is the last remaining patch of green from the old churchyard, a couple of tatty cypress trees growing in the shadow of the gaunt high rise the one remaining souvenir of Old St Paul's. They might have installed a fountain here and planted hedges, a tranquil oasis in the urban sprawl, but that would be to let him off the hook. The ugliness screams his guilt, the heart of the old village given over to cheap clothing and a Turkish barber. A labrador wearing a yellow dayglo jacket leads a woman holding a white cane towards the chain retailer that dominates the corner of the square and the clown envies her; at least she can only smell the shit. Argos, ancient capital of the eastern Peloponnese, seat of Diomedes enriched by Levantine trade, its sway extending over the Argolis and the lands east of Parnon, Cythera, Aegina and Sicyon. Today, it's just a logo slapped onto a lazy seventies brick box inside which Leonard Chester leafs through the thousand glossy pages of a ring bound catalogue. Chester, grey hair under a red baseball cap not here to buy anything, simply killing time. Almost eighty, he still lives with his one hundred and three-year-old mother, a woman born before the Great War, whose father died in the mud of Passchendaele and whose mother marched with Pankhurst. Leonard Chester turning the pages of bicycles, mattresses, vacuum cleaners, and skincare by Elizabeth Arden. At least it's warm in here. He sees they have *Baking with Mary Berry*.

"That'll cheer Mother up," he thinks, and grabs a chitty and a small blue pen.

Not caring if cars have to brake for him, the clown ambles back to the east side of the High Road, towards Birchington Road. Like a parasite on a sheep, a stall butts up between the bank on the northern corner of the junction and the shuttered up store next to it. Upturned cardboard boxes on a wooden pallet afford it some height; on these rest plastic crates filled with phone cases and knock-off wallets while faux Louis Vuitton bags and England shirts hang from a portable clothes rail. Under the wide, black umbrella that acts as a canopy, an old Romanian watches the tall, thin man in a great coat fraying at the hem, heading north one day, south the next like a pendulum, an achingly slow metronome marking the centuries. The clown glances at the stall, such as it is, passes the vacant shop and pauses outside another discount store. Confection, crisps and biscuits; toiletries, cleaning products and clothing; cushions, quilts and cheap plastic toys; hand written signs shouting the prices. A Pakistani shopkeeper wearing a mobile phone earpiece shouts at a woman in a headscarf for opening the plastic covering of some pillowcases, the woman yelling back in Serbian. The clown grabs a can of Pepsi Max from a red plastic drum, reaches deep into his pocket for a golden pound coin which he throws at the man who catches it, still remonstrating with the woman who tells him she will never shop here again. The man correcting her, she isn't shopping, she is sabotaging; the clown downing the drink in one then belching out the gas. He crushes the can and drop kicks it deftly into a nearby litter bin. From her buggy outside the shop, the two year old child of the Serbian woman stares in wonder at the bin where the can landed. The clown whispers to her:

"Practice".

The swineherd's feet thrust him along a track through woods which had long since been cleared by the time the developer George Duncan shook hands with General Arthur Upton, soldier, politician, cricketer and heir to the estate of Fulk Greville Howard; a man who took six catches in the inaugural gentlemen v players match at the MCC, the last at full stretch, falling over the boundary but tossing the ball to Major Lynford Streachy inside the bounds who held it. It was Duncan and his son John Wallace whose streets lined with Italianate villas first desecrated the land. Three hundred homes by 1854, and permission for the London and North Eastern Railway to gouge a deep and lasting scar where, decades earlier, there had been pasture, a handful of cottages and a smithy.

The clown looks back across the road to where William Henry Smith walked his dog through a churchyard. At least the Cock is still here. A business that has plied its trade on this same spot on the edge of Kilburn Square for five and a half centuries. He watched as woods were cleared, trenches dug and heavy stones packed around the uprights. Sturdy frames for the walls pegged together, roped to mules then hoisted into place. Wattle dipped in wet soil, dung, clay and straw to make a plaster, then woven in between vertical boards. Thatchers dressing the roof. Hammer taps, a small forge, the slow sawing of wood and the smell of freshly cut oak. No other building of any permanence for a mile west to Kensal or east to Hampstead save the priory, these roads too dangerous, the woods too easy for robbers make their lair. Here Turpin drank and Catesby conspired. Even Shakespeare stopped once to eat a veal pie and take a shit.

It was at the Cock that birds clawed at each other's heads and chests for money, giving the pub its name, but dogs fought here too. Point-headed bull mastiffs with savage teeth and powerful jaws set at one another in the old cockpit until one lay bleeding or an owner called the fight. Before that, they chained a bull to a pole, pug faced mutts mawing at the brute's head, pulling him down, tearing at his face while he tried to toss them away. Bears were harder to procure, though he was among the crowds throwing coins when they brought one in, a young female, when the pub was still a remote tavern in a clearing. The furious beast on her hind quarters, snarling at the starved hounds who yawed at their cage, the hatch lifted and the animals prowling as a pack. The bear jabbing as the first dog bit her, growling and swiping in fury, her chain clanking as the others took advantage of her momentary inattention, attacking her flank; the bear desperate, clawing, roaring, tossing and tumbling, shaking her great head and spraying the jeering crowd with blood and slather. Two dogs died that day before the bear bled out, a carcass of fur, flayed flesh and gore, a dog eye among the offal left in the sawdust. They tore the worm and rot infested building down a century ago and built a gin palace that kept the name, the only fighting in the new brick tavern between market porters and Hackney cabmen, rat catchers and carny barkers. Today, it's the last stop before the slab, a terminus for red faced men who die alone on mattresses drenched in urine, their bedsit carpets littered with encrusted takeaway boxes and chicken bones.

Inside the pub, John Mulligan waits for the cunts to show up with the money. He put in four hours work shoring up the foundations with a cunt behind the eyes from the night before, and it's been three days now. Cunts said they were waiting for a cheque but they had to cash it in at the pub in Kentish Town. Never used to be like this, no boy, this is fierce. John Mulligan staring at his pint of Carling like it spat at him, reaching in his trouser pocket for a packet of Benson. He pulls one out with his teeth and walks through the door into the sunlight. Cunt's ten minutes late already. Mulligan sucks smoke and tar deep into his frontal cortex and feels momentary sanctification as snatches of music waft over from the precinct. Fucking darkies singing to Jesus. Mulligan, who was absent from every mass since he fell off the boat in Liverpool in 1988, watches the cunt over the road dressed as a clown kick a can into a bin as a black 2011 Bentley Azure sweeps past, carrying Damaris Kostantides to his Grade II barn in Iver Heath after an hour with his Harley Street osteopath. Kostantides who imports minerals from Australia to Europe, whose company now owns over three hundred container ships in four continents, two years younger than John Mulligan from Newtownabbey who grubs around in construction ditches and waits three fucking days for the cunts to pay him. The Irishman spits in the direction of Kostantides 6.7 litre V8 automatic and cunts at the car, the day, himself and the man who may or may not turn up with fifty pounds. From across the road, the clown sees Mulligan, the square, the whole bankrupt and broken place. This long, grim ribbon of dreck. These poisoned people, this vile spew. The stink. The grey air. The bitter stench. The clown bares his teeth at stores selling joyless wares to those too desperate to shop anywhere else, live anywhere else, die anywhere else. Because ultimately, and no one can persuade him otherwise on this, he's been over it a thousand thousand times, if it weren't for him, this might all still be forest.

A brisk breeze gusts along the corridor formed by buildings on either side of the street. To the east, three storied Victorian brick terraces with sash windows stretch the length of the High Road. On the corners, elegant sturdy structures that were once banks and public houses, some of which remain. The homogeny punctuated only by the occasional modern apartment block, the Art Deco palace housing the Primark clothing store and the white stucco walls and domes of the National Club. Few tenants stick around for long; the clown has seen each of them come and go, everything and everyone replaceable, forgotten within a couple of generations, none immortal, not even him; and today the cathartic denouement where the world can see him get exactly what he deserves.

In the years that followed, he scanned every face he passed to find a likeness, but none came. What if she married again? Who would the man have been? He doubted it would have been another swineherd. Perhaps a hunter, at least while there was still forest to shoot in. How did she look at thirty? Forty? What pestilence took her? Did she find redemption? Was there time for her to make peace before God and apply herself, head bowed, to the priory church that stood where she once stroked his naked body with gentle fingers? Where is she now? Eternally blessed, or forever scourged as he should have been, a thousand years into her torment and a thousand into his own?

Abbess Wendreda led Godwyn along the stone corridor, her leather sandals clacking at her heels. On reaching an arched doorway, she pushed the heavy wood. Inside was a small chapel where three or four nuns, heads bowed in prayer sat before a painted fresco of the Annunciation.

Wendreda nodded and one of the women, a squat, red faced sister with a stern brow rose and came to the door.

"Thorhild, this is Godwyn. Show her around, please."

The woman looked at the new arrival, as if this were the last thing she wished to do. The abbess walked away, and with her, all connection to anything Godwyn knew.

"Come, oblate."

Thorhild's voice was sharp and she walked quickly, pointing out the library, dormitories and refectory matter-of-factly and without elaboration. In the kitchens, a fire glowed in the central hearth and two nuns chopped vegetables. One of the sisters looked over at Godwyn who, despite her simple clothes felt conspicuously worldly in their presence.

"What, do you covet the oblate, Eadgyth?" barked the older nun. Do you grieve the life you gave up for Christ? Give me your knife."

Eadgyth averted her eyes and her cheeks filled with colour as she held out her blade.

"But doesn't she have the most wonderful plumage?" Thorhild said, gripping a handful of the Godwyn's tight black curls and holding them, the corner of her mouth twitching. Staring at her, Thorhild removed her own coif, revealing a shock of steel grey matted with grease. Godwyn shrank at the sudden gesture and had no time to compose herself before Thorhild grabbed her own hideous mane in one hand and sawed it off at the scalp with the other, her eyes unblinking.

"That is what we do with hair, oblate."

Replacing her head covering over the remaining jag of grey, she wiped the blade on her wimple, handed it back to Eadgyth and threw the cuttings on the fire. They smelled of pig.

Opposite the Cock on the eastern side of the High Road is the black-painted facia of another loan shop, a bargaining house whose clerks wait with fingers that grasp more than they give for the needy to step inside. The shop's storerooms and safe deposit boxes groan with watches, rings and precious things. A gambling husband, a booze addled wife, a business partner who cut and ran; a hollow-eyed cashier holding up a gleaming keepsake to the bare light of a tungsten bulb, tipping coins from a leather pouch onto a glass counter that entombs the keepsakes of the poor and the lost. Barely a quarter of a mile from the shop where Emmanuel Gbeho tried to hock his watch, Angel Flores hopes to cash in the war medals belonging to the father who beat her and her sister Rosa. Her brother's eldest daughter, Carmela is getting married in Miami and she has no money for the flight. The medals prove worthless. The ones they gave you just for showing up. Two a penny. Forget that – ten a penny. Angel Flores, who vacuums corridors in the Hilton Metropole Hotel three miles south along the Edgware Road, has no idea that the plates – the blue and yellow ones with the terracotta bottoms that she uses day in day out – how could she know that just two of those stupid plates that were a wedding present to her parents José and Frieda could buy her a flight to Florida, and the whole set of six with the bowls and china cups she keeps on top of the wardrobe in the one bedroom flat on Willesden Lane could pay for every dress, tiara, roast pig, floral decoration and musician at Carmela and Domingo's wedding? She picks up the cigar box filled with ribbons and medallions while the pawnbroker turns his attention back to the sudoku puzzle in last night's *Standard*.

Next to the moneylender's is a Poundland discount store. Outside, twenty-five-year-old Armen Azaryan sits cross-legged on the pavement, his back resting against one of the advertising panels of a bus stop. Azaryan skinny and small in black jeans and a light grey zip up jacket, a black knitted hat with a white band shielding his ears from the wind. Clutched in cold fingers is a small paper cup from the Café Nero across the street, Azaryan hoping for the generous and kind to fill it with charity. Invisible Azaryan who passed all his money to the butcher Ferukhan for the number of the shadowy Belarussian, Domash. An early morning rendezvous in the parking lot behind the Zakrama supermarket in Minsk, thin men with knapsacks climbing the tailgate in darkness, Azaryan among them, a bucket for piss and sixty eight hours of night. The truck pulling out onto the E28 towards Berlin, the E30 to Amsterdam and the Hoek where it rolled onto a DFDS Seaways ferry, pallets of bauxite ore marked for a canning plant in Leicester. Arriving at the dock in Newcastle in the predawn January drizzle, the silver Volvo FH16 semi moving past the security checkpoints and on into the night, slipping into a warehouse in Monkwearmouth where seventeen men, weak from lack of food sleepwalked into a new world. Azaryan stumbling ten miles to the slip road of the southbound A1 where the driver of a truck filled with refrigerated chicken carcasses fetched him up and jettisoned him four hours later at Staples Corner, a mile or so north of the bus stop advertising *The Amazing Spiderman 2* where he now sits. The coffee has long since gone cold in his belly but his cup still hopes for a coin to christen it. Too hungry and cold to look for work or a hostel on the day he arrived, Azaryan curled up in the doorway of Argos to sleep. Here, youths came in the night and took his phone and the bag he brought from Yerevan, the card from Anush; no beautiful sentiment, but her writing. The clown passes by like everyone else. No sympathy. The queue for that is a long one, and it's never your turn.

Since the flight from the Cunebourne, the swineherd had not left Willesden except to dash across the fields and onto the road for help. Now, his feet impelled him towards Hendon, Stanmore and the villages and farmsteads beyond, unable to turn left or right nor deviate in any way from his predetermined destination, away from the woman who might well die without him. At Wæclingacaester, guards ushered him through the London Gate, but here his northward journey ended and he found shelter in the lea of a Roman wall that had stood here since before Alban was martyred. Here he slept poorly with only sacking to cover him before rousing, hungry and thirsty. The only direction his feet would take him was back through the gate again. He had no food, no water and no money. There was no work that he could carry out nor any home he could reach in which to lay his head. Yet he was alive. He sunk to his knees by the pedestrian gateway and put out an upturned hand. He had to get back to his family. Praying would have been disingenuous. There could be no heavenly banquet for him; in weakness and fear of the eternal fire, he had chosen to live on, a lesser evil than the furnace and a hope that he might find his way home. Hours passed and with only a few small coins and a hunk of stale bread thrown his way, he began the slow journey south. At Radlett, a woman took pity on him, bringing him ale and boiled cabbage which restored his energy a little. Here where the lane to Willesden joined Wæcling Strete, he tried again to turn towards his cottage but the curse threw him back to the road and pushed him on towards Westminster. This, it turned out, was his southerly resting place, his daily round echoing his final journey as a monk, to bring Augustine's Bible to

Westminster and return again to the abbey. Beneath the jetty where a boat took pilgrims across to Thorney Island, he slept. When he woke, there was a cloak around him. It was a Christian kindness which, though he knew he did not deserve, it was one he appreciated deeply. The curse propelled him, his brain not needing to think nor his feet doubting where they would fall. None recognised him at either terminus of his journey, for none were searching him, nor would they be looking for a swineherd, a beggar, an itinerant wanderer, a ghost. At times he rested along the way, sometimes for hours or, if rain or flood made the road impassable, days. And he wore the cloak for the next four centuries.

Outside the opticians next to Poundland, oblivious to the beggar at the bus stop, Daksha Joshi waits for his wife, Pearl to have some bifocals fitted. Inside, his eight-year-old daughter Kamila plays games on Pearl's phone while two year old Amit sits on her knee, blowing bubbles from his spittle. Joshi jabbing a cigarette between his lips. It's been a long day. The Good Samaritans were round again at crack of dawn, going through their finances, who was that for? And what about that one? and it all came out again and Pearl cried and he had to go outside for a walk up to Queens Park. Daksha Joshi, spending every penny the government gives to him, his wife and family on chatlines, flirting with drug addled mums in Liverpool, Burnley, or Swansea, trying to befriend bored whores with fake names, counselling them from his fifth floor Kilburn council flat; Daksha Joshi ejaculating trite homilies into their ears at a pound a minute while they fill in word searches and watch reruns on mute while the debt tower rises like a tsunami to annihilate him, Pearl, Kamila and Amit. Pearl who confiscated his phone because the lady said to, who can't see that he is ill, that he was ill long before they married in Gujarat two days after he landed after an eleven hour flight. It was the first time he set eyes on her. Daksha Joshi whose lip quivers when he talks, who has never worked, who sleeps all day and plays computer games all night draws on the cigarette and watches nineteen-year-old Nicole Braithwaite on her way to the chemist to buy hair colour, laughing into her phone. No phone of his own now, and no money till Pearl gives him some, her husband and oldest child, resentful at her, the do gooders who say they can pray their money worries away and the Masons who, he believes, ultimately organise everything. He logs Braithwaite's curves with greedy eyes until the ash burns his fingers. As he stamps out the butt, little Amit runs out and presses against his leg, arms up for a cuddle. Joshi takes his hand.

"Come on, let's get you back to mummy," and he leads his son back inside the opticians while Braithwaite pretends not to look at the clown outside Poundland, and wonders if he sees her.

Just past the opticians into which Daksha and Amit Joshi have just disappeared are a couple of shoe shops. Above the signage and flaking white paint, behind the net curtained sash window of a second storey flat, scenes from the biblical epic *King of Kings* throw light on the walls and bed where Kieran Monaghan lies back and reaches inside his pants. Monaghan's room a damp box where bedbugs no longer seek sanctuary in the creases of mattresses or seat cushions, roaming in brazen packs across the walls. Small brown smears mark where they have been beaten with a rolled up *Kerryman*, their bloated abdomens bursting onto the woodchip. Friday by Friday, the landlord sends one of his boys to collect the seventy pounds for Monaghan's bed, bills and fresh toilet paper. No work on Easter Saturday and

91

cement caked boots lie kicked over by the door. Monaghan not religious, but it feels profane to be nursing an erection as the Messiah staggers towards his execution at the hands of Roman and Jew. He tries to blank the voices out but it's no good, his heart's not in it.

"Fuck you, you little bastard!"

He reaches for the paper to murder a bug as it crawls quickly over the wall beside the bed and a roach already creeping across a picture of the victorious schoolboys from Pobalscoil Chorca Dhuibhne holding aloft the silver Hogan Cup scurries off onto the maroon carpet.

"Cunt!" Monaghan shouts, as Christ drags his burdensome cross slowly to the place of the skull, called Golgotha.

A Blue Vauxhall Astra carrying Carenza Philpott and her nine-year-old daughter Georgia to a playdate with Georgia's cousin April in Wealdstone lurches forwards, then cuts out as the lights turn green. The white DAF CF250 truck behind them hits the horn but the stalled car allows eighteen-year-old Jamaal White to run across the road and into McDonalds. Here, Wasim Ali, thirty-eight, his black hair greying at the temples takes White's order, pushing buttons on his console but wishing he wasn't. Behind White, pinchfaced Marie Johnstone wants to know if the cheeseburger he has just given her has pickles in it, because she asked for no pickles. Ali opening the yellow box and lifting the lid of the bun to reveal two grey green slivers of gherkin atop a shrivelled disk of beef. The teenager rolling her eyes and Ali barking at the Nigerian at the burger station behind him. Prudence Ajoade grins stupidly and tells Ali not to be so bossy. Ajoade's father paying her college fees and her rent while Ali who is still unmarried grafts for pennies, working shifts instead of studying, just to pay Siddiq for the room. The money Ajoade makes here is for what? The hairstyles she changes every week? A twenty-three-year-old duty manager reaches over Ali with a punnet or French fries and a Big Mac.

"Get with it, Wass."

She places the food on a tray for Jamaal White, then turns to the black girl and a Korean youth with thick lensed glasses frying chicken nuggets and apple pies.

"Hustle, hustle!"

She claps and disappears to the back office as Prudence Ajoade who has a small tribal scar on her left cheek grins at her like she is an entertainer, and continues frying burgers at the same languid pace, waiting for four o clock when her shift ends.

After her orientation, it was time for Godwyn to dress as befitted an oblate at Barking Abbey. Thorhild led her through lightless passages until they reached the garderobe, an airless room deep in beneath the church. As the nun lit a series of candles, an arched undercroft filled floor to ceiling with robes materialised around her. Thorhild looked at her charge, considering her shape and height. Grabbing a robe, she held it up against her. It was enormous. The nun snorted and climbed onto a stool to reach the upper rail on which more dark cassocks hung.

"This will do," she said, throwing a slightly smaller robe at Godwyn. It weighed heavy in her arms and to it was added a course woollen undershift that prickled her skin, a white wimple, a veil, a rope girdle and leather sandals. Thorhild clapped her hands:

"Quick girl, sloth is devilry, get dressed."

As the older nun watched, Godwyn stepped out of the simple gown that had been given to her at Albric's house and into the sacred clothing. The habit pulled her shoulders down and gaped around her sparrow's frame, dragging on the floor behind her. Godwyn pulled on the wimple and arranged the veil over her face. Tying the girdle as best she could, she slipped into the shoes. Thorhild rolled her eyes, rearranging the veil with rough hands and yanking the girdle tight. When Godwyn flinched, she smiled.

"A little pain serves only to remind us of the sufferings of our Lord."

And with that, she chivvied the oblate out and back along the passageways to the light.

Clement Durade cycles past on his way to cash in a prescription for sufficient opiates, barbiturates, pills and pastilles to counter the vapours, fainting and other hypochondria suffered by his mother Betty for another week. He came yesterday but forgot it was Good Friday, Durade pedalling quickly past McDonalds on a bicycle slightly too small for him. Useless Clement, his mother's sister calls him, the aunt who never had children, whose husband left her and whose only business now is Betty and the son who lives with and cares for her. Durade running late, his green jacket flapping in the slipstream. In their tumbledown townhouse on Brondesbury Villas, Betty watches weather reports wearing Balmain shoes, her lips painted red while upstairs another son, Florian lies on his bed as a DVD of *Prometheus* plays in the corner; Florian Durade, a terrified recluse, a hollow chested spectre with translucent skin and a voice so feeble that the noise of the world beyond his room would smother it. From outside the opticians on the east side of the street, the clown watches Durade's feet, a furious whir, running errands for Betty who he loves and hates, needs and resents, adores and fears, until the giant red bulk of buses obscure him from the picture.

Like a landbound Flying Dutchman, there was no journey's end nor any amelioration of the loss the swineherd felt on that first day. But he was alive. He bled and his heart beat, and it would continue beating for another ten centuries. He walked more quickly than his body wanted, his feet tripping over the ruts and rocks. With each step, the years loomed before him. Maybe this was hell after all, and the Devil had tricked him into choosing the only destiny fitting for him. A wretched rag of a man, hop skipping to nowhere with nothing to do when he arrived; a life on endless repeat, powerless to change anything; a speck of dust drifting down through the dark earth, its only weight the memories it holds, falling forever.

Easter Saturday. The Christ holed up in the tomb; the one full day in the calendar where God is dead, or at least his son. It seems the perfect day for it; a day off for everyone. The clown looks over at the McDonalds building, its curved fascia wrapping round the corner of Victoria Road, the words 'Trinity House' still embossed on the brick. Formerly the Trinity House School, latterly a furniture store, now a fast food restaurant. Nothing stays the same, only God goes on. Over on the east side of the street, a fashion outlet and a phone store stand at either corner of Quex Road, another of Powell Cotton's vanities. A crossroads, although the clown has already promised his soul to the Devil, and today the Dark Lord is calling in the debt.

Behind the distant cotton candy of a cherry tree on Quex Road, the clown can just make out the Catholic church of the Sacred Heart of Jesus. A chapel and monastery was founded by the Fathers known as the Oblates of Mary who laid their cornerstone a hundred and fifty years earlier, their mission to save the souls of Irish railway workers who swarmed, shovels in hand, to the metropolis. A century or so later, the clown fell in with three thousand mourners who followed a coffin along the High Road and turned up this street, the casket draped in the flag of Ireland, so light that it contained more soul than man. The body, when it lived, belonged to Michael Gaughan, volunteer in the Clann na Éireann, a prisoner in Parkhurst who starved in solidarity with the car bombing Price sisters, renegade soldiers demanding political status and transfer to an Irish jail. Gaughan's skin shrivelled and shrank until one day, six correctional officers held him down, dragged him by the hair, forced his head back over the bedrail and placed a wooden block between his teeth. Through a hole in the wood they pushed a tube so roughly that the man's throat bled. Seventeen times over the next two months, they roughhoused him with their tube until one day they pushed it down so savagely that it hit a lung, filling his bronchioles with liquid milk and eggs, drowning him. Unable to follow any further once the parade deviated from the main thoroughfare, the clown watched the crowds walk solemnly up Quex Road for a requiem at the church, a foretaste of the fifty thousand men, women and children who would turn up to hear Dáithí Ó Conaill stand by the coffin at the Leigue cemetery in Ballina, scarlet with fury, denouncing Gaughan's jailers as the vampires of a discredited empire.

Lost in a time when life moved at a more languid pace, the clown rests against a pole on the corner of Quex Road whose decommissioned traffic lights have been bound in black polythene. Long days spent in the abbey scriptorium with nothing to distract him than the rasping, rhythmic song of ink scratching across vellum. He remembers the zeal with which he approached his work, his bright-eyed readiness to learn, copying in hand drawn vulgate the words of the beloved disciple. He remembers poring over the pages, astonished that the Holy Lamb of God should die for so lowly a sinner as he. And now, a thousand years of canker have collected around his soul, ossifying over the centuries. He feels his sin a deadweight within him, a leaden bolus he can never cough up or bleed out. He looks up as Miguel Velasco and José Cruz pull a pirated copy of *Pacific Rim* from a red shoulder bag and show it to Felicia Arkle, an administrative assistant from Barbados employed by Camden Social Services. Arkle doesn't know the film but thinks her nephew Rhys would enjoy it, and it's his birthday in a few days.

"Five pound" says Velasco in a low monotone.

"Three for twelve" adds Cruz, pulling out *XMen, Robocop* and *Jack Ryan*.

"This one will do," says Arkle who wants the transaction to be over, to minimise the time spent with men who can also sell her drugs brought to London in a swallowed prophylactic then shat into a pan in a terraced council house in Becton. Arkle reaching into her purse for a blue and green banknote and shoving the DVD deep into her bag, wishing already that she had never engaged with these baseball-hatted banditti.

As the months passed, the young oblate moved through the hours as if on rails. She was tutored patiently by an elderly nun named Caenfrith who taught her the Latin alphabet, the two of them sitting on wooden stools in the courtyard. Caenfrith had the girl pour ash on the ground, then drew each letter with a long stick, speaking its name. Her pupil would smooth over the ash with a broom, then attempt to draw the shapes herself, Caenfrith coaxing her and never chiding when she drew her 'e' upside down, or placed the shoulder of the 'r' to the left. Sometimes, she was given needlework; sewing orphreys onto priests' chasubles. The work was simple if monotonous, affixing strips of white, green or brown cloth with tiny stitches to the hem of the garment. Sewing afforded the nuns time to pray and it was this that governed their days, an almost never-ending round of chants, invocations and plainsong. They pleaded ceaselessly for the souls of the abbey's benefactors, the life of King Æthelred and his son Edmund Ironside, and for protection from Cnut's Danes who were feared to be launching a raid on the south. It felt strange to never be hungry, to be fed, for her body to fill out beneath the plain robes, to never be groped or manhandled, thrown onto a straw bed covered in rags and penetrated. Lustre came to her face, the oblate became a novice, the novice learned the words of ten of the Psalms, then twenty, then fifty, took vows and became a nun.

As Felicia Arkle hurries away, Kaitlyn Eastwood carries her Costa Coffee almond flat white past the clown to a side door on Quex Road. Here, she climbs threadbare steps to the second floor of Merlin House, an ugly nineteen seventies block that squats above the fashion store on the corner. The company Eastwood works for services properties for absent landlords, sending cheap Romanian labour to fix problems as best they can while creaming off a tidy profit. This is not why she left Australia. Her desk doesn't even have a window and they share a kitchen with whoever is renting the other units, a revolving door of men and women with broken English who disappear into locked offices. A man with a greying beard and a belly always stares at her. Eastwood can feel his eyes on her when she makes coffee from the machine, which is why she has taken to wearing baggy jumpers and paying for take-outs from the café across the road. Back home in Tasmania, waves lap a long beach as gulls pick pristine sand for mussels and clams while labradors and collies chase balls excitedly in the surf. Here in London, her fingernails need cleaning every day and the cleansing pads she uses on her face turn black. She misses her dog, her mum, her church. Eastwood sits back down at her laptop as buses rumble on the street beneath and opens Facebook to look at pictures of Lara and Maddy's twenty first party in Taroona.

North. South is Tyburn. This way St. Albans. Tyburn where the adulterer Dereham and the Saint Campion were strung from the tree, St. Albans where the executioner of the eponymous saint threw down his sword and begged to be slain in his place. As he walks, the clown kicks the blossoms that litter the pavement. Army boots that have seen some road; pulled from a dead labourer knocked down by a tow truck outside the Green Man in Paddington in the early hours of a January morning, not the driver's fault but he should have stopped. The clown only had time to take the boots before others came running. North to St. Albans. Then south to Westminster. East to Northminster or south to Eastminster would make a change, but where would the burn be? South to Westminster. Then north again to St. Albans. To Wæclingacaester. To Verulamium, again and again and againium. The same same samium. The clown looks west up Victoria Road and back at the gaunt Kilburn Square tower, taking it in one last time. What a bastard he thinks. Kilburn a never-ending cuntknuckle. And on he walks, over the junction of Quex Road towards the phone shop on the other corner. However many circles of hell there are, he must be near the centre.

In those first days, the swineherd followed where his feet took him, collapsing where they stopped on the outskirts of

Wæclingacaester or on the banks of the Tybourne stream. Each dawn, he was lifted to his feet and carried in the direction from which he had come. Should flood or frost make travel impossible, he was ushered to a place where he could hole up until the road was clear. Grief stemmed his appetite, he had no thought of food, just a deep sadness that would not lift, of what he had lost and what he had become. If it was cold, he shivered, if he was thirsty, his tongue swelled and the discomfort remained, so it made sense to attend to it. New foods and drinks arrived infrequently from the continent or further afield and, even if he could afford them, he bored of them all in time. His hair and nails did not grow, he did not need to shave nor did he age. After the river failed to kill him, he dragged the short blade he carried in his belt across his wrists, but though he bled, the wounds healed before his astonished eyes. He assumed Godwyn would not grieve him and that, should they ever meet, begging her forgiveness would be as pointless as the hope that she would grant it him.

In the phone shop on the corner, Ali Iqbal explains the advantages of a Samsung Galaxy S6 over his customer's three year old Sony Xperia Z2, Iqbal's fervour rivalling that of the men hoping to convert the infidel Archie Hatton. Maryam Yahya simply wanting a phone that lets her see photos of her nephews and nieces in Tikrit, and which she can use to talk to her sister Sanaa free of charge. Iqbal showing her apps, screens and widgets, flicking his finger across the phone's illuminated blue screen, Yahya feigning wonder, the anxiety rising, waiting for the man to finish talking. The clown has neither phone nor any need of one. No phone number and no address either. He has no driver's license nor any ID. He has no friends to call, no treasures that need a house in which to store them, and nothing to keep. Iqbal's phone may be a repository of all human knowledge, but can it tell you the tree where Turpin hid? The grave of John the Cooper buried by his wife and lover behind the barn near Smyrna Road? Can it tell you the plot of the novel which a drunken Oliver Goldsmith shared with him in the Harp and Horn before he left the manuscript in a carriage and never revisited it? Can it describe the stink of dead fish when drought dried up the river in 1622, the melancholy of a plague house, the everyday reek of sweat and piss before the days of public sanitation? Can a device in the palm of your hand adequately relate the tune of the reel danced by the Macey sisters at the Essoldo Theatre, the howl of wolves in ancient forest, or plainsong echoing off abbey walls before the Conquest? As a novice, he spent three years inscribing vellum with the words of the fisherman John, words now available to all with a few taps on a screen. In multiple tongues. And he's had time to learn them.

Mit Eifer hab' ich mich
der Studien beflissen;
Zwar weiß' ich viel,
doch möcht' ich alles wissen.

In study, I applied myself with zeal; much I know, yet want to know it all. Always more to learn, and thirty lifetimes in which to learn it. The clown wonders what became of his own precious pages after Cromwell's death angels rode along Watling Street and took sledgehammers to the presbytery, nave and chapter house; men running, filling carts with books and gold, boys crying, the splinter of headstones and crack of masonry. The horror of Alban's shrine ransacked, of Amphibalus' limestone frippery reduced to a stump; the rapacious hunt for treasure, for anything of value that might be sold to enrich the coffers of a lustful king whose desire for Ann Boleyn had cut the umbilicus, leaving an innocent multitude destitute. The building remained, gaunt and stripped of finery, stones left unadorned, pale squares where looted hangings, tapestries and paintings once hung. The clown arrived at night once the rape was complete, and the weeping was so loud and so sorrowful that he heard it long before he reached the city's ancient walls.

Tony Wu throws the stub of a Galoise Blonde onto the pavement, crushes it with the toe of a fake alligator skin boot and steps into a gaming arcade that hides between the phone shop and an optician. The only customer, Wu does not acknowledge the Ethiopian cashier who is absorbed in a game of Tetris on her mobile phone and doesn't look up. Tony Wu, forty, slim with a black leather jacket and jeans and a drooping Mandarin moustache. Import, export; mainly phones, chargers, and GPS; plugging himself in to a flashing one armed bandit called Lucky Seven; twenty pounds in and forty more in his back pocket if the luck fails. Wu's head throbbing from the stress of it all. Tiny Cheo and that fag brother of his calling twenty times a day and the ship still somewhere south of Suez. Diazepam washed down with a Red Stripe helped a little. 'Do not operate machinery'. He sneers as the twenty rattles up to twenty seven and he rubs the back of his neck where it hurts. Bonus symbols. Free spins. He smacks the button, licking his lips. Up she goes. Digits flicker quickly as they race towards the magical fifty and for a moment, Wu is weightless, fearless. Tomorrow his shoulder will ache again and another bitch from the HMRC will call and so will his son, asking why he didn't wire the money; Soon Yi's birthday and who else is looking after her while Marco is in jail?

At the cashier's desk, the Ethiopian rearranges coloured oblongs and squares as they drop from the top of her screen and passes three hundred points for the first time. An ad interrupts the game and she takes a bite of an orange Club biscuit, while on Tony Wu's machine, the number settles at ninety six pounds. Wu is free from all of it. No grownup children back in Macau, the idiot Rudi and the delinquent Marco, no Rita demanding Western Union money transfers, no unpaid taxes nor problems with the Home Office, just adrenaline and his body suspended in space; only the machine anchoring him to the bedrock of the earth. He hits the button and the lines spin again.

On the western side of the road that links the execution ground of traitors and villains to the city ransacked by Boudicca and her Iceni hordes, Raymond Purcell walks into the Halifax building society with a cheque from his mother. She is the only person who ever sends him cheques, filling out the slip in blue biro, tearing it off, placing it in a brown manilla envelope with a blue second class stamp and posting it to 178 Ashford Court, Cricklewood, London NW16BU. Genevieve Purcell, unable to work out how to send money via the internet, too many codes and then she has to find the card reader. They never give her enough time to react and the panic sets in, clumsy fingers entering numbers wrong and fear that she'll end up enriching a wholly different person, that the sky will fall in. And so she writes a cheque instead and posts it to her son. Grateful as he is for the money, Purcell waits months before cashing in the things, only walking into the Santander on the High Road when he has at least one other transaction to take care of, usually another cheque from his mother. Today, there is no queue and he walks up to the cashier, an Indian woman in her late thirties in a grey suit bearing a plastic name badge, and hands her some banknotes from a work trip to Doha. As Puja Ramaswamy taps on her keyboard to find the exchange rate, the bank fills with people and a queue forms behind Purcell, the transaction taking longer than he thought. Now five people stand in line behind him, Purcell feeling their frustration and telling Ramaswamy that it's OK, he can come back later; the cashier not caring about the queue, she's paid by the hour, not the customer. Purcell sweating, asking her to give him the money back, Ramaswamy shrugging, pushing the notes back through the tray and asking if there is anything else she can help him with. Purcell grabbing the riyals and leaving, hating Ramaswamy, hating the people behind him and hating his mother for sending him the stupid money.

The evening meal finished, Godwyn rose with her board and cup to clean it.

"Stop."

The voice of Thorhild.

"Come".

She followed the older nun out of the refectory, along a passageway and down the stone steps that led to the sacristy and other store rooms. The flame of Thorhild's candle rose tall with no breeze to disturb it and they entered a small room in which stood a wooden table and two stools. An office of sorts, otherwise the place was completely bare. It was cold.

"Sit".

Godwyn sat, Thorhild walking around the table.

"We shall see how well you have learned your Psalms, child."

Fetching up a bale of cord, the nun dropped it on the table in front of the girl. The rope had knots along its length, a kind of prayer rosary.

"*Dominus regit me*. Now."

The younger nun reeling off the lines of the song

confidently in Latin. She loved the words, and found comfort in them, the Lord her shepherd, but before she had passed the fourth verse, Thorhild stopped her.

"*Qui habitat*".

The ninety-first Psalm. Again, she knew the words. Again she was interrupted.

"*Deus noster refugium et virtus*".

Psalm 46, aborted by Thorhild after the third verse. It was only a matter of time, not all of the book had been committed to memory, and she would inevitably fail. That fall came with Psalm 14.

"*Dixit insipens in corde suo.*" Thorhild impatient.

"*Dixit insipens in corde suo non est Deus*," Godwyn began.

"No!" Thorhild slamming her fist down on the table in fury or triumph. "That is the fifty third Psalm."

"The two are near identical", Godwyn protested.

"How dare you answer back girl!" Thorhild's face red with venom. "Strip."

The younger nun not comprehending. Thorhild spitting the words,

"Remove your clothing."

The girl remained rooted to her seat in fear. Thorhild stood so suddenly that her stool fell. Grabbing Godwyn's habit, she wrenched it up with such force that the girl was lifted with it. Naked, she crossed her arms over one another, clasping her shoulders in protection from what might come next. Thorhild now grabbing the cord with one hand and Godwyn's head with the other, pressing it into the table, shouting each word of the psalm as she whipped her.

"*Dixit. Insipiens. In corde. Suo.*" The pain intense. *"Non. Est. Deus. Corrupti. Sunt."* Thorhild grunting the words, beads of sweat forming on her brow despite the cold. "*Et. Abominabiles. Facti. Sunt.*"

On the beating went as Godwyn gripped the table, her

flesh burning from the lashes, her lips mouthing the words of the psalm that consoled her, Yea, though I walk through the valley of the shadow of death, I will fear no evil: for thou art with me and thy rod and thy staff comfort me. The table falling, and with it, the girl who curled herself up on the cold flags, still mouthing her prayer. Thorhild now bent double, catching her breath. A door opening. Ænfled hearing the table fall wanting to see what had caused it.

"The child needed some of the Lord's precious discipline," Thorhild told her matter of factly, straightening herself and beginning to coil the rope.

"Get dressed girl, and learn your Scripture."

As the older nun placed the cord back on a rusted nail hammered into the wall, Godwyn crawled to her feet. She fetched up her clothing with shaking hands, her back red and stinging so badly that all she wanted to do was remain lying on the cold stones. Ænfled helped her on with her habit and led her to the nuns' dormitory. Here she bathed her with cool water, applied dock leaves to her welts and bound her with linen bandages, saying nothing, her silence kinder than any words.

Somewhere near here, before the expansion of the city when this was all parkland and pasture owned by Littles, Liddells and Howards, there had been a smithy. Three or four men working the forge, and a cottage next door where the smith lived with three children and a dark haired wife. The clown would see the woman staring from the window as he passed, feeling her eyes on his skin. One time, she was waiting for him and walked with him, telling him things he shouldn't have known, and he felt her desire. A week or so later, she was there again. Her face flushed, her shoulders rising and falling as she breathed. He did not know how long she had been looking out for him by the road, as it was already evening and the light failing. She pulled him into the shadows, grabbing his hair and kissing him so violently that his lips hurt. He felt nothing, neither pity nor desire, and pulled away, wiping his mouth. Her head dropped and she didn't speak. He thought of the smith and the children he'd seen many times playing in front of the house. Whatever it was the woman needed, he couldn't give. Holding her by the shoulders, he whispered in her ear something that only she heard. A few days later, the smith himself confronted him on the street, companions at either shoulder, one carrying an iron bar. The man accused the clown of everything he had not done but had been invited to do. The smith had seen the way his wife looked at the clown, the way her face flushed when his mane was spoken. A crack of metal, the smith's fists pounding at his chest, oaths and spittle from the thugs accompanying him. He played dead, more for the sake of the smith who seemed a good man, and it's not as if he didn't need punishing. Within a year, the woman was cradling another child, her hair as curly and red as her father's. The smithy has long since been swallowed by a block that runs between Quex Road and Kingsgate Place; two shops selling and reconditioning laptops and games consoles; a mobile phone outlet, a cheap jewellery store and a discount clothing chain. On the first floor are a number of import-export, accountants and conveyancers', not that anyone looks up. Who knows what you might tread in?

Judit Ferencz walks out of the discount clothing store, a plastic carrier bag holding a twelve pound ninety nine black skirt, and tucks her Marc Jacob's purse back into her fake Hermès bag. She is livid. József has gone to his friend's place in Brighton. For Pesach. Brighton. Who goes to Brighton for Passover? Grandma and Grandpa Donát are coming all the way from Debrecen, arriving tonight, praise God, and her oldest son won't be there to greet them. Nor has he been wearing his kippah recently. And what's the use of a family business when there's no family to run it? As she passes Victor Sërbo, sitting in a red sleeping bag wearing a black jacket and grey woollen hat and hoping for alms, she fishes in her bag for the phone which has started to vibrate. József is such a beautiful boy too, blonde like a Norwegian and always dreaming, drawing pictures for her; her angel. Maybe that's why she said yes to art school, because the other thing would crush him, the paperwork and rubber stamping; the transactional minutiae of house surveys and property sales. Judit Ferencz was weak and now József has forgotten he is her family, that God forbid, there is religious meaning behind the food she is preparing, that there is pride in who you are. Pride in Grandpa Donát who arrived aged fourteen in Oświęcim in November 1944 with his parents and two younger siblings, and left naked and alone, half as heavy and twice as old. This is why we celebrate, Judit Ferencz finding the phone and it's still ringing and it is him and her heart melts. Her angel of life. Praise God, praise God, praise God.

Having failed to drown himself or bleed to death, the swineherd took to more subtle methods. He ignored the groans of his stomach and refused to feed it. As he starved, his north and southward travels grew more laborious. His concentration dropped and his limbs grew thin. Though he had never been full of face, his cheeks fell in and his teeth loosened. The skin pulled taut and thin around his ribs and the vertebrae protruded. He ceased shitting and his vision blurred. But still he walked these roads, trying to cheat the reaper and freefall into the hell he knew awaited him. One night in July as he approached the Knight's Bridge, he fell. A horse trampled him, cracking his ribcage, but he was already unconscious, face down in the ordure at the road's edge. He dreamed he was on a hard floor under a bluish light. With him was Godwyn, nursing a child as strange figures crowded round them. A moment of joy before he was snapped awake, his clothes clean and his body hale. He licked his tongue around his gums; the teeth were firm and his belly ceased to grumble. Pink light announced the dawn over Lundenwic and he continued his journey south to Thorney Island, as cursed and unkillable as he'd ever been.

As Judit Ferencz talks to her boychick, she steps out of the way of Amber Jamieson who is in the middle of an episode. Jamieson can neither hear the traffic nor an ambulance siren on Belsize Road, nor does she register the animated Muslim preachers or the Pentecostal choir, both of whose gods might soon be in battle over the eternal rights to her soul. Head down, no bag, no coat despite the chill, Jamieson wears a formal shirt top, jeggings and boots; who co-ordinates when the journey's end is the grey-brown ooze at the bottom of a fast moving river? On a white laminated bedsit console lie the fluoxetine pills she hasn't taken for two days. The agency didn't call back and her twin sister has gone to Edinburgh for Easter without her. Then there's the rent she owes, but it's none of those, just an overwhelming heaviness, the weight, the lead in her soul that will sink her to the river bed and beyond, down into the soft, deep earth where at last she will rest. Amber Jamieson walking purposefully; finally, her life having meaning, knowing what it is she was born to do. This is her day and the clown's eyes follow her as she passes him, as if he envies her.

Before the Powell-Cottons signed over the land east of the road to developers, it was part of the estate of Oaklands Hall, home of Charles Hippopotamus Murray. The clown once played poker with Murray at the back of the Victoria Tavern and took two guineas off him, the twitch of the man's wax tipped moustaches too obvious a tell. Murray was a polyglot and adventurer who hunted buffalo with the Pawnee and survived an attack by two hundred Cheyenne. It was Murray who rode his horse to Oxford and back in sixteen hours, and who engaged Pacha Abbas to bring him a hippopotamus from the White Nile, a beast so exotic that when it reached London Zoo from Alexandria, Victoria herself brought her young brood to ogle at it. By the time the clown beat him at cards, Murray was consul to the Danish court and regaled the table with tales of a woman named Edith and his burgeoning friendship with the ailing Hans Christian Anderson.

Zig zagging his way to kill time, the clown crosses over to the west side of the High Road where tree lined Glengall Road leads up to the more salubrious residential suburb of Queen's Park. In the bookmaker's on the corner, a few down at heel men stare at a wall-mounted TV screen; dogs racing around a track at Towcester. Reynard's Boy wins by a head at 15-1 and as none of the men register emotion, none predicted the upset. The clown takes a chitty and pen from the counter, draws on it then hands it to one of the men. The others gather to see what he has scribbled and all three stare at him as he leaves the shop, the skirts of his coat stirring stale, dead air and fluttering some Gambling Anonymous leaflets in the rack by the door.

More than a century ago, this was a tobacconist's run by the Percy family. Hearing a forlorn wailing from an upstairs room, Mrs Percy ran from the shop to fetch a bobby who was chatting to a cabman on the street. According to the account in the *London Evening News*, the cries became so severe in tone and volume that three more constables clattered up the stairs, bursting through the locked door of the upstairs flat where the Farnell family lived with their three children. The men were met with a grisly scene; two children lying quietly on the bed with cords tied tightly round their little necks, the mother weeping and struggling against the policeman who was attempting to restrain her, kicking him and trying to bite his arms, asking him over and over to let the babes die so they will be happy. As she screamed, Constable Robert James pinched the infants' noses and breathed into their mouths, Dr Smith hurrying from Gascony Avenue with smelling salts, pushing on tiny chests until both children breathed freely and were taken to the Paddington Infirmary. Inspector Cooper arriving from Scotland Yard with notebook and pen, arresting Mrs Farnell for attempted murder, the woman screaming that Jack the Ripper would take her girls, that she was saving them from him. A letter from Mrs Farnell was later read out in court. Her husband was away on business, she believed people were trying to kill her, she had consumption and fretted over what would happen to her girls should she die while Charles was away. She had seen a ghost, her mother had died insane and she herself was, her letter said, out of her mind. The jury agreeing and a judge ordering the woman to be taken to Broadmoor where she died after forty four years spent weaving baskets and talking to the wallpaper.

Onward. The clown exits the bookmaker's and, taking one of the leaflets, folds it into a paper dart which he throws, the paper gliding along the High Road in the slipstream of a passing Toyota Previa. Watling Street after the Wæclingas, the tribe of Anglo Saxons who built their city from the rubble of Roman Verulamium and named it Wæclingacaester. Before that, the Romans had no name for their road, simply paving over a track used by the first Britons, striking north from Canterbury, fording the river at Westminster then north again to Viroconium Cornovioram. Over on the east side of the road, Paul Potter walks out of JD Sports with some new trainers. Sixty one and balding, his grey hair a fat tonsure, Potter carries the box of size ten Nu Balance running shoes which he will never run in, despite twenty-one-year-old Ashlee Domecq assuring him that they will help him set new PBs; Domecq's autism not picking up that Potter isn't an aspiring athlete and that he's recovering from a hernia operation. Paul Potter will take his new slippers in their red box to his one bedroom flat in Kilburn Vale, something comfy to wear while he makes a cup of tea, sits next to a sleeping cat on the couch and watches *Countdown*.

Thorhild marched ahead of them along the river bank, her sure footfalls contrasting with the ten or so apprehensive young women who followed after her like ducklings. Though summer, there was no warmth in the day and the cool of the woods made Godwyn hug herself, rubbing her arms with her hands as they walked. At a bend in the Roding River, Thorhild stopped, the women lining up behind her, unsure why they were here or what they would be asked to do. The nun looked left and right but there were neither wood cutters nor dogs to suggest the presence of others, and the only sound the song of nearby thrushes. With her back to the brook, Thorhild formed the younger women into a semicircle around her.

"You."

She pointed to Godwyn. A firm grasp pinched her shoulders as Thorhild pulled her forward. The older nun commanding two others to strip their sister, Godwyn covering herself, shivering, her skin unused to the elements.

"See the filth?" Thorhild asked. "The lord cleanses the soul, but to us falls the duty of cleaning the body." Then, matter of factly, "Get in, child."

Godwyn looked at the dark water, back to the pursed lips of Thorhild, then to the others who cast their eyes down so as not to see their sister's shame. Thorhild raised her eyes theatrically to the heavens, grabbed the girl roughly by the shoulders and shoved her so that she fell gracelessly into the flat waters at the river's edge with a loud smack, before disappearing out of view. For a moment, sight and sound vanished in the blackness, the chill gripping her, an explosion of pain in her lungs and nose. Finally, she clawed back to clean air again and was able to catch her breath, gasping and flailing to keep afloat, hair clinging to her face. Thorhild held out a thick branch which Godwyn mistook for a lifeline, grabbing at it. Instead, the nun jabbed it at her then pulled it away quickly.

"When I say so child," she said. Godwyn felt that she would drown, that the dark waters would pull her into the belly of the river. With what little breath she had left, she sputtered out a cry for help. Eadgyth made towards her but Thorhild slapped her hard across the cheek, the red rising instantly.

"Cleanliness. Chastity. Poverty. Prayer." Enunciating the words to the group as Godwyn's efforts weakened. A splash of oars. The prow of a wooden skiff turning the bend. Thorhild suddenly prodding the branch towards the girl but her previous efforts had pushed her out of reach. The men in the boat now rowing with urgency to the near lifeless body in the water, reaching for her as Thorhild wailed protestations, the girl was simply bathing, to let her be, that they were violating Scripture, these were Christ's saints and he alone would protect them. The men ignoring the dark habited harridan, hauling Godwyn's limp, brown body into their boat, one removing his cloak for her to lie on and the other wrapping her in his own and laying her among their cargo of plums and pears. When she opened her eyes, the tops of trees glided above her. Behind her, oars creaked steadily. An oaken face leaned over her.

"She's awake," and then the voice of Thorhild and the wails of the other nuns from afar. She looked over the side of the boat where the older nun was jogging along the river bank, hurling fury at the rescuers as her charges trotted behind her, lifting their habits so as not to trip over tree roots. She felt a sharp pain in her side and brought her hand up. Blood. The branch wielded by Thorhild had stabbed her. The effort to stay awake was too great and she fell back into unconsciousness.

Once, this block with its chain fashion, discount clothing and cell phones was a grand fin de siècle emporium. Here in 1897, the merchant, Benjamin Beardmore Evans opened his draper's; in a few short years his store haemorrhaging along the High Road until it had consumed eight shop fronts. Evans a purveyor of Egyptian cotton sheets, shoes made from crocodiles' skins and ornaments fashioned out of lapis lazuli. For fifty yards, his store's grand windows displayed leather bags from the Levant, Venetian glass lanterns and Parisienne couture until a dropped Westminster on a chintz cushion sent up a thin wire of smoke as red teeth bore through thin fabric. The iridescent orange tip tunnelling a tiny black-rimmed hole into the dusty goose down which flinched as the heat tore into it, small flames glowing and plenty for them to eat. Seventeen-year-old Emily Harriman taking a break from plumping and sweeping the soft furnishings, dozing, cigarette in hand over her copy of *Home Chat*. The cushion properly alight by now, but too hot to smoke, fire making light work of the chaise's silk cover, gorging on kapok and webbing, the heat burning Emily Harriman beneath her apron. Waking, the girl shrieked and patted out the flames on her clothing. She ran for the pail, water landing with a brown smack, the flames shrinking for a moment before falling back on their work. Now the whole couch was ablaze, Harriman crying with the fear of it, the carpet smoking too where molten resin dripped onto it.

"Fire Fire!" Emily Harriman hurrying down the wooden stairs as the inferno gathered its armies, others following, wanting to know how the blaze began. In the January afternoon gloom on the street below, an orange glow pulsed behind a second floor window. A shrill fire bell as staff and servants from forty departments on two stories filed out of the store founded thirteen years earlier by Beardmore Evans who, as it happens, was clean shaven. Barely fifteen minutes after Emily Harriman dropped ash on chintz, three more windows glowed red as bare headed shopgirls ran onto the street where a small crowd began to assemble. By now, curtains were ablaze and the fire bell continued as someone remembered the dog, the big black dog who slept by the hearth in the staff kitchen; did anyone think to look for him? Harriman running back inside despite a bobby shouting to keep away, up one, two, three, four half-flights of stairs dense with smoke, but the door was locked. Harriman pressing her shoulder on it as the dog whimpered on the other side but it was fast, the girl now stepping back and hurling herself at it, shrieking with fury at the fire and herself. The door shifting a little and Harrriman running at it again and again until one of the panels splintered and she could reach through. The dog barking in terror but the handle almost too hot to touch. Unable to turn it, Harriman using her boots to kick the lower panels of the door until the animal pushed through, yelping, bounding past her down the stairs, its claws skittering on the wood. Cheers as dog and shopgirl appeared out of the choking black fog. On the street, firemen had set up a long ladder and as the dog jumped around Emily Harriman and licked her hands, greedy flames leapt through every department of B.B. Evans store, devouring rolls of fabric, haberdashery, men's trousers and umbrellas; melting soap and glass and cracking ceramics. A group of men hurried to the stables at the rear of the building to free the horses, pulling at heavy green-painted doors and dragging the animals by the bridle. The northern end of the block now a furnace of black smoke and red rolling flame, and the police and fire brigade ordering people away from the building. The inferno a low, bass roar, hypnotic, dancing yellow dragons licking the roof, snaking around the ornate cornicing as men climbed ladders, directing their hoses into the furnace. The last fireman to leave, a wet towel over his face and a ragdoll body over his shoulder, all staff now accounted for. The early evening air had become a stench of burned rubber, paint and textiles cooking at a thousand degrees Fahrenheit, and the whole north end of the store now eaten by fire, only the brick façade remaining. People pointing as the wall itself began to buckle, running back to the safety of Glengall Road as the third storey frontage bowed outwards and bricks began raining onto the pavement beneath. The clown had joined the crowd, glad of the warmth, watching tall flames shoot high into the low canopy of night. Petting the dog, Emily Harriman felt an ache in her shoulder and a searing pain in the palm of her hand for the first time. As he passed by in the days that followed, the clown watched the bowler hatted Evans instructing the repair and rebuilding of his empire, noting the diligence and speed of the workmen. Months later, only the unmistakable smell of water on burnt wood, a reek that any number of coats of fresh paint could not mask. Today, much of the ground floor is taken up by a German discount grocery chain. No trace of Beardmore Evans' store remains, the smell of fire completely gone.

In the middle of the Great Middlesex Forest, on a spring day in the year Cnut acquired England's throne for the second time, a swineherd climbed a tree. He had not attempted such a feat before; his job had been to round up hogs and usher them to the beechmast that would fatten them. Pigs did not climb and the forest was so dense that scaling a tree offered little extra visibility. His climb was a solemn one. He had chosen the tallest trunk that had branches which he could grab hold of, working his way up like a rugged stair; an oak whose yellow flowers hung like tiny streamers. The man's feet slipped but he did not care, his one desire to go higher, as high as the tree would allow him. A mother starling squawked from her nest, flapping her wings at him, but he cared not whether she fled or fought. Higher. He looked down, the ground now a great distance from him and the sky showing more of its light. Hand over hand, he edged his way along a branch which began to bow under his weight. Closing his eyes, he let go, leant backwards and fell. The sound of men's voices brought him round, four faces looking down at him and one with his head on his breast, listening. Coppicers who had been working in the woods nearby and heard the thud.

"He's alive!"

Questions followed. Did he fall? Why had he climbed? Who were his people? He thanked them, but without cheer and they wondered at a man who might have died, yet took no joy in living; who simply walked away shaking his arms and rotating his hips a little, back along the road to Westminster.

Calvin Bennett-Anderson keeps to the line of his walk but the clown moves for no one, and Bennett-Anderson, dark grey hood and hands sunk deep in the pockets of his jeans waits until collision is imminent before side stepping, kissing his teeth. His brow creased into a frown, Bennett-Anderson turns and jabs his glare at the clown; the nineteen-year-old on his way to see Kadisha, mother of his son Kane, knowing she'll ask for money for baby clothes and nappies and spend it on weed. Swings and roundabouts. She let him keep a Biretta in her fridge and lied about an alibi, telling police he'd been with her all night; they watched *Real Housewives of Beverley Hills* then the baby was sick. Calvin helped her change the bed, then they ordered Domino's. The life she wished she had with him. Bennett-Anderson a moving target, his swagger betraying fear, keeping his head down because the streets are no longer safe. The war will never end; hatred like magma beneath the rat runs of council estates, erupting in chicken shops, bus stops and drive-by gunshots. Bennett-Anderson's ancestors shackled in pens and delivered to Dominican plantations like livestock, crushed by the slave owner and damned by lack of opportunity until they looked east for jobs and money and found neither. Bennett, a gout ridden profligate who plundered Tobago for its sugar, then raped a scullery maid who conceived the son who bore his name. Anderson, a Presbyterian molasses baron. Their blood mixed in 1990's Camden and Calvin Bennett-Anderson now walking the lands where Godwyn prayed, cussing the man she loved.

There was a time. By all that is good in Creation there was a time before. The tall pillared abbey in the greensward; the quiet unfolding of the daily horarium, cold stones beneath his sandalled feet. The cry of the miller's boy who had spilt a sack and was beaten, specks of dust caught in shafts of light from the chancel window, and sparrows in the roof beams. A time when this was real and it was beautiful; the quiet, the blessèd anointing stillness pouring through cracks into the glad, thirsty chamber of his soul, long before any tree still growing in this place took seed, when hump-shouldered oxen pulled simple ploughs across long fields and hermits lived by rivers. In those days, they say the Virgin herself walked in Willesden. On Assumption Day in the year 925, a woodcutter happened upon a woman in the forest. The woods were dense and, assuming she was a lost traveller, the man offered her bread and ale. The woman thanked him for his kindness, then pointed him to a crooked oak, telling him that this was the tree he should fell. The man assured her that it was useless timber, good only for burning, yet the stranger spoke with such authority that he buried his axe in the trunk until it had fallen. Only later when he had sawn it into logs and was splitting one for the fire did the blade hit against something smooth and dark, like polished stone. As he chipped, white wood fell away leaving a perfect statuette of a woman, a Madonna the colour of ebony, cradling an infant. Trees were cleared, a shrine built, the statue placed within an arched recess, Archbishop Athelm of Canterbury himself arriving in pomp to dedicate the new church to Our Lady of Willesden, pilgrims following him here in their tens of thousands as the centuries unfolded.

In the discount supermarket, Sammy Chin Li sits at the checkout scanning barcodes with a red laser, waiting for Norma to come back from her break. Soft skinned and fine haired like an animal that has never been outside, Chin Li is working his sixth consecutive shift, his doctorate on the biomechanics of polyvinyls and synthetic esters still unwritten. Chin Li choosing instead to wave packs of pretzels, weigh apples and manually type in the codes of poorly packed salamis, working every extra day that the bearded Moroccan, Shirhan offers him. Time and a half if he works the bank holiday. A large West Indian lady arrives to relieve him and Chin Li gets up, grabs his water bottle and shuffles away, pushing on the door that says 'employees only'. Chin Li not suspecting that later today, Shirhan will call him into his office, sit him down with a Diet Coke and tell him that things aren't working out, that the few minimum wage pounds trickling into his bank account every two weeks will cease. Too slow, too many errors, and an expired study visa that shows no hope of being renewed.

Rudderless and with no power to change the trajectory of his own life, the clown who waits his turn in the queue would swap with Chin Li in a heartbeat. Adeya Kinemba, in the middle of a phone conversation with her friend, Prudence Lingwe steps in front of him, her conversation making her immune from the resentment of those patiently waiting their turn.

"There is a queue you know."

Mary Martin, cross at the rudeness of the woman.

"Shut your mouth" says Kinemba, without turning around. And then to Lingwe, "Don't worry, she's only Irishwoman."

His lack of employment will leave Chin Li unable to pay rent, or the fees for his course at Kings College. His landlord will leave him on the steps of the Westminster Housing office, his possessions in six black refuse sacks. A kind minicab driver will take him for free to a church in Cricklewood where the pastor will usher him to on a camp bed in a store room at the back of the building, next to a folded up table tennis table and stacks of plastic chairs.

Where wild fruit and seeds grew by the lush banks of the Cunebourne stream, and bright fish hopped into Godwyn's net, wriggling and dying, their fillets cooked in an iron pot over red embers and eaten wrapped in the leaves of wild cabbages, the clown pays Chin Li for matches and places them in the pocket of his coat.

The abbey sanatorium was a simple room with two cots. Godwyn woke to find Ænfled leaning over her, applying a warm poultice of bran and herbs wrapped in linen to the wound beneath her ribs.

"Keep resting," she told her. The pain was bearable but she had no strength. Her muscles ached from her exertions in the water and she felt a fist clenching inside her forehead. Wendreda appeared behind Ænfled, lips pursed, her expression grave. She remained for a few moments, turned and left again. The hours faded in and out and nothing was asked of Godwyn nor could she have given anything. She was spent. Ænfled's kindness was an ever-present tonic and as the days passed, she revived to the point where she could sit up in bed and spoon thin soup from a wooden bowl.

"Do not worry, for I am with you," Ænfled said to her, quoting the prophet. "I will uphold you with my righteous right hand."

Godwyn took comfort from the words as the wounds scabbed, leaving a vivid pink welt against the dark skin. After two weeks, she made her first steps out of the quiet, curtained room; Ænfled and another sister supporting her on either side. The nuns had gathered in the sanctuary to welcome her with a sung matins, followed by prayers to the martyrs Valentina, Paula and Ennatha who perished under the emperor Galerius Valerius Maximinus. At their head were Wendreda and Abbot Ethelwold.

"Where is Thorhild" Godwyn whispered to Ænfled, who did not answer.

"It is wonderful that the Lord has chosen to return you to us, Godwyn," Wendreda said. "Christ is merciful."

She did not ask any more about Thorhild, nor did she see the nun again at the abbey.

Across the four lanes of the A5 from the supermarket where Sammy Chin Li works his final shift, the Earl Derby. Affixed to newly scrubbed brick, a gently swinging sign bears three stags' heads, the motif of the Derbyshire earls. Emblem: Argent on a bed azure, three bucks' heads caboshed or, a crescent for difference. Crest: On a chapeau gules turned up ermine, an eagle, wings expanded or, preying upon an infant proper swaddled of the first. Motto: Sans changer. The clown cracks a wry smile. Without changing. This hostelry that was lately the Golden Egg, before that the Goose and Granite only now adheres once again to the name given it when it opened on the High Road in 1884. The arms belonging to the earl of legend, a fourteenth century adulterer whose wife could provide no heir and who courted one of her ladies-in-waiting, a grateful Jezebel who bore him a son. The babe was dressed in noble robes then left in an eagle's nest to be serendipitously found, the earl and his barren countess adopting the miracle child and raising him as their own. Henry of Grosmont, first of his line, the champion of St Martin's Eve; five hundred men at arms and two thousand archers, their firebolts on point, the corpses of three thousand Flemings paying tribute to England's military hegemony. The earldom bestowed on Grosmont by a grateful Edward III. Earl John who took the coronet from the cold, pestilent head of his uncle in 1361, the third surviving son of the Plantagenet, Edward. Earl John of Ghent and so 'of Gaunt', warrior and trusted counsel to the child king, Richard. Earl Henry, the Lancastrian pretender, future king of the realm, crusher of the rebel Glendower. Richard, the final earl from that war torn, plague ridden century, progenitor of one king, two queens and a pair of dukes. And here, on ragged ground where Watling Street races through Kilburn is their legacy, a dining pub with bleached wooden settles, red leather sofas, and tables laid out with broadsheet newspapers. A temple of spirits and victuals inhabiting the dead shell of the pub whose innards it has eaten like a parasite. The clown peers through the window at those who the Earl Derby has drawn in with its promise of craft beers and American themed fare. Angeline Tousson and Mark Cadfield sit in a corner enjoying a glass of chilled Viognier, the bottle sitting next to their table in a bucket of ice. Two childless sybarites, he besotted and she enabling, junior producers at a TV channel where he watches her like his favourite show, studying the profile of her bosom as she passes, intoxicated by a lust that has no release. Lost, lost Mark Cadfield, bewitched by lips that demand kissing, breasts that beg to be freed and legs which belong wrapped around his own, Tousson's involuntary cries a whimper of ecstasy he will never hear. The clown laughs, his breath condensing on the window. He wipes it away, the movement catching Tousson's attention. She lifts her big ayes to him and smiles. Tousson who has slept with two men since she and Cadfield last had drinks together a month ago, one of them a busker whose charm waylaid her outside Brondesbury station. Yet to Cadfield, Tousson is Pavlova and Karenina; she is Bovary and Piaf, the man in love with an idea, convincing himself that they are kindred souls when she has never once imagined him naked. He glances again at the fat orbs contained beneath the satin sheen of her loose, short-sleeved top. Soon, he will offer her a gift, a framed photo of the two of them at Winter Wonderland. Tousson will lean across the table to hug but not kiss him, a wave of J'adore by Dior crashing on his face, and while they abandon themselves to a second bottle and order stuffed potato skins with sour cream and chorizo to share, Tousson will tell him about the busker, a throwaway line, a bit part in another story and the words will ricochet around the chamber of Cadfield's heart like a coin dropped in a copper cauldron, so loud that he will not hear the rest of her sentence; he will want to snatch the gift away and smash it against a wall and run from the pub, from northwest London, from the city, from the good earth, away.

The years passed and Godwyn had no desire to return to Lundenwic nor the wretched life she had led before Albric brought her here. It was her seventh summer and she knelt on the tessellated Roman floor of the Saints' Chapel, her lips moving through the nones, the three psalms and then the prayer of the blessed Basil:

"Forgive us our sins, and kill our fleshly lusts, that putting off the old man, we may put on the new, and may live for Thee our Master and Protector."

It was not the first time she had prayed it, the words falling frequently from her lips since she first called the abbey home. But today, she felt that she heard a small, delicate bell ring inside her as she mouthed the prayer. She no longer felt stained, or that her sins were unwashable. Her induction to the carnal act had come too soon, the raw frequency of her liaisons numbing her. But now she was a bride of Christ. By his wounds at Calvary he had redeemed her, a sinner. Out of his boundless goodness, he had spared her, she who had believed herself unworthy to even pray. She felt lifted and suddenly compelled. On the completion of her prayers, she hurried to the chapter house, where

Wendreda was discussing repairs to the tower with Abbot Ethelwold.

The clown plays with a small wooden wolf in his pocket, a plaything carved from an offcut of oak a millennium earlier as the door of the Earl Derby swings open and Ryan Capewell steps out into the fresh spring air, his shift over and yesterday's flowers in his hand to cheer up the flat. Capewell reaching for his phone with his free hand and fretting. In a few hours, he will greet his parents, Tom and Viv, flying in from Adelaide to stay at the first floor flat on Brondesbury Villas which he shares with Simon, a trainee barrister. Ryan on the couch and Simon in Barcelona for the weekend so Tom and Viv can have the room. Ryan Capewell, anxious that his mother will notice the one bedroom, the single king-sized bed, and that the truth will out. The talk he never wants to have will now take place after a thirty hour flight, his parents jetlagged and bewildered by the size of London. How he will he find the words, and in which order will they tumble from his mouth? How can they not know already? Simon's mum guessed when he was sixteen. Tom and Viv, elders at a Baptist church in the northern suburbs where Tom leads the Wednesday night men's fellowship, and Viv hosts a Tuesday morning Bible study as their raggedy West Highland terrier, Pops yips for treats under the kitchen table. Their beloved son who's not been to church since he landed. Free, finally from its gospel of hate, drinking from the debauched cup of the great Babylon. Tom and Viv Capewell, coming into land to a rainbow awakening. Their son cannot change them. If they see, they see; if they ask, he will tell. In a week, they'll be gone, touring the Yorkshire moors and the Dufftown distilleries in a rented Winnebago. Twelve thousand miles between them for a reason; Ryan Capewell distancing himself from the disappointment and shame they will carry back with them to Fremont. He puts the phone back in his pocket and heads to the bus stop with his flowers.

Two centuries before the clown's birth, Offa of Mercia was told by God to 'erect a fair monastery to the memory of the blessed Alban, in the place where he suffered martyrdom.' The king had no idea where this shrine of prayer should be located, and wandered around in a confused state until a light shone from heaven upon ground which, when opened, revealed the very bones of the saint. Offa used rubble from the ruins of Roman Verulamium to construct his church, the Anglo Saxons being poor builders and there being so much of the ancient city left dilapidated and derelict around them. In the same way Zerubbabel's roughshod and treasureless temple fell markedly short of Solomon's masterpiece, so the architecture of the abbey at St. Albans was a pale reflection of what might have been achieved centuries earlier under Roman direction. Assembled with red bricks, flint, and little artistry, the church contained true treasure, for the bones of the nation's first martyr were interred here. And while Alban's spirit had direct access to the Almighty, his bones held special power for the brothers and sisters who lived here. They were imperishable, the young Benedictine was told. They lived and had lived since the saint died seven hundred years earlier. In what manner they lived, he did not know, but as a young novice, he marvelled at a human whose spirit might endure through the centuries. Back then, Alban's remains were kept in a simple stone ossuary, just as St. Peter's in Westminster treasured a strap from the sandal of the apostle – with Peter being a more prominent saint, his hair, bone and teeth had all been requisitioned by the time that church was completed.

The monastery at Westminster was smaller; St. Albans was England's principal Benedictine house and its satellites poor in comparison. St. Peter's too had been requisitioned from the ruins of a nearby town and the Roman style copied. Doors and ceilings had arches but were made of simple brick and rubble, and its tiled floors and rough stone slabs bore few adornments. The monastery had been built on the island where the Tybourne forked before joining the Thames. Ælfwig was an astute abbot who used friendship with England's nobles to acquire the great estates of Brickendon and Kelvedon, both of which allowed the abbey to thrive. Here at Westminster, Ælfwig established Wessex's first and finest library. A little to the east was the settlement of Lundenwic, an impoverished town at the northern extremity of Wessex. These two churches will both will outlast the clown, both more glorious now than a millennium earlier, and the God in whose name they were built still worshipped, even here on this degenerate streak of blacktop between Cricklewood and Maida Vale. The things that last. Going out like Samson would be nice, he thinks. Take the fuckers with him. He hopes his plan won't disappoint; it's going to be a blast.

Across the road, another hole in the wall for thirsty travellers. A whitewashed facade, yellow flowers in hanging baskets and dense frosted glass windows making it impossible for the passer-by to peer into the gloom within. A couple of white chairs on the pavement for good measure, comfort for devotees of nicotine and tar. Above the gilt lettered crimson sign that spans the width of the building's exterior sits the heraldic arms of the worshipful company of coopers, established 1422. The clown remembers the year, the old king victorious at Meaux,

127

holding aloft the bastard's head. Henry's premature death at Vincennes just months later and his ague and pox riddled body embalmed and brought in solemn procession to Westminster where his infant son was sworn in as king. At the time, this was still forest and road; no Kilburn to speak of, just the priory and a few cottages. Shield: on a chevron sable between three annulets or, a royne between two broad axes azure, thereon three lilies argent. Crest: a demi heathcock, winged, or, helm and mantling double argent. Motto: Love as Brethren. The pub a twentieth century whimsy opening in the last year of the old century under the name Prince of Wales in honour of the future king. No barrel makers drank here, but in former times, the clown watched men shape casks over steam in the sheds behind the Red Lion. Workers fitting hoops with an adze and smoothing them with a topping plane, a chiv perfecting the curved ends of the staves ready for a croze to cut grooves for the caskhead. He saw men apply hoops and smooth the insides with a roundshave, hammering rivets on an anvil. An intricate business, the coopers working mechanically; dowelling stocks boring holes in the heads, a swift shaving the sides of the caskhead and a bow saw cutting it to size. He watched the man with a heading knife shape the edges to fit the groove, a hammer and driver fixing hoops into their final positions. A forgotten craft; barrels now cast from aluminium in a purpose built 1600m^2 facility in the shadow of the Europoort that shits them out like pellets, eight thousand a day.

Michael Whelan and Nolan Finnegan smoke on the pavement outside the pub. Whelan wearing the fine head of hair that is the badge of the alcoholic male and a suit jacket to prove he's decent; large pink ears flat against his breeze block head. Finnegan in woolly hat and glasses, long black puffer keeping the breeze out. Whelan looking into the middle distance drawing hot smoke through a Marlboro Light, Finnegan clutching a half-finished pint of Strongbow and swaying slightly. Both at mass at the Sacred Heart earlier as they missed it yesterday. Barely a handful of the faithful scattered in the temple on Quex Road. Whelan in a sombre mood that he can't quite explain. Finnegan waiting patiently beside him, occasionally sipping from his glass.

"A terrible business. Brutal. The things they did to yerman."

Whelan who's taken a few beatings reflecting on cords embedded with flint and bone, tearing into human flesh.

"Cunts didn't hold back in them days. No boy. Rip a fella's back off."

Whelan taking a last toke on his firestick.

"Jaysus. That would have been a long walk now. I've carried a fella on the shoulders more than once, deadweight he is, and the cunt would have weighed more than that."

Finnegan nodding. Whelan always right; that's why he followed him all the way from Drumree to build Brent Cross and stayed. Whelan throws his butt onto the pavement and the two men return to their stools in the otherwise empty bar and drink to the poor fucker, Christ, solemnly, and in silence.

He was not a swineherd for long. Wandering became his work, a ceaseless toil, and in those early days, a never ending search for the ones he had lost. He had been a monk, but the faith he had never questioned was now meaningless. Who needs hope when they have certainty? He was damned, had been damned from the first, is still damned and will always be damned. As he walked from the ancient walls of Wæclingacaester to where the Tybourne forked around Thorney Island, he begged for alms. The flakes of silver that counted then as coins soon added up, and he emptied his pouch into the cupped hands of a woodsman in the village of Radlett and bought himself a bow. In the half century or so before the Conquest, the woods were a larder from which all could feed. Restricted as he was to the path and a few paces east and west from it, he could still bag enough game to eat should the mood take him, or better still, sell in the towns and villages through which he passed. Money was what he needed. Money bought him ale, women and a few precious moments of oblivion. His first shots were wild and loose, but he had time and with that, a man learns to regulate his breaths, to think like his quarry, to quieten any impatient impulse. He bagged mallards, teal, doves and partridges, cursing the ones which fell too far into the forest for him to fetch. But once William slew Harald at Hastings, the new king coveted England's game for himself, and the forest where once even a beggar could gather sticks to sell became a forbidden garden, with death to all who stole from it.

A life of solitude. She had heard stories of the Desert Fathers; Isaac who scattered ashes from the incense on his bread so that he would gain no pleasure from eating; Pambo who only wore clothes so ragged, they could lie discarded outside his cell for three days without being stolen, and Sarah who lived by a river, yet never once regarded it in case her attention should be taken from her prayers. Godwyn was not as noble as these saints, but she preferred her own company and prayer was what the nation needed. She had survived winters among the alleyways and wharves of Lundenwic, and now the wilderness was calling. Northwards, a great forest spread thirty miles in every direction from the banks of the Thames. She would find a clearing, build a shrine and pray until the Lord chose to kill her, or move her.

As the clown takes up his journey once again, a BMW Seven Series cruises north, past the two pubs, Brahim Jabrane driving his eight-year-old son, Karim. Personalised plates, V8 block and eight speed automatic transmission. Success doesn't recognise weekends, let alone bank holidays. It demands its ten thousand hours, and Karim must be half way there already. An afternoon at the Bushey Golf and Country Club practicing his long iron, no matter that it's Adel's party.

"If it were that easy, we'd all be at birthday parties filling our faces with cake. Get good at this son and life's one long party. Remember Dubai?"

Karim pictures the Jumeirah Beach Hotel with its kid's club where he met a German boy called Ulli and lent him his Wenlock plush Olympic mascot. That was on the first day while Brahim was still trying to find a golf course where they would let Karim practice his putting, finally settling on the Arabian Ranches. Karim never seeing Ulli or Wenlock again, he was up too early or home too late. Jabrane looking at his son through the rear view mirror; the kid loves it. Look at him. Can't wait to get the driver and crack the 45.93g of ionomer, urethane and rubber up the fairway, dad at his side, behind him, over him, measuring, analysing, recording him. Karim already entered for the 2017 IMG Academy Junior World Championships at La Jolla. Warm weather training in Palmares, Portugal over the February half term helped. It needed to; the kid's not a natural but he's a grafter. The black station wagon continues north carrying Karim and the American training clubs designed for his four foot one inch frame, Karim's head down, playing a game on his dad's phone while Talksport's Colin Murray dissects tomorrow's Premiership clashes between Everton and Manchester United, Southampton and Aston

Villa. The child catapults birds, not even thinking about golf, a game he doesn't especially like but plays because he has to, because he's always played it. What else would he do?

Henry of Grosmont came here once, guest of the Black Prince. The men planned to ride south to defend the Channel from French raiders, but allowed time to chase stags before the battle. A hunter lurking in the shadows with his bow saw the royal party arrive with men and dogs at the appointed spot on the road, which by then was known as Watling Street. In a century where little happened in such a sparsely populated place, a royal hunt was a spectacle not to be missed. They had been clearing trees for more than a century but the forest still had deep wood; places the sun never reached and where hunting threw up plentiful spoils, though the hunter was forbidden by the curse to tread there. Hiding his bow, he had climbed a tall sycamore to ensure he would not be seen. A pair of animals were spotted, horn blasts keeping the party informed of the beasts' movements; horse sweat steaming in the early chill on the roadway beneath him. While the Earl's huntsmen tracked their quarry, he and his company breakfasted in a clearing near the clean waters of the Cunebourne, messengers bringing news from the forest. A beast of suitable size and maturity had been followed to its lair, the lymerer marking the covert that harboured it. The "Hie Hie!" and the chase. From his vantage point, the huntsman could only hear, not see; a terrified hart double-backing on his own footfalls, smashing undergrowth and crashing through streams to hide his scent, dogs surrounding him, holding him at bay as his great shoulders heaved in exhaustion. Men on horses arriving in a great rabble of snorting; voices shouting and horns blowing the *Mort* in celebration. The prince arriving with his company to break the deer, spaying it with his sword, cutting it apart ceremoniously and dividing the meat among his hunters. The clown tries to remember the taste of venison. Sweet, with the texture of veal. He runs his tongue over yellowed teeth. He's tasted every food, almost all of it is joyless, but right now he would kill for a venison backstrap griddled over a birchwood fire.

The clown yawns. He had slept badly today as a vagrant from Stockton on Tees woke him on the offchance he had cigarette papers. His quarters changed frequently as the two cities at either end of his perambulations expanded in restless exuberance, burying what had gone before in a never ending carnival of development and destruction. At first, he slept behind the old Roman wall of what had been Verulamium and a boat shed where the Tybourne stream forked around Thorney. His journey never allowed him to reach the sanctuary of either abbey, nor the hospitality which might be afforded him there. Though the London Gate still stands, the city of St. Albans has grown around it, and Watling Street no longer travels there. Centuries ago, his northern terminus switched St. Stephen's churchyard, where he slept in the porch. A nineteenth century verger took exception to the green haired vagrant who he would need to step over on his way to matins. The curse favouring the churchman, it moved him to the outhouse of the old leper hospital. When they tore this down, a nearby tithe barn served his requirements for the next century and a half. Since then, a series of canvas tents among the trees behind St. Stephen's provide his northern rest. Nothing inside them to steal, and if he's discovered, the tent moves; his feet always find it. No need of any tents tonight; let the foxes have them.

The great church of St. Peter in Westminster also rejected any permanent shelter. Streams were filled in, the island anchoring itself to the northern shore of the Thames. Boat sheds were repurposed into animal pens, then torn down. The clown slept in the lea of taverns, under tarpaulins in stationary wagons, beneath the first of Westminster's bridges or in the doorways of shops; wherever he fell. This morning, he woke up in a sleeping bag on a bed of flattened cardboard by the doors of the Victoria Palace Theatre. The Metropolitan Police are more assiduous than the Hertfordshire Constabulary and he is frequently shaken down at 2am and asked why he hasn't tried his luck at a shelter. An inconvenience that makes the night longer, but a curse is a curse. He has money to check into a penthouse in the Shard, but getting there is the problem, plus it would only be for a few hours before he needed to make his way north. It would have been a pleasant send-off; like a last meal for a condemned prisoner. No such luck. At least he'll never have to see any of it again; every step a point from which he will never return. Only forwards now. Forwards to St. Albans.

The clown looks up and down the High Road. What a mess, the poor clutching plastic carrier bags, waddling mothers in pursuit of red-faced children, skinny addicts, brown, white, black; rudderless ships crashing into one another, foundering in seas of penury and dependence. He thinks of the crackhead who jumped him at Kilburn High Road station, a small Jamaican hoodlum demanding money on an empty platform at six in the morning, a pointed spike held in his bony fingers, threatening to pop the clown's eye. The skinny man claimed he had a gun in his pocket, the clown certain it was just a sawn off metal pipe pointing at him through the nylon, grinning back at him. Not that a real gun could have killed him, not that anything can kill him, he'd fallen from enough bridges, swallowed enough pills and hanged from enough trees. He planned what he would do. He would wait for the train to arrive and once the doors opened, push the fool into the carriage so far that he'd fall backwards, cracking his head on the floor. Cracking the head of a crackhead. There was a poetry to it. As the train hurtled out of the tunnel under the A5, a sudden change of plan. He flung himself in front of it, the horror on the driver's face a picture, the eight carriages clattering past and screeching to a halt, oblivious. The cab door opening and the clown picking himself up and climbing back onto the platform to the open-mouthed terror of his attacker and reaching into his pocket for banknotes.

"How much are you after?"

The Jamaican taking to his heels, not knowing if he was tripping or already dead, up the steps to the streetlight.

With Ethelwold's blessing, the decision was made. In early spring 1013, aged around twenty, Godwyn set off for the river with Ænfled and an earnest monk named Ecceard who spoke little. A boatman's oars flitted like wings across the surface of the Thames. As they passed the wooden wharves and under the staves of Lundenwic's bridge, Godwyn was jolted back to the days before Albric found her. Now though, she wore a woollen robe, her hair was clean and cropped short beneath her wimple and her belly was far from famished. She could read. The boats and those who clustered about them on the shore, hauling sacks and crates and shouting were a distant world slipping by her, a wound that had healed. As they glided on towards Westminster, Ænfled asked Ecceard about the abbey. He spoke surprisingly loudly, with a resounding bass. Ælfwig was abbot there, he said, and their library was filled with great treasure.

"Great treasure," Ænfled repeated to Godwyn. At the chalk wharf a little beyond the abbey, the boat turned north into the Westbourne. Cows drank in the shallow reedpools and two crows on the grassy bank fought over a wriggling slowworm. In the boat, each kept their own thoughts, the plash plash of the oars drawing them forwards. As they passed under the Knights' Bridge, the river narrowed, meandering through deep oak forest. Here the air was cooler and Godwyn pulled up her hood. Further upriver, the Westbourne was too shallow to navigate and the boatman moored alongside a small jetty where a track led into a clearing. Here, the river was known as the Cunebourne and Ecceard helped steady the boat while the women disembarked. Gathering the tools which he had brought with him – an iron axe, some fishing nets, a handsaw and a bale of bedstraw, he followed after them. They walked along a trackway, Ænfled stopping occasionally to gather fat headed mushrooms from the forest floor. Where the path met Wæcling Strete, a herd of wild pigs crossed in front of them, dark skinned and startled. When they reached the planked bridge over the Cunebourne, they stopped. This was the place. Easy to find but still wholly remote. No buildings, just brooding verdure high and wide and deep. Rather than continue across the bridge, the three pilgrims walked away from the road, along the river and into the wood, mosses and lichens cushioning their steps. Hazels and holly nestled among the taller trees and catkins dangled from low boughs. Ecceard went first, pressing on into the forest as the women followed him in silence. A small clearing opened up, bordered by a curve in the river, and snowdrops peaked above the grass.

The Cunebourne here was at its widest, its surface glassy until it rolled over a clump of large boulders, bark and small tree branches bumping against the natural dam, unable to pass. The flow of the river was a constant and calming song; its water was clean and there would be trout. Ecceard laid out the tools that Godwyn would need to build shelter and make fire.

"Birch is good timber, and you have willow for wattle," he bellowed, and she noticed that his eyes closed when he spoke.

"Pray for us Godwyn," Ænfled entreated her. "Pray for Æthelred, Edmund and the safety of the English, as we shall pray for you."

She took Godwyn's hands in hers, squeezed them gently then let them go. Godwyn nodded and looked down. Ænfled glanced quickly at Ecceard who stepped back, bowed then turned towards the road. The nun picked a single snowdrop from a clump at the foot of a slender alder and carried it away with her, following the tall monk into the gloom beyond the glade.

The clown kicks a can that clatters across the paving stones. A woman stares disapprovingly as if he were the one who dropped it. He catches up with the can and kicks it back towards the woman who swears at him in Polish under her breath. Lewis Westbury, paper under his arm kicks the can onto the road where a blue Volkswagen Caddy carrying two Ukrainian window cleaners on their way to Holborn crushes it flat. The freesheet which Westbury picked up at Euston Station is already a day old but fat with stories of human tragedy. A ten-year-old-boy fighting for his life after a hit and run in Clapham, a Muslim shopkeeper in Glasgow stabbed to death for his religious views and a terror suspect shot and arrested at a tram stop in Brussels. Outside the hairdressers next to the Earl Derby, Westbury sidesteps Maggie Hicks on a mobility scooter, morbidly obese and crippled with MS. Inside the hairdressers, Joshiwanee Sittak waits her turn, eight miscarried infants and a ninth now dying inside her womb. Tragedy everywhere. As Westbury ambles through Kilburn on his way to the Jubilee Line tube station, a light aircraft carrying a patient from a car wreck in rural Alabama crashes into woods, killing all four passengers, while in southeastern Bangalore, a thirty-four-year-old motorcyclist dies when he is hit by an out of control garbage truck.

Godwyn arranged the birch poles she had cut from the woods against the hollow of a great oak. Taking some thinner willow, she fed twigs between the rods as if she were weaving a basket. It was slow work and she prayed as her fingers moved, keeping the hours despite her toil, the verses committed to memory as no book would survive the damp of the forest. Nearby, a small fire crackled. It was monotonous labour but there were many hours in the day at this time of year, and her hands worked busily. By nightfall, a woven wall fanned out around the hollow, enclosing a small shelter. The ground inside was dry and so she laid down her bedding sack until she had found enough wood to build the raised dais that would serve as her bed. Mud and mosses would need to be pressed in amongst the wattle to keep away the rain, and the fire needed to be moved inside. Suddenly she felt eyes upon her. Turning, she saw a shape on the edge of the forest. A wolf. She froze, sweat trickling down her back. The axe was out of reach, her knife too. She swallowed, throat dry, not daring to move. Two more wolves slunk into view, tongues lolling, adding to the menace, the three of them now shoulder to shoulder. Across the brook, another two paced along the bank, watching her. Her skin prickled. As the first animal stepped forwards, boldly, she reached for a stave burning in the fire. The wood was hot in her hand but she jabbed it at him, roaring. The wolf stepped back, alarmed as the others watched. The recluse waved her flaming staff in their direction and roared again. The wolves understood fire, and knew it to be an animal they could not fight. Reluctantly, they wheeled around, back into the woods. Godwyn remained there, her heart pummelling like rain on a tent hide, her lips moving silently in gratitude. When she dropped the log, her hand had blistered. Today, an Ocado delivery truck idles on the site of this ancient stand-off, its driver unaware of the great tree that stood ten centuries before, nor the silent prayers of thanks that were offered up here.

Next to the Coopers Arms, another Poundland discount store; shelves filled with cheap household cleaner, made in China plastic toys and knock-off Easter eggs. Adding to the drear, a loan shark plies its trade in a building across the road, its cheerful signage belying repayments that hobble those too poor or too overwhelmed to meet them. The suburb like an empty purse, an entire quarter of London so heavily in the red that only moneylenders and betting shops turn a profit, a miserable strip of beggars and graspers, a desperate confederacy of the lost deluding themselves that the rainbow ends in Kilburn, that there is gold to be unearthed here. No Roman stopped at this place to do more than evacuate his bowels; there was nothing worth stopping for. The blessed hermit only came to its brook as there was no one here to disturb her reveries, and so it might have remained. Did Godwyn spend three years by a river praying so that Errol Baynard could push on a glass door, sit himself on a chair and take out a two and a half thousand pound payday loan for his daughter's wedding which he has no hope or expectation of ever repaying?

The clown sniffs the cool air on this, the Saturday before Easter, the day after Christ was abandoned to devils and his body broken by whips and nails. He descended into hell, though what he did there and who he saw were not recorded. What horror for the damned to see the virtuous Son of God walking among them, no hope of redemption, an eternity of their own poor choices revisiting them. Did Christ feel convicted by his own failure? For these were his children too, his sheep who had strayed irredeemably far from the pen, no shepherd to usher them home. The clown now walking the cold earth on this Easter Saturday, broken and damned, surrounded by crimes of his own doing, harrowing his own hell. A few more hours and he'll be down there, the demons stoking the fire in readiness for his arrival. He breathes in the cumin, coriander and garam masala leeching from the Pakistani grocers a couple of stores up from the Poundland. Just another weekend for these temples of commerce, the street as busy as any Saturday. He pushes a yellowed fingernail into his nostril and scrapes at a tag of hardened mucous. It hangs satisfyingly and flits in the light breeze, connected to his finger by residual moisture. He inspects it; grey, green and black. It was never black back then. He shakes his finger as Daniel Potter walks out of the discount store, barking instructions into his mobile phone. Potter who did not speak to his mother Mary for fifteen years because she disapproved of his marriage to Shireen, twice divorced and who had two children in tow.

"She'll take what she needs and move on," she told him. But the old lady was wrong. Shireen always needed more, Potter spending all he earned on keeping her, her two brats, and Trisha whom he had impregnated five years earlier. And now she's dead and the old witch didn't leave a penny in her will to the son who she nursed and cleaned, fed and dressed; who she fetched from school and took on holidays that she could barely afford. Because fifteen years ago, he turned his back on her and married the woman who she called 'the harlot'. Her blackheart son, Daniel Potter now with a solicitor in his pay to ensure he grasps what is rightfully his from the dead woman's hands. He shouts into the phone as he passes the clown who imagines a world with no God; death no different to the eternity before birth, the dreariest of all ends. The Vikings saw life as a sparrow flying out of the dark night and into a banqueting hall. As it flies, it witnesses the heat and light, smelling the glory of the great feast, before gliding out into the never-ending black. Finally, the flake is free from the clown's finger, dropping quickly to the ground where it rests among the blossoms.

In Godwyn's third year of solitude, the Viking Sveyn Forkbeard marched on Lundenwic. With Norsemen overrunning the forts at either end of its bridge, the city had never been in greater peril. An ally of the English king, the saintly Norwegian prince, Haraldsson wove wicker roofshields for his boats, tied hawsers to the wooden posts of the bridge and commanded his men to row. Ropes strained against the timbers and the bridge groaned as Forkbeard's warriors rained down arrows, the stout roofs deflecting them and protecting the fleet. While Godwyn prayed for the safety of her nation and its king, the bridge yawed then gave a terrible shriek before crashing into the river, hurling men, shields and spears into the maelstrom. The cries of the Vikings were as pitiful as their battle roar had been dreadful. Æthelred now stormed the fort at Southwark, putting the invaders to flight. The hermit of course knew none of this. Her days were quiet, and to ponder if the Lord had seen fit to answer her prayers seemed like vanity. She baked bread in a small oven made from piled stones, fished with a pole, recited those passages of Scripture which she had committed to memory and prayed for Æthelred who now found himself king of a nation which, had it not been for Haraldsson's heroics and her own prayers, might have suddenly and dramatically become part of Denmark.

The sight of an Arabic man at his stall lifts the clown's spirits. Wedged in the recess between the Pakistani grocer and a bakery; the man's small table of wares forms the terminus of the great trade roads which have wound their way west from the Orient since the days when Moluccan sultans watched their spice ships leave the port of Sunda Kalapa, laden with cinnamon and cloves, skirting around warrior islands guarded by fierce Majapahit, datus, rajahs, huangs and lakans, finally making weary landfall at Dagon under the watchful eye of the Chittagong Mughals. Here, the company would be met by turbanned Karakorum Mongols on stout, short-legged horses; wisps of beard, packs of tea, porcelain, metalwork and frankincense; jewellery and sandalwood; amber and jade. And, of course the textile that gave this many fingered route snaking from the tips of Asia to the heart of Christendom its name, bales of brilliantly coloured silks strapped to the haunches of their pack animals. South around the Indies, stopping for fresh jars of water and salted provision gifted by the Chola kings in their Arikamedu stronghold. Ten days at sea until the lookout would spy the coast of Arabia Felix, leeward of the Island of Diodorus, sailing under warm, friendly winds to Kolzum where Saladin himself picked over the spoils. It was here that Bedouin merchants loaded their camels and brought spices, textiles and their own trinkets of amethyst and glass to the Mediterranean shore, laying out their oriental treasure on wide rugs and filling leather bags with ducats, thalers and doubloons. The clown glances at the wares being offered today and sniffs in disdain. No glorious craftsmanship from the east, simply cheap facsimiles, tchotchkes that had little worth even before they were copied and mass produced in dismal factories in Nanjing, an overseer barking time; bowing to the gods of cost saving and productivity. The man whose ancestors may once have been Bedouin stares at the screen of his mobile phone and cannot see the clown beneath the green awning of the Pakistani grocery, judging him.

It was the hour between nones and vespers. The seasons had moved but each day turned to its own rhythms. Today, a light fall of rain in the morning, and now a sharp breeze. Autumn. A small fire burned in the stone hearth and Godwyn sipped nettle broth from an iron pot, watching it. No news came her way, as none visited and only the miller, a handful of people at Barking and a few client priests at Westminster knew her whereabouts. An envoy from St. Peter's crept through the woods once a year on St. Sylvester's Eve, careful not to interrupt the nun's devotions, simply observing that she still lived.

As flames snaked around a willow log and the soup warmed her hands, Godwyn's mind wandered from her prayers to the jetties. The stench of fish and hides and excrement bobbing on the foreshore. The man was Italian and spoke no English, a boy of eighteen or nineteen; mannered and well-dressed, not like the usual roughnecks. He had taken her hand confidently, looking her in the eye. His smile won her trust and she walked with him away from the river. He had rooms above a tavern on Eastcheap and they sat in a downstairs nook where he fed her bread, cheese and watered ale until she became sleepy. His brows were refined, his nose angular and his chin strong. She imagined his home; his brothers and sisters, the servants who would come running at his whistle. To her, he seemed like a prince. What she didn't think to ask was why he broke bread and drank with a wild haired and penniless pauper barely out of her childhood, a girl he had bought for three pennies on the wharfside, or why he had chosen one of the few inns in Lundenwic whose rooms had locking doors.

He led her upstairs and kissed the side of her face. Suddenly, she felt a sharp pain. He had bitten her ear and she cried out. Throwing her on the bed, he loosened the leather belt from around his cloak, whipping her with it. Godwyn spun away, trying to evade the lashes as they rained down on her. The young man laughed. It was a game. Ripping off the linen tunic that served as his undergarment, he stood naked, his body pale and yet to be grown into. She held up a pillow against the blows as red welts showed on her face and shoulders, the tip of the belt curling around to her back. She cried out for help and he rushed at her, placing a hand over her mouth. Godwyn bit down on the flesh of his palm and he jerked it away before punching her. She blacked out. When she came to, she felt that she was being ripped in two, as if someone were trying to split her like a log. Her whole body moved back and forth, her face abrading against the bedding as he grunted behind her, her hair in his hands, jerking her head back. He would kill her. With what little strength she had, Godwyn clenched every muscle in her body, hurling her hips from left to right. The man cried out and let go of her hair, pushing her away but still she thrashed. He beat her with his fists until, with a preternatural flourish, she threw him off her. He landed badly, his back catching the corner of a table and she fell with him. He screamed, clutching his shoulder. Finally free, Godwyn grasped the key and rattled it in the lock with hands that shook. Moaning, he began hauling himself towards her. The key turned, she swept his cloak from the floor and fled down the stairs and onto the street. Later, she sold the garment for a guinea and threw the key in the river. Later still, she discovered that the Italian had paid the hag at the bar a shilling to ignore any shouts that came from the room. The log shifted in the fire sending up a shower of sparks. Godwyn sipped the broth and readied herself for vespers.

Ernesto Farzi walks past the bakery towards Maida Vale, face almost as white as the clown's. He hasn't shaved, his five-o-clock shadow blue beneath the foundation and talcum, his eyebrows tweezed into great arches. Ernesto Farzi, head held high in three quarter length tweed coat, large leather handbag and slingbacks. Trousers too short, ending above the ankles, Farzi looking straight ahead so as not to make eye contact with the haters; children laughing from the top deck of buses, throwing apple cores at him. Each time he leaves his flat on Shoot Up Hill, he dives into a hole in the ice and swims under it until he re-emerges in the third floor flat on the corner of Kingsgate and Quex. An engineer working on a nearby junction box grins at him as he passes. Two men wheeling a large trolley filled with pallets into the bakery block the pavement, Farzi waiting patiently for the obstacle to clear before he continues swimming to Pauline. Maybe they'll play *vingt -et-un* and eat Madeira cake chased down with a glass of Vermouth or Dubonnet, then he'll bring out the pills and they'll wake up on Monday.

145

In the bakery window, cakes and a sign for Mövenpick ice cream. Inside, Polish girls brew sweet, mint tea for the Arabic men who congregate here. Refugees from Damascus and Basra, Abyssinia and Khartoum. Men who once spent their afternoons outside Levantine coffee shops, sipping gahwa harvested from the peaceful earth of Eritrea. The beans roasted on a brazier then crushed with a pestle, the mud brick black with residue. The course ground powder boiled in a clay jebena, cooled then boiled again and strained through horsehair into cups without handles, frankincense and gum Arabic burning nearby. A little sugar, or salt, or niter kibbeh. The coffee brewed three times, first the *awel*, then the *kale'i* and lastly, the *bereka* – the blessed one. Skinny men who once sat cross legged around open fires in Asmara, Aleppo, Addis Ababa and Baghdad, fleeing the Caliphate, Ali Jaweesh, the dictator Afewerki and Al Qaida in their thousands, boarding ragged boats that fell apart in the Middle Sea long before they reached the coast of Italy. The long journey north to the Sangatte favela, washing from a single tap behind a disused boatyard and running from police who chased them with tasers, like rangers. The dispossessed of the Horn of Africa and the Fertile Crescent, roaming the concrete Serengeti like apes in a park. Not even a fire, just meagre handouts from charity workers who visit once a day as drivers wait in line for the *Spirit of Britain* to haul them and their cargo to Dover, locking their doors, fearful that brown-skinned men driven by the hope of work, housing, and education cling to the underbelly of their vehicles or climb into their trailers. The clown watches the men in the bakery, most simply sitting and not speaking, glad to be in the promised land. The aroma of freshly baked bread swirls around him, permeating the thick fibres of his trench coat, passing through paper skin and wafting

146

between ancient bones. Finding no home there, it continues on in search of someone who might appreciate it.

It was late autumn and the woods lighter with the early leaf fall. The path was wet with mulch as the autumn had been wetter than usual, and spongy brackets of fungus clung to the lower trunks. The Benedictine wandered through the great forest that hemmed in Wæclingacaester, stopping at every oak until he found what he was looking for. Gall wasps had laid eggs in leaf buds back in the spring and instead of acorns, round oak apples had formed, shielding and feeding the grubs. In the summer, adult wasps had bored their way out and flown off into the forest, leaving hard brown casings clinging to the trees with the last of the tawny leaves. At each provident tree, the Benedictine filled his pouch with galls, adding to those he had already collected then returned to the abbey in time for nones. Once his prayers had been completed, he made his way into the scriptorium. A single flame guttered from its tallow and, lighting a squat candle from it, he placed it on the desk. In the abbey church, boys were singing in preparation for Martinmas; their shrill voices floating in and out of range. The monk took a small hammer to the oak apples, smashing them. Fetching an earthenware jar, he filled it with the broken galls and emptied a skin of rainwater into it, allowing the nuts to soften and infuse. From a silken purse, he shook out some precious gum Arabic; brown crystals that had been collected from acacia trees in Byzantium tinkling into a pestle where he crushed them into a pale powder. Once pulverised, he sieved the gum into another bowl, crushed again what was left and repeated his labours until the dust was as fine and soft as talcum. This he mixed with water in a small phial and left to thicken until the following day when his labour would be completed.

147

The punch of composite leather on concrete paving slabs announces the approach of Nico Pirez, thirteen and Luke Fisher, twelve; Fisher guiding a basketball to the ground and back to his waiting palm like it is attached to string as the two boys pass a cheap homeware outlet, a fashion store and the bakery. Without looking, Fisher pushes the ball with his right hand towards his left heel where it smacks the ground, rebounding behind his left hip where his left hand launches it effortlessly back towards his right heel and so he walks, the ball dancing between his legs without breaking stride. Nico Perez envying his friend, never needing to tell his parents where he is, staying out till after eleven on school nights, arcing shots at the hoop on Sumatra Road in the orange glow of streetlights. The freedom. Perez resenting that he has to be home by six to do homework and practice piano; that his phone will chime any minute now, Alessandra Perez telling him what time he needs to be home to eat and what chores need doing beforehand. Fisher envying him back. Envying him the people at home who care for him, who want him there, who care about his future success. Who's he going to tell when he nails ten straight three pointers that no one else sees? The basketball doesn't love him, and even after he has spent the requisite number of hours perfecting his crossover, or his shoulder fake, or his no-look pass; whatever magic that will one day eclipse the elbow pass of Jason 'White Chocolate' Williams, there will still be a black hole that basketball can't fill. He can't read music. He's never heard of Brahms but he'd love someone to book him a piano lesson, to tell him to eat his peas and send him to bed at 9.30 without his phone. The clown watches them as they pass. We all want what we don't have.

The following day after nones, the Benedictine poured the sodden galls into a bowl using a scrap of linen as a strainer, brown liquid trickling through the cloth. Taking a small pouch of iron sulphate, he tapped some crystals into the mixture, alchemy turning the brown to black instantly. To this, he added some of the gum arabic which, by now, had the consistency of translucent tar. Stirring it with a slender wooden stick until it blended with the ink, the process was complete. The monk settled at the writing stand on his bench and opened Augustine's magnificent codex, an ancient leatherbound book lettered by the saint himself and which had only recently been brought to the abbey for safekeeping. Its pages undulated and the illustrations shone despite their great age. Carefully dipping a swan feather pen into the solution, the Benedictine tapped it and drew the nib gently across a page, the encaustum burning into the parchment as he copied almost exactly words etched by Augustine some five hundred years earlier. He had been part way through the ninth chapter of John when the inkwell ran dry. "*Scimus autem quia peccatores Deus non audit: sed si quis Dei cultor est, et voluntatem ejus facit, hunc exaudit.*" We know that God does not listen to sinners. He listens to the godly one who does his will. The quill tapping and stroking Vulgate onto the page, the scribe blowing on his fingers to warm them as, far away, the boys resumed their singing.

Next to the homeware store is a hair salon outside which a woman sits, her body rocking as she begs for alms. Romani and full faced, she wears a patterned black and white headscarf which, the clown presumes, she brought with her from Transylvania, Armenia, or Bessarabia; an ancient homeland east of the Danube. Protruding from her thick, warm black coat is a leg amputated below the knee, the woman's skirt hitched high to show a pristine white bandage. An opportunist panhandler; hands clasped in prayer, head nodding rhythmically as she cries in theatrical distress in her mother tongue. The clown is not buying it. This wretched drag of tarmacadam a collecting place for the destitute; waifs who fate has thrown into the city's corners; shadowpeople floored by meth amphetamine and crack cocaine, living a half-life in doorways, on night buses and in Salvation Army shelters. The few pennies pressed into vagabond palms by the charitable finding their way to the dealer, the shopkeeper who sells them white cider by the litre or the backstreet bookmaker. But this bozgoroaică, who would heap coins at her feet if she had two and not one? Mend her and you break her. Perhaps her handlers took the leg off themselves to guarantee a better return. Maybe her tears are real. The clown looks back at the ribbon of A5 as it stretches south towards Tyburn and the triumphal arch of white Carrara marble where the road meets the green of Hyde Park. How far would Amber Jamieson have reached by now? he wonders. He'd seen the hollow stare of the walking dead many times over. Would Jamieson turn back, seeking shelter in a chain café, shivering; no pennies for a drink because the dead carry no money? No. She was going to the bottom. Checking out. There but for the curse, he'd be gone too. Not long now, he thinks. If he had a watch, he would check it, but what's the point? Time is for people with things to do.

Brenda Corrigan, short dyed red hair and grey jacket bends down to whisper something into the beggarwoman's ear, then reaches into her black patent leather shoulder bag as the clown crosses the road, a Honda 50 narrowly missing him and the rider raising a hand in disbelief at a man so cavalier about his own safety. Here, a blind arm called the Terrace points a blunt finger towards Ryde House, a greybrown nineteen sixties monolith piling immigrant tenants over nine dreary floors. On floor three, behind a balcony filled with portable laundry rails and children's bicycles, in the lounge of her three bedroom council flat, Farah Alam serves her three offspring burgers made from Welsh lamb killed in the Halal way and drenched in 89p Iceland tomato ketchup. Hakan nine, Nihat seven and Birsen, five grab the soft, white, sugar-infused buns and stuff them into their mouths, not looking at their mother who shakes oven chips from a tray onto their plates. Their gaze instead on an electronic tablet made by Apple in California, and which is balanced against some bottles of oil and a basket containing receipts and money off coupons to be redeemed at Lidl and Asda. The animated frames of *Max Steel* flash across the screen, a boy hero pitted against the forces of darkness intent on seizing his father's secret. Farah Alam places the empty metal baking tray in the sink, rinses it and turns back to her brood.

"You know what day it is tomorrow?" No response. "It's Easter Sunday."

The glazed look of children whose attention is elsewhere. Max now in Turbo Mode against Miles Dredd.

"Easter Sunday" repeats Farah Alam. "Hakan."

Her elder son looking up momentarily.

"And yesterday was Good Friday"

"What's good about it?" the boy asks.

His sister Birsen answers.

"It's because there was no school."

Max looking like he is taking a beating. Bored with boy television, Birsen walks round the table and hugs her mother's legs, a signal for Alam to hoist her small daughter into the air and cuddle her.

"Good Friday is the day the Jews killed Jesus."

"How did they kill him mama?"

151

Farah Alam chews her lip.

"Oh, they, you know, they just killed him. And that's why the Christians had a holiday yesterday. It's why you're weren't at school."

"Do the Jews have a holiday too?"

"They had a holiday already. Still do."

"Why did they kill him mama?"

"Well, he said some things they didn't like, and so they killed him. But after he died, there were stories that he was alive again."

"Alive again?"

Birsen Alam giggles. She does not understand how a dead man can be alive again.

"The Christians said he was alive again, and if he could do that, he must be God."

"Mama stop talking we can't hear." The petulant Nihat.

"Mummy, can you play with me?"

Birsen bored with the Christ story and wanting to play a game where her mother is a teacher and she is Elsa, the ice princess from the movie *Frozen*.

On the street beneath their tower, Carl Johnson walks resolutely; his white Staffie, Petra straining at the lead. Carl Johnson, twenty five pounds from the invalidity benefit awarded to his sixty-nine-year-old mother in his pocket, lips pursed, heading towards William Hill to put twenty each way on Swift Imelda at the 13.30 race at Lingfield. Jobless Carl Johnson, ignorant of events that played out in Palestine one thousand nine hundred and eighty one years earlier; unaware that Christ died for him, that the flesh ripping scourge and the bone splitting nails were for his unswerving love for the twenty-three-year-old man who rolls twenty joints a day, who believes in alien life, crop circles and who is convinced that when he was on a school trip to Wales, the trees talked to him. Carl Johnson, beloved child of God who is watched, cared about and fretted over by his benign, all-loving father in heaven walks towards the bookmaker's to wager money on a horse which, a furlong into the race, will swallow her own tongue.

Albric came to the river once, discreetly, by road. He saddled a horse and rode the five and a half miles to the plank bridge over the burn where he tethered his animal to a young aspen. Creeping through trees on the opposite side of the river, he spotted Godwyn washing vestments on a flat rock; her lips moving in prayer but the words inaudible from such a distance. By now, he had ushered two more waifs the way of Wendreda; one a thief and the other a wretched girl in her third trimester who was dragged from Lundenwic's river into which she had waded until the waters closed over her head. The babe came early and was lost but the girl stayed with Albric's family while she grieved. These were turbulent times. Lundenwic had needed to defend itself from Forkbeard's Vikings, and on St Michael's Day 1014, a great wave thundered in from the west, drowning villages miles inland, ruining crops and condemning thousands to a life of desperate penury. How much of this did Godwyn know? he wondered. She lived a primitive existence, but danger was everywhere. Truly, God was harrowing the English and its people never needed her prayers more. On his way back to Lundenwic, the merchant stopped in at the mill and left a bundle of clean clothing, soap made from lye and a tinderbox, buying the miller's discretion with a flagon of sweet wine. Godwyn knew nothing of the wave that hit with such force that coastal rocks from Cornwall to Scotland were flung miles inland and whose floodwaters consumed the marshy coast of Holland, never to recede. She also knew nothing of any invasion, nor the immediate danger facing the nation for which she prayed. She met no one. Her companions were the birds. She trapped fish and squirrels and grew herbs. This was her third life, and though it was a rude and solitary one, she preferred it. On the street, hunger gnawed at her daily. In the abbey she was safe but the memory of Thorhild infected the place, a stain that could not be cleaned. Here, she had been renewed; cleansed of her past. Her sins were those of the mind. She had no one to rob, kill or bear false witness to, and though she had no notion of what perils threatened her country, her king, or the great monastic houses of England, to pray for their wellbeing was her sole purpose. God knew the details, she was simply his maidservant.

Occasionally, the clown spouted popular rhyme or coaxed music out of the small pipe which he kept in his coat. Most of the time, he made money by juggling. He'd had enough time to practice. Seven oranges, lemons or whatever he could put his hands to. Once he hung a bag of mice around his neck and threw the beasties into the air, their legs and tails flailing as they flew and fell. He earned good money that way. Then one evening in the great depression that followed the Napoleonic wars, he was attacked by three drunken soldiers, a bearded private sinking a knife up to the shaft in his chest and the clown grinning at him, the man losing his mettle as has everyone since. Now it's just another trick. Off the main drag is the best place; it doesn't do to have spectators. Outside the door of Ryde House, a few men loiter, some smoking, some talking on mobile phones. Most work at city banks where messages are passed in secret, whispered in corridors and elevators but never written down. This adventure isn't in the guide books; participation by invitation only and entry isn't cheap – four crisp red banknotes bearing the face of Sir John Houblon.

The clown looks at today's adversaries; one of them can't be more than nineteen, bravado bringing him here. That and the promise of a kick you can't get anywhere else in this city, at least not without getting banged up for thirty years. An ample bellied man in Ralph Lauren chinos and blue Charles Truitt shirt produces a blade and tests it with his thumb, drawing blood. Light brown hair slicked back, confident; he seems like the alpha. The man grimaces, baring his teeth and the youth flinches; his first rodeo. Stainless steel flashes as it reflects the white sky and business begins. A man's got to live. The same rules as usual; anywhere in the torso, up to the hilt. Heart, lungs, stomach. Cash up front, no refunds if – he grins at each of them – you can't stomach it. The clown collects a thousand pounds in notes from hands that try not to shake and the big man licks his lips, grips the knife handle and adjusts his stance, as if there's a proper way to do this. The others form a semicircle around him, staring at the clown who pockets the cash and dreams of the sex he'll be having later under a railway arch, a last hurrah before the drop. He opens his coat and waits for the pain; brief, clean, and sanctifying; the breath drawing out of him, the noise of the city momentarily dissipating, a gasp as the blade is retracted quickly, dripping with gore before being handed to the next assailant, a balding man in a dark suit who purses dry lips and stares at the bloody weapon in his hand before plunging it into the clown's stomach. It beats feeding pigs or shooting rabbits; the men's faces a picture. The bald one so pale, it's like he's the one who's bleeding out. The clown falls to his knees for added theatre as two more men plunge the blade into his abdomen until it's the turn of the novice to finish him off. He takes the knife and his hand shakes as if he has the palsy. Blood bubbles from the clown's mouth and he gurgles, almost a death rattle. Immediately the young man soils himself, drops the knife and stumbles back to the road. As the clown lies in a pool of his own blood, the fat man takes a cloth from leather pouch, cleans the blade and places it back in his backpack. Only a knife in his flesh can punish him, only this can offer him the faintest sense of a debt being paid. Even then, he always gets up, walks away and lives another day. While the men change into fresh shirts, the clown feels strength returning. Staggering to his feet, he clicks his bones and walks back out onto the High Road, money in his pockets that he no longer needs, wounds healing like they always do because a deal is a deal, a curse is a curse and death only comes at its appointed time.

Vespers had been sung in the abbey church which, in those days, was built from the rubble of old Verulamium. The walls were thick and the structure simple with rounded arches and a wood roof keeping the worst of the weather away. At one end, a squat tower made a crude attempt to reach closer to God, and beneath this, a stone sarcophagus held the earthly remains of the martyr, Alban. Two transepts either side of the tomb and the chancel beyond formed the shape of a long cross if viewed from above which, at the time, was only possible by God, his angels, and the bats, bees, and birds. The brothers had finished singing in the nave and were filing out along the east cloister which was lit by a great brazier in the centre of the courtyard, past the chapter house to the newly completed novices' dormitory. Leofstan was speaking in hushed tones with Ædwald the prior and Osfrith the novice master. The Danes who posed a near constant threat to the English were coming again; sword wielding warriors whose longships shone with gold, some even carrying bulls to add to the terror. The monks whispered about fearless men of metal, windborne lions and rapacious wolves. They were Anakites and Nephilim, Leofstan said, and so fleet of foot that they scorned the speed of the Saxons who hoped to repel them. The great Bible of Augustine must be moved. Westminster was strong and its island offered better defence; the book would be safe there. Who should carry it there was the subject of the men's conversation. As the Benedictine passed, all three turned to him and watched him disappear with the others, beyond the reach of the firelight.

Fresh from his knifing, the clown catches his breath against the window of a Thai restaurant on the corner of the Terrace and the High Road. Inside, Michael Huxley and his wife Christine are finishing the second of three courses. Christine beginning with four skewers of chicken seasoned with a satay sauce, Michael choosing a clear, piquant tom yum soup with prawns. The two now picking at the last morsels of a green curry with chicken (Michael) and a beef Pad Thai (Christine). Charlotte and Tom raved about the place, and it's only a quick hop from Queens Park. Basic, they said; no frills but they know how to cook and it's clean. Michelle Thonglau arrives to take their plates away. Eighteen, slim with long black hair shining like it is polished, a white shirt too large for her, pencil black mini skirt and black leggings. Michael Huxley looking at her face, briefly; the girl seems bored, going through the motions, her mind somewhere else. Christine Huxley talking about swimming lessons for Bonnie. The only class nearby for children her age is at 5.30am, but her teacher thinks that, with proper training, she might represent Brent. Thonglau returning with a Cilio 18/10 stainless steel table crumb remover, and as she busses the table, her breasts accidentally brush against Michael Huxley. Instantly he feels blood rush to his loins as pressure builds against the green and blue tartan design cotton stretch hipster underpants that Christine bought in a pack of three from Next.

"Simon takes Benedict to Swiss Cottage pool at 5.30 every Saturday, and he says they just go to bed earlier on Friday, but we could always take it in turns, and who knows? She may find that when it gets serious, she doesn't like it as much."

Michael Huxley looking at Christine patting her mouth with the salmon pink table napkin and seeing lines around her eyes and the shiny deep grey patches under them, the wrinkles by the side of her mouth, the heavy shoulders that used to be so slim. He looks away. Michelle Thonglau now laughing with an older Thai woman – possibly the owner. He wouldn't have looked twice at her before, but now he's fixated with her bosom, trying to figure out how big her breasts are beneath the billowing cotton of her work shirt.

"Cameron and Daisy have started drama classes at the Tricycle on Wednesdays after school, but that clashes with Zumba. Then again, they do them on Saturday mornings too, so that would mean going straight on from swimming which might be too much for Bonnie."

Michelle Thonglau returning with some dessert menus, innocent of the storm that she is creating in bespectacled Michael Huxley, forty-one; thinning on top but not enough to shave it. Christine Huxley picking up the menu greedily, as if this in itself were something sweet to be devoured. Her gaze averted, Michael Huxley stares at Thonglau's upper body while she takes an order from another table, his eyes trying to penetrate the thick white cotton. He swallows and picks up the menu. Thonglau walks past again, suddenly statuesque, Huxley not listening as Christine details the intricacies of their children's Saturday mornings, his focus now solely on the contents of Michelle Thonglau's blouse.

"Then again, she might want to do ballet this term, but they do that at the O2 as well. You're very quiet Michael."

Huxley raising his eyebrows in faux defence and taking a gulp of Singha beer to rid his throat from the clag that has collected there.

"I can take her swimming."

He smiles and gets up to excuse himself. Thonglau no longer in the restaurant; she must be in the kitchen. The loo a single small cubicle with a sink outside. Huxley bolts the door, pushes down his jeans and boxers, closes his eyes and begins his fast journey to rapture, feasting on a naked Michelle Thonglau of his imagination. His balls tighten as a child's voice outside the door asks his daddy why they can't go in.

"Because someone's in there, Barney. We have to wait for them to finish."

Michael Huxley stopping for a moment as Thonglau reclines, half undressed on a white bed, hoping they'll leave. Peace. He grabs himself again.

"I don't want to wait daddy."

Huxley clenching a fist and pressing it to the top of his forehead. He pulls up his jeans, flushes the lavatory and unlocks the door. A man in a leather jacket; unshaven with a whiff of tobacco holding the hand of a small blond boy. Back at the table, Christine Huxley has decided what she is having – tempura banana with coconut ice cream. Michelle Thonglau who is a student of business and administration at the College of North West London and who still lives with her parents in Hendon returns and smiles. She waits, nubile, flat bellied, intoxicating; Christine handing her the menu, Michael aching to be left alone with her compliant, willing body.

"Michael, dessert?"

Huxley breaking from his trance, mumbling an order for a black coffee. Christine Huxley looking tired, her skin no longer pearlescent and her voice now a shrill clarion, a sharp atonal blare that cuts through the excited chatter of infants. On the next table, the man in the leather jacket returns and begins feeding chips to his son while the couple sitting with them teach their six-year-old how to eat with chopsticks. Tonight in her bed, Michelle Thonglau will imagine that the slim dad with the stubble, the laughter lines and leather jacket who called her 'Sweetheart', whose breath smelled of cigarettes and who has a son called Barney is riding her up to the balls. Michael Huxley toys with his beer glass as Christine checks on her iPhone for the times of the drama classes on Saturdays at the O2 Centre on Finchley Road.

A web of messengers conveying news that Forkbeard and his Viking hordes were preparing their fleet at Jomsborg invoked terror in the uncertain middle months of 1015; men hurrying Augustine's vellum codex bound with calves' leather across sunken tracks between fields, through fords waist deep with recent rain, the Bible even spending the night in a moorland cave as wolves howled at a blood moon. England's great ecclesiastical treasure had been hidden most recently in the abbey of St. Benet where it had been brought when rumours of a Norse invasion panicked Lindisfarne. Illuminated with cochineal, vermillion and verdigris and leafed with gold, Augustine's Bible was secreted in the traveling bags of wondering clerics, first to Repton, then Hinckley, then Ely; flitting between Mercia, Northumbria and Wessex until it reached Yarmouth. The brothers here wrapped it in a sheep's skin and hurried it in relay to the Benedictine abbey of Wæclingacaester where it had spent the past two months. Here, the Benedictine had pored over it in the abbey scriptorium, tracing his finger over cursives applied with a reed pen in Italy four hundred years before, the drolleries at the margins of the pages, the rinceau borders. Now the book was to be wrapped up once again to continue its flight from the Vikings.

The clown peers through the window of the Thai restaurant. He saw Michelle Thonglau when she was a baby in a high chair at the back of the restaurant. She was there as a toddler, a child doing her homework at a table before the restaurant opened in the evening. While most who rent rooms in and around the High Road are simply waiting to earn enough money to escape, some live their entire lives here. Trapped here; too poor or just too stuck. He looks around. Who knows where any of these fuckers are from? They blow in and they blow out, just like they have always have, and none have overstayed their welcome longer than him. Twelve-year-old Brahim Jama walks out of the KFC next to the Thai restaurant. With him is his cousin Mohamed Noor, the same age but half his size, Noor holding a large red and white punnet bearing the face of Harland Sanders. Jama tall for his age and big with it, grey tracksuit bottoms, a baggy burnt orange t-shirt and a giant bustle backside, the boy waving his arms to propel him along. Noor skipping beside his cousin as they pass the clown, telling Jama that *Spiderman 2* was the biggest movie that has ever been shot in New York City. Jama refusing to believe him, needing to be right and for Noor to be wrong; the smaller boy asking what film was bigger? What movie shot in New York had a bigger budget or took longer to film? Jama punching Noor in the arm, almost upending the bucket of legs and wings and making the smaller boy cry out. Jama who will grow up to drive fork lift trucks around a warehouse in Park Royal while Noor will escape, study robotics at UCL and play the cello.

161

The evening repast had been interrupted by the arrival of a breathless scout; the Danish fleet had set sail bound for Mercia. The great Bible was wrapped hastily in skins, the Benedictine given bread, victuals and a small flask of ale in readiness for his journey south to the abbey at Westminster. They sang Matins and lauds at three, after which he fetched his cloak and stepped into the dark of the pre-dawn, the boy Ealdræd pulling the beam across the abbey gates and wishing him travelling mercies. The night was chosen as it was clear, the moon waxing gibbous affording him good light and surer footfalls. A day to reach Westminster, a day or two spent with the brothers there and a day to return. From here, a lay brother would take the Bible to Canterbury. This final journey would not be completed until the old king Æthelred had died, a peace forged and Cnut crowned king of all England by Bishop Lyfing at the Kings Stone on the banks of the River Thames, the king's hand resting on its vellum cover. By then, the Benedictine too would be dead.

The clown watches Brahim Jama waddle away to eat chicken wings with his cousin and looks into the Subway next door, the acrid stench of sweet, chemically infused bread gusting across the pavement. Fifty-two-year-old Scot McCabe hurries past, glancing in at the yellow and green, the smell awakening his hunger. Nine days without solid food, McCabe is fasting; a devotee of a shyster named Bragg who claims to be one hundred and sixty years old, drinks apple cider vinegar and once abstained from food for forty days before shitting mercury into a cup. One hundred and sixty years old. What crime does a man need to commit to deserve that? The clown can't remember when he last ate, or what. The body goes on because it must, but not for long. Today he goes back to black.

Silver shards of light sliced through the cloud as the

Benedictine walked. Behind him, the sleeping city; the only visible light a torch burning at its southern gate, receding with every footstep. The road passed under the birdpecked corpse of a thief hanging from a gallows, his bared teeth glinting in the moonlight. The Benedictine shuddered and hurried on. At the bottom of Holmhurst Hill, the track passed through open country for about a mile until forest engulfed it. Around one shoulder hung a leather bag in which was wrapped the Bible. Over his other shoulder, a knapsack with food and drink for the journey. The woods closed around him, too dark for his eyes to accustom but the road was mercifully straight. Owls close-by and distant wolves the only animals announcing themselves to the traveller. After an hour or so, dawn lifted slowly and hares grazed by the roadside, stoats hurried across the path and ponderous badgers waited for him to pass. A fox stepped quickly back into a thicket, watching him. By the time the sun had been up an hour, he was on the edge of a clearing, a village called Little Stanmore in the hundred of Gore; no inn but some cottages. An old woman fetching a pail of water from a stream offered him a cup of warm sheep's milk. Two children marvelled at his feet, for few wore sandals at that time, and none of them infants.

"Are you rich?" they asked him.

"I am rich in spirit," he replied, and believed it, for he had yet to meet any who might undo what the Spirit had wrought in his young life. The woman brought him a crust of barley loaf and some dripping; it was a good breakfast and he left as the rest of the village was waking.

In the halal butcher that forms part of a ragged row of nondescript shops on the east side of the High Road, Abdul Sayyid waits as a young man in a blue coat chops at lamb shank with a cleaver. Sayyid timid, like his family. Bookish factotums, reckoners and bean counters; cowards who failed to fight either the infidel, the Russians nor the British Expeditionary Force. Men who hung back behind their desks, heads down, their soft hands unused to farm work, and daggers that only ever cut paneer. Abdul Sayyid flinching as the cleaver hacks through bone, turning instead to the shelves of imported cans and packages from Pakistan; giant drums of ghee, ten kilo bags of rice, chickpeas and cardamum seeds. How does it end? Sayyid sick of pleasing. He loves Sabhia but they never do anything, or go anywhere that isn't halal. One day, he'd love to have a week that isn't arranged around family and the mosque, to board a jetplane, drink gin and tonic with a slice of lemon and land in Las Vegas with Sabhia; his wife wearing a fashionable dress and sunglasses instead of a niqab. He'd love to ride in a limo to Bellagio, marvel at the fountains, eat generous piles of pancakes and feel the thrill of throwing down a hundred dollars on a blackjack table. Just once. Would God hate him? Is that so unforgivable a dream? His phone buzzes. Sabhia. Her aunties need picking up from Heathrow and Siddiq is in Borehamwood all day. And can he bring okra and dates? The blade cracks down on a sheep's pelvis like a full stop and Sayyid agrees to grab the extra food that wasn't on the list, and the two aunties.

Next to the butcher, a Chinese herbalist and next to this, a locksmith outside which Stuart Hitchin waits anxiously at a bus stop, a large wheeled case containing only the most necessary of his worldly possessions. The rest can wait. What a dick. He can't believe he got played. And he's never going to drink again, that goes without saying. Change his name too if he has to. Proper muppet. Two weeks earlier, he fell into an after-hours speakeasy on West End Lane, lust-fuelled largesse paying for cocktails, the girl he'd just met that evening hanging on every word. Sex a given; he had her. Hitchin checking up and down the High Road and wishing the bus would get a fucking move on. He steps back from the edge of the road and hovers under the awning of the Asian grocer. A woman's raised voice breaking the ambiance of the bar. Hitchin cocky and emboldened with booze. A man's hand on a woman's throat, gobbing off at her and Big Stuart wading in, grabbing the man's wrist.

"That's enough fella."

The man holding up his watch, its strap broken. The room suddenly quiet. Three men between Hitchin and the door. The girl he was with afraid too, wanting to leave, his courage draining with every second. The man putting his face close to Hitchin's.

"How much do you think that'll cost to fix, knight on a white horse?"

Hitchin suggesting twenty.

"It's just a strap."

The man grinning at the others.

"Just a strap."

His mates laughing. Menace, not derision.

"More like two hundred."

"I've not got two hundred, mate."

"How much have you got?"

Hitchin reaching for his wallet, his hand shaking despite the tequila, counting notes.

"Ninety five."

The man snatching it from him.

"We'll collect the rest later."

The woman who'd been attacked looking at him, impassive, in on the scam. The old Cockney behind the bar who he'd been joking with earlier whispering to him:

"You'd better go. And you'd better pay."

The girl he was with grabbing her things, wanting to get out, the moment broken, not even a goodbye as she jumped in an uber. Hitchin didn't even know her name let alone her number. Just met her. Then a few days later, a knock on his door in Dennington Park Road. Two men, shaven headed wearing puffer jackets, demanding two hundred pounds. Hitchin explaining that he'd already paid nearly a hundred. The men sneering. That was for emotional damages. They need two hundred for the watch. Hitchin fumbling for cash while his brain tried to catch up. Had someone followed him home? He counted out the notes.

"That's us done right?"

"That's us just started, Stuart. See you next week."

Valuables and a few clothes thrown in a case, fearful he's being tailed, his route planned, 16 to Victoria, lose them in the mêlée in the station then grab a tube to Euston and a train up to Manchester, to the single back bedroom at his sister's house, big Stuart Hitchin, hiding and scared. The clown watches him and climbs onto a 189 travelling the other way. Upstairs, seventeen-year-old Christopher "Cashmoney" White stares out of the window, a drawstring JD sports bag taking up the spare seat next to him. The bus being relatively full and not wishing to stand, the clown takes the bag, throws it onto the floor in the aisle and sits down. White looking at the skinny man in the seat next to him with fury and fear.

"Be my guest." says the clown, swinging his legs aside so that White can reclaim his lost baggage.

It had been an early start to the day as it was midsummer. A Wednesday. Prime at sunrise; Godwyn reflecting on Alban whose day it was. She knew little of the saint, only that he was the nation's first martyr, and the abbey built around his shrine was one of the great Benedictine houses of Mercia. She had fished a little; the mayfly nymphs settling on the water to sun their wings attracted trout. At around nine it was terce, the recitation of the one hundred and twentieth psalm, *Ad Dominum*. "When I was in trouble, I called upon the Lord, and he saved me," a hymn of St Ambrose, spoken not sung as with many pleasures, she found singing too joyous for one with so much to forgive. Godwyn gathered nettles and cabbage and chopped them for later. Fetching up a couple of squirrel skins, she began stitching them into a blanket while the light was still good. Noon was the hour of nones, the one hundred and twenty sixth psalm, "They that sow in tears shall reap in joy." While she prayed, she washed her pot in the river in readiness for boiling a stew, her cowl up to protect her from the heat of the sun. Nearby, a wide willow cast welcome shade. Out of nowhere, a voice.

"Hail!"

She rose to her feet and made for her shelter but the intruder followed. She tuned, entreating him.

"Please, come no further."

A man. A monk in the brown robes of a Benedictine; the first person she had spoken to in over three years. He was tall and his voice was kind.

The fishers of men are out today, eager for a catch. Passion Week, the last truly religious festival in the calendar. Easter still a holiday. A holy day. Standing patiently in the cut-through to the church carpark on the west side of the street are the D'Souzas. Bruno, fifty one, in a sombre navy suit and tie, and his sons, Eduardo and Felipe, fifteen and twelve. Eduardo tall for his age, six foot three and chubby, a grey jumper with a dark blue panel around the shoulders, his navy blazer giving the impression that this is a school day. Maybe it is. Felipe smartly dressed too, standing with his family next to a display of *Watchtower* magazines. The clown watches them from his perch on the bus. The older boy wanting to be invisible; he sticks out enough as it is, keeping vigil because of his family. His friends are spending their Saturday playing Xbox, kicking a ball in the park or hanging around the Apple Store in Brent Cross. Right now, he could be at a Brazilian ju jitsu class but instead, he stands in the middle of Kilburn in dreadful ill-fitting clothes bought by his mother, his only prayer that no one he knows sees him. Felipe excited, beaming; a pleaser, wanting to be liked, the virtue sanctifying him; idolising his father and older brother, wishing he could chat to passers-by and be anointed by their gratitude, but waiting in silence instead for the rest of the one hundred and forty four thousand to join them. Eduardo checks his watch. Still two more hours. He rolls his shoulders and yawns as the bus crawls past.

The hunter stood by the wayside, pointed his bow at the skies and took aim. A flock of seven swans. He drew back the taut pig gut and released his bolt. Its sharpened antler bone tip piercing one of the birds under the wing, killing her instantly. Too heavy to glide, she tumbled gracelessly, cracking through the canopy of a beech tree and thumping onto the forest floor. A heavy-boned dog bounded into the woods; a companion of sorts but a means to an end. The hunter unable leave the path but the dog under no such curse, returning with the swan's neck in its mouth, the body dragging behind it. He slung the bird over his neck, knowing it would fetch good money at the market where the east-west track crossed Watling Street at Paddington. He patted the dog who he had named Rollo like the fifteen before him, Rollo the name he would have given his son, a boy who, even if he had lived would be long dead, whose great grandchildren would also now be in their graves. What if it had been a girl? Matilda. Gone now. Perhaps not even surviving her own birth. Somewhere, his wife and child are buried but he is doomed never to find them nor join them. A man with no last will and testament, as he has nothing to leave and who plans to be cremated, his ashes rising to the heavens from which has been barred, scattered on winds to an ocean he has never seen and mountains he will never climb.

Nightfall. The forest behind him and now the single stone slab across the Westbourne known as the Knight's Bridge ahead of him. The road continued south to the great river, a few houses but none lit, most now sleeping until the sun rose. Try as he might, the Benedictine could not avert his mind from the nun by the river. Every contemplation, however virtuous led back to her, and he was glad of the distraction provided by the city. Two soldiers stepped away from a fire at the roadside, one coughing into a rag, the other asking his business. When shown the edge of the great book wrapped in its fleece, he nodded the monk towards the ferryboat and peered more vigilantly into the gloom to see if any followed. The boy Ælfric was asleep in the boat but scrambled awake as a guard shook him. Placing a cushion in the prow for his passenger, he began the short journey across the Tybourne to Thorney Island.

A tattooist and an empty store on the west side, a wig shop, a stationer's and a dentist to the east. There were no rules against using public transport, but waiting at lights was intolerable. Walking, though ultimately slower, led to more opportunity. On a bus, he watched everything through a screen; outside he could smell the destitution, the fear, the avarice. He preferred to be among the shoeless and shillingless on the street than to steam past them in a charabanc with everyone glued to a phone or a freesheet.

In a cramped one bedroom flat above the dentist's, Marcus Forster wearing a tweed jacket, corduroy trousers and sporting a fine Edwardian beard rummages through jigsaw pieces on his coffee table. He finished the last puzzle, five hundred pieces of a half-timbered thatched cottage in Shropshire and gave it back to the animal charity shop next door, and now he is working away at a thousand piece lighthouse in the Frisian Islands. His *Times Atlas of the World* informs him that the islands lie off the west coast of Denmark, Germany and Holland at a latitude of around 54° north, roughly level with Whitby. An atlas because Forster has no computer, nor even any internet; his two rooms cluttered with brown furniture, antiques, and oil paintings culled from charity shops. A grandfather clock keeps a serene beat as sirens and car horns pass on the street below. Fifty-year-old Marcus Forster who still calls his eighty-three-year-old mother "Mummy", who eats supper and describes himself as a homosexual, never gay, who has no mobile phone and watches the five channels available on a television wired to a wall pokes around with his finger to find a piece of sky with at least one outie and two innies. A large ginger house cat, Mr Quivers purrs on the settee while Classic FM plays a Beethoven piano concerto by the Moscow RTV Symphony Orchestra on the nineteen sixties Bakelite radio which Forster calls his wireless. Above them, the ceiling has pock marks where Forster hits it with a broom handle during manic episodes, raging at the music played by the man upstairs who he hates. Forster who has never worked, waits for a call from his dealer on his landline. The HIV meds affect his libido, but it's nothing that a puff or two of methamphetamine can't put back in order. There. Now he needs two outies with a corner between them.

At St. Peter's, the Benedictine was welcomed warmly, Abbot Ælfwig thanking him for his endeavour, praising God for his safe passage and personally taking Augustine's bible to the abbey library. The monks had all eaten and most were asleep, but the visitor was given a hasty meal of dark bread and curds in the kitchen where the embers of a fire still offered a little heat.

The abbey rose at four and though it was summer, dawn was still an hour away. Here on the island, the singing was simpler and the readings delivered by a faltering monk with a high vocal tone, as if the man were terrified of what the passage might unfold and what its words might mean to them. Once the prayers were over, the Benedictine was ushered to the library. Augustine's treasure had been brought from the sacristy where it had been kept overnight, a windowless strongroom deep in the bowels of the monastery. Until its arrival, the abbey scriveners had been working on the great Psalter of Bosworth, a grand book financed by wealthy patrons who hoped the project might protect them and their nation from attacks by the Danes. Now Westminster's monks pored over the ancient codex, touching with tentative fingers words that had been lettered by the hand of saint himself. The Benedictine shared his own strokes and admired the scrolls which they showed him, his lips moving silently as he spoke the words. The elderly scribe, Eadgar who was training an apprentice, Ælstan brought the Benedictine a square of goatskin parchment and a quill pen, a great honour. The old monk opened Augustine's Bible at the third chapter of the Second Epistle of Peter.

171

"This is the verse we will copy," he said, and with a shaking hand, he gestured to Ælstan to give his seat to the visitor. Then, looking at the Benedictine,

"Write".

As a tall candle guttered, he took the quill and dipped it in the dark vial of gall nut, copperas and gum arabic and began painting letters on the skin. *Unum vero hoc non lateat.* He felt the breath of the apprentice, a man older than himself, leaning over him, as if trying to inhale his craft. None spoke. The pen scratched and when he had finished, he sat back, fanning the wet script. He stood and stepped aside. Uncertain, the apprentice looked around at the others.

"Go on" said Ælfwig impatiently, motioning to the chair. The monk sat and took the quill.

"If your hand is going to shake so, we should keep with Eadgar." Ælfwig's eyes rolling for effect.

The monk wrote well, absorbing himself in the scriptwork. He placed more flourishes than the Benedictine might, showing off with the kind of unnecessary frippery that could delay the completion a manuscript considerably.

"Well, we are none of us Augustines," Ælfwig concluded, but rolled up Ælstan's parchment and handed it to the Benedictine to take with him to show the brothers back at Wæclingacaester.

The clown tires of the bus and saunters down the stairs. As they are not at an official stop, he hits the red button that opens the doors in an emergency and steps out as the driver swears at him from behind the safety glass. Across on the east side of the road, Jeanette Pirsig walks briskly into the charity shop next to the dental surgery above which Marcus Forster is slowly piecing together a lighthouse on the Frisian island of Wangerooge. Pirsig is cross, not that it's the shop's fault. Someone, and she's not pointing any fingers, has mislaid, thrown away or hidden the two thirty pound tickets for tomorrow's Jason Donovan concert at the Hammersmith Apollo that were attached to the fridge. She's asked her five-year-old, Megan who assures her that neither she nor any of her friends saw, opened, drew on or cut up the envelope containing two printed and embossed tickets to the concert. And Megan wouldn't lie, she's a good girl. John is still at work and when she called him out of a meeting because it was urgent – how else was she going to get hold of him? It would take the house burning down or Fudge dying before he put her first during work hours, but sometimes it would be nice if he could prioritise her, or at least realise how frantic she is that it's barely twenty four hours until Donovan will stride onto the Apollo stage wearing a pale linen suit and white T-shirt, and she still has NO IDEA WHERE THE TICKETS ARE – when she called John out of the meeting, he simply told her to search in all the places where she had already looked. All she can think, and if he bothered calling her, she would tell him, is that they were somehow still in the pocket of the jeans that she dumped here yesterday with everything else. But who knows what happens to donated items after you drop them off? If it's anything like the Oxfam over the road, they ship it to some kind of central warehouse where they sort and distribute the good stuff to the shops a bit more evenly. The lady there told Pirsig this when she asked why none of the things she donates ever seem to make it into the shop, let alone the window, not that she's suspicious, why should she be? People like that don't steal the best items for themselves, or throw it in the trash, but the shoes were Russell and Bromley and it would have been nice to see them on display. The lady behind the till is chatting to an older black man who she appears to know and as time ticks, Pirsig instinctively hates them both. Finally the woman looks up.

173

Jeanette Pirsig explaining that her feckless husband John might have left the tickets for Jason Donovan in the back pocket of some trousers which he hasn't worn for months, and could she just have a quick look? The woman at the till disappearing through a door, returning a few moments later and inviting Pirsig to look for the bag herself in a giant stock room filled with boxes and piles, a handful of volunteers picking over the spoils. Pirsig seeing the bag and lunging at it, a sudden and dramatic move that makes the others look up, but she doesn't care about them, only Jason Donovan crooning *Ten Good Reasons*, Donovan with his blond flick, wide eyed Donovan duetting *Especially for You* with a backing vocalist, of 1989, of being at Chesham High, reading *Smash Hits* and *Seventeen* with Tracey Pelham and Ruth Flitton and kissing Lee Marcus in Lowndes Park because he had cigarettes and rode a motorbike. Pirsig not caring about the eyes that are upon her, rummaging through work shirts and trainers and VHS videos until she finds the jeans and feels in the pockets. A receipt from Homebase, a parking voucher and a couple of plant markers.

"Fucking hell!"

She stares at the bag as the volunteers in the room look at her, then turn away to give her a moment. Several weeks ago, while she was playing with Siobhan from next door who never says please and actually ASKS for food and juice when it's not even her house, Megan brushed against the fridge where Jeannette Pirsig had attached the tickets with a ceramic fridge magnet in the shape of a cupcake. The envelope fell to the floor along with a photograph of Megan's cousin in Australia and a newssheet from her school. Pirsig's sister Marie who was minding Megan at the time saw the papers on the floor and, not realising they had once been attached to the fridge, placed them on top of it, meaning to but forgetting to tell Jeannette Pirsig that they were there. Pirsig will not find the tickets until long after the show. She cannot call Ticketmaster because she bought them from a tout on eBay, and so she will make her way to the Apollo a few hours before the concert begins and pay eighty pounds to a man who looks like a car thief while John stays at home minding Megan. "At least we'll save on babysitting and one of us will see the show." And despite the brilliance of Donovan, she will remain cross, cross with John, cross that it had to be like this, that this always happens to them. Cross.

Though his cot in the Westminster dormitory afforded him comfort, the Benedictine could not sleep, and not because of the loud exhalations of the brothers who slept nearby. He had left the path and seen forbidden fruit. He wondered how that fruit might taste and the face of the blessed sister stood before him, more beautiful than holy, and he felt warmed by her. He admonished himself for thinking this way. She was untouchable, and he forbidden to touch. He began reciting psalms to still his mind and send him to sleep, but the demons in his soul showed her to him over and again, an upturned face, a shoulder the colour of maple, her soft lips. He begged the Lord to quieten his thoughts and only an attempt to name the kings of Israel and Judah in alphabetical order rent him away from the Cunebourne stream and sent him into a light but dream-filled sleep.

While Jeanette Pirsig has been in the charity shop, the clown has gathered a small crowd of bystanders who listen as he plays *The Cat and Bells* on his tin whistle, a few of them throwing coins at his feet. Pirsig exits the shop and passes the shell of the Citizens Advice Bureau on the corner of Kingsgate Place. Kings after the Georges whose coffers swelled with coins paid by travellers on the High Road; gate after the old tollhouse which moved here a century and a half ago. Who cares if the gate was first built in the time of Anne and moved here when Victoria was Queen? The building has long since been dismantled, taken to Shoot Up Hill, decommissioned and demolished. The heavenly tollgate remains standing, of this the clown is certain, and having avoided it once, he will now find his way permanently barred. He looks up and down the High Road; an almost endless strip of Arabic greengrocers and hardware stores, beauty clinics and charity shops. Just a couple of streets back from the main drag, houses fetch millions and those who live here have Hampstead and Marylebone, Brent Cross and Westfield as their playground. Those with cars drive away from the dreck, those who don't take cabs, while the detritus washes up on the polluted shores of the A5. Rain on this road. The clown hoiks up a gobbet that tastes of chalk and bile. Rain on the hypocrites and whores. Rain on the promise breakers. Rain on the cheats and the card sharps, the gossips and those who bear false witness. Rain on the usurers, the tamperers of scales and the exploiters of the weak. Rain on the violators of good, on the selfish, the greedy and the cruel. Rain on the pederasts and philolasts, on the vampires who suck and suck, long after the carcass is dry. To the rock with them. He has a whistle. Let the melody bewitch them. Compel their feet and draw them on. Over the hill and past the fields. Across the brook and through the trees to a gaping hole in the cliff that sucks them in like a riptide and slams on their godforsaken tails. He spits at passing refuse truck. A stain on this beautiful land. A stain that can never be cleaned. The clown crosses the High Road, ankle deep in the filth of his own sin, and all the rains of the earth cannot wash him clean.

Hunting did not last. Once the clearances began and the land gave way to pasture in the reign of the third Henry, there was little need of a bow. The hunter had learned to snare using horsehair traps, mainly rabbits and hares, cooking what he needed on a fire lit by striking the back of his knife with a rock on some wood shavings which he kept in a dry pouch. The rest he could easily sell. On this day, he had a couple of hares and was tying them to a pole to take with him to the Cock where they would be strung up in a back room and bought by any who knew what to ask for. Preoccupied, he did not see the reeve and two constables approaching on horseback, and had no time to untie or hide his haul. These were the king's woods they told him, demanding to know where he had obtained the animals. Lying served no purpose, and while Rollo barked and whined, the hunter was led with a rope around his waist towards the lane that cut through the woods to Willesden. No sooner had they turned off the main track where today a bookmaker takes money from grey, hollow-faced men than he vanished from the end of the rope. Not comprehending, the men returned to find their quarry striding purposefully towards Hendon, hound at his heel. Apprehending him again, they ordered the poacher to walk in front of the horses so that they might keep an eye on him. Again they turned into the lane but had not gone twenty paces before the man vanished like an apparition. After several oaths and imprecations to the Virgin, the men concluded that it must be witchcraft, that the man before them was demon-possessed, a necromancer who must be burned. Resolving that Newgate Gaol was the best place to hold the prisoner before his inevitable death on a bonfire, the lawmen caught up with the hunter once again. This time, they slung him across a horse and tied him to the saddle, making any escape impossible. But no sooner had they turned south towards the city than their captive was standing behind them again, untied. They beat him with sticks and cudgels, the dog sinking his jaws in the reeve's leg in a desperate bid to save his master. One of the constables took out his knife and in one swift movement, sliced the beast's throat. Rollo slumped to the ground, a pool of blood darkening the earth around him. Next to his dog, the hunter lay a graceless heap on the dirt. The constables scooped up his broken body and slung him over the horse once again, roping him fast while the reeve attended to the wound on his own leg. One of the men even gripped the hunter's belt with his hand as they began their southward trail. The posse had not gone ten paces when the constable's hand was grasping air and the hunter was behind them, bending over the corpse of his dog. At this, one of the constables sank to his knees in prayer, convinced that the man was an angel and that they would be punished for harrying him. The reeve was less superstitious, but also feared what he had seen; this certainly was no ordinary poacher and though the dog had proven mortal, its owner seemed indestructible. Conferring, he and the other constable decided that if it was impossible to bring the prisoner to trial in the city, justice would have to meet him in the field. The reeve pointed his sword at the hunter's chest and ordered him to his knees. When he failed to obey the constable pushed him down, harshly. A hemp rope was thrown over a branch then looped around the hunter's neck. By now, the other constable was shouting prayers to the saints to save them all; the man was a wight, he would curse them and rob them of their souls. Turning on his heels he saddled his mare and rode away towards Willesden. Together, the reeve and his henchman hauled on the rope, grunting with exertion as the hunter's body lifted until his legs straightened and his toes cleared the ground. He twitched for around a minute until he was fully strangled. Rather than drop him, the men bound the rope around the tree to keep their victim suspended. As they watched his limp body hanging, the reeve uttered a short prayer from the epistle to the Romans:

"I am convinced that neither death, nor life, nor angels, nor rulers, nor things present, nor things to come, nor powers, nor height, nor depth, nor anything else in all creation, will be able to separate us from the love of God in Christ Jesus our Lord."

The two men mounted their horses and trotted away, reassured that whatever tricks the man who they had punished for hunting in King Henry's land had played on them, he was as mortal as the rest of us. Once the plodding of their horses could no longer be heard above the sounds of the birds and the breeze, the hunter's eyes opened. Reaching into his shirt he pulled out a knife, sliced the rope above his neck and collapsed on the ground as if his body had forgotten how to support itself. He soon roused. Hauling himself to his feet, he lifted the deadweight of his dog and moved him away from the road. Hunting had lost its lustre. He might not die but encounters such as this took their toll. The dog had been good and quiet company, and he knew that his confiscated hares would be eaten by the reeve and his constable, that the king would never hear of this trespass. But if he couldn't be a hunter, what could he be? A raven landed near the corpse of his dog and he began walking northwards again before the bird began pecking out the animal's eyes.

Where Kingsgate Place meets the High Road, Bharti Athinareyanan squeezes mangos under the green awning of the Al-Rouche supermarket; just her and the boys now, but no money for food. A violent husband, scared children and a restraining order paid for by her parents in Kolkata. Peace for the time being, but no money. Baldeep controlling the finances just like he controls everything, and now he's refusing to pay her until he can see the sons who are so terrified of him that Pankaj still wets the bed. In a single room in a Neasden share house, Baldeep Athinareyanan forks last night's lamb bhuna from a foil tray, finalising a plan to take the boys back to India. His wife not realising that he keeps the children's passports in the safe at the cab office. Athinareyanan deciding to play nice, to stop asking to see Pankaj and his cry-baby brother, Priya, and when the order expires, he'll fetch them from school, take them somewhere that bitch will never find them, and turn them into men. Bharti Athinareyanan who weighs barely six stone, praying for fortitude, wondering how to feed her children for another day with the few coins left in her purse, and with no idea of the storm that is about to engulf her family.

Three men riding horses along the ancient forest track came upon a miller carrying grain and milk in his oxcart. Dunheld, son of eoldorman Odred and leader of the three ordered the man to stop and tell him his business. The miller was afraid. He knew nothing, he said, the monk Ecceard having rewarded his silence. But the miller had children too, and when Dunheld drew his knife and the blade flashed, his resolve weakened. His sacks contained milled wheat, and with it was a pitcher of goats' milk for the hermit girl who lived in the woods. He had brought them from his mill which was in the direction of Mapesbury.

"The hermit girl who lives in the woods?" Dunheld looking at his companions who grinned back at him. "Tell me more about this angel."

Sensing bad intent, the miller babbled, his sentences a confused fog. He did not know where she was, she moved

180

about. Who knew where she'd be one day to the next? Dunheld dismounting and the man taking a step or two backwards. The ealdorman's son measuring out his words.

"Where will you leave the grain and the milk today?"

Dunheld's companions Uthred and Edgar now also dismounting. All three taller, broader and younger than the miller who struggled to speak. Dunheld grabbed him by the course cloth of his shirt, his mouth inches away from the man's face.

"Lead me to her."

The miller, who also had a wife and aged parents to feed, had no need of heroics. Mumbling a prayer, he walked slowly back along the track, Dunheld and his cousins now back on their horses, following the miller's ox. Their leader stopped and turned to face his companions.

"I think I had best go alone."

Uthred and Edgar fell back, despondent. Pulling a mouse carcass from a leather pouch, Dunheld whistled. A hawk flew down from the high branches and settled on his master's arm, tearing at the mouseflesh.

"There you go my beauty. There you go."

Where Lady Sarah Salusbury walked guests through the leafy parkland of a noble house called the Elms, they built the Gaumont State theatre, a building so tall that only the seventeen storey Kilburn Square tower affords a loftier lookout. In a Kilburn of modest necklines and floral dresses flared at the calf; of bowler hats, black umbrellas and omnibuses, the clown watched the theatre take shape. An homage to the Empire State, hence its name; the exterior clad in cream ceramic tiles, its tower lit with red neon and a giant Wurlitzer organ drawing people in their thousands to this hitherto unloved corner of northwest London. The gypsy, Reinhardt once played here accompanied by

Stephane Grappelli, sweat flying as he worked the guitar, the clown standing in the shadows at the back of the auditorium remembering the elms that once grew here, the elegant park and the forest where he drove pigs through snow to feast on the crab apples buried beneath. In the fifties, Sinatra, Jerry Lee Lewis and Buddy Holly came here, just another hop on a European tour, but all three gunning for it nonetheless, Lewis as raw and ragey is if it properly mattered. Maybe it did. On the street outside, Ronnie Wood bummed a roll up and gave him tickets to the show. The clown had no one to bring, sold his passes to a Sikh and spent the money on a Nigerian courtesan with a fondness for opium and gold. He lost count of the young renegades he watched on the Gaumont stage, thumbing their noses at a world they'd barely seen twenty three years of. But he was forever twenty three; forever angry at how things had turned out. These wild spirits gave it voice and he grieved when the bands stopped coming and the building fell into disrepair. First a bingo hall and now a Pentecostal church. Plenty of spirit still, but nothing that reaches deep into a man's soul like a possessed maven, one foot on the piano, battering the keys and telling the rapt crowd why they were alive, why they fought and what it all meant. That was a time.

Three young men in drainpipe trousers and artfully designed hair walk towards him past the old cinema; one wearing Ray-Bans, another in a leather biker jacket and the third in a long tail coat, their soundcheck at the Good Ship in the bag and now a quick Subway before heading into town to kill time. None of the men local but the Ship one of many venues in northwest London with a stage and a sound desk, pubs whose toilet doors are smothered in stickers, a single drumkit shared between five bands and nowhere to load and unload without getting clamped. The clown watches the men ambling up the High Road in winkle picker boots, adding colour to the street despite the blackness of their clothing. Who cares if they never hit the big time? Compared to most of the walking dead he passes every day, they've already made it.

The Benedictine spent a couple of days on Thorney Island, sharing his own strokes and drinking warm ale in the gloaming, for the days were long and relatively humid. Now, on his journey back north, the air seemed suddenly sweeter despite horse and cattle shitfalls underfoot. He crossed the Knight's Bridge in the early morning and the planks across the Cunebourne an hour or so later. Trees either side of him; no houses, a distant mill and the air still. Smoke from a fire beyond the fields wriggled into a white sky, sparrows sang and a crow cawed. A little ahead of him, a mare stood tethered to a tree, sweat clinging to her flanks, her tail flicking away horseflies. A hawk gripped the saddle and eyed him, suspiciously. The monk looked around. Who could be visiting the recluse? And why? Something felt wrong. Where now buses roar past a kebab shop and a Turkish barber's close to the Overground station, he stepped off the road, concerned. Dry twigs crackled beneath his feet as he pushed through the undergrowth to the clearing by the river. A woman's cry. His pace picking up. A man's tone, the Benedictine running now, an impulse; two figures beneath the trees, one white the other darker, smaller, struggling. Closer now, a man intent, insistent, powerful; grabbing the wrists of the beautiful grace child who lay on the cold earth, robes hitched up to her haunches. A roar as the Benedictine hurled himself at her attacker. The man stunned and unprepared; his tunic half off, no weapon to hand, grabbed and thrown aside like a dog; his assailant kicking him like he would kill him; the brute stumbling away, swearing curses at

183

them both, vowing to return with men, swords and dogs. He wiped blood from his mouth and, looking at the red on his hand, turned back to the road.

The clown finds a gap between a metallic green Range Rover Epoque and a dark grey Citroen Berlingo and crosses back to the east side of the street, to a shop which sells fancy dress, balloons and other party paraphernalia. He peers in at the masks. Barak Obama, Queen Elizabeth and David Cameron. They even have a monk's habit, made from cheap brown polyester in a factory in Guangzhou. A tailor at the abbey would take the twill weave and sew long robes with loose sleeves and a hood, a small unglazed window providing the requisite light for his work. This nylon chasuble with its cincture approximated a Franciscan's robe; St. Francis and Friar Tuck perhaps the only monks most can recall, and he two hundred years older than both. What has he achieved? He's seen men turn coal and iron into steel, use steam to power engines, send ships to the farthest corners of the earth and harness lightning to illuminate cities. He has seen them fling wires across oceans, transmit radio signals, moving images on celluloid and connect computers invisibly through air. Meanwhile, he has walked from Westminster to St. Albans and back over one hundred and fifty thousand times. His job, if you could call it that, had been to pray for the safety of the nation and for the benefactors who sent money to the abbey. Those men and women were long dead and the nation could pray for itself. The cassock in the party store was what they deserved. A fake copy, devoid of any spiritual meaning. A going through the motions. If it wasn't his last day, he might have bought it.

"Are you hurt?" he asked.

Godwyn stepped out of the shelter into which she had recently fled naked and ruined. Now she was clothed again, but her face had lost much of its colour.

"You are an angel," she told him.

"An angel?" He laughed.

She looked at a streak of red on his hand.

"You bleed."

His knuckles had caught the man's teeth and the graze bled.

"Who was he?" the Benedictine asked.

"A demon sent by Satan to test me. Come."

Godwyn led and he followed.

"Here is clean water. Sit."

She gestured to an upturned log near to where some water bubbled up from a pile of stones and he sat, obediently. Picking yarrow leaves from a pouch around her waist, Godwyn took his wounded hand, her cool fingers providing their own balm. He took her other hand.

"You shake."

"My heart beats so quickly."

"You have seen violence."

Silence while she bathed the wound.

"Your hand shakes too," she said.

"I've never struck a man. It is not in Benedict's rule."

She laughed like water, covering her face with both hands.

"I'm sorry."

Her face flushed.

"You have your colour back."

"I wish you would not look." She ripped a strip from the hem of her robe. "Only the world cares how it looks."

As Godwyn bound his hand, he felt time stop. The crow and the sparrows and the stream suspended; the world in stasis, his face so close to hers he could feel her breath. She

185

looked up suddenly, everything happening as if ordained, as if no decision were made nor needed making; lips touching, eyes closing, the wattle door of her cell shutting behind them. They fell on a bed of straw covered with furs, the warmth of her beneath him, his teeth knocking against hers as they kissed, laughing, filling his lungs with her scent. The act itself messy, uncoordinated and short lived, he holding her in his arms, nuzzling her ear with his nose, whispering to her, his hands running over the newness, drinking her.

In a flat above the party shop, Denzil Urquhart attempts to tie a tie for the first time, an hour before his grandfather is laid to rest at Kensal Green. Grandpa Lenny who brought transports from America to Britain after the war and wound up driving trains for British Rail. There had always been Africans in London; moors who arrived on trade ships and remained in the city, some wandering north up Watling Street to see what opportunity lay there. Lenny Urquhart was one of the first Caribbeans he had met, save from a few escaped slaves who had boarded ships filled with molasses and worked their passage to England. Urquhart from a proud Adventist family, believing his new nation would embrace him, grateful to him for his Herculean wartime efforts. All they saw was a black face, a man who, despite his raincoat and trilby hat was unutterably foreign, and they refused him lodgings. At the Anglican church he visited on his arrival, Urquhart was the only black man in a sea of white.

"Lovely to see you," they said, shaking his hand as he as he left. "But don't come back."

Lenny's nephew Robert is doing the talk, thank God. Denzil's not one for words and his sisters don't feel confident either. Edwin's a platform announcer at Piccadilly Circus, so he'll ace it, if a eulogy can be aced. The two ends of the tie hang around Denzil Urquhart's shoulders in the bathroom of his sister Chantell's flat. He looks in the mirror blankly as if someone has asked him to prove Fermat's Last Theorem, or the structure of DNA. He wraps one end around the other and loops it over but the whole thing collapses again.

"There must be tutorials online," Chantell tells him, but it can't be that hard, Denzil Urquhart sensing his own uselessness; can't get a job, can't get laid, squatting at his sister's place at twenty two, feeling every inch the waste of space his Year 10 teacher said he was.

"FUCK!!" Grandpa Lenny would have done this with his eyes closed.

"Come on."

Chantell taking both ends of the tie and trying to make a Windsor knot. She can't and laughs at how something that should be so simple is beyond them, the failure of the sibling who Urquhart has long looked up to making him feel immeasurably better.

"Just wear a black rollneck, Denz. No one will care."

From the eastern side of the street, the clown has a better view of the great nineteen thirties portico of the State. Wedged between the old theatre and what was once a corner tavern is a café where Mañuel dos Santos, short sleeved white shirt and black hair combed and oiled, is the only customer. A small espresso remains untouched in its white cup and saucer in front of him as dos Santos reads the copy of *Folha de S.Paolo* sent to him by his niece, Gabriella. Gaúcho is dead. Dos Santos reading the obituary of Luís Carlos Tóffoli, legendary centre forward for Palmeiras. Gaúcho, the cowboy. Dos Santos remembers the game against Flamengo in November 1988, not that he was there; like millions of his compatriots, he was crammed into a café, glued to a TV. Sao Paolo versus Rio, his own side in the belly of the beast, the gigantic Maracaña stadium. Flamengo still a goal down until a minute into time added on, Bebeto in the number nine shirt clipping a flailing Zetti who had rushed off his line to intercept; the keeper writhing in agony as players huddled around and team physios made their way onto the field with a stretcher. Gaúcho taking Zetti's shirt with seconds remaining, all his team needing to do was cling on, and victory would be theirs. Seconds later, a corner to Flamengo, a desperate diving header from Bebeto that ricocheted across the goal line, bouncing into the back of the net, the final whistle blowing almost immediately, and now Gaúcho the centre forward in the firing line of five penalties from some of the finest strikers in South America. Adair placing the ball on the spot, the big defender shooting low and left but Gaúcho somehow getting a hand to it and turning it past the post. Euphoria in the café. Zanata from Palmeiras shooting low and right, goalkeeper Zé Carlos at full stretch, unable to stop Palmeiras going one up. The café erupting once more. Bebeto, the striker who took Zetti out of the game and brought his team level in its dying seconds shooting top right as Gaúcho dived left; Bebeto for a moment the hero of Rio, the stadium deafening in support for the home team. Amauri for Palmeiras who later shone at Juventus shooting top left, the ball simply too fast for Zé Carlos who threw himself in its way fractions of a second too late. Leonardo shooting top right, Gaúcho's outstretched and gloveless hand almost in reach, the second for Flamengo. Midfielder Fabio Bandeira skying the ball over Zé Carlos' crossbar and now Renato, wrongfooting Gaúcho and driving the ball down the centre, Flamengo inching in front, 3:2. Zé Carlos, crouching on his goal line, arms outstretched, white gloves like wingtips, the plume of hair, a raptor ready to spring on the ball released from the boot of Ederval Luiz Lourenço da Conceição, the green-shirted giant known to the faithful as Tato. The ball shot high and left while the keeper stayed low, Tato levelling the scores. Zico for Flamengo slotting the ball so fast and low and left that Gaúcho had no chance, then Gaúcho himself, back in attack, cannoning the ball into the net like Adair, Zé Carlos guessing the trajectory but arriving too late intervene. 4:4. Zinho stepping up for Flamengo, just twenty-one years old and driving the ball to the left where Gaúcho leapt, parrying it away, the thump of his bare palms on the synthetic leather audible across the stadium, the gasp of disappointment from fifty thousand Cariocas in the stands. Gaúcho clapping his team mates, urging them on as midfielder Heraldo shot hard and fast to the bottom left, Zé Carlos' gamble to go right failing, the victory finally theirs. The inestimable joy as the Bar da Praça exploded, men hugging and kissing strangers, the endless Antarticas that followed, the parties that continued all the next day and a hangover that lasted into the weekend. And Gaúcho now dead, his emaciated body saturated with Dipheriline and Heparin, the cells that encrusted his prostate overwhelming his blood and his bones. Mañuel dos Santos takes a sip of coffee and stares at the picture of the smiling, dark haired man in the black and red shirt from three decades earlier. Gaúcho the incredible, hero of Maracaña, sobriquet after sobriquet, idol of the rubio y negro, the lone highlight in this, Palmeiras "lost decade". Tóffoli may have pulled on other team shirts in his career but for dos Santos, he was always Palmeiras. Fifty two. The old man shakes his head and reaches in his pocket for some rolling tobacco. This needs a cigarette.

The monk had been watching Godwyn as she slept. Her eyes opened, acclimatising. She looked at him for a few moments and her lids closed again as she buried her head into his chest and he kissed her forehead gently. When she next woke, she sat up and stretched.

"I was not your first."

His eyes searching hers.

"We should eat, Benedictine."

"Who are you?"

"I am one who was lost, yet was found. Whose life was no better than death and who, by the grace of God, was given life."

"I thought I had ruined you."

"Perhaps. Or perhaps you have saved me."

"There is food in my sack," he whispered.

She reached inside the leather bag and pulled out a small parchment scroll.

"A letter!"

He reached out to take it from her.

"Just dull script. A sample from Westminster to take to the brothers at Wæclingacaester."

Godwyn unfolding it, he kissing her shoulder, her arm, any skin that came near his mouth.

"Stop, Benedictine." Then reading aloud:

"*Unum vero hoc non lateat vos, carissimi, quia unus dies apud Dominum sicut mille anni, et mille anni sicut dies unus.*" She turned to him. "And if this day could last a thousand years, would you keep it?"

"A thousand thousand."

He ran a finger over the arc of her shoulder to where a red scar streaked across her ribs, watching her eyelids closing, safe but lost, ending and beginning, rescued and ruined. Their vows now broken, a coal fallen from the fire, an egg that had dropped from the nest. He slept, a falling leaf never wanting to land. A man's face, a dagger raised and driven home. Waking with a start, he saw Godwyn leaning over him, naked, her hand on his chest, her face a perfect mirror of the love he felt. She kissed him and he slept again.

The clown passes a shoe shop and the heart clinic with its incongruous corrugated blue cladding. He stops outside a laptop repair centre where a Pakistani man scrolls through his phone behind the counter. When the clown he first trod these roads, there was no Pakistan, or none that any in England had heard of. Boats crossed the channel, or the North Sea, or traversed the open water to Ireland. They knew of France and Spain, of Rome, Greece, Egypt and the Levant. The Danes to the north were a permanent menace while the Celts kept to themselves on the western fringes. But the Asiatic hordes; the Ashanti, Yoruba, Igbo and Mandé who later toiled in New World plantations; the Aztecs, Incas and Mayans who built cities and sacrificed children to the sun were all unknown, yet their offspring tread these roads. This man, hunched over a glass counter filled with reconditioned iPhones, Samsung Galaxys and Xperia Neos, who knows what relation he is to the Umayyid Caliphs? The Shah Miris? The Delhi Sultanate and the Hindu Shahis? Were his forebears the Mughals who built Lahore, the Āryāvartan scribes who wrote the first Vedas? Were they bean counters for the East India Company, valiant foot soldiers for King George V in his war against Japan? The man in the shop stretches and yawns and reaches beneath the counter for a packet of custard creams.

Godwyn was dressed again and had been busy while he slept.
"There was a hare in the trap, we shall have breakfast."
"What hour is it?"
"A night and almost half a day since we lay down."

191

A bubbling stew with goatsbeard root and nettle leaves poured into a wooden bowl with rough grey bread. She spooned the broth into his mouth, spilling it. He laughed.

"Have I fed you well Benedictine?"

He wiped his mouth.

"I am Wulfstan."

She lifted the spoon to his mouth again.

"They call me Godwyn."

"And what is this place?" he asked.

She looked around at the trees and the stream.

This is the Cunebourne stream but as far as a name, it has none."

Taking some hare's meat from a flat stone that served as plate, he fed her.

"Men will come. Your attacker will return and I do not rate my chances against a posse bearing swords. They will see it as unfinished business. We must leave."

By the time of the Protector, Kilburn such as it was consisted of farmland; lonely fields bordering the High Road and stretching as far as West End Lane. The landlord of the Cock lived in a house with five hearths while others grazed horses or grubbed turnips from the muddy earth. Beneath the clay lie bridle bits, clout nails and coins bearing the heads of Charles II, William and Mary, and Anne. Perhaps a glass bottle dropped by a ploughman, a knife rusted beyond recognition, the broken blade of a scythe. By the time of the fourth George, the estate and its scattering of cottages was sold to a surveyor named Ware who parcelled it up, selling it to developers whose streets still scar the greensward. An ancient yew which had stood since the clown first walked these roads found itself among the earliest trees felled to make way for a village now consumed by a city that must continuously eat itself just to keep growing.

Before bombs fell and drove him from the city, the painter, Houthuesen would sit somewhere near here with his easel. One day, he asked the clown to stop for a few moments so he could sketch him. Seeing the face paint and emerald hair, the Dutchman wondered if he was on his way to a party.

"No," said the clown. "Are you?"

The Dutchman laughed.

"I am not dressed to entertain, but you on the other hand…"

His hand drawing bold strokes as he bit his upper lip.

"Yes, yes, so no party? You are part of a circus?"

The clown gazed at the painter. He had never seen an image of himself on paper, canvas nor even a photograph, only reflections. No, he was not part of a circus.

"I have never painted a clown. You are my first."

Houthuesen, whose studio was a few paces from the spot where the Benedictine had first met Godwyn became a prodigious painter of clowns, most of them abstract marionettes in yellow and red, but one of them a green-haired whiteface, the canvas kept in a basement on Greville Road throughout the war years where it was eaten by damp and mould and later burned by the artist.

A copse on the other side of the track. Breathless, they sank to the ground beneath an ancient beech, laughing, the danger thrilling them, kissing again, lying on dry leaf litter, the Benedictine rolling on top of Godwyn, their movements frantic, he kissing her, lying next to her, ruined forever, but elated. Later, they found shelter in a stone bothy, a place for keeping pigs where they lay on dry straw, her head nestled under his chin as mice rustled in the dark; two prodigals on the run from a father who would never take them back. Her smell so sweet that it was the only air he wanted to breathe, her voice the only plainsong his ear desired to hear.

Long before they built the late Victorian terrace whose ground floor is now despoiled with low rent shops and cafés, there was a hunting box here; a high-roofed wooden kennel where Charles II kept his dogs. Not that the king ever hunted in these woods, preferring instead to ride through the great park that had been laid out around his newly restored palace at Windsor. Nor were the dogs spaniels, which were only good for hunting birds. Here, the king kept the deerhounds used by his favourites, most notably the rake, Buckingham, a man whose mortal sins outnumbered the venial; an atheist and blasphemer who drank, gambled and screwed his way through the six decades of his adult life with an absence of any style, grace or humanity that would make such transgressions forgivable, or at the very least admirable. A boor who thought nothing of drinking a companion unconscious while a friend broke into the man's house, raped his wife then dragged the woman to the inn so that Buckingham could ruin her too. The clown passed the duke a number of times on the road, and noted that he always talked as other men listened.

"Entertain us jester!" he cried once as they passed on Shoot up Hill, followed by a sotto voce "This'll be sport" to his companions. At this, the clown lowered his breeches in full sight of the men, grabbed himself and took aim at the Duke, a jet of urine landing on his face and clothing with a satisfying patter. Disgusted, the blueblood reached for a silk handkerchief to wipe urine from his lips as the clown bared his teeth and the men on horseback heard a low aspirated exhale, a bitter, wretched sound like gas escaping from a corpse.

"Whip him!" cried Buckingham.

No sooner had the command been given than the crack of cord echoed off the nearby trees. The pain was energising; punishment for his true crime earned by pissing on a rapist, the cords wrapping around his body and legs, a great red welt rising beneath the white paint on his face, wounds which would heal but would never absolve the one guiltier than all who persecuted him, deserving of their condemnation, willing it. And if he could take a cunt like Buckingham down with him, all the better.

As the clown passes a hair salon next door to the laptop repair shop, he hears a shriek; another lost spirit haunting the lanes of Kilburn and Cricklewood. A face painted red and spitting, a witch; a black woman spooking children with her hoodoo, her clothing red too, a wide-eyed fury, as if Hell just spat her out to terrify a town. He can't remember when she arrived, or where from; she blew in one day and stayed, spewing her gospel of rage. The woman stops outside the salon window, her headdress adorned with red flowers and feathers dyed red, stepping towards a passing mother and child, hissing at the infant. The mother shouting back and the woman unleashing a tirade of Yoruba and Creole, a cocktail of curses as the girl in the salon walks over to the window for a better view. The clown has no idea what the woman is saying, who damned her, or for how long. An obayifo, living out her days on the same shit filled road he's walked since it was a track across a river passing through the forest. Maybe she's eternal. God help her. When they opened the synagogue on Harrow Road at the close of the previous century, he saw a man he recognised. Not his face nor his walk, but like the woman who rages at the passing

195

hordes on this sacred weekend, a lost wayfarer, a shadow, a husk where once a soul had resided. A body going through the motions, alive but unliving, a shape, a geist, a Jew whose eyes looked through him, his coat torn and his hat dishevelled, uttering something which, had he been closer or listened more carefully, he would have heard was cracked and whispered Aramaic. A shoemaker who had been among the crowd in the City of God, jeering at the stricken Christ as he stumbled with his crossbeam along the way of tears that led to Calvary. A zealot who, when the doomed prisoner sank to his knees and Roman guards thrust Simon forward to carry his load, struck him hard in the face.

"Go on quicker Jesus!" he scolded. "Why do you loiter?"

And Christ with blood and dust caked to the sweat on his bruised brow looking him in the eye with weary dispassion,

"I shall rest awhile, but you Cartaphilus, you shall go on until the last day."

Just another Jew among the Sephards and Ashkenazis celebrating the grand opening of the new temple, stepping away from the crowds and climbing into a hackney carriage driven by a bone thin cabman who whipped his black horse and drove it through the crowds with a "Har! Har!" The wheels sparking off the cobbles, a ringleted ancient criss-crossing the goy globe, forever forsaken, never resting, never dying, the horror, the horror.

An hour before sundown, horses. Three men stumbling through trees with axes and staves, calling for the holy recluse but she had gone. All that was left was some charred wood, a hare's bones and a small lean-to beneath a wide oak. Hammer blows on the hut smashing wattle, feet kicking over the rude stone altar and simple vases of sweet violet, butterbur and star of Bethlehem. A man hitching up his tunic and defecating at the mouth of the dwelling, wiping himself clean with a fistful of dock. Their work done, the men left the glade as the Benedictine and his hermit bride ran through trees, her hand in his, following where he led, gone. As the red witch's voice is consumed by Police sirens and motorbike exhaust, the clown looks over at the junction of Willesden Lane. A fork in the track through the forest where a thousand years ago today, the blade of Athelstan Dunheld gored him and left him to bleed out on the path. It's the last time he will see it. He breathes in and looks up at the blank sky. Nothing, just a vague elation that it will end. A thousand years is but a day, his wonderings simply the appetiser to an all-you-can-eat buffet of eternity.

In the rush to fill Kilburn's green with terraces in the time of Victoria, Lady Salusbury's elegant lodge was sold and demolished. Speed and poor quality materials condemned the terrace that replaced it before it was twenty years old when a new, sturdier row was built. The Victoria Hotel held the corner for a century, even after the rest of the block was razed to build the Gaumont State. The clown knew the old prize fighter who ran the pub; a wiry Kerryman called Keene who battered Sambo Sutton, then made his money promoting bouts, some of them at the Victoria. He continued drinking here when labourers building the M1 needed a home from home and the pub changed its name to Biddy Mulligan's. Biddy Mulligan, pride of the Coombe, a fictitious Dublin street hawker whose quick wit lit up the music halls and variety theatres of the nineteen thirties. A wild place; an embassy for the dispossessed and a collecting point for the Cause. Raffles every night, a jar rattling at each table, "for the children". The clown wasn't there when a loyalist bomb ripped a hole in the building on a December Saturday in 1975. Alexander

Brown and his accomplices, furious that Michael Gaughan's body had been serenaded by a piper to the Sacred Heart church in June of the previous year; angry that the Irish wanted control over the province; raging at the tens of thousands of pounds pouring into the IRA kitty from collecting tins in Kilburn pubs decided to take action. The clown had no loyalty to Ireland; he simply enjoyed a drink, and had Brown blown him up, he'd have returned the next day with no hard feelings. After all, it wouldn't have been the first time he'd died on this corner. Once the Irish had either returned home, died of cirrhosis or otherwise ceased to be of profit to the landlords, the old Victoria tavern became a bar for drunk hoodlums from the Antipodes. Now it's a bookies, another scab on this pock ridden quarter that festers in the ancient forest like an infected sore.

They ran. Darting through trees, the sound of the stream fading behind them. In the glade where Godwyn had lived and prayed and where sparrows still nested, bluebottles began feeding on human ordure. And when the miller came to leave the sack of grain at the secret place, he saw last week's still there and feared what might have befallen the nun by the river.

As she waits at the lights to cross the lane where herdsmen once drove cattle to Willesden, Yamilé Haroun in black abaya and grey khimar talks into her mobile phone to her sister Amina in Hamburg. Two women from the city of Kassala on the banks of the Merab river, dry for most of the year until rain falls in July and August, mud brown water surging under the low bridge as long horned cattle gather at its banks to drink. Kassala where mules draw flat-topped carts laden with bananas and white robed men sell dates, baobab fruit, and peanuts from brown sacks in the market.

Kassala, legendary land of Punt where Solomon had his mines and Prester Johannes, mystic patriarch and bloodline of magi entertained Umiyyad sultans, reclining on a bed of leopard fur in a cave filled with gold, myrrh and ivory, attended to by Nubian whores. Haroun's husband Abdalla who she met at the university now cleans schools in Hounslow for eight pounds an hour while he qualifies as a civil engineer, while Amina's son Ismail just completed his Abitur and landed an apprenticeship at a fleet management company, Allah be praised. Yamilé Haroun missing the colour, the call to prayer and the smell of sandalwood, khumra and bakhoor. The green man ushers her across the wide junction of Willesden Lane, air dense with diesel fumes, the roar of buses and Amina's unspoken pity.

The clown has no idea of his age, nor any memory of his childhood. He was brought as a child to the monastery where saints days, not birthdays were celebrated. By his own reckoning, he was around twenty three when he stepped off the road and began the course that would determine his next millennium. His deathday his child's birthday, a way of marking off the years, decades and centuries; anniversaries met with gloom rather than rejoicing as he pondered what he had lost. Voices punished him daily and on this day, they yammered more than the rest. He feels for the matches in his pocket, reassured by the certainty that it will all soon end.

Here, where the demon cursed him, pilgrims once turned on their journey to the shrine at Willesden, a solemn trickle of penitents that filled the centuries until footsoldiers of the vandal Cromwell ransacked the sacred church of St. Mary. Men tearing the black Madonna from her alcove and burning it with other sacred statuary before a baying crowd of Protestants who had gathered near Cromwell's palace; the sweating, ulcerous and urine reeking mob inhaling

199

sweet, woody notes of *Diospyros ebenum* from the blazing virgin into its lungs, smoke rising as Cromwell on his hustings raged in righteous fury, hurling words at a Heaven that had long ago abandoned him.

Hair scaped back into a high ponytail, Dawn McReady, three years clean pushes a buggy round the fashion store on the corner where Willesden Lane joins the High Road. Nothing lasts for long; people a blur and shops gone in an eyeblink. Buildings linger but it's hard to remember what came before when they change hands ten times in a century, sometimes in a decade. All that has endured as long as him is the road, the kink where it crosses the Cunebourne and the names of the places it passes through. The pubs offer a measure of continuity; the Cock, the Red Lion, the Old Bell, the Black Lion. Some of which have been serving ale and sweeping up drunks at the end of the night for over half a millennium, though the original buildings have long since been replaced. This shop on the corner? Who knows how long it will endure. A blip, gone, the sign changed, forgotten, demolished, built over and reborn for a new generation of passers-by who will never know its past life. The ten or so years it sold bridesmaids dresses; the French clothing store that came before it, the shop after shop after shop that preceded these, stretching back to the reign of Victoria when a three storey terrace of ten homes was erected using pale yellow brick and featuring gothic arched windows with wrought iron balustrades along their roof terraces. Detached homes with well-kept front lawns set back from the road that were demolished to build the terrace, a stone at the junction of Willesden Lane marking eleven and a half miles to Watford and two and a half to London. In the time of William IV, a corner of a field that had only just begun to relinquish its pastures to the builders. A lone cottage at the century's turn; before that, hay fields, then nothing save the endless wood. The years moving so fast now that the street changes its appearance like a magic lantern. McReady pushes her son, Alfie towards the Tricycle Theatre for his Mini Maestros session, ready to face off the mums who will look at her tattoos, hear her accent and judge her. Nothing those pampered bitches can say or do will change how she feels. She pays her one hundred and twenty pounds for the term, and Alfie gets to bang a drum, rattle castanets and sing while she cradles a black americano in the theatre café, watching the gaggle of mothers through a barricade of pushchairs which she will never be able to penetrate. The clown wishes there were more like her, that some of them would stick around longer, that the world would stop fucking strobing for just a moment.

"Wait here," he said and Godwyn drifted back to sleep, cells in her belly beginning to knit. At the manor house at Willesden, a steward had neither room nor alms for a cleric. The Benedictine assured him that he was his humble servant, that he could turn his hand to any number of tasks, however menial, kneeling before him and asking him to make him his bondsman, and his wife his bondswoman.

"The monk has a wife?"

A brief wait as the man conferred with his lord; pigs that needed feeding, goats and sheep to milk and no questions asked that did not need asking. He handed the Benedictine a goad and pointed to a parcel of land at the forest's edge beyond the wooden palings of the village. Taking his head in his hands, the steward commanded him, "Build your home."

It does no good, and no resolution ever comes from it, but each time he passes this junction the clown stops at the same thought. What if the child had lived? He's asked himself the question a hundred thousand times but it comforts him, the knowledge that a small part of him might have endured. Was mortal. He cannot help the indulgence, brooding as he has done every day since Dunheld took his life and the demon handed it back to him. He knew it would have been a son; the size of the bump and the way a stone moved in small circles when they suspended it on a string above Godwyn's belly. Her skin was dry, she craved cheese and there was no sickness. But what became of the child? How did he grow? Did he know that he was loved, if only from afar by his father? Could he throw a ball? Fire an arrow? Skin a deer? How did his mother cope as he grew into a man, or did she remarry? Did he become a soldier, make his way to Lundenwic, or beyond, to France? Did he make a fortune in trade and become a great man at court? Or did he wonder the streets, desperate and poor and riddled with sores for the few pitiful years God gave him? Did he ever wonder who his father was? What did his mother tell him? This he knew. How the boy must have hated him. For decades, he watched out for him, looking for Godwyn in the face of men he met who would have been twenty, thirty, forty. At eighty he gave up, for few lived to such great age. All he had then was an ache, a son who might have been, who might have planted his seed in others who today walk these very roads. He hoped his child had found peace, someone to love, a sense of belonging and purpose; this man he never knew, would never know, could only guess at, whose heart he had no doubt broken and who had broken his own. Other days, he wondered if he had a daughter who might have become a queen, a duchess, a wife, a harlot, or any gradation in between. On darker days, he imagined an infant wrapped in blood and rags and thrown into a pit where dank earth was piled over it. His child. His flesh and blood. Him.

A crossroads. A fitting place for a man to do business with the Devil. Opposite Willesden Lane, tree lined Gascony Avenue heads east towards West Hampstead. The clown leaves the scene of his cursing and passes the empty unit on the corner where a failed discount store has cleared out its wares ready for the next opportunist to squat within its walls. He crosses the junction and continues past the dry cleaners to a Nigerian restaurant above which, in a dingy third floor bedsit lit by a bare bulb, Mariana Ruiz prays for the first time. She's recited many prayers; as a child you couldn't get through the school day without multiple incantations to God, Jesus and Mary, but all of them just words, the things that needed to be said before a lesson began, or you could eat. Ruiz is not even sure who she should pray to; all she has is faint hope and a belief that she's run out of options. Desperate times demand desperate measures, she tells herself as she settles at a table with a mug of instant coffee. It doesn't feel right at the table; too cosy, so she moves over to the unmade bed and sits on it. The mess seems disrespectful. She neatens the duvet, placing the stuffed rabbit on the pillow. There. Maybe she should kneel? Maria Ruiz gets onto her knees by her bed, clasps her hands together and closes her eyes. She still has no idea if this is right or why she is even going through with it. She thinks of her mother in the public hospital in Braga and her fingers clench tighter together.

"Dear God. Tell me what to do. Tell me what to do. Tell me what to do."

Abbot Leofstan walked through the gates of the abbey at Wæclingacaester. Chickens strutted in the road which remained empty east and west. Wulfstan should have returned two days earlier, but none had seen him. Within the abbey compound, a posse of monks readied themselves to head south to see if they could find their brother or learn his whereabouts. Perhaps he had been detained at Westminster, or met with wolves or bandits in the forest. What had become of the Bible? The abbot admonished himself for placing an object above the life of a man. Had Augustine's book become an idol? No, it was God's word they were protecting. Whatever the good deeds of Christ's followers, whatever the miracles, without the texts that spoke of those wonders, how would the faith survive? A bee buzzed around his lips, tasting the sweet trace of a cup of mead. He batted it away. Where was he? They had lost another of their number years before, Eofred, but the man had been spotted alive and well in Lundenwic where by all accounts he had made his fortune. Clasping his hands, Leofstan prayed a short, fretful prayer before returning inside to oversee the departure of the search party.

The clown looks across to the west side of the street to a small tree that stands outside the fashion store and the butcher's next to it. Bedecked with flowers and handwritten tributes; a shrine to a young woman gunned down a millennium after he too was left for dead. Hoodlums whose need for revenge outmatched their aim; the bullets of their Mach 10s meant for the South Kilburn Mandem who loitered on the corner, but flying wide of the mark and taking an innocent to her tomb. Partly obscured by the grief tree, seventy-eight-year-old Dennis Prosser walks out of the butcher's with a slight limp carrying two chops in a blue and white striped plastic bag, one for him and the other for Imani, the wife for whom he provides but with whom he doesn't live. Imani yet to tell her family that she has married a British man. A Christian. Prosser's wife sending his money to her sister in Jordan every month, "for medicine." Prosser toiling at the Tesco Metro near the Old Bell and yet to tell his wife that he's had to take out a loan to cover the payments. Still, they'll have Easter Day together which is something; Prosser who might have retired ten years ago had he not sat next to Imani at a residents' association meeting, who still works because he has to, because his wife's sister is sick.

The Jew, Heilemann set up his stall in Chelsea in 1845, before changing his name to Hillman to fare better with the pig-loving British; moving his cleavers, hooks and blocks to the High Road almost a century ago. There had been a butcher here before him, two in fact, and before these a photographic studio presided over by the son of John Jabez Edwin Mayall, the man who sat the grimacing racist, Marx on a wooden armchair in his studio, the revolutionary's hand inside his jacket as if reaching for his manifesto, though more likely his cigars, capturing him for eternity. Gold art deco lettering on polished blue bears the name of Hillman's store, a throwback to when the shop next door was a wine merchant, an agency upstairs provided domestic servants to Kilburn's mansion dwellers, and gas lamps stood on an island in the middle of the wide, unpaved road. Only the undertaker, Crook and the four taverns have been here this long. Ale, meat and death the only survivors in a city that eats its own children.

The men filed out of the abbey gate and headed south towards the forest. Three monks, not expecting to meet many on the road, but stopping each one they passed. In Hendon, they spent the night in one of the manor barns. The straw was soft, and a serving girl with a lazy eye brought a large board with bread and sheep's cheese. None on the road had seen their lost brother, though they remembered him at Stanmore. Now and again, the men called his name but the only replies from the forest either side of them were the occasional croaks of crows.

"What are we to suppose has become of him?" asked Osfrith. None wanted to say the worst.

"I say he's been delayed at Westminster. There will be much to see," suggested Caelstan. "And much that might forestall his return. Cnut's navy may have reached the Thames."

Silence as the monks considered what this could mean, and the terror of what they might be walking into. Their meal finished, they prayed, each finding bedspace in the hay stalls.

In the Blitz, a new playground opened up every time a bomb fell; craters to climb into, beams and girders to swing from. In July 1944, Kilburn's last convent, the hospital known as St. Peter's was struck. The same St. Peter whose house at Westminster permitted the nun, Godwyn to live in seclusion by the Cunebourne, and whose priory was built on land where she had once prayed. A last thread connecting him to the time before had been severed. Four V1 flying bombs in a little over a week, the fourth coming in from the east, making a left turn over Kilburn, appearing to circle overhead then exploding in the garden behind the convent on Mortimer Crescent. An earlier raid had already condemned the building, the intact rooms above ground now storing furniture from bombed out homes. The nuns had been at mass in a basement linen room when the bomb fell; the sisters screaming in panic as a candlestick flying through their makeshift wartime chapel cracked into the celebrant's nose, breaking it. Though many homes nearby were destroyed, the nuns escaped harm, emerging from the dust in time to see Orwell staggering from his house with a wheelbarrow, the writer searching desperately through rubble for his only manuscript of *Animal Farm*. The bomb craters proved too compelling a playground for ten-year-old Dennis Prosser who obeyed a dare, falling through rotten floor boards into the cellar of a home whose ruined, wallpapered walls saw sunlight for the first time. Prosser landing on a shattered spline of timber, skewering his leg and crying out. The clown heard him but was unable to leave his path, unable to fetch help, return with hope or make it better. At least if the boy was crying, he was alive. Across the road, Prosser limps past the decorated tree and waits for the lights to turn red, a Waitrose lorry obscuring him from view.

The three monks walked on towards Westminster, passing uneventfully the place where their brother stepped off the road, into the arms of a woman and away from the rule of Benedict. No trace remained of his having been here nor was there anything to alert them to any misrule, the skirmish having taken place away from the road. It was the season for pollen and Osfrith sneezed, his eyes streaming and his allergy to birch making the journey tougher than expected. They could hear the stream to their left, passing parallel to the road a short way off into the trees. Ahead of them, horses. Athelstan Dunheld with the brothers, Uthred and Edgar. The men wheeled their horses to a stop and looked the brethren up and down, Dunheld circling them on his tawny mare.

"Where to brothers?"

Caelstan began, hesitatingly.

"We…" Osfrith's hand on his chest stopping him.

"To Westminster," the older monk said. "It is our custom to dwell a few weeks each year in our sister house. You may have seen our brother? He journeyed this way three days ago." Seeing how Dunheld's face was bruised, he added "You've seen battle, sir."

Dunheld reached down and grabbed Osfrith by the throat, a move so swift and shocking on a holy man that the other monks shrank back a few paces.

"Tell your brother that if I see him again, I will put out his eyes, tear his limbs from his body and flay him. I will be wolf to his lamb, lion to his fawn, and I will avenge."

At this point, Osfrith let out a sneeze and, unable or unwilling to cup his hands to his face, mucus splashed on Dunheld's hand. He let go of Osfrith's cassock, stared at the glistening secretion and wiped it on his tunic in disgust.

"Bless you," whispered Caelstan, and genuflected.

Dunheld spat on the ground.

"Godspeed your journey, brothers," he said. A hawk flew from the forest and hovered above him and his two companions as they trotted slowly away.

Caelstan and Ealdred placed their hands on Osfrith. The monk had never been manhandled in this way and shook. Ealdred sang comforting words from Psalm 35, David begging God to brandish spear and javelin against those who pursued him. Their brother Wulfstan had passed this way and somehow, he had bested the noble rider. What in God's name had brought this about? Wulfstan was a man of peace and prayer, armed only with a paring knife and a priceless Bible. There had to be a virtue behind his actions, even if it were a misplaced one. Where was he now? And had the great treasure of Augustine survived the altercation? The men walked on with more questions than answers, south towards Westminster.

Next to the restaurant outside which the clown stands watching Dennis Prosser, a jewellers' still bears signage from another century. GW & AE Thomson, the lettering attached to an iron trellis above a first floor window. Below this are the golden balls of the pawnbroker and two capitalised words, CASH LENT. A clock bearing the jeweller's name juts out above the street, locked at a quarter to four; its machinery long since seizing, time for some never moving on. A faded sign which claims that diamonds are forever now bears only the ghost of a ring, white space where the jewel once belonged. Inside is a mess of trinkets; a glass case filled with watches on the countertop resembling more a lost and found box than a retail display. Lillian King, ninety five, has travelled here by bus from Colindale, her frame tiny but her diction clear so that the Asian man behind the counter can hear her. King needing to know how to wind up her twenty-five-year-old Timex, because it has stopped. The bearded man behind the counter looks at the watch while his colleague rocks on a chair beside him, grinning. The man must be a simpleton, King thinks, and admires the bearded man for giving him work. Perhaps he is family. He seems happy in this Aladdin's cave; alarm clocks and tired, unfashionable baubles arranged haphazardly around them.

"It won't wind," King says, as if speaking to a child. The man opens the casing with the tip of a penknife and removes a small, flat metal disk. He looks up at Lillian King.

"The battery is dead."

Then, reaching into a drawer for a new one, he inserts it, clipping the cap back on. Checking his own watch, he resets the time. The idiot lets out a shrill laugh and Lillian King looks at him indignantly. Rudeness is still rudeness. She thanks the man who mended her watch politely, takes out her purse and asks him how much she owes. The shopkeeper waves away her question like someone from the old world; his dilapidated emporium and its ancient customer a haven from the rush and roar on the street outside.

As the boy rowed the travellers from St. Albans across the river to the abbey, he told them what he could about the brother from Wæclingacaester who had passed this way a week earlier carrying a great treasure. Osfrith's heart jolted. At least the book was safe and, like Leofstan, he scolded himself for placing Augustine's Bible ahead of the life of a monk. Was Wulfstan in good health, he asked. If Athelstan Dunheld sported such wounds, it seemed unlikely that their brother could have come away unscathed.

"He was weary from the road," the boy told him, the water sloshing against the side of the boat as the oars dipped expertly across the surface. "But otherwise, he seemed well. Has something happened to him?"

Unwilling to share their mission, Osfrith pointed out the shape of the abbey buildings, and how similar they were to their own church at Wæclingacaester.

"A veritable home from home," he said, his smile belying the fear he felt in his heart.

Crossing the road is the only east west travel permitted to the clown, and his north south journeys contain many zigzags as he tacks from shore to shore. Crossing over to the west, he peers though the window of Woody's Grill where Frazer Stockman, forty eight, sits phone in hand, studying the profile of a pretty twenty-seven-year-old real estate agent from Hong Kong, a half-eaten lamb shawarma in front of him. Weng Wei at a party, posing in a white one-piece at the pool of the Indigo Hotel, with her girlfriends at a restaurant in the Kwei Chung Plaza. Wei's profile not set to private, which to Stockman means she is game; she wants to be seen and so approaching her is no different to walking up to her at a bar. He messages her, commenting on the hotel. How did she enjoy the Indicolite restaurant? What is the property market like in Kowloon? How's the weather there in March? Stockman's own profile picture ten years old now. Blond and strong-jawed, he no longer works for the MOD but Facebook doesn't need to know that, and though he's greyer now, he's still a catch. Stockman moves from Hong Kong to Thailand. Kalaya Pongprayoon seems nice. Petite, just how he likes them. He has a trip to Asia planned for July, destination thus far unknown, to be dictated by the willingness of any potential playmate to meet him. And though he's had adventures, he rarely gets beyond dinner and drinks and listening to stories. A girl in Ho Chi Minh brought her cat on the date; a physiotherapist in Manila put her leg behind her head in a nightclub, and a beautiful lawyer in Macau reeked of onions. Stockman always picking up the cheque and brushing himself down because one of them, one day will be the one. The waitress at Woody's asks if he has finished his lunch. He has. As she walks away, he watches her; admiring her figure though he's not really into Turkish girls. Even so, he wouldn't say no. Back to his phone; Kalaya Kalaya Kalaya. Bit too skinny. He keeps scrolling.

Osfrith and his party were greeted warmly by Abbot Ælfwig at Westminster. The brothers took their cloaks and fetched again the great Bible from the sacristy. The book was opened at Psalm 61: "I will abide in thy tabernacle forever: I will trust in the covert of thy wings."

"One can only hope," Ælfwig smiled. Afterwards, he sat with his visitors in the cloisters; it was a warm evening and no need to light the brazier. In the bright, clear moonlight, pipistrelles flitted above them. None had seen or heard of Wulfstan since he departed here four days earlier. Perhaps he had travelled on to Lundenwic? Did he have family there? No, he was a foundling, brought up by a weaver and his wife before their own five children needed all their care and money. He arrived on a Tuesday aged somewhere between the age of seven and nine and had been trained in the art of scrivening. The men sipped weak ale and pondered. Osfrith sneezed. It seemed worse at night and by now, the rag he kept hidden in his cloak was sodden. Where was he? They couldn't have missed him on the road. The young men on horseback knew something, but who could force them to tell? At least the beating which Wulfstan gave to the man must have happened on his return journey. But the young monk who had lived at the abbey since childhood was neither prone to violence nor was outbursts of temper. What had driven him to lash out in this way?

Like themselves, the brothers at Westminster rarely ventured beyond their abbey; their calling to remain in seclusion from the world, praying for it ceaselessly. However, they did have a faint lead. Over the evening repast, a name was mentioned. A nun from Barking had been given permission by the abbey to live in a cell not far from the bridge across the Cunebourne, close to where the horsemen had accosted them. It was believed she lived here in perpetual devotion; a spy from St. Peter's coming once a year to check that she still lived. Might the recluse have seen something? With no one else living within a mile of her cell, the woman was perhaps the only one who could help. They agreed to leave at first light and see if a new day threw up any more answers. The nun's name was Godwyn, Ælfwig told them.

Easter the holiest of all days, the day the Christ resurrected, the hope for all the Christian dead who came after him and who hope to rise in the last days. A final escape from the pestilence, poverty and pain that choked, crippled and contained a human life around the first millennium. Thirty years was all a man could expect. If he did not die at birth, disease might take him as a child. If crops failed, few but the wealthiest ate, and medicine had moved on little since the time of the Caesars. Many died by Viking sword, drowned at sea or in rivers, or fell while building houses and churches. Death was everywhere, and everywhere life was spent in preparation for it, the eternity of the ever after vastly outmeasuring the eyeblink of a human life. The years the Benedictine spent at the abbey moved to the rhythm of saints whose days the church venerated, the lives of the virtuous dead a lesson to the errant living. Among the people, most tried to avoid sin; good works were encouraged, attending church a mandatory for all but the most reckless of souls. For this, a man could hope for three score years and ten while expecting to be taken considerably sooner. But not him. Condemned to live over thirty lifetimes, incarcerated in a body that never aged, cursed to remain Corpus intactus the day he saw a riderless horse tethered to a tree and stepped off the path, away from the everlasting light.

The clown takes his gaze from Fraser Stockman and dawdles near the trays of fruit outside the Arabic grocer next door, picking a grape from a plastic punnet. It is sweet to the taste; sweeter than the ones that grew in the monastery garden under the guidance of a monk named Alwin. Alongside yam, mango and dates – imports from the old and new world, the shop sells carrots, garlic and parsnip; cabbage, celery and leeks, all of which grew within the abbey gardens. In summer, pears, plums and peaches appear outside shops like this one, and now and again they might sell parsley, coriander and lettuce. All of these graced the monastery table, and with them radishes and shallots, poppy and marigold, figs, quince and mulberries. Alwin provided the abbey with chestnuts and hazelnuts, walnuts and almonds, and a brother named Sigebert tended bees, though honey was a delicacy to be enjoyed sparingly on account of its scarcity. A motorbike accelerating out of nearby Messina Avenue brings the clown back from the well-ordered beds of the abbey garden. He feels hungry, takes another grape, throws it as high as he can into the air and catches it in his mouth. Renée Guishon watches him as she passes on her way to the butchers and wonders what would make a man practice a thing like that.

"I've had a lot of time on my hands," he says, as Guishon hurries past, anxious that a stranger has talked to her, particularly one with white face paint and green hair.

Fearing the worst, the miller stepped off the road and pushed through the birch saplings. Some had been recently snapped and he proceeded with fretful feet and beating heart. What he saw confirmed his dread; the girl was gone. He did not stay long, a broken shelter and tumbled shrine telling him all he needed to know. That night, he remained kneeling by his bed long after the rest of the house was asleep, praying for his wretched soul and for the safety of the blessed nun who, until he had betrayed her to save his own family, lived in solitude by the river.

Terry Hopkins hovers by the lamp post outside the Arabic grocer's where a clown throws grapes into the air and catches them in his mouth. Hopkins reaching into the hessian satchel around his neck; his felt cap and corduroy jacket giving him the appearance of a college lecturer. In the bag are sheets of stickers which Hopkins is attaching carefully to lamp posts and traffic lights along the High Road. He affixes one on top of a torn away sticker promoting a metal band; a small white square bearing the name of his website, a repository of conspiracies and counter arguments which back up Hopkins' avowed belief that the earth is in fact flat. The clown has no access to the internet nor any wish to be sucked into Hopkins' orbit, but were he to type the link into a browser, he would find no shortage of evidence telling him that the spheroid earth is a mediaeval myth backed up by no science of repute. Hopkins is tired; he was up until 3am going down a wormhole with some Americans. How would a flat earth have gravity? they asked. He explained that up is always up wherever you are, that if the flat earth were propelled upwards in a direction perpendicular to its face, the force on it would feel like gravity. Up is relative, they told him; it is not necessarily above your head. Lie on your back and up is above your chest. Floating in space with no objects from which to take bearings, where is up? A wag asked if he'd graduated from middle school, the kind of ad hominem argument he has come expect from trolls. Some still think that he and his cohorts are Creationists who believe the earth is covered by a dome in which the sun and moon are both contained. How does his infinite acceleration theory sit with this? The chatter was generally benign, and several fellow flat earthers chimed in with suggestions. Hopkins knows his stickers won't convince anyone, but at the very least, the world will know that not everyone agrees with the scientific orthodoxy; that it is healthy to ask questions, to challenge the "official" version of any event, to not be such cattle. The clown admires the man; he remembers when the earth really was flat, before the navigator El Cano returned from the

215

dead, limping home to Seville after an odyssey that took in the Spice Islands, Patagonia and Cape Verde, proving by his own heroic circumnavigation that the earth was in fact a giant ball. Here in twenty-first century Kilburn, with space travel, the internet and the wonders of modern science, it is Hopkins who is the pioneer.

Tired of being shaken down by the king's men and unable to stray into the woods to retrieve game without a dog, the hunter's time carrying a bow and a quiver of arrows lasted no more than a couple of centuries. Besides, the number of pilgrims travelling to the shrine at Willesden had increased considerably, and both the Cock and the Red Lion had been rebuilt to accommodate them. With so much traffic on the road, few animals ventured close enough to its edges for him to prey on them, and he considered what an itinerant ghost might do for money and food. It was a wet morning in February, not long after the great plague, and the hunter had not killed for some time. Sheltering under a large beech, he watched a party approach from the north with considerable fanfare. A cumbersome carriage pulled by six slow horses struggled with the ruts in the road. The vehicle was festooned with ribbons, streamers and pennants, and musicians walked before it, their timbrels jangling and the melody from a lute evaporating quickly on the gusts of drizzle. Dancing behind them was a figure in striped hose with bells at the corners of his tunic. The man's cowl was red and another bell jangled at the point of his hood. He twirled a baton at the end of which was a carved wooden skull, and on his shoulder sat a small ape who chattered and clapped. The hunter watched, spellbound as the posse neared him, great wheels creaking and crashing through the puddles and bog that Watling Street became in winter. Who was this man? His purpose seemed solely to entertain, and none took much notice of him. Seeing the hunter watching him, the jester reached into his tunic and produced three silver balls, their lustre brilliant in the dull forest. He threw them high into the air, catching and casting them over and again. At the end of the show, he picked two out of the air and the ape pulled his hood open to land the third. In the carriage, England's king sat with his queen, Margaret and their son Edward while stern-faced guards in mail helmets with longswords at the ready walked slowly alongside. The hunter cared nothing for kings; his focus was on the juggler who seemed more spirit than man, who kept a macaque and danced along the road to London. The man pretended to throw a ball at the hunter who flinched, his palm opening and the ball clinging to it through what dark art the hunter could only guess at. The jester grinned and recited a riddle.

"For you, hunter: three headless men played at the ball; one handless man served them all. One mouthless man stood and laughed" – he staggered for effect – "as a cripple dragged his cloak."

The hunter felt a quickening as the red and gold charabanc rumbled on towards Westminster. He reached into his pouch for three smooth pebbles which he would usually place in a slingshot to kill a rabbit. He threw all three in the air, catching none. He tried again and failed again. No matter. Time was on his side. He picked up the rocks and cast them once more to the skies.

Having disembarked on the north shore of the river, the monks picked up the track that would lead them home. Osfrith was deep in thought. He was a man of prayer and contemplation, not a detective and certainly not someone who could inhabit the minds of others to unpick their thoughts and motivations. What he did know was that he

217

had no reason to suspect Wulfstan of subterfuge. The monk had not asked to take the Bible to Westminster; Leofstan chose him for the task as he, of all people at the abbey would cherish the care and craft that had gone into the book's production. If the man had disappeared, it was most likely through accident, or foul play. But his treasure had been delivered, this they knew; Ælfwig had been excited to show them the precious codex. Their brother carried nothing of value on him, and Benedictines by their nature had sworn to be forever poor. An accident then, but not on the road; they would have seen him, or at least those in the villages they passed would have heard of the incident. Perhaps he had got lost in the forest at night and a wolf had taken him? But where would they begin looking? The wildwoods stretched ahead and either side with only a few small clearings for over a hundred square miles. The monks could not delay their return for fear of worrying Leofstan further, but the irresolution niggled Osfrith. Another sneeze shook his body but the brothers had long since ceased blessing him. If there were a body, a hunting party or a woodcutter would retrieve it. If there were foul play, it would out. The men who they had met on the road knew something, but their paths were unlikely to cross a second time. Perhaps the nun would have answers. He blew his nose with his fingers and they continued on towards Hendon.

Two storeys above the African cosmetics store outside which Terry Hopkins affixes another sticker to a lamppost, Farouk Asselah watches *Heroes of Telemark* on free to air TV in the bedroom of his share house. Ibrahim Bouras in leggings and slipper socks pushes on the door without knocking and peers in, glass of sugared tea in his hand.

"Why do you watch this shit?"

Asselah shrugging and clearing files from a chair so Bouras can sit down, but Bouras waves a hand, he isn't stopping.

"My TV is forty six inch, Netflix, YouTube, Amazon Prime. You can watch everything, man."

Asselah smiles,

"It's all TV."

He doesn't care what's on, it's company while he studies for his computer science masters at the University of Westminster.

"How much that cost you?"

Bouras with a point to prove. The set didn't cost Asselah anything; he found on the pavement outside a shop on Cricklewood Broadway and carried it home on the offchance it worked.

"You found it in the trash, man?" Bouras delighted. "It's because no one watches this shit any more. You know how many channels I have? Guess."

Asselah doesn't want to guess.

"Go on man, guess."

Asselah guesses thirty, Bouras throws his head back, laughing like a benign king.

"Try three hundred, and keep counting."

Like it matters. Both men at the bottom of the residential food chain. Broken down bedsits with a shared kitchen above a shop selling blue wigs and fake eyelashes. Bouras walks into Asselah's room; he has seen something that demands inspection and pulls out the *Bourne Ultimatum* from a shelf filled with DVDs.

"You know you can get this shit for free man?"

He regales Asselah, who is a friend of his little brother Mahmoud, of a website that lets you download every Bourne movie free of charge.

"They just rip it man. No one pays for movies anymore."

Asselah pretends to care. He's just here for his degree. Netflix can wait until he graduates. One day, he'll sit poolside in a giant villa earned with his own money, watching every movie he's ever dreamed of on whatever state of the art device he has to hand while Bouras will be boasting to the next tenant about his espresso machine, or an app that dims his lights. Asselah humouring the man because he is his brother's friend, and Bouras sucking his teeth at how far short Asselah is falling as a human. He leaves and Asselah feels his neighbour's pity, turning it into energy. Above the DVDs on a shelving unit scavenged from a skip are text books with a combined worth of over a thousand pounds. These are his investment, and if he reads them, absorbs them and implements their teaching, he will escape this room and the smell of ammonia that pervades it. He scoops up the last forkful of a Pot Noodle that has long since gone cold and turns another page.

Copper plates in a barrel of wine, the verdigris crust scraped off and mixed with lead oxide and egg yolk, then pasted on. Once it was green, it remained green, never fading. And just as the clown's hair never grew and his skin did not age, his bones had not grown stiff with arthritis, rheumatism or ague. His eyes did not fail and his lungs and heart kept strong. The hood which he wore as a hunter was already green and to this he added bells. He whittled a pipe which he learned to play, trilling the tunes sung by travelling troubadours he met on the road, or by drunks in Kilburn's well-stocked taverns. A nightingale sang in the woods and he learned his song. Some days, he sat on the bridge and echoed the music of the water as it trilled under the road, a few hundred yards upstream from where he met the woman who, centuries later, he still mourned. Coins and food for doggerel while he learned the sleight of hand that kept travellers entertained and his belly full. As he strode through the centuries, he acquired new tricks; he walked on his hands, learned the Jew's harp, the harmonica and the ukulele. Ten thousand hours they say. Try five million. He learned the click language of the Sandawe from a freed slave who drank absinthe and played songs from his homeland on a zeze. He could throw a deck of cards in the air and catch them in the box and hide a sovereign under a cup in a way that no one could guess its whereabouts. When he encountered the first travelling clowns two centuries ago, he applied lead paint to his face, blacked his lips and ringed his eyes. A mask to hide behind, a face to cover the one Godwyn knew, which she loved and he detests; a burial. The jester was the making of him, not that he needed one; it gave him something resembling a purpose, and it sure as hell killed the time. Like a lifer who studies for endless degrees which he will never use, the clown collected tricks. But all the time he wandered at the riddle. Headless men, a handless man and a cripple dragging his cloak. Were they letters? Shapes? Names? Countries? Now and then, if he saw a person he considered wise, he asked, but none knew and the answer hovered just out of reach, like a shadow.

As the clown passes the wig shop, he looks across the street where tree lined Messina Avenue heads east away from the High Road, skirting the southern edge of Grange Park, a lone expanse of green in the metropolitan sprawl. High on the wall above the money transfer shop on the corner, those who have time can make out what looks like a box of matches painted onto the brick. The clown remembers when men on ladders with cans of paint created murals, the new advertisements slapped on top of the old, only to be replaced when it was felt that passers-by needed a new message. Layer upon layer upon layer, the old forgotten, buried behind the new. On this wall, the layers have become exposed. Gillette, Players cigarettes, Vicks Vapour Rub, Shamrock Tobacco, Sunlight Soap, no one dreaming that they would still haunt the High Road, their messages lost ghosts that cling on through the centuries.

As Osfrith, Caelstan and Ealdred crossed back over the Cunebourne bridge, they paused. All they could see was a nondescript patch of trees, bracken and leaf litter, but this was the place. If they could find the nun who lived by the brook, maybe she could give them news of their lost brother. Tentatively, they stepped off the road and pushed through the foliage. Another world greeted them. A desecrated shrine, the remains of a stove and a ruined shelter, but no clue as to whether the blessed hermit had survived the attack. Osfrith looked around him. Vernal in the midsummer afternoon, this had clearly been a place of contemplation. Near the broken door of Godwyn's shelter, maggots wriggled over human excrement. Finding no body nor evidence of bloodshed, the monks assembled by the ruined altar. Had the men they had met on the road done this? Or worse – might this be the work of their own brother? The horror made Osfrith shudder. Now two saints had been lost and as the water meandered towards the bridge behind them, he quoted from a Psalm:

"Shew me thy ways, O LORD; teach me thy paths. Lead me in thy truth, and teach me: for thou art the God of my salvation; on thee do I wait all the day."

It felt an appropriate word for the uncertainty they were all feeling. Just as they were about to leave, Ealdred knelt down and called Osfrith over. On the grass in front of him were two flat stones, each with a small pile of hare's bones and a crust of meat juices.

"Two plates, not one. What kind of hermit entertains guests at her bower?" he asked. The others stared at the remains. Osfrith looked around him. Whoever had eaten these meals had broken bread in peace. If their brother had been the guest, why the desecration? Had others come to wreak destruction on this holy place? They were not sleuths. Their concern was for their brother who, for all they knew, had never been here. A crow called from the birch branches. If only the birds could talk, Osfrith thought. Still, if Wulfstan lived, he had agency. He could return or remain where he was, a lost sheep away from the safety of the fold and, like the father of the prodigal in the parable, they must await his return. The men said a final prayer for the safety of their lost brother, then continued their northward journey.

In the staffroom of the money transfer shop on the corner, Domenica Alvarez stares at her phone. Hindsight on her Words with Friends game shows that she could have scored thirty four points, not twenty three. What is a zyme? She reaches in her bag for lip liner and a mirror and begins applying it. She's worked here for three months and the others in her team seem nice; the guys a little flirty, Beatriz a bit of a ball breaker. With the hustlers who come in here, she has to be. Every day another scammer. Beatriz is Colombiana too but from Bogotá, Alvarez is from the north. Taking out some mascara, she paints her lashes. Ronnie pushes the door open, asking if she's seen Beatriz. She hasn't.

"Looking gorgeous," he adds, before shutting her in again. Alvarez packs away her make up and pouts at the glass. She may not have always been called Domenica, but she has always been her, even when she ran around the streets of Medellin and answered to Carlito. Ronnie, Gus and Daniel need never know how awkward, shy Carlito made a one way trip to a clinic in New Mexico aged twenty two, or how Domenica boarded a jet for Heathrow so overjoyed with her new life that she could have probably flown to London using her own wings. An E, a D, a W, a Y and three I's. Ay ay ay.

A small demesne at the edge of the woods, a home built inexpertly with their own hands, the Benedictine felling and sawing poles, Godwyn cutting sticks and mixing clay and manure for the walls. It was hard work but righteous, and the sun burned. When the day's toil had ended, they buried their faces in the cool water of the River Brent where it meandered through the woods behind their cottage. A simple timber hut; rushes on the floor and a fire pit, a pallet for a bed and whatever sheep's wool, fur and feathers that could be sewn into a sack to lie on. Unused to manual labour, the Benedictine's hands blistered, splintered and bled, but it was theirs. A plot to plant barley, rye and beans; a place to begin on terms decided by themselves, not others. A home.

An Aston Martin DB7 convertible pulls up at the lights, its top down despite the chill. Twenty-eight-year-old Ashrif Hussain at the wheel; next to him his friend Sultan Sharif, the vehicle's stereo blasting out breakbeats. The two men on their way to Hussain's home on the outskirts of Milton Keynes; Hussein whose father owns a nationwide network of pharmacies and sent his son to Winchester College. The music detonates against the cold stones outside the wig shop and an empty store next door, its sign ripped away to reveal stained plaster and studs where a fascia should have been. As he pours water from a cheap plastic kettle into a chipped mug, Farouk Asselah looks down from his window at the source of the noise. On the pavement below, he sees a green haired man in clown make up begin to move his shoulders robotically, then step forward and back in a skipping motion as two Arabic men in a stationery convertible look on. The clown flips into a handstand, takes one hand away theatrically and bounces, the hand actually leaving the ground. He lands on the ball of his back and immediately begins flaring, his legs windmilling around his arms, his coat a flag in a wind of his own making. His body twists as shoulder, back, head and hands push up against the ground, keeping him in motion. Standing on both hands again, the clown freezes, crossing his leg so the foot rests on his thigh at a jaunty angle before dropping to his shoulders where he spins so ferociously that his body becomes airborne, a green whirligig, arms and legs indistinguishable; a shape propelled by its own velocity, finally jumping back to upright. Hussain and Sharif sit mesmerised. By now the lights have turned green and the driver of a white Sprinter behind them hits the horn. Ashleigh Connor corralling her daughters towards TKMaxx pulls a two pound coin from the pocket of her puffer jacket and presses it into the palm of the clown who clicks his ancient bones back into place.

"You earned that, mate."

Their marriage was a hurried affair, with no guests. Cynefrith meeting them in the church porch, no dowry given and none taken. Words from Scripture recited quickly, not read; the priest taken aback that the rude swineherd and the servant girl he was marrying mouthed along to the Vulgate and knew each word as well as he. A cloth draped over their clasped hands, Cynefrith pronouncing them man and wife, looking anxiously beyond them and into the trees should any eavesdroppers be watching. The formality over, the priest hurried away along the path to his home, leaving

225

the two of them at the door, married. Taking the bluestone pendant from his neck, the swineherd placed it over Godwyn's head:

"*Vulnerasti cor meum soror mea sponsa, vulnerasti cor meum in uno oculorum tuorum, et in uno crinecolli tui.*"

She clasped it in her hand:

"Thou hast ravished my heart, my sister, my spouse; thou hast ravished my heart with one of thine eyes, with one chain of thy neck.

"Till death part us," he said to her.

"Till death part us," she replied.

The swineherd kissed his bride and she returned his kiss, amazed at a love borne of such joyful serendipity; this happiness which neither of them had words to express, only the movement of their lips against each other's.

Slightly dizzy from his latest caper, the clown rests against a traffic light pole and reflects on a certainty about which he has no doubt. Had he restrained himself, had he not placed his lips near the inflamed face of Godwyn and not touched her chin with his finger; had he denied his beating heart and rising blood and turned away, hurrying back to the road and the safety of the abbey, none of this would have happened. He looks north beyond the bridges at the distant towers of Watling Gardens estate on Shoot Up Hill, east at the loan shop and another vacant store, then south to the twin peaks of Gaumont State and the Kilburn Square Tower. Had he shown greater fortitude, deported himself like a Benedictine, not an impulsive, carnal creature, he would be centuries dead, his bones eaten by acid soil or turned to powder in a tomb. What might he have achieved had he lived out his days in Wæclingacaester? A Bible as magnificent as Augustine's? Most likely not, but the words he patiently copied would have been useful to many, and valued by God. Bread and vegetables to eat, sometimes cheese; meat at Christmas, a fish; expecting death from thirty and old at forty. Only his soul will have remained eternal. Eternity can have it, he has no use for it.

Behind the late Victorian terrace of shops that line this particular western stretch of the A5, the nineteenth century builder, Buckley laid out seven fine town houses and in patriotic zeal named them Waterloo Cottages. This was 1815, the jubilation of those who stayed home matching the gloom of those who returned from their war to find an England that had moved on without them; conscripts who missed the sure food and family of the regiment, who struggled with the bloodletting they had seen and whose petty felonies first filled county jail cells, then prison hulks at Deptford and Chatham before they were poured into converted merchantmen and blown by trade winds to convict jails at the ends of the empire. The clown drank and played craps with them in the gin shops that proliferated every corner. When drunk, these men sang with one another; songs that lifted their spirits while they tamped the cannons at Salamanca as shells flung up earth, rock and splintered wood. One played *Cogagh na Sith* on a penny whistle, the ancient *War or Peace* that he had heard a regimental piper skirl at Corunna. The piper was killed and a second man took up the tune as England's men pushed forward in the frenzy of battle. He too fell, a third piper stepping in to complete the reel. None of the returnees could afford to live in Waterloo Cottages, grubbing around instead on the margins, scrounging, poaching and thieving their passage to the gallows or another world. They'd feel at home on this road with its flattened punnets of chicken shop fries, driven over by heavy wheels. However many new layers are laid down on the old, the scum always rises. This wretched and ruined place, he'll not miss it.

Shielded by a clump of Khejri trees across the dusty road from the primary school in Feench Village on the outskirts of Jodhpur, Abdul Ahmed, his brother and a number of other men in short sleeved cotton shirts work their looms in a large workshop covered with plastic sheeting. As Joshi shouts orders, a woman sings in Hindi through the radio while the men weave coloured cords of jute across taut vertical warps, bashing the weft down with a block of wood as slowly, a red, white and brown kilim pattern grows. In another room, Pankaj Saleem sits cross-legged on the stone tiled floor, hitting a small chisel with a wooden mallet to carve the shisham wood that will make the stool whose kilim upholstery is being finished next door.

An ox tethered to a wooden cart waits patiently outside as two men lift stools, benches and carved shisham cabinets onto the flatbed while the moustachioed factory owner, Sanjeed Amma looks on. The items will make their way through pale blue painted streets to the railway station at Jodhpur, then to the depot in Delhi where Mr R.L. Singh will pack them into wooden crates and ship them half way across the world to Tilbury, a Luton van bringing them to a shop on the Kilburn High Road where any who value the ancient craftsmanship of the Rajahs can buy them for upward of five hundred pounds. Nestled between an empty store and an anonymous grocer's, the handmade ottomans will sit alongside treasures from Afghanistan, Pakistan and Turkmenistan, a shop as out of place among the detritus on this stretch of High Road as an Anglo Saxon. The clown runs his finger across the velvet texture of a Persian rug displayed outside the shop. He remembers when people made things, before the machines, when there were

228

workshops and forges, the sound of spinning wheels and tailors' shears on wooden worktops, of hammers on brass and saws ripping through wood. Today, a few back street mechanics and phone technicians fix things, a couple of chefs and bakers practice their craft, the rest of these shops palm off their mass produced consumables, pressing a button to make a cappuccino or decorating a pre-prepared pizza base. The kilim woven by Mr Amma's men in the dust of Rajasthan is a pattern barely changed for millennia. The clown feels in his pocket for the carved wooden wolf which he had made for his son, crafted centuries before anyone had heard of the Rajahs and their blue city in the Thar Desert. He turns it in his fingers and thinks again of the one for whom it was intended.

The first monks from Westminster arrived a few weeks later. A distraught miller on the road had stopped a party of merchants on horseback heading south. The nun who lived by the river had failed to collect the grain which he left hidden for her. He had walked into the woods to find her, but found her gone and her shelter and shrine in ruins. The man knew that the hermit was under the stewardship of the abbey, and that she prayed for the wellbeing of its brothers as well as for the souls of their dead patrons. He seemed grief-stricken. Moved, the travellers stopped at Westminster on their way to Lundenwic, passing their message on to the youth who ferried pilgrims across to Thorney Island. The brothers who inspected what was left of Godwyn's cell took their findings back to the abbey where Ælfwig concluded that there had been some kind of violation, possibly a fatal one, and a mass was sung in Godwyn's memory. Some spoke of beatification and a letter was written to the bishop. As he read it by candlelight in the Abbey at Canterbury on St Swithin's day 1015, Godwyn was lying beneath her

Benedictine, her eyes rolled back and her face flushed, her breaths quickening. Within a year of the loss of their saint, plans were drawn up for a monastic house, a nunnery to honour the shrine that had been raided and ruined.

In the kitchen of the restaurant next to the shop selling furniture from central Asia, Ryo Inoguchi wipes the chopping board and takes beef and onion from a stainless steel fridge. Gyunabe, his grandmother Fumiko's recipe. Fumiko whose husband Hiroshi went down with the Yamato as the Japanese fought to control the island of Okinawa, who raised three children on her own, repairing clothes in a booth at the railway station by day and cooking in an orphanage at night. Gyunabe; beef and onion stewed in miso paste, a recipe from the revolution that swept through late nineteenth century merchant class kitchens. With the Buddhists no longer holding power and a tsunami of western thought flooding the nation, the taboo of eating beef was lifted and roadside izakayas across the country began serving the new beef and rice bowl – Gyudon. This was the meal Inoguchi's mother would make for him and his sister Kashi when they returned from school in Yamakita. A pound of ribeye steak chilled until stiff but not frozen, which he slices thinly with a Misono blade, the tip of his tongue poking from the corner of his mouth as he works. Nice and even; the thinner the slice the less chewy it will be, cutting the strips cross ways; done. An onion chopped with the deft guillotine blows of a second, larger knife and scraped across the board into a bowl. A bunch of spring onions sliced into thin, diagonal slivers. As rice steams in the cooker, he throws a cup of dashi soup stock into a fry pan followed by a lug of sake, mirin, and light soy sauce, and a tablespoons or two of sugar. The daishi a family recipe too, a combination of kelp, bonito flakes, dried anchovy and shiitake mushroom. Inoguchi adding the onion with chopsticks, being careful to separate the layers; the strips of meat laid on top, a lid placed over them and the heat turned up a little. While the meat browns, he wipes his knives and checks his messages; Lena has gone to Westfield with Ana, Inoguchi now skimming off the scum and fat with a fine mesh spoon and setting the pan to simmer. An egg cracks into a bowl and he beats it with the chopsticks, drizzling it over the beef and onion until it sets. Pushing it into a plastic punnet, he garnishes the Gyudon with the spring onion and some beni shoga ginger before popping on the lid and placing it in a white plastic bag with a box of steamed short grain rice. The bag is handed to a man in a motorcycle helmet for delivery to an address in West Hampstead. No one comes in to eat any more; there's nowhere to park in the day and the High Road is too dangerous for diners at night. Ryo Inoguchi preparing takeaway dinners to be enjoyed in front of *Orange is the New Black*, *Grey's Anatomy* and *Suits*. He picks up a knife to wipe it again. Let the muggers come for him; he has a blade hidden in his sock and he'll dice and slice anyone who tries to get a piece of him on his walk home to Cricklewood. Maybe even cook them in a gyudon. He grins and looks at the next order.

They lay on straw covered in sheepskins under woollen blankets. Embers glowed in the firepit and he kissed her, still revelling in the newness. He had never lain with a woman and she had seldom gleaned an ounce of pleasure from her liaisons, had never lost herself in bone shuddering joy. His weight over her, she believed herself safe and loved. When it was over, she lay her head on his shoulder, her fingers drawing circles on his chest, his skin a musical instrument, the woman beside him plucking melodies on its wires.

"What are you thinking?"

He was quiet for a few moments.

"I made vows."

She exhaled and continued circling his skin.

"To be chaste," he said and laughed through his nose. Her hand reached down to the curls of hair at his groin.

"What is chastity?" He turned to face her. Two dark eyes looked up at him. "We are chaste," she continued. "Not celibate, but not profligate. You are mine and I am yours. Did he not send you to me?"

"I longed for you from the moment I saw you. Even as a monk. That was not chaste. I wished to see what was under here, to touch you here." He ran his hand across her belly. "Had you not been attacked, I might still have returned. You invaded my thoughts. I could not meditate without thinking of what you were doing by the river."

"Are we to be damned for turning our backs on our calling?"

"I did not choose to become a Benedictine, I was raised one. And now…"

"And now?"

She rolled on top of him and kissed his lips, the bluestone wolf around her neck hopping on his chest as she rose and fell. He closed his eyes as the bliss began to overwhelm him. The two of them were all that mattered now in this world. As she moved above him, he clung to her and she gripped him. An owl called in the beechwood and another answered. They had saved each other, they had damned each other.

Mustafa Huq walks around the corner of Messina Avenue onto the High Road wearing a black bomber jacket over a light brown jellabiya, 'Raw Blue' emblazoned on his back and his grey buzz cut growing out. Here, where the old National Club dominates an entire city block, two penitents fled through trees. Before the young birds who had watched from their nests had time to fly or the fallow deer fawns who had scattered into the woods as they ran were fully grown, men hacked a path to the river, and carts carrying sawn stone rolled along the trackway. Pits were dug, lines measured and the once tranquil glade rang to the sound of master masons and joiners. Hundreds of men busy at work where before, there had been a spring, a river, a small lean-to against a hollow oak, and a solitary penitent at prayer. A swineherd watched from the track as seasons turned, walls grew, paths were laid and a garden planted. By June of the following year, a grand priory stood where Godwyn had built her cell, and where a Benedictine had gazed at specks of pollen and dust passing through shards of sunlight, caressing Godwyn's naked shoulder as she slept. The following month, a delegation from Westminster arrived; three nuns walking ahead of an ornate carriage drawn by horses in which sat archbishop Lyfing himself, his long face crowned with a pointed golden mitre. Lyfing's alb was white and he wore a bejewelled cincture, a linen maniple embroidered with gold crosses and he carried a bone handled crozier. In contrast, the women; two short, one tall, wore long habits of undyed wool, white cloth wimples and rough sandals. Brothers from the abbey brought up the rear, walking solemnly as the sun reached its apex on the third day of July in the year of our Lord 1017. Inside the church which still smelled of felled oak and stone dust, Lyfing stood on the chancel steps and preached on Levitical vows, and read the Corinthian epistle in which the apostle exhorts those who are unmarried to remain celibate. The name they gave the convent that replaced Godwyn's crude stone shrine was St. Peter's, in honour of the mother church. A splinter of Christ's cross was placed in a small teak box and presented to the abbess, a woman called Geatfleda who was the tallest of the three and whose voice was as deep as a man's. The relic was treasured and displayed at a special mass on St. Peter's Day until the priory was dissolved in the time of Cromwell's purge. The sisters turned the glade into a formal vegetable garden and continued to venerate Godwyn who, they said, had been taken alive to heaven like Enoch and Elijah, for none knew where she had gone, or why, only that she was never seen again.

The long, cream coloured neoclassical building on the corner of Messina Avenue and the High Road replaced a fine mansion called the Grange. The house sat in grounds which formed part of the Little Estate, the last of Kilburn's pasturelands to be developed. The building boasts arched, stain glassed windows and a copper dome surmounted by a lantern and was once the Grange Cinema and is now home to a Brazilian church. The clown watches people wandering in and out of the swing doors even though it's a Saturday, though they'd need to meet every day for a century to clean the place of the sins that its bricks have borne witness to. Many of them while it has been a church. A renegade priest named Goodman preached prosperity in the twilight years of the last century, urging his flock to praise God with their chequebooks, not just their hymnbooks. Goodman wearing made to measure suits, rejoicing in the wealth that poured into his sacred coffers. A priest convicting and absolving as the Spirit moved him, speeding away from what little faith he possessed in a Ferrari, young women in the seat next to him purring into his ear and calling him Daddy G; a shyster who ended the Millennium in grey sweatpants slopping out a Wormwood Scrubs jail cell.

A swineherd wandered through the forest with a reed basket hanging from a pole. Halting beneath an oak, he placed the pannier on the ground and struck the boughs until acorns began falling. Gathering them, he shovelled his harvest into the basket with both hands. The woods were silent, the swineherd's footfalls and the nuts rattling as he walked the only sound. He met no other travellers and felt no sense of the Spirit which had previously ordered his days. No matins, lauds or vespers here in the forest, no divine instruction, no sense of anything other than the expanse of the world and his own smallness within it, a man gathering acorns in the great belt of green. He grabbed his basket and set off to feed the pigs before returning to the hut where a woman stirred pottage over a fire.

The clown often entered the cinema in the Grange's nineteen twenties heyday, his feet padding along plush red carpet as far as the curse would allow him, pulling up short at a giant balustraded staircase spiralling past ornate panelling and plasterwork to a balcony above the giant auditorium. Here, he would have seen thick gold curtains parting to reveal the matinee, Lillian Gish in *Way Down East*, Douglas Fairbanks in *The Mark of Zorro*, Bebe Daniels in *Sinners in Heaven*; air dense with woodbines, the giant organ rising to a crescendo at the point where all seemed lost, audiences waiting for the day to be saved and lovers' hands creeping under clothing in the blackness.

Instead, he waited outside, watching the audience trickle out, some continuing what they started, finding a wall away from the lamplight, others whistling for a cab or queueing for an omnibus, stamping the cold from their feet, faces glowing from ninety minutes' escape from the leaden mantle which life had laid on them. Unemployment, pestilence and death. Let them screw in the shadows, they needed all the pleasure they could get.

July and August were the months of hunger. Barns that had been filled with the previous year's harvest were all but empty, and the poor eked what little they could from the dry land. Wulfstan and Godwyn were fortunate; the lord of Willesden was kind and shared from his storehouses, even though they were newcomers. The man who had been brought up as a monastery scribe worked hard marshalling the lord's pigs. The beasts roamed wild; quick, lean bodies on long legs, gorging on a woodland mast of beech nuts and acorns. Too much discipline and they would frighten, too little and they would refuse to move to the next feeding place. Godwyn milked, swept the lord's home, helped with the harvest and made herself useful to the women of the manor. The two rarely saw one another during the day, but when they did, he was always caught off guard. Her poise, the grace of her walk and the music of her laugh intoxicated him. At night, he buried himself into her, wishing he could climb his whole being inside her, to curl up in her kind womb and sleep.

She passed him near the church, carrying a spray of dog roses, foxgloves and vetch, an explosion of pink. St. Mary's was a simple building with small arched windows set high in its mudstone walls and, putting his firewood down, the swineherd followed her through the tall oaken door, watching as she arranged the flowers in a vase near the stone altar slab. Standing behind her, he placed his arms around her waist.

"Stop!" Her cry was out of surprise and fear, and uttered before she could even think. "It's a church!"

"There is no God" he whispered.

"Get thee behind me, Benedictine."

Her words urgent, sharp.

"Here I am", he smiled.

She turned, her face flushed.

"There is a God, and he sees us and he saw us and he will judge us."

"Then let us give him something to judge."

She pressed her head against his chest and her hands gripped his arms.

"We are wicked," she whispered as their lips touched. No one came in, and the secrecy and scandal thrilled them. Afterwards, they sat together on a wooden bench looking up at the wildflowers.

"Are we damned?" she asked.

"We were always damned."

"Does not God forgive?"

Behind them, the door opened and Cynefrith bustled in. Looking up, he saw the pink display.

"Wonderful," he said. "It is as if they are blushing."

They left quietly, he to the woodpile and she to the cows.

The Grange had been a sturdy mid-century pile set back from the road; home to a man who made carriages for the Queen. Where local roughnecks now get high on nitrous oxide in the park, his weathered hands tended salmon pink Boscobels and yellow Gloire de Dijons in a walled rose garden. In the latter part of the last century, this had been a wild place. The owner and impresario was an Irish strongman who tore out the guts of the cinema that had replaced the house and filled it with rock and roll. When he wasn't lifting truck axles loaded with weights or pulling a cart filled with ten men using a rope clenched between his teeth, the man threw his doors open to skinny boys and peroxide blondes who graced the stage of what became known as the National. For the clown, the queues outside provided a captive audience. One night, he juggled tangerines and the singer of the band walked past, pausing to watch his impromptu performance. As fans screamed in the presence of their idol, the man told the clown to meet him backstage afterwards. A fangirl with dark red lips and black eye make-up was so besotted with the singer she offered the clown a blowjob if he took her with him. While her friend saved her place in the queue, they snuck into an alcove in the alley that runs along the side of the club where the clown leant against a battered black door while she unbuttoned him. Nothing.

"You not into girls, sweetheart?"

The truth wouldn't have helped. He was so bored. Worn down by the lack of anything new under the godforsaken stars. He'd like for once to jostle shoulder to shoulder with the sweating crowd inside the club, to feel elation and escape, not to be jerked off in a doorway or snort coke in a dressing room with a skinny Scottish rock star. He touched her head tenderly.

"I'm not going backstage afterwards."

She looked up, confused, her hands still gripping his thighs.

"Why not? It's the fucking JAMS?" like he was crazy. He shrugged, packing himself away then reached into his pocket and took out a tangerine.

"Would you like an orange?"

"No, I want to see fucking Jim and William and Bobby."

"I'll take you back."

"I fucking need a wee now," the girl pulling down her pants and squatting on the pavement.

"Sorry", though he wasn't.

"Fuck off."

He turned back to the road leaving the girl to the pale, black-clad saints who would later grace the National stage. It feels like last week, but she's forty five now. He still knows her.

One Sunday after mass, a swineherd and a milkmaid walked arm in arm into the woods. Here, they picked fat blackberries from bramble bushes, their fingers staining red with the juice. This being a Sabbath, there was no work but the hazelnuts were ripe too and it seemed a sin to leave them all for the pigs. Later, they sat in a small clearing where he cracked nuts between two stones, picking the fatty kernels from the shattered shells and feeding them to her.

"What do you know of me, Benedictine?"

He looked up at her and smiled, the lines in the corner of his eyes creasing.

"That you are beautiful. And you are good. A saint."

"A saint I am not."

He continued cracking the nuts.

She pulled her knees up to her chest.

"Truly, I do not know who I am."

He looked up again in case there was more.

"All I know is who I was, where I've been and where I am now."

"You were a saint. A nun from the convent at Barking. Your cell was by the Cunebourne stream where I found you.

She laughed.

"Found me."

"Saved you. Damned you. Damned us both."

"That was the end, Benedictine. You did not see the beginning, only what I had become."

"Godwyn…"

"That is not my name."

He stopped shelling the nuts and looked at her, not understanding.

"See, you like me less already."

"Not Godwyn? Then who?"

"Beloved," she took his hand. "You ask questions whose answer might distress you."

He took her other hand.

"Speak. Nothing you are or you have been can change how I feel."

She laughed again and he felt uncomfortable, as if he were being kept from a joke.

"Speak or be silent," he said, letting go of her hands. He placed a nut in his mouth and continued shelling. After a few moments he looked up at her. Tears streamed from her eyes and she wept quietly. Placing the cloth that contained the nuts to one side, he sat next to her, his arm around her shoulders.

"What is it, Godwyn?" he asked, kindly.

"I am not Godwyn!" she screamed, and the tears and snot came with renewed force, her shoulders heaving in great sobs. He listened and he learned. The father, the uncles, the orphan left to steal or starve. The wharf at Westminster, the inns and back streets of the great city and the men in their hundreds whose coins kept her belly full enough to live another day. He learned of beatings, broken ribs and bruises, of the nothingness she felt; a directionless puppet with nowhere to be nor any time at which to be there. She had no idea of her age, neither then nor now. He knew of the abbey at Barking, the years by the river, but nothing of what came before. He let the information settle.

"If you are not Godwyn, who are you?"

She looked directly into his eyes.

"Laila," she said. "My mother named me Laila."

He looked at the woman who he loved, who he could not unlove, who had nothing left from her previous world save some scars and her name. He had killed Godwyn and desecrated her shrine and he would no doubt pay the price, in this world or the next. He learned all she knew about her mother, how the woman had had been captured and brought from the coast of Morocco in a ship filled with captured slaves, then married to the brother of the boatswain.

"Laila."

He enjoyed the sound of the word on his lips. Pushing her back on the soft beechmast, he kissed her damp face, and she kissed him.

On the west side of the street opposite the old club, Burton Road leads up towards Queens Park. On the corner is a pub called the Kingdom. The clown walks in and pulls up a stool by the bar. No kingdom for him, just a dark infinity, the not knowing and not being for an eternity, an end, a final point in time where the beat of his footfalls will cease. While a meat-faced youth with badly cut hair pours him a double shot of Bells, Musicians from a ceilidh band assemble a drumkit on a low stage. Nearby, two men, one in a cap and the other in a leather jacket sip pints of strong lager at separate tables. Cap reads a paper, the *Leitrim Observer*; jacket stares ahead of him, a ghost. An older woman appears behind the bar from a back room and regards the clown, though not with any joy. He beckons to her and she leans forward, nodding as he whispers. He sips the whisky and the ball of fire rides down to his belly as Cap begins a coughing fit. The man is almost choking and his face turns vermilion. Jacket doesn't look up. Who would miss him? Who even knows he's here? Yet one day, decades earlier, he placed a cap on his head, looked in a mirror and thought, "that'll do." In the same way the other man will have tried on the jacket, turned this way then that, considered the cut, the width it leant to his shoulders; who knows when it was, but the blood beat faster, keener. Now they're two shells beached on the shore of the Kingdom, stuck. The clown downs another slug and, lips still burning, walks back onto the street. North, across Burton Road, past the handbag shop, past the discount store where Bianca Yidefonso is on the phone to Emily Savage for the third time today. Yidefonso trying to sound cheerful but she's worn out. Savage's brother won't take his sister's calls. Every so often he just stops picking up, and there's no way Emily Savage is getting a train and two buses all the way to Luton to try and find him. Not with her hip. And then there is all the fish from the man who came round last Tuesday. She still doesn't know what she's going to do with it; her freezer is full and it won't keep. If she can't get rid of it, it'll start to smell.

"Why did you buy the fish?" Yidefonso asked her.

"Because it was cheap".

Today it's Domino, the Bassett Hound who Savage has struggled to walk since the operation. He's scratching the paint off the door and whining. Yidefonso yes yesses, promising she'll be round later to walk Domino, but Savage doesn't thank her, warning her that she'll be watching the news at six, so to come before then.

"And bring some bags to take away the fish."

Yidefonso with a child of her own and a job, who offered to help her neighbour as an act of charity, not knowing that there are as many people to leech on kindness and hoover up generosity as there are those ready to help them; Savage the parasite and Yidefonso the host. A pox on all of them. A fire. Let it burn.

A siren smashes through hard air, bouncing off brick, stone and blacktop. Caucasian woman, white, late twenties, fell from a third floor window. Possible trauma to brain, fractured pelvis, lacerations to face and shoulders, hypertrophic and atrophic scars on forearm.

"Stay with me Daniela."

Samuel Devars driving and Megan Foote pumping Daniela Fon's chest as 0.9 saline is delivered by IV through a canula in the back of Fon's right hand. Fon high on ketamine, sitting on the balcony at Kenny's place on the Templar House Estate; didn't even scream when she rocked backwards, lost her balance and experienced the ecstasy of weightlessness for a nanosecond until her shoulder impacted the dull grass.

"Shoot up Hill, ennit?" Devars grins.

Foote not replying. She's breathing into Fon's mouth, trying to restart her cooked heart.

"Couldn't have picked a better road, eh?"

Devars pleased with his joke. Foote pumping the chest again.

"Just fucking drive, Sammy."

The vehicle rushes past the clown, creating its own weather system, throwing up blossoms and crisp packets and billowing his coat, the shrill doppler of the klaxon drowning out all other noise. He dances to its atonal tune as one more life teeters on the brink and cars and buses crawl to the edge of the High Road like they are parting a wound. Drama over, he walks on.

Yassin Ahamed drives his 4.97 rated Toyota Prius south along the A5 past a clown in an army green greatcoat who leans on a lamppost outside the discount store next to a handbag shop on the western side of Kilburn High Road. Ahamed explaining to John Jeffries who he collected from

Luton airport and who showed interest in Ahamed's home country of Somalia that the place is "completely fucked." Ahamed who escaped to the Dadaab refugee camp in Kenya at eighteen, spent two years kicking a ball around with other men and eating food provided by the UN, telling John Jeffries who imports shoes from Indonesia about the cartel of warlords who defend their tribes with guns, machetes and bombs, turning the economic desert that was once a proud country into a killzone. A place where nothing can get started because all aid is hoarded by war dogs who guard their power with avaricious zeal. Somalia with its three hundred mile strip of unbroken beaches, the longest coastline in Africa, a potential tourist mecca collapsing beneath the unending bombardment of Al Shabab.

"It wouldn't happen if we had more women in power," Ahamed says. "We need to kill the old men."

Jeffries nodding, not knowing that he is being driven by White Star General, an anonymous Youtuber with twenty five thousand followers who hang on his every warlike pronouncement, his calls to kill the old guard, to hack them to pieces in their beds, to liberate Somalia so one day he, his brothers his sisters and his cousins can re-enter paradise. The clown watches Ahamed as the Prius crawls slowly behind an Argos semi-trailer. He sees fury and fire in the man's face and resents him. Resents his ardour. He feels nothing but a slow, seething disdain. Tired of this world, apart from it yet still somehow part of it, the last leaf of autumn that has clung on until winter, soon to be terminally disconnected. Others' joy only heightens the loss and lack of any of his own. He balls a fist in his pocket, wanting to hurt something, or for something to hurt him. To feel something, anything before he leaves the earth forever. He feels the box of matches in his pocket. Nearly time.

When the runaways arrived in need of work in Midsummer, the pigs were still being fattened for autumn. July was the month of haymaking, a cruel harvest that brought neither food nor succour, only winter feed for the animals. Men, women and children gathered at sun up for the reaping and the swineherd was assigned to a narrow field measuring a chain by a furlong and given a scythe. It was heavy labour for a man unused to it, especially when the sun rose to its zenith, and the long blade brutally sharp. He swung his hips as the carl had shown him, sweeping the cutting edge with the movement of his body. Dry stalks fell to his left, leaving just a short bristle clinging to the earth. His shoulders ached but he found the rhythm absorbing; the swoosh as the blade cut into stalks of wild meadow grass, clover and thistle and the metallic sing as it rose again. Behind him, women gathered the hay into bundles and a scattering of children tidied and played.

An acre was enough for a single reaper to mow with a blade, and longer than it was wide to save the man from turning too frequently. When he was thirsty, which was often, he drank ale from a flask and at midday, they gathered under a solitary oak to eat dark bread with cows' cheese. In the days that followed, the hay was turned daily to dry it while Cynefrith prayed to stay the rains; a ruined hay crop making for a gloomy winter as animals that could not be fed would need to be slaughtered. A week later, he helped pile the bundles onto an ox cart and followed it to the corner of a field where it was stacked on a bed of bracken, opportunist swallows picking over the leavings. Despite the blisters and calluses on his hands and the ache in his bones, he felt useful in a way he never had at the abbey. There, he had prayed without knowing if any of his prayers were answered, drawing letters on parchment with no idea who would read them or what hope they might take from them. Here in Willesden, the hay was cut and stacked by Lammas, the animals could eat throughout the winter, and all agreed that the work had been completed well. The clown looks west up Dyne Road. Where he chased pigs a thousand Julys ago, a Cash Converters and a tobacconist. Behind these, the nineteen fifties sprawl of James Stewart House. The fields were in a clearing somewhere beyond, and he remembers bumblebees taking their last sip of clover before a scythe fell on summer grass, and wonders if there are still hayfields in Willesden, or any bees.

Here on the west side of the street next to the discount store where Bianca Yidefonso wishes she hadn't picked up the call from Emily Savage, Martine Brooks sits with her sister Tilly in a café, the wall behind them dominated by a giant chart mapping out the origins of the universe. Tilly who left home at sixteen and lived on a canal boat in Leicester with a bunch of hippies, still pink haired but married with children, suddenly the sensible one. They sip lattes and nibble on carrot cake, Tilly's ratty terrier, Angus underneath the table sniffing for crumbs. Martine still brown from the cruise, already two and a half years into the two the doctor gave her, and living her best life. Spending it all now because she's single and has no children, so what's the point of leaving anything in the bank? She shows Tilly pictures of Steve who's sixty but looks forty five and who she hit it off with. The two of them in Malta, a friendly cat on Mykonos, a badly framed photo of the Acropolis and the golden dome in the old city of Jerusalem.

"Are you seeing him again?" Tilly asks.

"He's allergic to cats."

Martine now the rebel, about to start immunotherapy and who knows what happens after that. A dark skinned man looks over from the table in the corner and smiles. Tilly looks at her sister.

"He's nice."

"He's gay, Matilda."

"You don't know that."

"No straight man wears salmon. Anyway, I've had a few winks from this guy."

She shows her sister her phone.

"Stop it! He looks like Dad!"

Martine snatching the phone back.

"No he does not!" She swipes the screen. "Ooh, he does a bit."

"What's his name, it's not Richard?" Tilly looking up at her sister. "It's not! It is! You're dating our father!"

Martine Brooks howling with laughter and Tilly laughing too, the child who once hated being in her family now terrified of being alone, of never having moments like this again.

With the hay stacked, the men began their weary journey home to the village. A churl named Alfred stopped the swineherd.

"Where do you think you are going?"

The man's tone was unfriendly. The swineherd was going home to the village to eat and sleep, like the others, he told him.

"The rick needs guarding," Alfred said, "and they've asked me to tell you that it is your watch."

With that he turned and followed the others, all of them in jovial mood as the work had been completed without incident.

Hungry and tired, the swineherd turned back to the hay mountain. He sank to his haunches and leaned against it. Light was beginning to fail and curious bats flitted around.

Crickets chirruped and nightjars churred as he tried to make himself comfortable. Hours passed but none came to relieve him. His joints ached especially when he moved after being still for a while, and his belly ground with no food in it. He craved sleep but sleep he would not, the hay needed guarding. For the first time since leaving the abbey, he prayed the divine office, not with any heart, more a going through the motions; a way to keep time. First, vespers as the sun dipped orange over the woods. Then compline as dusk turned to dark, the time most souls would make for their beds. By midnight or thereabouts, he had given up hope of being relieved and recited the Scripture for matins and lauds. This was the hardest watch. His eye sockets hurt and he decided to get to his feet, pacing around so as to keep himself awake. Psalm 148, praising God for "the beasts, and all cattle; creeping things and flying fowl," his meditations interrupted by the shrill screech of foxes.

Before the dawn, corn bunting and linnets began their song, joined soon after by blackbirds and wrens. The swineherd had never wanted time to hasten as much as he did now. With first light came prime, at which he recited the first chapter of James, "blessed is the man that endureth temptation: for when he is tried, he shall receive the crown of life." With the dawn came new energy, and new hunger. When would the men relieve him? When would the day watch take over from the night? With the sun climbing in the east, he made a decision, he would run to the village and ask who was to guard the hay by day, and if it was he, to fetch vittles and return to his duties. How much hay could be stolen in the half hour it would take him? When he reached their hut, Godwyn flew at him, furious. Where had he been? What could have taken him all night? She thought he had been killed, and then clung to him, weeping with relief.

248

On entering the village, a woodcutter named Eadric was at the smithy, sharpening his axe.

"How was the hay?"

The smith laughed.

"Hay still there?"

Another worker called Beostan. The youth next to him laughing too. And then it dawned on him. This was why no one had relieved him. He felt foolish and tired.

"Your wife was worried about you," grinned Beostan. In the distance, he saw Alfred with some other men. They too turned to look at him, pointing.

Still warm from the whisky, the clown passes the café where Martine Brooks drinks coffee with her sister, and the Asian cash and carry which, in a former life had been the shoemakers, Waugh and Co. He looks in at the Iranian café next door. It was Iranians who got as close as him to immortality. Or were they Iraqis? Adam, Noah, Methuselah; those antediluvian ancients who lived long centuries in the land between the rivers. Adam, the first man, still fecund at his eviction from the garden, fathering sons with Eve and procuring food by the sweat of his brow from a land of thistle and thorn for another nine centuries. And Noah, who, unlike him, did nothing to displease God, whose giant floating menagerie repopulated the drowned earth, a paradise which he called home for nine hundred and fifty years. Methuselah, the most ancient of all, a man who appeared blameless yet was forced to eat, sleep and copulate over and again for almost ten centuries, a life on permanent repeat, never leaving his homeland, simply enduring, wearying of everything and everyone; an existence devoid of surprise or novelty, of watching everyone born before him die. Such is the prize for the last man standing, the hollow victory of one who has lost everything, who has long since given up living and who simply takes up space on the earth, a husk. In the Vandalia Senior Centre in Brooklyn, the blind daughter of Alabama sharecroppers, Susannah Jones, sips tea with her carer. One of only two people still alive who was born in the nineteenth century, the year Monet painted his lilies, the Boers besieged Ladysmith and Victoria laid the foundation stone of the London museum that still bears the names of her and her beloved husband. A mere child born a blink ago. 6 July 1899, a Thursday. It was wet, and a Hackney carriage overturned on the corner of Shoot Up Hill and Mill Lane, throwing a woman to the ground and concussing her. How the biblical ancients fared for almost a millennia of monotony, he cannot imagine. More a subsistence than a life, men rattling around their lush, Mesopotamian paddocks, herding goats and sheep in a time before the wheel, before iron smelting, before the domestication of the camel, before Mesolithic labourers hauled bluestone slabs from the Pembroke mountains and rolled them on sawn trees to barges at the mouth of the River Severn; a time where change was imperceptible and the land in which they died resembled almost exactly the one of their birth. The clown looks around. A Pakistani grocery. Another café next door to it. Over on the east side of the road, the alleyway where a girl called Stacey Valentine offered him sexual favours in exchange for a backstage pass in 1987. The Chinese restaurant on the corner. A thousand years ago, this was beechwood, as silent and changeless as Noah's fields. Woodpigeons cooing, a distant axe on the base of a sapling, leaves rustling in the early afternoon breeze. A National Express coach to Loughborough via Milton Keynes Coachway, Northampton North Gate and Leicester St. Margaret's Bus Station rolls past on the road where he once travelled clutching a Bible wrapped in calfskin. And he now thirty years older than Methuselah, in a land changed beyond imagination. The last woman from the nineteenth century. Ha! The last man from the eleventh wipes snot from his nose, kicks a crushed can of Special Brew into the gutter and walks on.

In the royal port of Jomsborg, final preparations were being made as men rolled barrels up gangplanks onto the boats. The great woollen sails were fetched from the long barn which had kept them dry throughout the winter. Wool because it stretches in the wind and withstands any sudden strain on the rigging, smeared animal fat to proof it and ochre for sheer drama. Horsehair ropes provided the rigging, with stronger cord made from walrus hide for the halyard. Salt beef and mead in the butts, sacks of henbane for courage and animal skins for shelter and warmth if they couldn't make safe haven by nightfall. Crowds gathering hours before the ships were finally ready, both to see Denmark's men off on their voyage and to catch a glimpse of the young prince. Cnut as yet untested, the opportunity to lead the fleet to England and glory a ruse by his brother Harald to keep him away from the Danish throne. The Vikings themselves now filling the quayside and fanning out in a great sea; rivers of warriors between the sheds and wool stores, not a thrall nor a freedman among them, a picked host whose number increased as the hour for launch neared. A priest on the quayside stirring the men with David's attack on Ammon, invoking the gods of the Edda to help Jesus bless their mission to conquer the great island to the west. A loud cheer as the crowd parted and finally, Cnut and his men passing through on horseback. The soldiers fearless, death bringing glory and for the victorious, the chance to turn their longswords into ploughshares, to till England's greensward and raise families. The spirit of the bears and wolves in whose skins they wrapped themselves were with them. The wind smacking into in the sails would send them skipping across the Vestrsaer where they would hit Tarkhum so hard that stones would shatter and the gods would hear. Fire and fury on Æthelred and his weak and undefended realm.

The clown is hungry. He's not eaten since the morning, and though he cannot starve and food is joyless, he looks around for options. On the corner of the alley which loops around the back of the old cinema is a Chinese. Behind him is the Iranian restaurant and next to that, an Irish café and a chicken shop. In this beleaguered strip of city, he's spoilt for choice with fayre from the earth's four corners. Refugees from the empire and other satellites who bought stoves and pans when they made landfall, stocked up at a cash and carry in Park Royal and tried to replicate the recipes from home. Art on the walls that never changes, sticky floors, laminated menus in poorly written English and bare-bulbed toilets which smell of naphthalene. Food by the poor for the poor, overlooked by the moneyed cognoscenti who hole up at the Black Lion or the North London Tavern. Once, crowds came to Kilburn for the State, or the Theatre Royal, or the National. Those days are gone. Kilburn is no "must see" on any tourist trail; the only people who dine here are those who live nearby, or are passing through, hungry and far from home; the food a distress purchase to be eaten in a car or at a bus stop. The clown walks into the Iranian restaurant. Or maybe it's Afghan. A home from home for émigrés from Central Asia and the Levant. Not that he cares. Food is fuel.

For a time, he was not the only clown in town. A troupe of Pierrots could often be seen here, their flowing white silk capes and pantaloons, pointed hats and white face paint adding glorious if fleeting theatre to the Edwardian suburb. These were professionals; performers who had studied the Commedia dell'arte and whose slapstick brought joy to music halls across the metropolis. One of their number must have lived in a flat across from the cinema and they would often retire there to drink. One hot summer night after a show at the Theatre Royal in Belsize Road, they gave an impromptu performance here on the street. "Pelissier and his Kilburn Follies", among them Gwennie Mars, a runaway in a clown suit whose twist on music hall songs and Shakespeare plays had crowds howling for more. Mars was among the entertainers that night; her wild spirit only accentuating the deadness he felt inside. So much life and only a mortal coil in which to live it, while he had done nothing but whine, kvetch and bellyache for the centuries since his curse. She was a true clown, he an imposter who turned tricks to kill time. At the end of her routine, Mars saw him in the crowd and curtsied, and he felt blessed. He grabbed a hat from the man next to him and placed it on his own head as she watched. Lifting it, a pigeon flapped away. If nothing else, he had put in the years.

In the restaurant, a quiet man brings him small plates and naan bread. At the next table, Salim and Yasmin Ormazd sit in silence, eating skewers of minced sheep, the only other people in the restaurant. The clown wonders why they came in. Were they more bored of their own four walls than they are of one another? No children to keep them busy and no conversation left, rattling around in the shell of their marriage until one of them succumbs to carcinogens and dies intubated in a shared NHS ward in Northwick Park. The clown looks down at his food. A shish kebab with a side of okra. Is this what Methuselah had to make do with day in, day out for ten centuries? Lamb and flatbread. At least he had wine which is more than the poor bastards have now in their shitforsaken desert. Named a giant bottle after the man, no doubt because he drunk himself stupid to forget. Anything to get high and escape the endless drip drip drip of a life on loop. You eat, you shit, you work every day; and every night you suck from the vine to obliterate the dread of another fucking dawn.

As summer turned to autumn; the swineherd threw himself at whatever work they gave him, shovelling out pens, fetching straw for the animals and chasing swine through the pannage. Godwyn eased milk from the teats of goats into wooden pails with hands red from cold and the pair spent nights around their fire, fat from a snared bird cracking yellow as it dripped into the ash. While nettles and dandelion boiled in a pot, Godwyn span wool caught on briar and blackthorn, and when their meal was complete, they lay next to one another. A thousand years before, when Cymbeline was king of the Catuvellauni, a track had already been cut through the forest to the Roman stronghold of Verulamium. The king would recognise the land where the runaway Benedictines held one another on a straw bed covered with fur, though many trees had been felled and land set to pasture. But were the ancient king to pass today where car horns and sirens drown the noise of birdsong, teenagers in sports casual gather in doorways of fried chicken shops and the penniless and pitiful beg for alms, he would think he had been taken to an afterlife as hellish as it were foreign. The clown looks up at two blossoming trees outside the Chinese restaurant. An aeroplane crosses the sky. A Ryanair jet en route to Birmingham from Ibiza. He has never travelled by plane, nor train, nor ship. A landbound pilgrim, every day a Via Dolorosa, every step bringing him closer to death and the fire. Just an hour or so until his final curtain; his exit a far greater show than his entry; a spectacle worthy of the playbills they used to stick on the walls of the Kilburn Empire and on the omnibuses that sputtered along the High Road. He breathes in and feels sanctified by the plane's roar, the smell of truck fumes, and the shattered splines of glass in the shadows of the kerb.

Keira Hartley sucks on a milkshake in Rose's café next to the Iranian restaurant. Sitting with her back to the window, Hartley's grandmother Pat is talking about Robbie. Keira's uncle moved back to Connemara a year ago with Aunty Rachel and the girls. She never liked Tansy and Miraid who always made a mess in her room, never cleared it up and let her carry the can. She and Pat are waiting for Keira's mother Sash to come past on the 32 bus on her way home to Colindale. She'll call when she's near so her mother and fifteen year old daughter can jump on with her. Suddenly, Keira sits up and her mouth opens. Pat doesn't notice, she is in full flow – the wee'uns were like sacrificial lambs, should never have let them on the field, none of them had played before and those other wee girls had been flicking hurleys since they were in the crib. Keira not listening. Ashley Barron has just walked past wearing black suede Puma Rihanna creepers. She grabs her phone to tell Angel and Blainey.

"Is that your mum?" Pat asks. Ashley knew Keira was getting creepers, and she's only had them a day. Literally one day. Eighty pounds they cost her, and now Ashley has exactly the same shoes.

"FFS. I bet her dad bought her them," Blainey tells her, throwing in some vomit emojis. Ashley Barron whose father lives in Qatar and guilt shops for his daughters while Keira used her own money, money she earned from service washes in the launderette her Auntie Sonia owns in Burnt

Oak. Suddenly the trainers she loved and which felt special seem ordinary, just another pair of shoes to walk through the piss, dog shit and spat out gum that litter every road that leads from Rose's café.

"You know Alban was only a Christian for a week?"

The swineherd lay next to his wife in the dark pre-dawn, unable to sleep. She murmured enough for him to continue. It was a story he had been told as a child on entering the abbey.

"Imagine an England with no believers. It was then that Alban lived in the old city that stood before Wæclingacaester. A good man, but pagan as all who dwelled in the land were in those days."

At some point she fell asleep, but he told the story anyway, sharing his pride that the saint's shrine was at "our abbey." He repeated the words in his head. It was no longer his, and had never been hers. He would never return and the loss quickened in him. His scriptorium. His writing desk. The cot where he lay alongside Ulfred and Cuthbert. The sonorous echo of voices through stone passages, gone. He looked at her but her eyes were closed, sensing none of his sadness. He spiralled between lost and broken, found and healed and remained awake as Godwyn's body rose and fell, her head against his shoulder, his breaths keeping time with hers. Having never felt less or lacking, he now felt whole, that this woman with all her complexity, virtue and transgression completed him. Forwards was the only way. Alban had been Christian for just a few days. The Benedictine had managed twenty three years. Maybe that would count for something at the reckoning. God may have abandoned him, but the woman clung to him as he clung to her. Unforgivable in his own eyes, there must have been some good still in him, or she would not have seen it. A

Westbound Jubilee Line train to Stanmore thunders over the spot where the tang of woodsmoke and the sleeper at his side lulled him. Nineteen-year-old Shakar Williams walking through the train's seven carriages shaking a paper cup, asking passengers if they can spare any change to get him into a night shelter. No shelter will feel as safe, no arms as loving, no bed as warm as the one in the hut by the Brent River where Godwyn slept.

His meal over, the clown steps back out onto the pavement, takes a yoyo from his pocket and lets it drop. The silicon ball falls and spins. With deft movements of his fingers, he creates a triangular window from which the whirling diabolo hangs. Ahmed Ibram, five, tugs on his mother Haneen's arm as they pass. She turns as the clown flicks back the yoyo and flings it above his head, kinking the string with a finger so the ball jerks back on itself, straddling the taut line and rolling towards him. The clown's hands move in a blur as others stop to watch, a crowd attracting a crowd, his hands forming an impossible cats' cradle as the red spinning ball hops over the wires. He throws the yoyo and catches it still spinning, then takes a second from his pocket, the two balls duelling as he dances. A coin falls his feet, and another. It takes more skill and practice, and there's a lot less money than a stabbing, but it kills time. In the moment when the yoyo remains static in space and he controls the strings and where and when they move, everything stops. He forgets in the same way methamphetamine or opioids numb his memory, and clarity comes. Three headless men played at the ball; one handless man served them all. One mouthless man stood and laughed as a cripple dragged his cloak. The baubles spin and flash at the end of their strings. Where was his king to bedazzle? His painted coach and four? Where was his monkey? A

Romanian delivery driver tosses a pound coin at the clown, bowing politely as he steps away. Ahmed Ibram asks his mother for a yoyo. The clown snatches both of his out of the air and thrusts them back into his pockets. The small crowd that stopped to admire the spectacle applauds and disperses, and Karl Epsen waiting in a white Transit for traffic to move honks his horn. A Boeing 757 from Gatwick bound for the Emirates adds its high-pitched scream to the mêlée, the jetstream scratching out one of the last remaining patches of blue in the sky. How long was the forest here before he first travelled it? he wonders. A thousand years? Ten? Before Roman cohorts beat a road though it with their picks and shovels, what had been its loudest sound? An oak falling? Thunder? A bear's roar? Silent centuries stretching unendingly back through time before he stepped off the road, saw two dark bewitching eyes, and fell.

Æthelred Unred, unready not from lack of forward planning but his failure to take wise counsel. His son, Ironside, indomitable, whose throne only deferred to the Danes because death met him before he could fully vanquish them. Cnut whose Vikings harried west, east, south and north wreaking terror on the land. Harefoot and Harthacnut who quarrelled over their father's realm, the saintly Confessor and Earl Harold who fell with his nation to the Conqueror. The Domesday count. Rufus, slain by a hunter's arrow and replaced by his brother Henry, a priory built on Godwyn's land. Stephen who fought his cousin Matilda to keep England's crown. The Angevins; Henry with his troublesome saint, the crusading Lionheart, reckless John who signed away his privilege at Runnymede. The child who ruled in the shadow of Pembroke and de Burgh, the first clearings made in the great forest. Earl Simon who helmed England until the blood heir, Edward slew him at

Evesham, a stone bridge built across the Cunebourne. Edward the son who ruled with his lover, de Gaveston; a single cottage on the High Road. Isabella and her worthless favourite who ruled for Edward's son, a boy whose own seed routed the French at Crécy with archers who knew him as the Black Prince. A mill turning on Shoot up Hill and a great pestilence which killed three of Canterbury's bishops within a twelvemonth. John of Gaunt ruling for the tyrant Richard until he came of age. Henry of Agincourt whose soldiers grieved his untimely death, and the infant son whose regent, Bedford burned the French saint Jeanne. The first flagon of ale sold at the Red Lion. Edward the usurper, thrust onto the throne by the kingmaker, Warwick; the hunchback brother who smothered his nephews; the Cock opening its doors on the western edge of the High Road and twenty houses lining the Kilburn street. The Tudor and his son, Bluff King Hal whose troops despoiled Kilburn's priory of both wealth and purpose. Edward. Lady Jane who fell to Bloody Mary, the Virgin who ruled England when the Old Bell was new. James then Charles, the Puritan protector and his hermit son; Charles then James. Hunters in the forest, the priory a crumbling ruin by a river, three pubs and a scattering of homes. William and Mary, Anne and four Georges, medicinal springs and pleasure gardens; a church and a village square. Victoria. Railways, the sale of estatelands, the spread of terrace and villa; light industry, schools, churches and temples; the influx of empire. From village to town, town to suburb. The lothario, Edward; theatres, cinemas and omnibuses; the George of the first war and the George of the second, between them the lovesick Edward who escaped both. Elizabeth of the IRA and the migrant hordes, the poverty and pools of piss, the internet cafes and chicken shops, the barbers and bookies, the filth and fumes and fucked fuckery of this unloved and unlovely quarter. Easter Saturday, that godless day. Look at the clown, knee deep in shit and still walking. He shakes his coat and coins rattle in his pocket. He looks up at the brick wall of an anodyne block of flats rising above the east side of the street. This was once shops. But he raged at the shops because they had been houses, at the houses as they had been paddock, at the paddock as it had been trees and at the trees because they closed in on him like a tunnel, an unending green prison, a gangplank with no darkness after the drop. He raged at himself for lighting the touch paper, tripping the wire, kicking the hornets' nest or whatever it was he did that spawned this beshitten corner of creation at which, even in his final hour, he still rages.

On granite slab, the skald bard Ottar scratched runes. Æthelred and his son Edmund had quarrelled over succession. The young price felt throneworthy, yet the old lion chose to rule on. With division in the English court, the time for invasion was opportune.

"Cnut, helmed one,

the ship batterer,

no king younger than he had ever cast off from his country,

hacking the hard-cased ships,

risking all as red shields raged along the shore."

On the beach near Cromer, a young boy saw a sail, then another. As the horizon filled, he ran to the priest's house. A bell rang and fire burst into life on Beacon Hill, an unending chain of bonfires north to Lincoln, south to Wæclingacaester and on to Lundenwic as people along the coastlands fled into the forests, burying their treasures as they ran.

The clown looks over to the east side of the street at the apartment block whose ground floor is a dance studio, closed for the holiday. Upstairs in a second storey flat, George Carmichael deals cards in a room thick with the fug of hand rolled cigarettes. Seven other men sit around a table covered in a blue cloth with an oval drawn around it by hand in chalk. Fifty pounds buy-in, two pound minimum bet, unlimited rebuys. Carmichael knows Wedgy and Charlie; Charlie's brought a couple of blokes from the depot and then there's Ashif and his brothers. He sets the pack in the centre of the table and burns a card, placing it face down next to the pile. The men look at what fate has dealt them and the bets begin. Wedgy is small blind and places a pound on the baize in front of him. Charlie pushes two pounds over the chalk line and the others around the table add theirs. The flop, George flipping two of the three cards over with the third like a croupier. Three of hearts, seven of clubs, king of diamonds. Nothing unless you already have a three, king, seven or some other pair. Wedgy folding, Carmichael telling him he could have checked. Charlie pushing in two more pounds. Black Ralph is in too. Scotch John folds. Ashif who lives in one of the flats downstairs upping the bet to four and his two brothers matching him.

"We got a cartel here?" Wedgy looking over at them.

"Play your hand, man," says Ashif.

Carmichael folds. Charlie puts in two more to match the brothers, Ralph folds. Four men in the game. Carmichael burns a card and turns over the fourth. Nine of clubs. Charlie tokes on a menthol, Ralph rolls one for himself. John cracks open a can of Carling. Charlie checks, Ashif playing another two pounds, matched by both his brothers.

"Fuck's sake. You can think for yourself boys."

Ralph not happy with the open brackets close brackets shit going on at the other end of the table. Charlie checking

261

his hand. King of spades and two of clubs. Best he can hope for is another king, or a two, three or seven so he has two pairs. Ashif must have something. Maybe two pairs already. He drinks from a can of Bulmer's and pushes two more pounds on the table. Fifty per cent chance. Or just under. Fifth card. Six of hearts. Charlie's heart sinks. Back to a pair of kings. He checks. Ashif checks. His brothers too.

"Well there's a fucking surprise," Ralph shaking his head.

"If you're not in the game, you shouldn't be commenting," George Carmichael says firmly. "Charlie?"

Charlie flips over his pair of kings. Ashif has nothing. A couple of twos. The brother next to him also has nothing, although he does have four clubs. The last brother has three threes. A set.

"Are you fucking kidding me?" Scotch John looking to George. "Three fucking musketeers, all for one and one for all?"

"Five of you three of us," says Ashif calmly as he pulls the coins down the table to his brother.

"George are you seeing this?" Ralph righteously annoyed at the cartel.

"Sorry boys, there's no rules against it."

Carmichael lights a slim Panetella as Wedgy shuffles and a brown skinned man named Sharzad stacks forty two pound coins in piles in front of him.

"John, Charlie, you in?"

Ralph wanting to beat the men at their game. Charlie shaking his head.

"How about I buy you a pint when I clean up?"

Ralph snorts and looks down the table. The men aren't even drinking. One of them has a can of Rubicon, and he hates them.

"Less talking more playing eh, fellas?"

Carmichael calling order as Wedgy deals. Outside, the clown looks up at the window. Every now and then he joins them, but only when the big money is in town. The message finds him and he pulls up a chair, knowing he can't lose; the poorer the cards, the keener he feels, emotion not something he takes for granted in a world to which he has become utterly desensitised. Having a Moroccan clear him out of a thousand pounds generates a high that no royal flush, no alleyway bunk up or even a knife's blade can match. To lose is to die, and he feels mortal.

Cnut's longboats surged towards the coast of Kent, sails fat with wind until the port of Sandwich hove into view. Skirting the sand and shingle spits in the bay, sails dropped and men wrestled with oars, steering their prows towards the mouth of the Stour where, four centuries earlier, Augustine too had landed. Flat hulls beached in the low tide as men swarmed over the sides, climbing hand over hand down knotted ropes into thigh deep water. Ten thousand harriers wading through slosh which, two years earlier, had witnessed horror. Cnut's father, Forkbeard had died and the young prince was sworn king of the Angles by the Witan. At Whitby, Cnut took two hundred men and women hostage; their safety guaranteed so long as English loyalty favoured him and not the coward Æthelred as king. When the treacherous English brought Æthelred back from France where he had fled from the Danes, Cnut raged. Loading their human cargo, Denmark's men thrust oars deep into the sea, driving their war boats down the coast at speed to Kent. Here, Cnut extracted bloody revenge; axes chopped at hostages' hands while iron knives sliced off noses and ears. Deaf to their piteous screams as English blood stained English stones, Cnut saw that revenge was done, and as he turned the Danish fleet back to Jomsborg, he vowed to return as king.

Today, there would be no fight, simply the rounding up of those animals which remained once the sighting of Cnut's sailtops had sent locals fleeing in blind terror. The only soul they met was an old woman in cloak and hood, wandering the shoreline near the river's mouth. The ancient begged for alms and when they asked her why she did not till the soil, she held out stumps where hands had been. Æthelred and his thanes had removed to Wessex, she told them; there was nothing to be won here in Kent, and none but the cripples who God had spared to show his great mercy. Cnut's ships did not remain in the bay for long, and the fleet hauled south, round the corner of Britain towards the setting sun.

The clown falls in behind the Greek Cypriot, Vasselis Diligiannis who is being pushed in an NHS wheelchair by his granddaughter, Alison past the Nisa Local supermarket and a Turkish Grill.

"This'll do Dede."

Diligiannis swearing in Greek.

"Oi Toúrkoi eínai gouroúnia!" The Turks are pigs. The old man still in the womb when his mother saw George I assassinated outside the White Tower in Thessaloniki, the anarchist Schinas shooting the king in the back at point blank range as he promenaded with his secretary, Frangoudis. The screams of passers-by, many who did not know their king was among them; Georgios shunning the presence of guards, allowing a couple of gendarmes to walk a short distance behind him. Men struggling to keep their horses still as others rushed to the fallen monarch who died instantly. Schinas hustled away to torture and death while Diligiannis' mother Maroussa felt the first of her birth pains, hurrying into a café on Pavlou Mela and crouching in the washrooms, flies buzzing around her in the stench of the squatting pans, a waitress running to fetch one of the few doctors nearby who wasn't tending to the dead king. A makeshift gurney in one of the booths and the life of a tiny boy, Vasselis after the Café Vasselis and Giorgios in honour of the king. One hundred and two years later, Vasselis' mind is still sharp. He needs a piss but he won't go into a Turkish café. Or if he did, he'd piss on the floor. Fucking Turks. The old man was already living in Shepherds Bush when the coup happened, the pigs invading and making their landgrab. Kristina turns the chair to face the Chinese restaurant.

"Speedy Noodles?"

"Chinks are better than Turks."

"You can't say that, Dede. And it's just a piss."

The old man beyond caring what anyone thinks.

"I say what I like."

"We'll go to Nando's" Kristina says, and pushes the chair past the giant Paddy Power on the corner of Buckley Road. Her phone rings and while she answers, the old man sees the clown and grins.

"Got any smokes, boss?"

The clown wiggles the fingers on both hands for effect then pulls a Benson from his sleeve. The old man cackles and coughs, catching the cigarette and stashing it in the folds of his blanket for later, winking as he rolls away.

A single decker 316 bus approaches the stop outside the bookmakers which dominates the corner, and Bernie McFadzean waits to climb on. Slightly built, clean shaven with mousy grey uncut hair, McFadzean is somewhere between sixty and seventy. His clothes are tatty; a threadbare grey suit jacket over a beige jumper and a shirt with a collar. Gas squeals out of the bus's airbrakes as people assemble near the door in a loose huddle. The clown remembers when people queued, when there were conductors who marshalled their passengers like troops, hanging off the corner pole at the back of red Routemasters. Now it's a scrum. The front door swings open for embarking and Abija Adebole, fifteen, hood up, jumps out as Harriet Estridge, sixty two jumps back in shock, staring in disgust at Adebole who saunters away, not caring at the indignation of white women. She shakes her head at people exiting through the wrong door and mutters something to the driver, a Ghanaian woman who stares ahead of her behind protective glass, neither engaging nor caring as others climb on, tapping plastic cards on a yellow pad by the driver's window. McFadzean shuffles with them but at the last moment turns away, as if this were the wrong bus, as if he'd made a mistake. But it's always the wrong bus. The clown has seen him fail to board a 189, a 414, a 332, a 16, a 245, a 266, a 260, and a 460 at every stop between here and Cricklewood Broadway, his pockets empty, another lost ghost in a century filled with them. McFadzean walks away, head jerking as he admonishes himself, the bus, the world. Not that anyone cares. Who makes a note of the lunatics and the lost? The paper people who flit and flap as the world rushes on, whose voices evaporate and whose shadows have more life than they do.

The swineherd and his bride lay under a wayfaring tree on a warm Sunday afternoon in late summer. On the branches above them, red necked swallows and sand martens prepared for their long journey south. At the foot of the tree, some traveller's joy had begun its own slow creep upwards, its spidery flowers a splash of white against the green.

"Where will our journey take us?" the swineherd asked; he who had never ventured north of Wæclingacaester nor south of Westminster. The birds above their heads would soon begin the first leg of a heroic voyage that would take them across the Channel to the maze of streets clustering around the Romanesque towers of old Notre-Dame. From here, they would fly to Rome, its Coliseum and Pantheon in ruins and the new city hugging its ancient and uncherished edifices. On across the Great Central Sea to Carthage at its southern shore, the once noble city now a sprawling ruin, its history forgotten by those who farmed around its ransacked temples and broken pillars. As the weeks passed, the swallows would fly south to Egypt, swooping over pyramids whose polished limestone patina had long since been stripped, landing on a minaret in the gleaming new city of Cairo. They would cross the great desert at night and see dawn breaking over the Songhai Empire, gliding on thermals through the dark heart of Africa. Resting on the branches of Kikula trees high above the Congo forest over a month after leaving England, they would prepare for their final descent to Great Zimbabwe, the fabulous city of gold whose temples worshipped the moon. A pale moon was already visible in the sky above where they lay.

"We are having a child."

His reverie broken, he turned to look at Godwyn. Smiling, she placed her hands on her belly.

"A child?"

"A child!"

So this would be their adventure. Embracing her, the swineherd covered her face in kisses as tears fell, and he adored her.

Next to the flats where Ashrif, Sharzad and Hamid Khan continue to divest George Carmichael and the others of

267

their money is a boarded up yard that will soon be the gated entry to portered apartments overlooking the park. The clown looks at the work in progress. Flats which, by some alchemic abracadabra and sleight of hand from the realtors will not be marketed as Kilburn, but the more salubrious West Hampstead. Kilburn too dreary, too impoverished, too clogged with fried chicken and betting shops, weighed down by Asian grocers and Irish pubs, held in a stranglehold by the ever present threat of switchblades, Mach 10s and house breakers; sirens rushing through like a shrill, urban Scirocco. Let these apartments fix their gaze towards West Hampstead, turning their backs on the strip of low rent shops that front the High Road, a permanent menacing din that no electronic wrought iron gates can possibly keep out. Unloved Kilburn, adrift on the far shore of cash-strapped Camden, the High Road forming its eastern border with Brent. Out of sight, an outlier left to rot, broken paving slabs patched with blacktop; a mattress left next to a council refuse bin and a KFC cup kicked along the pavement by a white-faced, green-haired clown.

The Benedictine had not travelled these roads until he was sent on his errand. He had no need. He walked the many lanes to and from the abbey, the Saxon city a honeycomb of streets within its defensive stockade; taverns, a mint and a bustling market place. Few travelled further than the farms that grew barley and hops and grazed cattle on land cleared by the ancient Britons under the guidance of their Roman overlords. Now, every stone, every spray canned wall, every flapping hoarding is logged; every mile trodden by his ancient feet. Monk. Swineherd. Huntsman. Jester, on his final journey north. Thomas MacHenry limps out of the bookies on the corner of Buckley Road and heads south towards the Kingdom. Sixty-six years old, a navvy from Sligo, his leg smashed when a crane cable snapped in the rush to finish the Jubilee Line in '77. MacHenry escaping the worst of it, but the pallet had bricks on, and enough of them dumped on him to cripple him. By then, he'd met Colleen who cut hair. Thomas MacHenry who lost his foreman's job because he failed a breath test, who drove bin lorries until they tested him again after a night in the Galtymore. Some painting and decorating, a few odd jobs for a couple of landlords; cash in hand and advances on work not yet done as he'd already drunk or gambled the money. McHenry ambling along, his pate polished red and his hair white. Once, a man in his forties was venerable. A man aged sixty was almost unheard of. For hundreds of years, most people the clown knew died in their thirties; there were almost none who were old. People lived to procreate and, if blessed, survived to see their grandchildren. The clown passes MacHenry, a man long past any usefulness, eager to drink his sick money in a joyless, windowless room. A grave on the man, pissing away the years God gave him in a porcelain urinal at the back of a pub. The undertaker's across the junction with Buckley Road has buried half of Kilburn, and men in black will come for MacHenry. A hurried eulogy. A wake in a dreary pub, thick cut sandwiches, pies; beer to toast the deceased, and done. The clown takes a cigarette from a pack with his teeth and lights it with one of the matches. Leaning against the window of the betting shop, he blows a smoke ring that rises and wavers before dissipating in the windrush of a passing Argos truck. He blows another. A brief flourish before the fade. Ilona Szabó looks over as she crosses the junction and sees a ring of smoke hover and then and evaporate above a clown's head. Hands thrust deep in his pockets, the clown begins to tap dance. Szabó smiles self-consciously, but rather than stop and watch the show, she walks on, taking out her phone to check things that don't need checking.

Fire beacons along the south coast tracked the Viking fleet as it passed into the Channel, Ironside's army shadowing the invaders. Finally, the great horde of Norsemen passed up the river Frome to Wareham, men delirious on hallucinogenic herbs and wrapped in animal skins, barely human, charging through the shallows with blind, ferocious rage. Later, Ottar who had sailed with them committed the invasion to verse:
"Cnut! Armour-clad
the sail stretched above you.
Great king,
bloodshedder, shield smasher.
You crashed forward onto the shingle.
See the ravenous Dane-king bravely batters with his blade English mailcoats."

As he dances, the clown's mind tries to unlock the riddle again. He has had almost six hundred years, years in which humans have walked on the moon, created vaccines and split atoms, and still the answer evades him. Who were the headless men who played at the ball? Not men, that was for sure. Pegs? Were they stumps? Or fingers? And the handless man? A clock might have no hands, so might an arm but what has arms but no hands? A chair and a shirt. What is the ball? Some fruit are round; a ball of wool – a head too is round like a ball. Might the ball be the head of one of the headless men? He wonders what has no mouth but laughs. Is it an echo? And the cripple who drags his cloak will be a bent or broken thing, its cloak perhaps a butterfly's wings. However many tricks he's learned, he feels a poor cousin to the riddler. However much he trains his hands and feet to obey his will, his mind remains dull. A few others stop to watch him dance, his body lifting and falling as his feet fly out in a rhythmic blur, transporting this unremarkable corner into something magical; a burst of choreographed colour that fades like a Roman candle as the clown stops, blows his nose with his fingers and continues along the road where Gaius Suetonius Paulinus defeated Boudica's Iceni when it was still a grassy track through the woods. Beneath his feet, should anyone care to remove the slabs outside the shabby internet cafe opposite the betting shop and excavate fifteen feet through the silt and shit and London clay; should they dig below the pipes and cables in the dark earth below the Saxon level, a thousand years below, under Roman slabs placed in the early centuries of the common era and into the ancient compacted mud, they might find the golden amulets and torcs of Britons who fell defending their island forest. On the paving stones high above, three pigeons peck at a thrown away punnet of chips, finding their own gold.

The clown does not remember his parents, nor the day he arrived at the abbey or who brought him. He did not know for certain that he was christened Wulfstan at birth, or that he was ever baptised. The Benedictines cared for him and taught him. Orphans and foundlings were not exempt from the rigours of the order, even at the tender age of seven, and throughout the remainder of his childhood, he rose for matins at midnight and lauds at three, standing in pitch darkness and mumbling words of cod Latin of which he understood nothing. A few hours' sleep until prime, the first service after sunrise. A reflection on Christ before the proconsul, Pilate which happened at around this hour. On this day as every one that followed it, the monks retired to the chapter house where they gathered in a circle around Abbot Leofstan. The abbot reading aloud the life of Mary as this was her saint's day, the pious elder quoting from St. Bede whose avowed belief it was that by meditating upon Christ's incarnation, devotion is kindled, and that by remembering the example of the Mother of God, the Christian is encouraged to lead a life of virtue. It being the first of the month, the day was known as calends, a vestige from the patricians who, when they were not building roads and villas or minting coins, liked to organise time. The clown remembers laundering undergarments in lye, his arms aching and his fingers red, though these early days blend and jump around when he tries to pin them down. At nine they broke for terce and contemplated both Pilate's judgement and the descent of the Holy Spirit at Pentecost, both believed to have taken place at around 9am. The child wrung sodden clothing until his forearms burned, and then sext, the noontide prayer where the brothers remembered Christ at his hour of crucifixion. A meal eaten in silence, plates to rinse and floors to scrub. The hour of three they called none, the ninth hour of the day at which time Christ gave up his Spirit; the monks gathering in solemn reflection as the Gospel account was recited in Latin. Once the clothes had been draped over ropes in the kitchen where an open fire slowly dried their fibres, he was ushered to vespers at which God was glorified for the created earth and all that it provided. At eight, the day died, and with it the brothers who saw sleep as a daily death to the temptations of the world beyond the abbey walls. This was the hour they called compline and, the toil of the day over, the boy took in his surroundings, the shapes each monk lent to the room, the tone of their voices, the aching, sleep-deprived fatigue of his own frame. These were his first memories. No mother, no father, no sister, no brother. He did not remember the hut in the dense weald, the mother who died the day she bore him as a solar storm turned English skies green and pink.

No memory of the charcoal burner who fathered him and struggled to feed and clothe his son or find a new wife to care for them, who walked into the woods one day and returned without him. The weaver's wife foraging for sticks who found the babe shivering in a hollow made from the raised roots of an oak, the infant clutching a small stylised wolf carved from bluejohn, and who named him after the pendant. A woman who did what she could for him until, on the first day of the second millennium, she laid him as Hannah had with Samuel at the steps of the great church.

The clown waits at the corner of Buckley Road, yet another smart street of tree lined terraces. Over on the east side of the High Road, a boarded up shop front next to the internet café and a Caribbean restaurant; satellite dishes affixed to the red Victorian bricks above. He's never travelled, but he's heard the stories. Yerevan with its Blue Mosque, the basilicas of old Jerusalem, the Tiger's Nest in Bhutan. Sacred Uluru, the ziggurat of Chichén Itzá and the mud minaret of Agadez. He met travellers who had seen the antiquities of Greece and Rome while they were the artefacts du jour; men who had marvelled at the temples of Petra and been becalmed in the Sargasso Sea. How many pilgrims to this infected rash of Brent borderland returned to Palermo, or Beijing, or the Dakotas with camera rolls filled with anodyne grocers, hair salons and pound stores? These aren't the colourful traders making up a lively medina. There is no history to them; instead they are artless shop fronts devoid of soul; conduits of joyless commerce that change with the calendar. Trash on the ground and in the gutters, the broken minded wandering aimlessly, pockets full of government money to spend on carbohydrate, sugar and fat. The clown looks around. A man with a NHS crutch leans against the bus shelter outside the bookmakers, his

273

drawstring tracksuit pants pulled up around his great, white t-shirted belly. He spits a bolus in the direction of the shops and it smacks against the window of a passing black cab and dribbles down the pane. The passenger, a woman in her mid-sixties looks up, horrified. At least she can escape. He farts and flaps the skirts of his coat in her direction.

Across Buckley Road, past the undertakers, past another Asian grocer's and a shop where zero hours contractors from whichever diaspora spawned them wire money home, Dean Sefton waits at the counter of the pharmacy, still wearing his ring. A whole year since Alyssia left, but he just can't slip it off, even now she's driven herself and everything she owns to Mansfield. And the more he delays divorce, the more she hates him. Sefton an optimist. A romantic. A husband who said "I do" and meant it, who loves his wife. A dad whose grown-up children still live in their three bedroomed villa near the pocket park on Streatley Road, and who still reaches out an arm every morning as he wakes in case she is there. Sinusitis. Sefton's face aching from his ear to his eye socket to his jaw. Unbelievable the pain. You get run down and the bugs creep in, and next thing you know you're waiting for a small, bespectacled Indian woman to hand you a white paper bag containing Flonase and some antibiotics.

"Mr Sefton?" the woman asks, even though he was the only one in the shop when he handed her the prescription from Dr Ashkar, and no one has been in since. The woman explaining the dosage, Sefton grabbing the bag, almost glad to have a new focus, to make selling the house, figuring out where Evan and Kate are going to live and how he'll pay for everything secondary priorities.

"Don't take tablets on an empty stomach," the woman warns and suddenly, he pities her; the white coat she is wearing, the formality in this otherwise empty drugstore set amongst the internet cafés and betting shops, a tide of filth shoring up against the metal shutters every night. The shutters of his heart lock just as tightly, and whatever brickbats the legal shitshow throws at him are left in a heap at his own door to be dealt with later. Sefton walks out of the shop and almost collides with a clown who wears no ring, has no marital trauma nor any disease, just a centuries old fury, an eternal flame in the hypocaust of his soul that fired into life the day he failed to reach his screaming, birthtorn woman; every blighted building, every broken life, every discarded beer can, cigarette butt, jet of vomit and car horn adding timber to the furnace. The clown neatly sidesteps Dean Sefton and the mess of another man's tragedy, and walks slowly on to his own reckoning.

By September, the pigs were as fat as they needed to be; keeping them alive any longer was wasteful unless a sow or boar was needed for breeding. Vast as the forest was, coppicing had created its own hedges, a natural barrier through which the pigs could not pass. The slaughterman came at the beginning of the month and most of the workers spent their day rounding up the animals with sticks, careful not to panic them, prodding them enough so that they knew to move. The swineherd followed the others, his first slaughter, Godwyn followed behind with the other women, the two of them apart but part of something, accepted. Children joined in the chase, squealing as the animals fled through the trees. Once they had separated a sow from the herd, they closed in on her, cutting off her retreat and driving her towards the pen – a few crude posts hammered into the ground with hazel poles placed lengthways. Corralled, the terrified beast bucked her head but the slaughterman was swift. Grabbing her round the shoulders, he pressed her down with his whole weight, drawing a blade quickly across her throat. She fell and he lay with her, still, as a woman placed a bowl beneath the wound. The blood filled it slowly, too precious a sacrament to waste. Later, the women would steep it in oatmeal then wrap it in gut to make sausage. A wooden sledge was brought, four men lifting the great carcass on to it and dragging it to a nearby fire where they singed away the hair. Once the pig had been hauled to the manor kitchen to be scrubbed and butchered, the swineherd headed back into the woods with the others to track down another animal too old or too weak to live another winter.

Death. The clown tries to imagine it without God. Shoah. The pit. The grave. The place of the dead in Hebrew Scripture. Darkness and gnashing of teeth; punishment and woe, grief and despair. Then the Greek Testament; my father's house has many rooms. A heavenly host. Eternal life to the elect, a lake of sulphur and fire for the lost and casting into the sea with a millstone for all who cause a little one to turn away.

Ten centuries of rebellion come at a price. The day he stepped off the road, raised fists to another and followed through his carnal lusts with a penitent by an idyllic stream, he damned himself, and her. Smashing each of the sacred ten edicts chiselled on Sinai stone, he was the sinner of sinners. He the arch adulterer. Coveting what was God's, he stole it. How was his pretence at holy orders not taking that blessed name in vain? Now he placed Godwyn as his god, the one pure good that had never failed him. Five commandments broken already. Godwyn's vows stolen, her sacred pledge. Six. Murderer, he had killed the saint she was, and the anchorite he had been, seven. Every Sabbath was now desecrated as each day is like the hundreds of thousands preceding it. Eight. The name of his blood parents dishonoured by the godlessness of their child. Nine. He, the ultimate false witness, ten out of ten. Sabbath breaker, prodigal, adulterer and idol maker, God denier, coveter and blasphemer; liar, killer, thief. He will walk to the end of the road and keep walking to the end of days where unquenchable fire rages; he will burn and keep burning. As for redemption, that ship sailed when he made his choice. "I stand at the door and knock," says the Lord, but the clown can't hear the knock. How can he? He doesn't have a door.

Even two hundred and fifty years ago, there was no settlement to speak of here. Crops were too seasonal for workers to settle, and the views too poor and plain for the upper classes. Only a scattering of houses and a few cottages tailed along the road around which Kilburn now sprawls. A tollhouse took money, a smithy shod horses and the four taverns afforded travellers some basic rest as they approached the city. It was around this time that Turpin rode through on his journey to York. It was night, and the clown was asleep beneath the ancient wall of St. Albans, otherwise he might have seen the man, cloak flapping in his slipstream. If it ever happened. He observed plenty of robberies on the road and saw glory in none of them. Armed gangs on horseback hiding just out of sight; cowards who terrified coachmen with sudden violence, robbing their victims with dispassionate efficacy. There was no romance in any of it, and those writers who attached any were fantasists who had never been held at the point of a flintlock. Worse were the footpads, thugs who sprang out at carriages sometimes twenty strong, most armed and unafraid to shoot. Lowlife brigands who lived to drink and brawl and rob, most of whom ended up hanging from the tree at Tyburn, five at a time before they were thirty. Close to this spot, he watched a brazen band of robbers hold up a stage in the middle of the afternoon. The men were skinny and ragged with a pair of pistols between them, a confederacy of thieves who planned to divide the spoils. The coachman cracked his whip at one of the gunmen, the fortuitous cord wrapping round his thighs, felling him, the man yelping on the ground as his cohorts stepped back. A pistol fired but missed its mark, the bullet boring a hole in an elm. A passenger leant out of the carriage with his own gun, took aim and shot his would-be attacker in the shoulder, incapacitating him. The man felled by the whip tried desperately to reload his gun, but by now, the passenger was on top of him, pointing a silver pistol at his head. Now without any armed advantage and despite outnumbering their victims five to one, if you include the gentleman's wife who was curled up on the carriage floor praying; the rest of the band fled into the woods. While the captured footpad was ordered to lie face down on the ground, the coachman grabbed the gun from the man's injured companion and began trussing up the bandits with the help of his passenger, a master mason. Many words were spoken between the four; the attackers now victims and their intended dupes now their masters. Once the robbers were face down in the dirt, hands tied behind their backs, the mason nodded at the coachman who took out his whip again and let rip fifteen or twenty cracks on the men until his face was red and his strength gone. The clown remembers the shrieks and wails, the coachman kicking the men's raw and bloodied bodies to the roadside where they would either die or wriggle free and plan the next chapter in their short and sordid lives.

On his way back from the forest, the swineherd looked in on the wooden shelters topped with branches and birch bark that served as a milking shed. Godwyn was sitting on a sawn log, easing milk from the teat of a patient goat into a pail. She smiled at him. He emptied a bag at her feet: wood mushrooms, thick white stalks and bulbous heads which they could roast later. A child ran from the direction of the village, a red-faced girl of around eleven.

"The Danes have landed!" She caught her breath. "Two hundred ships off the coast of Wessex. Ironside is battling him." Wessex then, not Kent or Lundenwic. Augustine's book long gone from his possession but safe for now. Milk continued squirting into the pail. The swineherd gathered up the mushrooms as the child ran off to tell the woodsmen, the miller and anyone she met on the road that Cnut and his horde of berserkers were coming to feed them to the wolves and the birds.

To the clown's knowledge, the first Baron Clyde never drank in Kilburn; he was rarely in the country. A gun for hire after his exploits on the Peninsular, Sir Colin Campbell saw action in China, the Punjab, Balaclava and Lucknow. Victoria called him her Scottish Lion and relaxed among the pear trees of Osborne House or strolled along the Dee at Balmoral while the rifle butts of Sir Colin's infantry smashed the skulls of Sikhs, Russians and Chinamen. The clown waits for a silver Ford Focus and unemployed Alastair Munroe on a tatty twenty-five-year-old bicycle to pass before crossing the street and walking into the pub that bears the baron's name. The whitewashed three storey tavern which has only stood on the High Road for a century or so is empty save for a single lost saint staring at the bar. Wooden chairs and tables, a tricolour; dark green beer-soiled carpet and the walls an unspeakable orange. A cave. The clown pulls up a stool and an Irishman from Mayo pours a Three Barrels neat into a tumbler. The clown swills the liquor around his tongue, letting it burn the inside of his cheeks before swallowing while the bartender stands, sleeves rolled up, both hands on the counter where a copy of the *Daily Mail* lies open. Momentary absolution. A barely audible TV screen plays Setanta Sports, otherwise silence. The clown leans over to his fellow drinker, a thickset man with bushy red brows and a red, inexpressive face, and whispers in his ear. The man's eyes widen and his mouth turns into a slow grin. He nods and as the clown turns back to his drink, the man takes out an old Nokia cell phone and begins tapping it with fingers caked in London clay.

The clown steps out of the pub and looks at the building dominating the west side of the street. Where the Ancient Order of Foresters built their hall almost a century ago is now a theatre. Ancient! The building is barely as old as the pub, and the order itself a nineteenth century whimsy. The clown has no idea who these foresters were; fantasists who concocted their club, built a home in Kilburn from which to carry out their do-gooding and who bore no relation to the husbanders who once managed the weald. But until they turned it into a playhouse, this was one of the few reminders to the casual pilgrim that the land upon which they trod was once trees. Abbey Road and Kilburn Priory told of the church. Springfield Lane and Wells Court of the sacred waters. Reminders, faint as they were, of woods, a river, and a green glade where a blessed paraclete interceded by a sacred brook.

A bull, wide eyed with terror, burst through the briar hedge of the Harrier's Field west of the town where Ironside camped with his sleeping army. As the English slumbered, ships beyond number glided up the River Frome, dawn sun glinting off ten thousand helmets.

Unaware of the exact nature of the fight that awaited him at so early an hour, Ironside rallied his sluggish nobles. These commandeered their barely woken men into a warhedge; young soldiers clad head to knee in suits of ringed mail, their shields overlapping five hundred shoulder widths wide on the banks of the river, spears pointing towards the enemy. Behind them, the second rank, four thousand strong; a rabble of untrained men corralled by their chieftains, some with spear or battle axe in hand; others with bows of yew, ash or elm, iron tipped arrows pulled taut. At the rear, Ironside and his nobles surrounded by a guard of housecarls, invisible. In the nearby woods, horses tethered to young saplings stood ready to help the English commanders flee, or ride away in triumph. A single yell from Ælfwold, a sturdy blacksmith with a long red plait and a scarred and crooked jaw, an axe that came too close as he defended Lundenwic against Forkbeard the day the bridge fell. English warriors had repelled the invaders before and they would again. Ælfwold's shout meeting with others as Ironside's soldiers began jeering at the Norsemen who dared to threaten Wessex, blood and courage rising with the volume of the Saxon war cry. But then the sight of the ten thousand, the Viking shieldwall moving inexorably towards them at the head of a force so ferocious and vast that the land seethed with them; men blanketing the fields as far as the river. This was no army or navy, more a herd, a locust swarm. The men would engulf them, walk over them and continue moving until the entire land was scourged; not even the trees could stand against them. As the invaders moved ever closer, some of Ironside's men involuntarily evacuated; the huddle of men behind shields reeking of shit and piss. England's army found itself rooted to the Wessex earth as Cnut's men bellowed like a human thunderclap, many warriors foregoing any armour and cladding themselves instead with animal hides, fearless in the certainty that Odin and his war maidens rode with them. Despite its terror, the warhedge holding firm. A loose volley of English arrows and spears failing to dent the relentless advance as the Danish line narrowed into a wedge to penetrate the English wall, Cnut's entire army forming a single determined spearhead. Chaos among Ironside's men; shouts, the metallic clash of swords and then the grunts and gasps of the fight, only the cries of the fallen interrupting the almost silent exertion of battle. Slowly, the enemy trampled through the Harrier's Field leaving dead in their thousands, Ironside fleeing on his mare as warriors from across the North Sea rounded up every woman, child, sheep, goat and cow from the villages through which they passed. By evening, flames tore into wattle walls and straw rooves, colouring the night as orange as the dawn. In the words of Ottar:

"Great commander of the wind,
Widowbane,
Cnut the young prince.
Thunder filled white wings
through the sealanes.
Wareham woke to terror
as Norseblades fell,
Ironside no match for the seastained travellers
and the bloodbird fed."

Claire Murphy stands in the doorway of the unisex hair salon with her eleven year old grandson, Damon. The boy needs his hair cutting and here's as good as any. Ten pounds, and its close by. Damon squashes a discarded cigarette with the toe of his trainer, smearing brown weeds of tobacco over the pavement and shredding the foam fibres of the butt. Claire is chatting to Noleen who she's not seen since Ellie's christening three years ago. Damon is her daughter's boy, a quiet child, more inside himself than out, who rarely speaks. She misses her granddaughters, Chloe and Ellie but Martin married an American.

"She'll take you away to New York City" Claire told him. "And what happened? The wee'un was only two and just starting to chat and the big girl five and doing her ballet classes and gym."

"It won't be forever mam," he told her, "we'll just see how it goes." Claire begins to tear up and Noleen finds a tissue in her bag. Teary Clairey. That's what Damon's dad calls his mother-in-law, and the lad looks at his nan welling up again. He begins eviscerating the stub of a roll-up but the skinny roach makes for a less satisfying project. Amanda works for Louis Vuitton in New York and always brings Claire a purse or a beany for Brian when she visits, Claire showing them to everyone, letting them know that these aren't cheap knock-offs, they're the real thing, hating her daughter-in-law for taking her son and his family away, and loving her for what she brings home. As Claire dries her eyes and Noleen listens, the clown positions a can of Strongbow between his toe and heel, flicks it above his head, catches it on his knee then bounces it to the other knee before kicking it in a high arc out into the street where it lands in the flatbed of a passing dropside Transit belonging to a team of Polish landscape gardeners. Damon stares wide eyed at the spectacle, and looks to the two women to see if they saw it too. They continue chatting about his Auntie Amanda, oblivious.

Before the Brothers Grimm journeyed through their own forest, before they penetrated deep into the German urwald, knocked at the door of every woodcutter's hut and listened to the ancient tales; before a princess pricked her finger on a needle and a century of thorns engulfed her palace; before a red caped child took a basket of cakes to her grandmother, he lived. Before the catechisms and confessions of the Catholic church, the Saxon tales held firm. He believed what he was told; there were goblins and dragons, green men roamed the forest and it was ogres and giants, not glaciers or wind who shaped the land. When he arrived at the abbey, it was God who had created the heavens and the earth but there were sprites and fairies if you looked hard enough. The devil still rides these roads, the same demon who tricked Rotkäppchen, but at least she had the freedom to leave the path. He remains bound to it. No wolf can tempt him to his doom, he is the wolf, has always been the wolf, the rotting apple in the sack, the dark space at the edge of the story.

Bradley Simmons waits at the bar of the Black Lion, a giant Victorian arts and crafts ale house with ceramic tiled floor, etched glass windows, and ornate plasterwork on the high ceilings. They began building the original pub in the year of the great fire. The pestilent city had buried its dead the previous year and the clown passed workmen on the High Road, leaning on their adzes and staring at a great pall rising to the south. As he neared London, carts and people on foot passed him, parents holding babies, a pathetic mass clutching what they could in order to rescue it from the flames. On he walked as the air grew unnaturally hot; dense with the stench of burned timber, boiling slurry and molten lead. At the river, overladen lighters moved steadily, west to

Barking or east to Tilbury and the sea. At Westminster, few remained, the clerics and scholars having fled and only a handful of supernumeraries left to beat away the flames should the wind fan them this far west. Even at a distance, the heat reddened his face under the greasepaint and he watched a wall of flame tear into the old church at Temple. Beyond, towering tongues of fire wrestled above the spire of Old St Paul's and every now and again the crash of timbers and roof tiles interrupted the fire's low roar. An explosion to the east, small posses of men blowing up homes, inns, shops and churches to create firebreaks; the streets all but empty. A lone figure, hopped slowly, one legged, hood up against the thick brown miasma, his arm extended for assistance; a cripple looking in appalled horror at the jester, for it was clearly a jester, walking, duty bound, deeper into the path of the inferno.

Long before it became a gastropub for the middle classes of northwest London, or its seventies heyday as a spit and sawdust tavern for fighting Irish, the Black Lion was still a lively place. A dandy called Jellicoe drank Madeira from a conch and a Covent Garden opera singer who loved sherry sang impromptu arias. Oscar Wilde drank here and the philandering son of Victoria sat in a corner with Lily Langtree and introduced himself as Baxter. Bradley Simmonds who has never given in to an impulsive oration nor drunk fortified wine from a shell waits as the young Estonian woman behind the curved wooden bar pulls a pint of Peroni from giant copper taps. She has already poured a glass of Chardonnay for Soph and apple juices for Rosie and Zach. Salmon linguini, roast cod and a couple of children's bologneses are on the way. The clown watches from outside. Once, a man could get killed here but as with anything true, real and good, they fucked it up. Simmonds brings the drinks over to Soph who reads the *Observer* while their children sit on cushions in the corner, colouring pictures on their own paper menus. Simmonds, tanned from a recent shoot in South Africa, the rolling green of the Dolphin Coast doubling as Home Counties England. Two weeks in the Oyster Box in Durban while they began post production on a commercial for a sugared breakfast cereal masquerading as health food. Simmonds calm and assured, a man who gets things done, who people trust, who Soph trusts; a lothario who removes his wedding ring as soon as he boards the plane because what happens on location stays there. Soph reads a piece about Kim Kardashian's lavish Bel-Air baby shower, her disapproval rising, these *nouveau* nobodies with their ridiculously named progeny, as if she herself is a better, wiser human; a woman whose accomplishments are more earned, who has no idea of the philanderer with whom she shares a bed or the impending firestorm of their own that no charm offensive, no water cannon of apology nor contrition will ever quench. The clown looks as Simmonds brings drinks to the table with a smile as fake as his fidelity and considers taking a piss in a corner of the bar like he might have done a century or so earlier. It's too much effort and he walks on.

The swineherd emerged from the forest with firewood, a short axe, and a skin which he had filled with bilberries. When he reached the palings that skirted the village, the crooked and toothless Alcuin pulled open the gate and he nodded his thanks. Two children, the sons of the miller ran up to him, red faced and breathless.

"The bishop is here," they blurted and began dragging him with them but he shook himself free; he had no business with a bishop and hung back. To his right was a curved grassy embankment topped with another fence; a crude defensive earthwork for the village within. The children ran on ahead, thrilled that an eminent stranger had blessed them with his regal presence. A narrow mud-compacted lane ran between the earthwork and the outer perimeter, climbing a slight gradient to a second gate that led into the village proper. Here, a tall, square, half-timbered manor circled by its own fence sat apart from the other houses. Two white horses tethered to a post stood patiently; a young man with the brown habit and tonsure of the Benedictines waiting with them. An old woman, Æthelflæd hobbled over to the swineherd; the men who were in with the lord had spoken to her, asking her if they had seen a hermit girl.

"If she was living among us here, she'd be a pretty sorry hermit!" she laughed.

The swineherd nodded, but his heart sank. Few women were as distinctive to look at as Godwyn, and the steward knew that the two incomers had once had a religious calling. He left his pile of logs at the smithy and hurried back through the woods to the hut by the Brent River. It was early November, four months since they had fled. The russet leaves of the forest had yet to fall and many boughs were still green. Godwyn was inside knitting and said nothing as he entered, bone needles working quickly, agitating the wool as much as guiding it into loops and knots. Seeing her safe, the swineherd walked back to the village where men had gathered to discuss the lost hermit. Had she been killed? Abducted? No one appeared to know that the woman they were looking for had the distinctive complexion of a Moroccan Berber, and none guessed that she might have been ruined by the man who now looked after their pigs, or that he too had once been a cleric. He had taken care to shave his tonsure as soon as he arrived in Willesden so as not to rouse suspicion, and how his gair grew in thick brown curls, making him indistinguishable from any other labourer. A man who had fought with Æthelred and had lost one of his hands suggested that the girl might have been a daughter of the royal family, and that this was why the men were looking for her. As more people gathered by the small patch of green where hens pecked for worms and grubs, the great door to the manor house opened and the lord and his steward walked out, accompanied by two clerics. One the swineherd didn't know, but the man wore a fine mantle and leather cap and might well have been a bishop. The other was unmistakable; Ælfwig, abbot of Westminster and custodian of Augustine's codex. The swineherd retreated to the back of the group of onlookers and pulled his hood over his head. Later, he learned the nature of the conference from the lord's steward. The men were indeed looking for Godwyn, though none here knew the peasant girl who milked their animals by this name, she was Edith, just as he was now Athelwold. The lord had offered to round up the womenfolk and have the cleric identify his lost saint, but Ælfwig had never seen the girl. None of them had, she had come from the abbey at Barking. None suspected that the swineherd's wife whose belly swelled with their first child had once taken holy orders, could read and write Latin and even spoke a few words of French. The steward looked the swineherd in the eye.

"You are good workers" he said. "What needs not be known need not be known."

There was more news. Wessex had submitted to Cnut. The traitor Streona had abandoned Æthelred, handing a fleet of forty English ships to the Danish prince. Cnut's warriors were now striding east into Mercia, their war axes red with the blood of England's fallen.

"Have men at the gates," the clerics had warned. "Bury your gold."

The swineherd returned to the hut and settled next to his wife. A small fire threw quick shadows across her face.

"Have they gone?" she asked. He nodded and watched her fingers work the wool. "Should we move on?"

He shook his head. That would arouse suspicion. Here, they were two honest labourers. They had arrived together as man and wife in the summer, and the lord was pleased with their work. No one guessed their story or what had happened at the Cunebourne shrine, and only the steward knew of their former vocation.

"We stay here," he told her. "This is our home."

The clown steps away from the pub. At least it's daylight. His journeying doesn't stop when darkness falls, and much of his to and fro has been through the dusk and into the night. These days, there is no night; the orange phosphorescence of streetlamps, the glare of headlights and yellow-lit windowpanes illuminating the dark earth and throwing up a dull brown fog that kills stars and keeps the city in gloaming until the sun rises. But when he first walked these roads in the days after the vernal equinox, night clung to them for twelve hours or more. If there were no clouds, even a crescent moon threw down a measure light by which to see, stars adding their own faint illumination. Should cloud hug the forest, his eyes adapted, making out the shapes where tree tops met the sky, but the going was slower even though he knew the road. Mercifully, the path was straight but no lights from buildings beckoned, for any cottars on his route were in bed by nightfall and rose with the sun. The only towns of any size were at the extremity of his journey, and the fires burning there some thirty miles apart. For centuries. By the time of the Plantagenet, the forest had been partly cleared and there was an abbey at Kilburn whose thin windows flickered with the candlelit compline, midnight office, matins and prime, the last human-made light in those early hours until the abbey at Westminster or the torches at the gates of St. Albans. He took with him a staff and a tinderbox and with these two, he strode between his two poles, curling up in his cloak in the porch of St Stephen's on the edge of Wæclingacaester or in the sheds on the banks of the Tybourne. Centuries of nothing and no one; he may as well have been trekking the Arctic wastes or the Arabian sands; a purposeless pilgrim, killing time because time refused to kill him. If he fell, he thanked the rock that tripped him. If a wolf howled, he welcomed the attack. If lightning raged in the forest, he urged the struck timber to topple on him. The monotony, the endless north and south through the great wood; the long, lightless nights; a thousand years of failure, of not forgetting and not wanting to forget; each day another lash, each night over too soon, serving up another day on the torturer's wheel.

Once the fattened hogs had been slaughtered, preparation for winter continued with the cull of any ailing or elderly livestock that might not make it through the months of frost. In the monastery, meat had been scarce; maybe an occasional squirrel, fish or fowl, slaughtered by a lay brother; it's skinned or defeathered cadaver tied with others to a pole then brought in to be cooked on the fire. The deathblow happening out of sight, an invisible knife or a twist of the wrist, but now he witnessed slaughter first-hand; the fear of the animal, the sudden panic, the kicking legs, the mess of it all and the charged moment when a life is taken. Later, when he hunted game, he prided himself on a clean kill, to never leave his prey like the nanny goat that wouldn't die, though its throat was slit, a rough-handed butcher stabbing her, the terrified bleating, the knife going in so deep that the man was punching her and none knew whether her twitching legs were from the force of his blows or because her heart still beat and her brain still sent messages to her legs to run. The pigs were hung in the rafters above a fire in the manor house to cure before being cooked in sausages and pies, some of the offal making its way to his own table.

Outside the modern, redbrick monolith that is Kilburn Medical Centre, Blessing Gyaman gesticulates her anger at her son's wife to Arnie Peaseman who she knows from church; her rage so voluble that it carries across four lanes of traffic to the eastern side of the street where the clown listens. The whore who Edison married has been sleeping with his best friend, and still he won't throw her out. Gyaman's finger jabbing at Peaseman as she shares what she would like to say to the daughter-in-law who assumes that it will be she who keeps the children should anything happen to their marriage, Gyaman wanting to take them herself, telling Peaseman how her son has been brainwashed by the woman; Blessing Gyaman's voice rising to a shrill pitch that causes passers-by to stop. Arnie Peaseman's toes clench in his trainers in case strangers think that he and Blessing are a couple, and that it is he who she is angry with, when he was only on his way up to Argos to buy a duvet cover. Gyaman oblivious to the looks cast their way, simply needing to vent and Arnie a pair of ears and a nodding head, though it might as well be anyone who knows Edison's situation, that Belinda is a harlot, a mendacious wife, a reckless and negligent mother or, to use Blessing Gyaman's words, a complete fucking bitch.

At least Gyaman has some fire in her. The clown breathes the same air into lungs that first drew breath when Æthelred was king. He longs for the keen cuts and heavy blows of a mortal span, even for a son with a whore for a wife; to genuinely feel care or concern, to believe that anything matters. He deserves this. A coward, an unman. A gap in buildings here on the east side of the street leads to a park whose cropped lawns he has never trodden and never will, a wide expanse of mown green where the coachmaker's house once stood. The clown turns and walks determinedly towards it, away from the road, away from a millennium of slavery to the mindless back and forth with no reason and no resolution, a human being reduced to a senseless drone. Away from chicken shop and barbershop and Middle Eastern grocery, away, away. He walks on, almost to prove a point, like a man whose bank card has been blocked but who keeps slotting it into the ATM; onwards until he evaporates from view, flung back to where he began on the cracked and gumstained slabs that serve as his rails, propelling him north until his worthless life finally runs out of road.

A century ago, Norman's Dining Rooms served quality fare to shoppers who saw Kilburn as a destination, a flourishing high street with over three hundred stores selling everything from bicycles to pianos, top hats to hearth rugs; and thousands of hungry shoppers needing victuals. Six pennies for a pie and two for a fin de siècle teacake. Excited chatter, ringing tills and the buzz of commerce. Shopgirls in white starch aprons, the shouts of cabmen, children criss-crossing the street on errands, the snorts of horses. A golden age perhaps, but life still grindingly short, pain untreated, housing squalid, crime undetected and the stench. And today, a blur of cafes, kebab shops and nail bars. Temporary tenants; retail outlets filling space, landlords taking money from the optimistic and the desperate who hope custom will find its way to them, who last a season then fail, the city moving on without them. He won't miss it. Not a piece of it. If he could take this irredeemable, irreparable, unsalvageable shitfest to hell with him, he would.

In mid-December, the steward of the manor sent messengers to all who worked in the fields and woods owned by the lord. They were permitted to keep twelve nights' dung at Christmas for their fires and their gardens, as well as milk from the seven days that followed. There were also to be twelve days of feasting to mark the festival, and on the final day, after the nobles and their wives had departed, it was the turn of the villeins, serfs and cottars to feast, though only the men; the woman would wait on them and eat later. The swineherd and his wife fasted the day before as was the custom, and entered the great hall of the manor to be greeted by a large fire, smoke disappearing into the gloom through a hole in the thatch. The musicians and dancers who had serenaded the bishop and other guests on previous days were gone and the food too was more in the spirit of leftovers than royal banquet. Even so, it was a spread such as the swineherd had never seen, having spent his youth in the austerity of holy orders. The walls hung with embroideries and cloths covered the tables. A half-eaten cow roasted on a spit above the fire, food was plentiful and horns were kept filled with wine. He ate beef from a wooden platter and cut into fowl pies hungrily. The steward recited an old poem and the men drank to the longer days and the slow greening of the forest. The swineherd watched Godwyn as she walked behind the benches which had been ranged in a square around the fire. Her face glowed pink and she looked at him as she poured wine into the cups. Fate had thrown them together but for what? Was the new which he had gained of greater value than the old he had lost? She was behind him now, filling his wooden beaker with ale, her bosom against his shoulder, her breath on his face.

"I love you" she whispered, and moved on around the table. He stared at the half-chewed ribs on his board. The year had begun in peacetime, in the dormitory of the monastery in which he had taken a vow of celibacy. Now within a twelvemonth, he was to be a father. Godwyn looked over at him again and smiled. The joy. The terrible, unutterable joy.

"With bloodsword, the Danekerl slew Wessex.
Fork tongued, the traitor Eadric
flew to Cnut's side.
Eadric, shipbringer,
betraying for a seat at the Viking feast,
England's king bitten by his own serpent.
See how the gods have given victory to the Danes.
Even English dogs follow them!"
Words from Ottar, chiselled into a runestone near Calne, now buried beneath an Asda carpark.

Five feet eleven; a healthy height for an eleventh century Anglo Saxon. Under the army great coat, a linen drawstring shirt, provenance unknown. Dun-coloured moleskin trousers hitched with a leather belt, steel capped black boots from a dead labourer, green hair gelled into spikes and white face paint. Born to peasants in around AD990 in woods near Wæclingacaester, found as an infant by a weaver's wife, abandoned at the abbey of St. Alban in 1000 and raised in the Benedictine tradition. A scribe, an expert in lettering entrusted to carry Augustine's Bible to Westminster to protect it from Cnut's Vikings. A monk who strayed from the path, intervened in the attack on a virtuous recluse then ruined her himself. An expectant father murdered, saved and cursed on the same day in the Spring of 1016. A liver of lifetimes, a perpetual pilgrim, a hollow casing for a calcified soul walking north on broken streets on the last day of the one thousand and twenty sixth year of his life. Outside the African restaurant on the east side of Kilburn High Road, green bags filled with trash huddle around a pole bearing information for drivers wishing to park, trash dumped by one of the tired looking concerns nearby, their waste now someone else's problem. Passers-by have adorned the tops of the refuse sacks with drinks cans, takeaway coffee cups and empty packs of cigarettes. Two days ago, it was the celebration of the angel's visit to Mary. Fear not, for thou hast found favour with God. Oh to be favoured. Lady Day, the first day of the year in the old calendar, when daffodils and crocuses sprouted in clumps by the way, violets and celandine clustered among oak roots and hedge sparrows flirted. Creation crawling out of its long sleep, a warming sun wiping the last of the frosts from the fields, moles throwing up brown barrows as they cleared their runs, pussy willow and catkins on the trees and piglets suckling in a row. The clown breathes in. Only the pink and white blossoms to mark the fresh year; nature now banished from this squalid quarter, its woods and fields given over to dreary commerce. Most of the traffic passing through is on its way to the rolling hills of Hertfordshire and Buckinghamshire to the north, or the opulence and decadence of the city, stopping only because accident or emergency demands it. The skin beneath his right eye twitches. He needs caffeine.

Some three centuries after his fall, a hunter approached St. Stephen's, the last church before the ancient trackway passed through the gates of St. Albans. The building was barely a century old, and like the abbey, many of its flints and bricks had been salvaged from the ruins of the Roman city. Though the woods were sparsely populated, his journey took him through a number of small settlements and isolated clearings, and on this particular day, people seemed to be grieving. He assumed the beloved king Edward had perished, but as he approached St. Albans as Wæclingacaester had become known, he heard wailing; not one or two voices, it was as if the entire city wept. At St. Stephens, a cart laden with what appeared at first to be slaughtered livestock was followed by a gaggle of women and infants, some shrieking, others sobbing quietly. The hunter waited by the road and saw that the cart carried bodies, not beasts. They were clothed, their exposed skin blackened and punctuated by red fistulas. In the churchyard, men hacked at hard ground with picks and spades, clearing a grave large enough to receive the dead which, by the roughest calculations, seemed to be at least fifteen people in a single day.

That night, as the hunter lay in an alcove inside the city wall, his sleep was interrupted by screams of grief and the constant creak of cartwheels as ever more dead were taken out of the city. The next day, he awoke to find a man lying close by, eyes rolled back and skin necrotic. The hunter reached for the man's money pouch and slipped it inside his own garment. After a moment or two, he withdrew the bag and untied it. Taking out a small golden coin, he placed it in the man's hand and closed it.

"To pay the sexton."

Grief followed him on his journey south. The fields around the city remained untended; carthorses waited for orders that never came, and cows grazed with no maids to milk them. Pestilence in St. Albans, in Radlett, in Stanmore.

Death on the road and in the fields, a plague like those which afflicted rebel Israel on the wilderness of Sinai; an invisible foe which could not be fought. The priory in Kilburn was set away from the road, but as he passed, a stream of afflicted pilgrims staggered or crawled towards its doors, death behind and ahead of them.

The stench of Lundenwic reached him long before he arrived at the Thames, and he stepped over bodies strewn across the road, some still living. A man reached up his hand from the filth of his pus-soaked rags and the hunter took it, kneeling.

"Take me with you," he begged, and buried his face in the fetid oil of the man's hair, weeping.

"Take me with you."

But no welts infected his white skin. In the months that followed as London's wretched populace shrank, no constriction tightened his lungs; under his flesh, the dark hue that gave this new and terrible disease its name did not appear. He would live, as he would throughout the plagues that followed. Death could not touch him and he was immune to its attacks. Everyone who he encountered on the road died in the end, and there were none he cared for enough to grieve save the child he never saw, the woman who he had loved, and the man he had been.

A small voice cuts through the ugliness of bus engines and motorbikes. A tiny girl in pigtails and red boots sitting up in a buggy pushed by her father.

"I love you," she repeats, over and again. "I love you I love you I love you I love you."

The clown stops to look and listen. The simple joy. The envy he feels for the man who says nothing but continues pushing his daughter past the Cash Converters and the Savers supermarket, towards the theatre. He might once

297

have had a child who might have cooed her adoration for him had he stayed, had he made one better choice. And had he picked death instead of this curse of centuries, had he been roasting in his well-deserved eternity, such would be the torment meted upon him by devils that he would have no space to grieve her.

"I love you I love you I love you I love you."

The clown blocks his ears and looks away.

Pretending once again to be loyal to the crown, the traitor, Streona rode out with sharpened sword and two henchmen to track down the brothers, Sigeferth and Morcar, thanes of the Seven Burghs. Jealous of their influence over Æthelred, he told the king that the men plotted treachery and, finding the brothers at Oxford, he silver tongued them to the place where he was lodging. Here he fed the thanes veal and poured good wine before his cohorts hacked them to death in their beds. Dragged from her home at Æthelred's behest, Sigeferth's widow was flung into the dungeon at Malmsbury. Here, Ironside visited her. Knowing Streona to be a snake, doubting any actual treachery by the brothers and pitying the widow, he brought her warm clothes and food. Ealdgyth's spirit impressed him. She spat at him, regaled him with a flurry of expletives which he had only heard from soldiers, and he loved her.

Without the old king's knowledge, Ironside married the woman who his father had confined, declaring himself Earl of the East Midlands at the wedding feast. Had Æthelred not died before the summer solstice, some say Ironside would have seized the throne anyway. Summoning his son to Lundenwic, the king wept pathetically at the betrayal. Ironside, whose brothers predeceased him, who was not raised for kingship but coveted it nonetheless, saw his father's weakened state, asked no blessing, kissed the king's hand and left, still a prince, but ready to rule.

On a 189 single decker heading north, Taj Crossley, eleven, on his way home from his grandmother's flat on the Abbey Road Estate. The boy sits with his forehead pressed against the window, the lenses of his glasses touching the pane. A week ago, Crossley was mugged for his phone. Two older teenagers on bikes blocking his way in Wembley Park as he walked home to a council block that overlooks the Metropolitan Line railway tracks. When they saw his 2010 Nokia, they laughed and gave it back, their mockery hurting more than if they had stolen it, and Crossley begged his mother Jackie for a new one. He can't even get the internet; there's no games and he has to borrow Jackie's or his big sister Leesa's when they're not on Instagram, which is never. The clown spots the bespectacled child looking gloomily out of the window and strikes a pose, head down elbows high, hands angled. One shoulder jerks up, then the other like a marionette. He flips up on his tiptoes then swings his body side to side without his head appearing to move. The boy watches bewitched, as does a Deliveroo courier loading his bike from the Moroccan Deli. Abdullahim Sheik, waiting outside the Islamic Education Centre across the road stops too, all staring at a white faced man with green hair moonwalking as his upper body moves robotically. No phone needed, the entertainment is there if you look for it. The clown shakes his shoulders loose and walks on past the Good Ship on the west side of the street. When he first met the pub's owner on the road, the man assumed he was in a band and asked him if he would like to play. The clown took out a tin whistle given him by a returning fusilier from Sebastopol and fired up the *Bonnie Dundee*, and *Farewell to*

Katrine, and though it was not what the man had been looking for, he bought him a pint and stood him a cigarette.

Knowing his father was weak with age, Ironside remained to defend Lundenwic should Cnut attack. The Viking army had no need of the city, and no wish to meet the full force of the English, though they could not have known that its soldiers were few and its leadership haphazard. The Danish horde crossed the Thames to the west at Wallingford where a gravel shoal allowed a man to pass in ankle deep water. In the January of 1016, Streona travelled up from Wessex with Cnut and raged with him through Eastern Mercia, slaying all who came before their swords. Terrified families who saw no sense in fighting the Norsemen fled into nearby woods as villages burned and prize animals roasted over fires fed with poles and thatch from plundered cottages. Winter bit hard that year and many froze or starved before they could reach the safety of the west. As ever, Ottar kept record.

"Bullmeat for the soldiers,
Odin feasted.
Cnut's men harried north.
None of the slayers
dined in the hall of the slain.
Æthelred, weak king
wept in his palace.
English hills shook with the roar of the valiant
while Cnut hammered the land."

The smell of malt has gone. It felt like an eyeblink but they brewed beer here for almost a century, and though it seems like yesterday, it's been a hundred years since the last drays left the building loaded up with barrels, and trucks carrying malt from the Grand Union Canal wharf in Acton rumbled along the High Road. They ripped the old building down and replaced it with shops and a fancy redbrick arcade, now a DIY store. Adrien Sholer, nineteen walks past, staring into the screen of his smartphone. Platinum blond cropped hair, nose piercing, sheepskin coat, long black skirt and Doc Marten boots. Sholer is on his way to Kilburn High Road station where a train will take him east to the bars of Hoxton and Shoreditch. The clown admires his chutzpah; a skirted man who isn't part of a religious order is a refreshing sight. A rare break from the day-in, day-out homogeny of jeans and puffers, burkhas and business suits; Sholer is a tonic in a quarter that had become a drab shadow long before he was born, standing out like an albino Zulu, a seven foot tall woman or a man with a healed axe wound from the Wars of the Roses. The clown is thankful for the colour; Sholer's presence is a gift. Clement Durade cycles back past, at speed, headphones plugged into Queen performing live at Montreux in 1984, his body in Kilburn but his spirit three decades and two thousand miles away, the clown envying a man's ability to free himself from the disease that infects these streets and everyone who treads them.

Ken Barnes steps out of the DIY store clutching a tin of varnish to repair the scratches which Joan's cat has made on the stair spindles. Now that his mother has died, Ken devotes himself to Joan, a ninety-five-year old spinster from Cricklewood whose father John died in the First Battle of the Somme, leaving his sixteen-year-old sweetheart alone to raise the child he had placed in her belly. Ken Barnes, whose mother also looked after Joan and would have wanted him to keep an eye on her. The clown watches as Michael Riordan, a pipefitter from Lismore pushes past Barnes on his way into the shop, Barnes neither calling out nor remonstrating. In fact, he apologises to the man. The clown would have challenged Riordan, if only for the devilry, to feel a blunt fist in his belly and righteous blood bursting from his nose. Barnes sorrying his way out of a situation that he did not even create, Christing his other cheek to the bully. The clown sneers at Barnes who smiles at him as he limps to the bus stop outside Brondesbury Station and whispers,

"Cunt."

The man who has failed to offer help or succour to a single soul since his own joy was ripped from him feels a pang of guilt at mocking a cripple on his way to his do-gooding. Barnes is no cunt, and he is too far away to hear. The word fizzles in the dead air, its aftertaste a slow, repulsive rot in the clown's mouth. He spits, but it tastes no better and in that moment, her realises something. Barnes is happy. In the cavernous chambers of his heart where, in Saxon times, a conscience once dwelled, a kneeling child lights a small candle that immediately goes out again.

Now married to a bride from one of Mercia's most prominent families, Ironside, Earl of the East Midlands marched north with his own army. Ice puddles cracked under soldiers' feet and jets of breath shot from horses' nostrils. Where vendors now sell e-liquids, phone covers and other trinkets on Kilburn High Road, a five thousand strong legion of Anglo Saxons tramped along Wæcling Strete. Passing through leafless forest that had remained unchanged for millennia, the men were an untidy bunch, no uniform as such, just mail shirts over knotted underclothes and woollen cloaks to warm them. No discipline either, for none had time or resource to train a militia. Instead, the men honed their warcraft in sporting matches where they fought, ran and rode against one another. The army made its first camp at Radlett and ate wheaten bread dipped in thin vegetable gruel and whatever the soldiers could shoot in the forest. Ironside and his knights bedded down in the manor house while the manor lands filled with a sea of tents. From here, they followed the road north, camping at Old Stratford and Stretton under Fosse as they passed deeper into Mercia, collecting men as they marched.

Next to the DIY store is another pawn shop. The clown has lost count of the moneylenders who proliferate this strip; one shuts and another opens, but there are always enough for the desperate hordes to hock their treasure. Kettles and shoes sit alongside medals from the Spanish Civil War. The clown once drank with a man in the Old Bell who had fought Franco. The soldier's hand shook so much that he spilled his beer, and he spoke quietly. His brother had been blown up at Jarama in '37; his headless, limbless torso dumped by the blast in a ditch off the Andalusia Road. The man lost hope, walked back to San Sebastian and boarded a container ship to Southampton, his mind as broken as his brother's corpse.

The clown, who is in no hurry today, saunters between backed up cars, buses and trucks to the east side of the High Road. Here, Zeinab Sulemani passes him on her way to the Qalam Education and Resource Centre, blue prayer robes and white hijab reminding him of women from long ago. A time when the road saw more foot traffic than wheels, before the dirt was asphalted over and bordered with pavements and trees. A time when oxen drew rough wooden carts chased by dogs and children, and all believed, all prayed, all feared the awful vengeance, the fiery pit and invoked daily prayers to protect themselves from the sweet, serpentine temptations of the evil one. He remembers a life that moved with the gentle rhythm of the seasons, a landscape drawn with haystacks, woodcutters and windmills; peddlers, dairymen and wandering priests; quack cures and fortune tellers. Where children once stopped to pick wildflowers, Sulemani passes a man who witnessed first-hand the Reformation and the Age of Enlightenment; who lived through the Industrial Revolution and the triumph of reason; who witnessed the jet age, the space age, the information age and whatever age we're in now. In Sulemani's village in Pakistan, they stone women for adultery. None of her family throw any rocks, they all work for tech companies in Lahore. In her shoulder bag she carries a smartphone and on her wrist is a Fitbit; Zeinab Sulemani reading the holy verses and obeying Allah, a medieval ambassador at the court of 2016.

The clown disappears under a red awning into the Italian café next to the Islamic centre which, in a previous century, had been a greengrocer owned by the Marks family; gas lamps illuminating the display of fruit on the pavement and an ornate cashier's cabin inside. Today, the interior is painted red and a clock in the shape of an anchor and a ship's wheel adorn the wall behind the counter. There's probably a story behind it, but he's not here for the décor. He orders a double espresso to go from a pretty teen in a white shirt, and the machine hisses and steams. An older woman sits in the window reading a free copy of the *Kilburn Times*. Police appealing after a man in his twenties was knifed in Brondesbury Villas in the early hours of Sunday morning. The paper doesn't say if the man lived or died or who they think knifed him. Every week another story of the fatherless footsoldiers bound by blood oath to a postcode; warring against their compatriots from a different tall tower, lives sacrificed on the streets where they fall or the jails where they grow fat and old. The girl takes the clown's coins and hands him a small disposable cup of black coffee. As he leaves, she calls after him.

"I like your boots."

He turns.

"I like your face."

She blushes and looks down. The woman rattles her paper and the clown moonwalks out of the café as the girl giggles.

Where Wæcling Strete crossed the Fosse Way, the two armies met. Those who had joined from Mercia saw their first Vikings and their courage drained. The rumours were true. Here were terrible man gods; warriors half animal, half human. In their wake lay the corpses of those they had slain; infants, women and ancients lying among the bodies as January winds buffeted smoke palls from sacked villages. Weary from the march and their nerve gone, Mercia's men abandoned Ironside to protect their families and their farms. Weakened, and knowing that he needed support from elsewhere, Ironside turned his horse away. Cnut's carnage against his father's kingdom would continue, but Ironside would need to push the invaders back another day.

The clown has not been kind for a millennium. He has not lifted a finger to help another. Why would he? No celestial banquet awaits the cursed one. Like a strangled man at the gallows, he is a body waiting for disposal, a spent soul already condemned. Why else would the demon have met him on the road? Not for him the Christian kindness of Ken Barnes. Fury is his north star, rage at what was torn from him, of an incomplete life, of business unfinished and no means of finishing it, least of all on the last day. The world changes but he remains, as bitter now as when he first fell.

The clown looks at the people on the street around him; an autistic girl holding the hands of two women as they attempt to cross the road; a bow legged old man with white beard and kufi; a young man with a grey backpack talking into his phone, all stuck in this place, they for one lifetime and he for thirty. Anger is his energy and purpose. To rage and nothing more. He once heard of a man in olden times who stood on a hill outside a town, roaring his fury like a great wind. Day and night the man howled his wrath until storm and gale shredded his cloak to weeds. When he finally died, his body remained upright, calcified into a tall stone, leaning towards the town. Years passed and the wind tore a gaping hole where the man's mouth had been, and as the storms ripped through it, his cries were heard once again. He is that man. He has lost everything but his rage, his ossification almost complete.

Outside the café, the clown skulls his coffee in a single gulp, scrunches up the cup and throws it in a high arc into a square metal council cart lined with green bags whose attendant leans on his broom while taking a call from his mother in Forest Hill. It was here that the white horse of the commissioner sent by Wolsey trotting ahead of the dun mare of his factotum passed him in the twenty-seventh year of Henry. The clown could not follow of course, but he heard of their business on his return the next day. The men were bound for the Nonnerie of Kilnbourne, the house built on the site of Godwyn's shrine and where a saintly sisterhood spent its days in prayer, caring for the sick and giving bed and board to travellers heading to and from the city. There was no violence, at least none of the physical kind. The women were simply told to leave while a meticulous audit was made of the priory's treasure. The house itself was found to have a monetary value of £74 7s.

11d., of which the rapacious king had no need. Just as when the prisoner Caratacus was paraded through the colonnaded streets of Rome and marvelled that Caesar in his palace should envy him his hut in Britain, the sisters must have wondered how England's great king could covet the beds and books and butter churns of their convent.

It was early May and the commissioner made detailed account, which he published in an inventory. Where Godwyn had only a rude hut and a simple stone shrine, the priory built on her glade boasted a church, three bedchambers, a buttery and a pantry. It had a larderhouse, a brewhouse and a bakehouse. Three more chambers provided beds for the men, of which the husbandman, the chaplain and the confessor were logged in the entry. In measured script, the factotum detailed the furnishings. In the middle chamber could be found "two bedsteddes of bordes, one fetherbedd, two matteres, two old cov'lettes and three wollen blankettes," as well as "a syller of old steyned worke and two peces of old hangings, paynted." Next to these, a price in shillings and pennies. The shameless robbery from the penitents continued as their library was ransacked. "Two bookes of *Legenda Aurea",* a collection of lives of the saints widely read in Europe after the invention of Guttenberg's press. One copy scrivened by .pair valued by the commissioners at just eight pennies. The men found other writing on paper and parchment, "two chestes wt div'se bookes p'teinynge to the chirche". Eight pennies. The priory was relieved of its "relique of the *holy crosse,* closed in silver and gilt, sett wt counterfeyte stones and perls," valued at three shillings and fourpence. A shard of wood from the tree to which Christ was nailed, encased in a bejewelled casket, deemed less valuable than the church clock whose price was given as five shillings.

There was no desecration of property, simply calculation, evaluation, the scratch of a pen on paper and some quiet conferring. The prioress who belonged to the noble house of Montagu and the two women who served with her were ordered to leave; the building and its chattels would be taken care of. The women who had lived under holy orders their entire adult lives and who had barely left the building since taking vows were abandoned to make of the world what they could, to fall on the kindness of strangers, and in some cases, beg. The clown saw one of the nuns on the road not long afterwards. She clutched a wooden cross in one hand and held out the other for coins and food. As he passed, he could hear the woman reciting a lament from the Book of Job:

"Pereat dies in qua natus sum et nox in qua dictum est conceptus est homo." Let the day perish wherein I was born, and the night in which it was said, 'There is a man child conceived.' Let that day be turned into darkness. From his throne in Hampton Court, Henry traded the lands of Kilnbourne for a manor across the Thames in Southwark, the patch of green by the river soon falling into the hands of a favoured courtier, Richard Neville, Earl of Warwick. Empty of its virgins, the priory building remained a blind witness, its sole value in the earth on which it stood, a home to no one. The Earls of Devonshire owned it for a time, then the Howards and finally the Uptons who signed it away to avaricious Victorians who laid the first streets, built houses and carved a railway where a black horse grazed and saints sang the hours. As he passed the holy mendicant, the clown felt no pity. He too had had his life ripped from him. If anything, he felt affinity. After five and a half centuries, he had learned that we deserve nothing, should expect nothing. The nun might have been forty, but when it came to suffering she was a novice.

Next to the Italian café is a burger bar. Some might wish for oysters, langoustines or sheep's hearts; angelhair pasta, patatas bravas or Yak's cheese. Some prefer slabs of nondescript bread, a squirt of coloured, sugared sauce and patties of the cheapest cuts of farmed meat, ground, compacted and fried; the food shovelled into a polystyrene box with pulverized, modified and reconstituted potato saturated in corn oil and deep fried. The tray will be discarded on the pavement, floating on the eddies of passing trucks until it disintegrates under the weight of a thousand wheels, its polycarbons floating into drains and out to sea where fish feed. A joyless fare, a cuisine local to nowhere; a low bar, a quick fix repeated across this whole drag, as if this is what people want, as if they have no desire for pide, mole, babouti or philly cheese-steak. The clown turns his back on the place and the heavy thrum of a BMW S1000R slows for the lights. Few sounds above the creak of tree boughs and leaves moving in the wind were audible on the ancient road. A hammer on a molten horseshoe at the forge. On a still day, the church bell at Willesden announcing the Sabbath. Wooden cogs straining as the great millwheel turned at the top of Shoot Up Hill, the hum of summer bees, the chatter of hedgerow birds, and the call of a wood pigeon to its mate. In the woods, an axe on birch, a warning shout from the woodcutter, the thrashing of branches through the canopy and the thud as timber thumped the forest floor. At night, the high pitched screech of a tawny owl and the yammer of foxes. Centuries of quiet, of seasons, of snowdrops in winter, primroses in spring, forget-me-nots in summer and autumn harebells; of sycamore wings and conkers, pink and white blossom and leaf fall. The trees have all gone, and new ones planted in their place; lone sentinels along the concrete strip. Most are planes planted in the previous century to

309

mimic the grand avenues of Paris; neat squares of gravel at their base, hemmed in by paving, their rotting leaves swept up by half-hearted council workers at the year's end. The motorcyclist turns the throttle and a 1000cc engine guns into action, roaring away towards Maida Vale. The sound is shrill and penetrating. Even in a city that sits under multiple flightpaths and where the noise of jackhammers, scaffolding poles or carpenters' drills add to the devil's cacophony, it drowns out everything. The clown cocks his fingers into an imaginary Glock and unloads into the back of the vanishing rider.

Godwyn lay awake on woollen sheets which she had spun and woven, under hareskin blankets she had sewn together. The swineherd slept at her side, weary from the day, warming her as the coals cooled. She felt breathless. She barely knew this man, yet clung to him in the same way she had to her prayers. She who had been so certain of her calling, now unsettled. God had been real, still was real, but Albric had chosen her. She had no part in her own rescue. What was she to do? Run back to the street and wait by the wharves with the other waifs? She had no choice. She was Christian by default but saw it as God's grace; just as the women who Albric had spoken about had been redeemed, so too had Christ washed her own soul clean. She missed the lightness, the certainty that she heard his voice, that he had called her to make up for her life of sin by living out her days by the river in an attitude of constant prayer.

She listened to the man's breaths. It had happened so suddenly and felt so right that she hadn't needed to even think, a decision already made. Just as Albric took her from one river, the Benedictine had taken her from another. She simply followed. A rootless, drifting soul; a feather in the breath of God. Aside from the man who lay next to her, none here knew who she was, but nor did she. She felt powerless and lost. Only the child growing in her belly anchored her. The baby, the man, this. Maybe it was all she needed. At least she was no longer alone. The hut was warm and the swineherd's eyes twitched as he dreamt.

On the corner where Palmerston Road joins the eastern side of the High Road is another pawn shop. Two stories above, with a clean view of the Nando restaurant on the opposite side of the junction, drama. Retired theatre nurse, Berenice Whalley is furious with her nephew; he has robbed her and she wants to call the police. Her downstairs neighbour Malcolm Stanwix is attempting to calm her down. Stanwix who persuaded the consultant at the Central Middlesex Hospital's Mary Seacole Ward that Whalley is eccentric, not crazy; she just forgot to take her meds for a couple of days which is why she had the incident. The consultant who wore a bowtie in a hospital, like he was a children's entertainer, would only let Whalley home once social services had vetted the flat to make sure she could cope on her own. Knowing that the envoys from Camden Council would take one look at the chaos and place her in a home, Whalley's nephew, Carlton let himself into the flat and cleared up Auntie Berenice's junk, purging the clutter which had taken her eighty seven years to curate. He put most of it in garbage bags which he left on the pavement at the entrance to Palmerston Road where they were rescued by Stanwix who brought them up to his flat. Now he's sitting with Whalley in her kitchen, sorting through the bags, helping the old Jamaican lady decide what to keep and what to discard. A stack of margarine tubs so old that the logos have faded.

"I need those."

A mountain of thin blue plastic bags.

"I'm keeping them."

A pile of *Kilburn Times*.

"I haven't read them."

Stanwix pulls out a circular rug with a gaping hole where water has rotted through, one of several mats that lay on the floor of Berenice Whalley's bathroom. He holds up the rug and speaks through the hole.

"I think we can get rid of this one can't we, Berenice?"

Whalley places a bony hand with crooked, arthritic fingers on the carpet.

"I worked to earn every pound that paid for that rug."

A ragged mess of patterned blue and yellow woven wool, paid for in the blood, vomit and gore which Berenice Whalley stared down daily before the voices in her head confined her, and keep confining her. Malcolm Stanwix looks nonplussed at Berenice and the rag of a rug.

"OK, let's keep the rug and lose half of the blue bags and all the newspapers?

"OK."

Progress.

Palmerston Road. A slum laid out in 1865 as migrants poured into the capital and the northwestern suburbs raced to throw up buildings quickly enough and basic enough to house them. To add polish to the fetid tenements stretching east from the High Road like ribbonworm, the street was given the name of the sitting Prime Minister. Unskilled labourers crowded into shabby, disease ridden rooms ten at a time, some with only rags to sleep on and holes dug into the boards to shit in. By September 1897, three families shared number 30, one belonging to a stableman at the brewery, another to an undertaker's apprentice and the third to a plate layer for the Midland Railway, a paranoid schizophrenic named Harris whose terrible crime won fame not just for Palmerston Road but for the whole of Kilburn. Harris driven mad by the certainty that his brother and his wife, Anne were lovers, returning drunk and enraged to the house one evening to find Anne and their young daughter barricaded in a cupboard. Harris grabbing an axe and smashing the door, dragging the pair from their sanctuary, a neighbour rushing in room and restraining the axeman, remaining until he had fallen asleep and a modicum of peace had returned.

Shortly before five in the morning, a scream. Harris had awoken and, remembering his ire, grabbed the axe like a fairy tale ogre and smashed it down on his son William's head as he and his sister slept beside their mother. The side of the axe head hitting the child, bruising him and the boy fleeing, crying out for help. Harris now attacking his daughter May, cutting her badly and, thinking that the child was dead, proceeding to butcher Anne, all but severing her head. Before she succumbed, the woman was able to cry out to a neighbour.

"Mr Young! Save us!"

The stableman hurrying to witness the horror, running out to the street to fetch a policeman to the house of horrors. Mrs Harris dead and blood drenched, Harris himself with his throat cut and the child, May, bleeding into the boards. The girl's injuries not as critical as they appeared, and Harris himself still breathed. They brought him before a judge once his wounds had been treated, but the man could no longer speak even to answer his name. They gave him pen and paper but he was illiterate. Instead, his brother and others described a loving and hardworking teetotaller. A good husband. A model man who had only recently fallen off the wagon. Despite their attestations, the Mute Murderer was found guilty and sentenced to hang, breaking down in tears of gratitude a week later when reprieve came, and he was sent to live out his days in an asylum. Harris' son, a ragged, dirt-soiled and underfed boy was sent to the workhouse in Tooting while his sister was spirited away to a relative in Oldham. Let him rot in his wordless cell. At least Harris saw his children, and knew they lived. He may even have grieved his wife. Life ends, but grief, the clown knows for certain, does not.

Left without an army, Ironside was in no position to repel the invaders. Cnut had a unified fighting force and everything to win. The myth of warriors who could cleave a man with a single axe blow, and who rode on the wings of gods proved an invincible shield. The Norsemen seemed impelled through Wessex and Mercia with supernatural vigour, their men arriving like thunder, axes held high, their frenzy and their number clearing villages as England fled before them.

Only Uthred of Northumbria came to Ironside's aid. Between them, the men raised a new northern army, but rather than chase down Vikings who, for now, had ceased their war, they turned instead on lands owned by Streona. Ironside's warriors rode through Staffordshire, Shropshire and Cheshire, avenging England and Æthelred. He who had handed Cnut the English fleet soon had no land of which to boast; his livestock slain, his farms burned and his children smothered in their beds. Streona's people were cut down as they ran, and his fields ploughed with salt. Bodies bled out where they fell, frozen corpses littering the land as there were none alive to bury them.

Palmerston Road today would be unrecognisable to James Harris and his family. A blind alley cut in two by nineteen sixties Oak House, a low rise utilitarian brick block forming part of the dreary Webheath Estate. At least the poor now have running water and shoes. The Lord Palmerston still hogs the corner, a grand stucco building with great arched windows and Italianate porticos; a Victorian gin palace for the wild and the weak. Back then, gangers on the railway drank here, hard faced navvies with shovels for hands; Irish and Scotch and the odd African adding a splash of colour. Pints of cheap brandy and gin to drown out the voices in his head, the accusing tongues that reminded him why all this was here. Where's the brook, Benedictine? Where was it that Godwyn lived? Where is the shrine to St. Peter? The cell by the river? What did you do Benedictine? Are you pleased with your handiwork? The clown once drank with a salt here who claimed he had escaped the colony at Van Diemen's Land, a hell at the bottom of the earth, somewhere south of the China Sea, he said. The man spoke of beatings and deprivations; savage dogs and naked blacks with spears. Though his trial was only temporary, he had seen great oceans, wild land and had smelled the oaken planks of a square-rigged merchantmen. Yet the clown had travelled more and seen less, his sphere of reference tiny, a monotonous back and forth where occasionally the world and its stories came to him and could be bought for the price of a milk stout.

The clown rattles the matches in his pocket. A fire. It was the only way to finish it. Steal some thunder from the Devil. When he first met him on the road, he assumed he had imagined the whole thing; it was only when he found he could neither drown, nor starve, nor venture east or west from the path that he knew the curse was real. This time, it will be a proper showdown, and one he'll be ready for. No ambush from drunken hoodlums or a botched cry for help; he has nothing to leave, nothing to say and no one to mourn him. A fire. A great conflagration, an earthly foretaste of the

315

diabolical holocaust, the eternal furnace that will torment him for a million lifetimes, a million million, and even then, only a moment logged in the great chronometer of eternity.

On the west side of the street opposite the entrance to Palmerston Road is another moneylender's. It is as if the whole town is exchanging its chattels for instant gain. Next door is another bookmaker, part of an offshore holding based in Gibraltar whose doors open in three locations here on the High Road, its screens, dockets and strip lighting a siren call to luckless men who lose ninety pounds to win ten. The clown walks in, takes a chitty and writes on it in ornate, cursive script. Pushing it under the protective glass at the counter, he stares up at the screen. The favourite, Baby Bach takes it by a head from Jovial Joey in the 1.45pm from Haydock. A lone voice in the corner of the near empty shop cheers, then erupts into a fit of coughing. A tenner to the girl behind the glass, then a Carling at the Colin Campbell if he doesn't croak before he gets there.

Out of options and with time running out, the clown steps in front of a police BMW520d patrol car which stops and activates its hazards. He walks around to the driver's door and taps it.

"Sir, step away from the vehicle."

Police sergeant Asif Ramoh not taking any chances with this green haired nutjob who is probably on ice. Detective Sergeant Karine Stanzl stepping out of the driver's door and walking over to the clown, who has stepped away from Ramoh.

"How can I help you today sir?"

Stanzl, matter of fact.

"If you have a question, ask a police officer," the clown tells her, politely.

"What's your question, sir?

From inside the car, Ramoh calls his boss to come away, but Stanzl has got this. The clown closing his eyes and reciting a riddle told him by Henry IV's jester, a man named Ralph of Amiens, almost six centuries earlier. He opens his eyes again.

"What does it mean?"

"Sir, has anyone committed a crime against you, because we're holding up traffic."

A couple of car horns register impatience as vehicles begin to back up.

"No crime, but you're a policeman, and so I'm asking."

"I'm a policewoman, sir."

Stanzl taking out her phone.

"A what? Three headless men?"

She types in the words.

"Three headless men, yes, playing at a ball."

The clown patient, prompting, while Stanzl takes down the riddle, and cars, buses and trucks tail back as far as Buckley Road. Stanzl hitting a link and reading, nodding.

"OK sir, it appears to be nonsense."

"Nonsense?"

The word itself making no sense.

"It's medieval," the policewoman adds. "It seems it was a fashion to create riddles with no meaning, where the riddle itself was the joke."

"A joke?"

The clown parroting Stanzl's words back at her. She continues to read.

"So a round square, a headless man wearing a hat, a blind person seeing – just clever nonsense is what it says here."

Clever nonsense. A joke.

"Will there be anything else, or are we all good?"

The clown nods without speaking.

"Can I ask you to step out of the road for your own safety unless you're crossing."

A statement more than a question, and Karine Stanzl walks back to her car and drives away, followed by a solid convoy of traffic. The clown looks up and down the High Road then whispers to himself:

"Da steh ich nun, ich armer Tor,
Und bin so klug als wie zuvor!"

So here I am, a poor fool,

And know no more than what I knew.

He shakes his head. "What a cunt."

Shortly after Christmas, the freeze set in. Willesden found itself surrounded by forest stripped bare of leaves; balls of twigs in the high branches where rooks had nested, and the distant echo of a woodcutter's axe. In the snow that had fallen on the manor lands, tracks of hares and the foxes who stalked them. Thick ice crusted at the pond's edge and only the ducks swimming kept the water in the middle from freezing. A flock of swans passed overhead looking for water too, airborne invaders from the Norselands, the winter air so cold and its snow so thick that the barn owl hunted by day. In their hut, the swineherd whittled at a piece of wood with a small blade while the woman wound flax on a spindle. A small fire burned in the hearth, but they could see their breath.

"What are you making?" she asked.

He held up the piece to the light.

"A wolf?" she asked.

"For our son."

"Our son! Will our daughter want a wolf?"

"It's a she wolf. The fiercest kind."

He admired his handiwork for a moment, then continued to carve as the fire cracked, the woman treasured him, and their child grew silently in the dark.

Inside the Nando's restaurant that had once been the Lord Palmerston, Michaela Dennis stares at her date Wanda's chips.

"Have one," Wanda says, but Dennis is on the final day of her Lenten fast, and it is chips that she has put to one side. Stupid time to go on a date really, but Wanda Abalos was a match, and it's been three weeks since she last heard from Jade. Abalos takes a paper napkin an begins folding it.

"My mum ran a restaurant back in the Philippines," she says. "She taught me how to fold napkins into swans."

And she begins turning and creasing the white tissue. Dennis wonders if her faith will be a deal breaker. Most people don't care, as long as they don't have to change. But some can be a bit defensive; Chloe called the church a bigoted, homophobic patriarchy run on money and rules; a toxic force of corruption. She only saw what she wanted, the greed and human rights abuses, paedophile priests and billionaire televangelists. She didn't see the quiet ones picking up the pieces unnoticed; clearing up mess, mending the broken and praying in silence. Wanda Abalos continues folding, shaking her head.

"No, not like that."

"Love the sinner, not the sin", a kind priest had told her, embedding the belief that what she felt was sinful, as if she woke one day and chose to prefer girls over men.

"Come on."

"God is OK if you stay celibate", the priest told her, as if the Creator of the universe obsesses over how men and women climax, and with whom. The chips look delicious. Wanda utters a strange, frustrated grunt and Michaela Dennis wanders if Abalos is autistic. She doesn't give a shit about swans, she just wants to connect.

"So, what are the people you work with like?"

Abalos shushes her with her hand.

"I've got this."

The chips wait to be eaten and Dennis waits patiently for love, for Jesus to reassure her that God made her just as he wanted, and for a swan to emerge from a recycled paper napkin in a Kilburn chicken shop.

The clown looks in at the two women, one earnestly folding paper, the other watching; a bowl of uneaten chips between them. He has hundreds of pounds in his pockets but free food tastes sweeter, and so he walks in and strides up to the table.

"Have you finished with these?"

Wanda Abalos not looking up, her head still in the dining room at the Grand Garden Oriental in Manila.

"Sure, go ahead," Dennis says.

The clown grabs a fistful and strides out, a female manager in pursuit.

"Excuse me?"

He turns, mouth full of fries.

"Excused."

The food is still warm. It tastes of kindness.

The cantor's voice intoned in Latin the Gospel of John, just a week or two before he left the abbey for the last time. Christ stripping off his outer robes, and wrapping a towel around his waist, fetching water, then kneeling at Peter's feet like a servant. The apostle uncomfortable, Christ admonishing him gently:

"*si non lavero te non habes partem mecum.*"

Peter demanding that the Son of God now wash his whole body, the penny finally dropping at the eleventh hour. Only this wasn't the eleventh hour. Peter going on to deny knowing Christ in Caiaphas' courtyard, the persistence of the servant girl's questioning throwing him into blind, ass-saving panic. No record of the man who his teacher and friend called 'Rock' at his crucifixion, shamed and hiding in an upper room while women watched at a distance as the Messiah bled out. Even for him, salvation.

Mehmet Güvenç flies south on his 200cc Suzuki Burgman scooter carrying divorce papers in his topbox. Wakely vs Falk. The fool Wakely met Angelica Falk at work, married her and moved into the flat she owned in Maida Vale, all within a sixmonth. Falk his boss and their courtship a fug of late nights, cheap wine and cigarettes, two lost and broken souls convincing one another that, in between the slobber and sex and weekends where they never left the bed, they had fallen in love. The marriage disintegrating on the white sand of Bali where they honeymooned, and Wakely, finally sober, realising that he had misstepped, tendering his resignation to both his job and the relationship. He and Angelica Falk flying home in separate rows of the same plane, Wakely desperate to get out of what he should never have got into, Falk too proud to admit defeat. And so the papers. Güvenç married with three children, beloved by Elçin who he has known since high school in Antalya. He passes a clown with spiked green hair and an army greatcoat outside Nando's, eating chips from his hand. This city man. So fucking crazy.

No one is from here. The clown has long known this. No family tree of any who live here today threads back through time to the cottages that clustered around the priory. There are no great Kilburn families, nor even any lesser ones whose line leads back to the Domesday count. Until they built St. Paul's church and laid out the square where today a seventeen storey tower glares down at a shabby market and an Argos store, there was no village. When they invented the motor car and had no need of horses, nor fields in which to grow hay, when they desecrated the farmland to turn a profit from their useless fields and built streets, factories and schools, people came from all points of the compass to live and work in them. The railways that brought them from Glasgow, Liverpool and Manchester spawned their own suburbs. Ships brought people from across the Empire and later, planes emptied willing workers onto the apron of London Airport, buses bringing the poor to Kilburn to fill dreary estates, while its smart villas became home to the affluent. The clown never met anyone whose family had been here longer than a generation. Only himself, the one constant; the one familiar face that all knew, few realising that he had been here for centuries and would remain for centuries after they died. A man eating Nando's chips who hunted in the forest, watched coachmen dig out carriages bogged in mud, passed indolent horses flicking their tails at flies and smoked a clay pipe with the tollkeeper.

With Streona's land laid waste, Uthred hurried back to defend his fief from the Vikings. Cnut had entered Northumbria but Uthred had no army to speak of with which to fight his enemy; the sea of warriors spread across his lands making him wonder if there were any left in Denmark. His choices were few. He could die defending the indefensible or submit to Cnut and plan escape later. As he rode out to make peace with the Dane, Uthred passed through Wighill in the wapentake of Ainsty. Here, he was ambushed; Thurbrand the Hold, an ally of Cnut cutting down the ealdorman and forty of his men with blades hammered in the forges of Jomsborg. Knowing that Uthred's loyalty was thin as the Yorkshire mists, Cnut had arranged the strike. Now the Viking, Erik Haakonarsson became ealdorman, and with the entire north of the country now under Danish rule, Cnut looked south.

A Turkish grill on the corner of Dyne road across the A5 from Nando's takes up the corner of a nondescript block that replaced a Victorian terrace in the early years of the last century. Before they knocked it down, the row had been home to a bordello; young women and some not so young in bodices cinched at the bust, floor length lace petticoats and with bright ribbons in their bonnets. Wayward shepherdesses forced by sad circumstance into bending over silk sheeted chaise longues, skirts above their heads and minds elsewhere. These were the middle years of a century where Spring Heeled Jack stalked the city, a man who could leap nine feet in a single bound, who attached iron claws to his fingers and slashed the throats of women. Terrible as this spectre might be, it was the violent boors on whose coins these women depended who were most to fear. Drunken johns with no need to pretend at the kind of affection they showed their wives; whose barked demands needed to be met, whose oily whiskers and foul breath repulsed the women, beatings commonplace. One girl, a teenager called Elsie May died here, bleeding out in a back room before a doctor could reach her, by which time the man, a gentleman in calfskin riding boots and nankeen trousers had long since returned to his rooms on Craven Park Road to take tea, read his paper and discuss the emancipation of slaves in the colonies with dinner guests. When the terrace was condemned and rebuilt, the shop on the corner became a cobbler's where, a hundred years after Elsie May had died, a cripple named Best repaired heels and resoled boots in a back room. The man reported locks breaking, tapping on doors and bulbs popping out of their sockets. The shopgirls who worked with him backed up his story; an unexplained knocking, a workbench smashing, and shoes leaping from their shelves. One morning, Best arrived to find nails scattered over the floor and when a flying hammer narrowly missed his head, he left the store after twenty years' service. "The Kilburn Poltergeist" shouted the headline in *The Willesden Chronicle,* and for months afterwards, buses slowed so that passengers could gawp at the haunted building.

The clown had often been in the brothel and knew Elsie May to look at, though he preferred passing time with a bosomy, yellow haired strumpet who called herself Anastasia in the fashion of the Russians, and who had a cracked laugh, a quick tongue and a love of gin. What God thought never crossed his mind. God had judged and he had forfeited his soul. Just as no amount of Lazaruses could rescue the rich man from the fire, the clown too remained irrevocably chained to his treadmill. He often hovered outside the shoe shop on his to-ing and fro-ing, in the hope that he might catch sight of another trapped soul doomed for immortality. After all, it might be Elsie May, and if she were willing, he had a pocket full of coins.

A few days before the vernal equinox of 1016, the Viking army began its long ride south. Erik Haakonarsson, Grand Earl of Norway and now ealdorman of Northumbria rode on a strong horse alongside Cnut, all conquering prince of Denmark. Later, Ottar carved runes on a soapstone pillar:

"South across shires
Cnut and his jarls on the wings of war gods.
Ironside cowering behind his wall;
the old king feeble,
drooling on a silken pillow
as war hordes descend.

Loud sings the elm bow;
thunderous the twenty thousand feet
marching to deal England her deathblow.
Æthelred shall be food for dogs,
Ironside, carrion for crows,
Lundenwic's river salted with tears."

In the Indian restaurant next to Nando's, Stephen Thoms waits on a high backed chair at an empty table for a takeaway Lamb Dansak, Peshwari nan and mattur paneer. Twenty-seven-year-old Thoms troubled by last night. His flatmate, Kameera came home in a strange mood, and was cross with him for eating the schnitzels which she had left in the fridge. Kameera wanted to go to the Black Lion with him after work and he had misunderstood.

"We never go out," she pleaded, like she was his girlfriend. Kameera; vivacious, pretty, petulant; Thoms in his dressing gown, ready for a quiet night in front of *Breaking Bad*.

"Sorry," he said and then Kameera, who he'd fancied for so long kissed him quietly on the lips and his head span because he'd secretly wanted this, but also because of Laura, precious Laura who he was marrying in four and a half months' time. The kiss wouldn't end. Kameera's eyes were shut and he could smell her hair. Her tongue against his, his hands on her shoulders. Wasn't she with a writer from GQ? And what would he tell Laura? What will he do? They don't have secrets. She pulled away and smiled.

"Well, that wasn't supposed to happen."

"I'll get dressed," he said, and pulled on clothes in a blur.

Thoms sat on his bed trying to make sense of what he had done. It was a moment of weakness. It meant nothing, certainly nothing he needed to tell Laura. Yet he was thrilled by it, that Kameera found him attractive. Wasn't his decision to let her move in spiced with the danger that this might happen? So now what? What if it happens again? She should move out. Once is a mistake, but a repeat would be unforgivable. When Thoms came back out, Kameera was in her robe on the couch, channel hopping.

"What about dinner?"

"What about it?" she said nonchalantly.

Was she high? As she made room for him on the sofa, her robe fell open and he could see one of her breasts. He reached for it and held it for a moment. Her hand brushed his crotch. This was really happening. Joy mixed with terror. His phone buzzed. Laura.

"I have to get this."

When he emerged from the bedroom having heard about Amanda's meltdown on the train, Kameera was curled up on the couch asleep. He sat next to her for a while and stroked her buttocks through the towelling, but it felt weird and he stopped. By morning she had put herself to bed and her door was locked.

She texted him the next day while he was at the Serpentine with Laura, asking if they were cool, and he was at a loss to know what to answer.

"Yeah, we're cool," he wrote, trying to affect insouciance he didn't feel. As he waits for his food, Thoms keeps thinking about Kameera's breast in his hand and her fingers on his groin. He takes his phone out again.

"Are u home?" and then "I want to kiss you again."

The line now permanently crossed, regardless of her response. Moments pass, then his phone vibrates.

"I'm with Daniel. Talk later."

A Pakistani man places a white plastic carrier bag on the counter and reads out Thoms' order in a monotone. He grabs it robotically and walks out of the restaurant, past the clown, to the flat on Dyne Road, as if he is still in the middle of a dream.

Like an unwelcome drinker when the lights have come on and the staff have placed chairs on tables and begun mopping the floors, the clown remains. He does nothing but outlive. Kill time. Endure. A man out of ideas and long past caring what any think of him. Sometimes he looks up at the sky and others stop to peer at whatever it is that he can see, invariably nothing. Other times, he falls to his knees, searching the ground with a patting hand. This too attracts helpers. He drops things deliberately which passers-by pick up for him and points at nothing. He is a nuisance. A body taking up space and which has long since served its usefulness; an overstayer. He would have taken something, but he wants to be awake; aware as he finally goes under, not lost in caverns measureless to man, a chaos of opioids swirling around a body he no longer inhabits. In the seventies, a businessman gave him LSD in exchange for a throttling. The clown had no idea if the man was angry or high, and his soft hands were barely strong enough to complete the job. Eventually his windpipe popped and he fell. Once he had recovered sufficiently, he swallowed the tab and began a bizarre and colourful journey. He could taste the noise of buses on the High Road and smell their redness. In fact, they were not buses at all, they were great crimson whales and the minicabs were dolphins. Wanting to swim with them, he climbed into their river. An electric milk float which he mistook for a beluga narrowly missed him, the milkman climbing out of his small electric truck to usher the clown back onto the pavement where he could continue his delirium in safety.

Having returned to Lundenwic, Ironside readied himself to harry Cnut once again. As the Danes closed in from the north, men from Mercia and Wessex hurried to defend their city and their realm. The way took many of them along Wæcling Strete and into the great forest. Some straggled, finding comfort in the inns of Wæclingacaester and delaying their journey. Slowly, they too headed south. Word reached the Middlesex Ealdorman, Odred Dunheld at his farm in Hendon, and he rallied his son Athelstan and his nephews, Uthred and Edgar. Between them, they raised a considerable force which camped where the track crossed the River Brent near Hendon and waited for the king's army to join them.

Chuck Konzauer is sweating. Not just because at five feet eight he weighs eighteen stone, or because of the Piri Piri chicken he ordered from Pepe's on the corner of Dyne Road. Gunther is telling him Eric's bee joke. The thing is, Gunther has hyped up the joke so much that Chuck now feels obliged to laugh, no matter what, and he's a bad actor. The walk from the apartment on Exeter Road was only half a mile but it nearly finished him. Back in Tucson, he drives everywhere; it's too damned hot to walk. Konzauer listens so hard that it hurts. It doesn't help that Gunther is German, not that it should affect anything, but Germans and jokes? How many German comedians does anyone know outside of Germany?

"Honestly," Gunther assures him, "it's the funniest joke. Everyone asks Eric to tell it to them, he tells it the best."

Sweat runs down Konzauer's temple. He wishes Eric were here, whoever he is. He met Gunther in Hamburg as a student, Konzauer on an exchange program from Indiana State and Gunther on the same corridor in his dorm just off the Wiesendamm. Eric works alongside Gunther at HSBC.

"A man is in a pub and the barman asks what he does for a living. 'I keep bees,' he says."

A bead of sweat snaking down Konzauer's back under his shirt.

"'You're kidding me,' the barman says. 'Joe over there keeps bees.'"

Konzauer calls over to a girl who is clearing the next table.

"Can I get a water please?" Then to Gunther: "Sorry, keep going, I'm loving this."

"So the barman brings Joe over and introduces them."

It's loud and a chair scrapes, and Konzauer strains to hear every word, so he doesn't miss anything.

"'How many bees do you have?' asks Joe. 'Around a hundred and fifty thousand' says the guy."

Is this the punchline?

"A hundred and fifty thousand!" blurts Konzauer. He has no idea if this is a lot or a little, or if you need to know anything about beekeeping to get the joke. When they weren't in class, he, Gunther and the others would buy cheap beers from Aldi and push each other home in shopping carts. They lived off Nudelsalat, Bratwurst, and Ritter Sport chocolate, slept off their hangovers then rented pedalos in the Stadtpark, lazing about on the sun-dappled waters of the Alster. A hundred and fifty thousand is not the punchline.

"'How many hives?' Asks Joe.

"'About five,' says the guy."

Konzauer laughs again, even though 'about five' isn't funny. He just wants the joke to end.

"'How many bees do you have?' asks the guy. 'About thirty million.'"

This has to be it, right? Thirty million is a huge number. Sweat is dripping into Konzauer's food and it's not even a hot day. His mouth hurts from grinning.

"'Thirty million?'" he checks with Gunther that he heard right, and looks into his eyes to see if there is any expectation there that he should be laughing. Gunther moved to London after he graduated twenty years ago, and now he's a senior cost consulting specialist at the bank. Konzauer traded Columbus for Arizona where he is sales director for a delivery company that restocks its customers' freezers with junk.

"'Thirty million?' says the guy, amazed. How many hives do you have?'"

"'Just one,'" he says.

"Just one!" Konzauer repeats and laughs in a way that he feels is appropriate. One does seem little for so many bees.

"'Yeah, bees. Fuck' em.'"

"Yeah, fuck 'em," says Konzauer, glad and relieved that the joke is over. But then he realises he missed it.

"Wait, 'fuck 'em', was that the bee guy or you?"

"The bee guy, that was the punchline. 'You have just one hive for thirty million bees?' 'Yeah, bees, fuck 'em.' You interrupted before the end.

"I'm sorry."

"It's better when Eric tells it."

Gunther sips his milkshake and changes the subject to what Monica is doing. On the last Saturday of his life, the clown watches from across the road, two men, one fat, one skinny. He envies them. He has eaten and drunk with thousands, but avoided friendships like he did marriages. Only Godwyn was a friend to him, a kind spirit who nurtured his own, who caressed his hair and slept with her head on his chest, who journeyed with him for such a short time, like a star which fades to black almost the moment the eye settles on it.

Mehmet Ali and his twin eight-year-olds, Youssef and Hamad walk into the fish and chip shop next to the Indian restaurant. With Saturday School over, it's time to eat. The two boys dressed identically; black parkas over white khameez and black and red trainers. Hair black and short; simple. Four hours of rules; do this, don't do this. No wiggle room and no interpretation. God created the world and the angel spoke to Mohammed, sallallahu 'alayhi wa sallam. Bearded men teaching law with authority, yearning for the old country, the peacefulness of village life; the sound of generators and goats. Affixed to the wall inside the shop is a poster of British river fish, none of which are sold or eaten here. Fish is halal and the treat comes once a week. Ali knows school is not football, or basketball, or judo, so the food is something the twins can look forward to. In Iraq, there was not much school to speak of. Dusty days in the trucks with his father and grandfather, transporting anything they could as far as Mosul or Basra, sometimes even the Red Sea coast or into Jordan. Mehmet Ali would sit up front, the old Tata throwing up clouds behind them and solitary herdsmen walking their flocks without haste across red roads. Now there's no truck. They had no medicine to save his grandparents, and Ali's father died with three soldiers and all five members of a family in a Toyota Hilux at a Mosul checkpoint when the truck behind detonated in a fireball. His mother lives here in their three roomed flat in South Kilburn; no life for any of them any more in Baghdad. Mehmet Ali orders two cod and chips, the boys can share. Youssef and Hamad try and see how many of the fish on the poster they know. The clown can reel them all off, even ruffe, bitterling and rudd, which is easily confused with roach. He occasionally caught one in the burn before Bazalgette encased it in a stone tunnel, funnelled sewage into it and buried it under the road.

Neither the swineherd nor Godwyn knew when they were born, though they guessed they were around the same age. All he could tell her was that he was from the woods, that his parentage was unknown. He had been left in the forest, the monks said. Maybe his mother had died giving birth to another baby and his father had married a woman who had no time for children; the evil stepmother of fairy tales. A boy could be sold as a slave at seven, so it was by God's grace that he was bought instead to the monastery gates by the poor weaver whose wife had found him as an infant, wretched, blue and sobbing.

Godwyn had been born into a family of robbers; her first memories the men who gathered at their home to share the spoils. She fed on scraps dropped by traders on the streets and lanes of Lundenwic, no mother to teach her and no brothers to protect her from the men who used her. Where others learned their family story and their place in the world from a mother and father, his teachers were the brothers of the abbey at Wæclingacaester, hers the street barkers, other runaways and sailors who paid to grunt and sweat on top of her. Yet destiny brought them together, then destined that they parted forever.

Nine hundred and ninety nine years, three hundred and sixty four days and twenty three hours. Less than an hour from the end; an hour before the fire. Ten centuries since he should have first begun his eternal torment, the clown's appointment nears. Whatever renegade he might have been back then, he now feels fully demon. Gladdened at first to have stayed his execution, he soon began counting down the days until his doom. Today is simply another day from which no joy can be gleaned. There is nothing and no one he would keep; the curse has made him a terror to children, a perpetual outcast, loveless and unloved, a dark revenant who sees only black. What was once monk is now husk; a human soul so fragile that it might be made from dust. The repetition has inured him, he is immune to the dance of the seasons, as each day plods mechanically after the other, light then dark, light then dark, light then dark. Can hell be any worse? The fire will sting but fear of death will be gone. Flames may lick his body for eternity but they can never consume it. Hell will be dreary with no more wandering, but it will at least be an end. He longs to be cut off and face the oblivion; the not being and not knowing, sucked by dark magnets into an unending vortex, rushing away from the light, the flame of life finally pinched out and death's torch ignited. That to him would be paradise.

As Cnut and Haakonarsson moved south with their army, news travelled ahead of them on the heels of fleeing English. By the time they were camped at Towcester, word was brought to the bed of Æthelred in his Westminster hall. The ailing king demanded to be dressed and his horse saddled despite cramps that clenched his belly. Home from punishing Streona, Ironside entreated his father to remain within the safety of the wall, but to no avail. Æthelred, not Ironside was Wessex's king, and Wessex's king would lead Wessex's army against the Danes. His men awaited his command and they would collect soldiers on the way, keen to set Vikings to flight back across the North Sea. The mass of men moved slowly north through the great forest but barely two miles from the city, the king slumped forwards on his horse and had to be held to prevent him falling. Earl Aldred volunteered to chaperone him back to Lundenwic while Ironside took command of the army, but seeing it as a portent from God, the king's son wheeled his horse around. The phalanx of English troops continued south along Wæcling Strete like a comet's tail as the half-hearted straggled and new arrivals joined the march, word spreading through villages that the city needed soldiers like fire in summer wind. This was the beleaguered nation's last stand, and every man should do his duty. Keen to join Ironside's army as it prepared to defend Lundenwic, Athelred Dunheld and his cousins saddled their horses and rode south into the forest.

The clown arrives at the corner of Netherwood Street where an unpretentious cafe serves generous all day breakfasts to hungry workers. At a table outside, Ray Greenaway smoked a Winston Blue. Grey hair and fluorescent orange jacket, Greenaway staring at his phone like it just spat at him, a mug of tea long since finished. Greenaway's mother demented with Alzheimer's and his brother riddled with pancreatic cancer. And now this. The council outsourcing to a private company to look after the parks and green spaces. Notice of possible redundancy. The fuckers. How many times do you need to be hit before the referee steps in?

Ken Barnes appears and leans in towards Greenaway:

"I remembered you, God, and I groaned;
I meditated, and my spirit grew faint.
You kept my eyes from closing;
I was too troubled to speak."

"Good for you mate."

Greenaway not interested in Barnes, nor his religion. Barnes continuing in perfect vulgate:

"*Cogitavi dies antiquos, et annos aeternos in mente habui et meditatus sum nocte cum corde meo.*"

334

The clown looking across at Barnes. A memory from the Saxon abbey. Words he had once sung at matins. He stares at Barnes as if he were some kind of angel, not a seventy-three-year-old man holding a plastic Tesco 'Bag for Life'. Barnes looks up at him.

"It's not your fault."

The clown not understanding. What, aside from everything, might not be his fault? Barnes raises a finger, thinking.

"It could have been 'it's not too late.'"

The man speaks quickly, like a rabbit might if it could talk. He looks up at the sky.

"I get them every so often. I think that's it."

Greenaway watches as Barnes walks away, back towards Nando's.

"What the fuck as that about?"

"I thought about the former days, the years of long ago; I remembered my songs in the night," the clown answers. "It's from Psalm 77."

"Is it? And how would you know that?"

"I'm a thousand years old."

Greenaway laughs.

"Yeah, I'm having a day like that."

The clown looks at the cigarette that is burning in the ashtray, unsmoked.

"Shame to waste it."

"Be my guest," offers Greenaway, then "at least it's not your fault."

The clown drags on the cigarette and stares at the small grey haired man limping away from him, plastic bag bumping at his knees.

Around the time that days began matching nights in length, Godwyn sat on a squat stool while the goat she called Whiteface stood dutifully on the wooden milking stand. Three kids scrabbled at the gate, weeping, but they would have to wait for their feed. Placing the pail of seeds and grain into which the animal could bury her face, Godwyn wiped the udder with a wet cloth. Grabbing two long teats, she squirted the first jets onto the ground, deliberately wasting them; the better milk came later. Deftly, thumbs placed where the teats joined the udder, she squeezed with each of her fingers, one after the other, draining them into the pail in a slow rhythm. Whiteface remained impassive, munching as Godwyn eased milk from her. Shaking the last drops, she heard a new sound that wasn't milk splashing into a bucket. Her legs felt wet and warm; liquid was pouring from her, drenching her shift under the rough outer garment. She stared down at a spreading dark stain. It was coming. Labour would begin soon but the goats still needed milking, then the cows. Godwyn tried to make herself comfortable as the wetness cooled until it was cold, micturate clinging to her legs all morning. After the third cow had trotted away, she made her way to the Brent River, wading up to her waist in its chill waters, cleaning herself. Placing both hands on her distended belly, she wondered what would become of the child. Its parents barely surviving, eking a living where they could, forever poor but together nonetheless; two threads woven into the same garment, two spirits, unshakable and inseparable, and now a third, be he boy or be she girl, beloved, their own, forever theirs.

As he crosses the junction with Netherwood Street, the clown glances east. Trees, a grey sky, ugliness beyond. What a slum. Everyone here would leave if they could; thousands trapped until fate or fortune deals them a lottery win, a jail term or a one way ticket to the Central Middlesex morgue.

He turns back to the High Road. Halal grocers, launderettes and barbershops; cripples pushing wheeled walkers, shabby ghosts clutching reused plastic bags filled with just enough to carry them through another day on this pissforsaken earth. Turn it back to forest. Behind him, the café where Ray Greenaway drowns his sorrows in tea; ahead of him, a middle eastern supermarket, its cardboard trays filled with lead infused apples, oranges and mangos destined for the skip unless they are robbed by vagrants or addicts. This end of Kilburn a shitshow of the transitory and tawdry. For a while, sturdy, red-bricked Netherwood House stood to the east of the road here; a grand nineteenth century pile torn down to build the street that took its name. Another dead end of Victorian tenements; beggars and burglars, hustlers and whores, crowded into dim rooms and left to fester; an infected wheal on the arse of the city; not even the notoriety of a murder to lift it from the monotony of copulation, starvation and death. The clown walks around a white council refuse truck and crosses over the High Road to another blind alley called Albion Mews, useful only for a piss or a quick two hander from a crackhead. Here on the corner, a vape shop peddling perfumed firesticks and other tobacconalia. It's what the place deserves; let it choke on the fumes.

Long after he had left Godwyn at the gates of Barking Abbey, Albric took confession in St Botolph's by the Bishop's Gate. Though he continued to bring lost girls into the care of Wendreda and deported himself with great virtue, his soul remained ragged and untidy. It was this he hoped to address in the confessional, a rude screen behind which sat a priest who he had never met, for St Botolph's was not a church he had been in before. The confession began slowly, then poured from his lips, the young priest nodding silently, hands clasped. Despite his wealth, Albric had neither robbed nor killed nor fornicated. His sin was one of abandonment and betrayal, for he had once worn the rough brown cassock and cowl of the Benedictines. Before he made his fortune importing cloth and fur, the man had been a monk. The flesh being weaker than the Spirit, he fell and fled to Lundenwic. Here, he boarded a trade ship bound for Seville, his knowledge of Latin a boon for the merchants with whom he sailed. Despite his great success, Albric's guilt never lifted, nor had he sought forgiveness; instead he scoured the city for wretched souls who money and influence might redeem. But still the shame of what he had done rested on him like a great misshapen rock that only God could cast away. Tired of carrying it and fearing it might break him, he walked into the church. The priest absolved him on condition of penance; he was to pray daily for forgiveness and continue his acts of charity; an ongoing work of reconciliation with his maker. As Albric raised himself from his knees, the priest threw in one last command, more a word of advice than a message from the Almighty.

"Forgive yourself," he told the penitent behind the screen.

The merchant had not always been Albric. When he had sung matins and lauds, vespers, nones and compline in the abbey of St. Alban, he had gone by the name of Eofred. His steps lightened by the priest's words, he made his way back to the river to continue absolving the city of its lost children.

Three teenage girls wait outside the vape shop for a sap to buy them a watermelon flavoured ecigarette, and spot the clown. The tall one with the nose ring is the boldest.

"Mate, could you go inside for us?"

The clown looks at the girls, then at the shop, then back at them.

"No."

"Fuck lot of use you are."

"Maybe," he says, flips onto his hands and continues walking. The pretty redhead in the middle with brown eyes and freckles calls him a cunt with the others, but her heart swims slightly as he passes, and she wishes the other two weren't there to spoil it. The clown drops back to his feet, continues past the fashion store next door and pulls open the door of a phone box. The stench of urine gusts at him and he peers at the patchwork of small cards blu-tacked to the wall above the phone. A curvaceous brunette called Kitty can offer him a massage. A stranger. He slots some coins into the machine and waits. A dial tone. He taps some numbers. A slurred voice that might be trying to be sultry answers. He hangs up and calls a number for Patti, a pneumatic blonde, her improbable statistics printed next to her phone number. He hopes she's lying, that she's forty and a little overweight. She answers. A smoker. He asks if she'd like to come to a party. Patti loves parties. She can be there in a couple of hours. She may, she may not. He doesn't really care either way, but one last tango might be nice.

Godwyn screamed again. The swineherd passed her a hot woollen rag from a pot on the fire and she pressed it between her legs to relax the muscles as the woman had told her. Her teeth bit on a leather strap as her great belly rose beneath her, taut and brown with dark marbling where the skin had stretched. She had been this way for twelve hours, the pain whiting out, bringing her to a place from which she never believed she could return, gripping the swineherd's hand, needing to hear his voice; tears stinging her eyes and snot clogging her nose. She'd taken nothing besides nettle tea all day and though her body convulsed, she had no power to resist or help it. The child would not out. The swineherd was no midwife and had no medicine beyond kindness and compassion. Now, Godwyn barely squeezed his hand as her body shook and she grimaced, no strength even to cry out. He kissed her, promised to return with help and ran from their hut in the woods to the village. Here, he was caught by the scruff of his cloak like a pilfering child. Alfred.

"Shouldn't you be with the pigs?"

"My wife is in her birth pains. She needs help."

"None of which is my business, swineherd."

The man dropped him and he bolted to the manor house, battering the door with his fists. A young serving girl appeared with hands covered in flour.

"The women have gone to Hampstead," she told him. It was a Tuesday, market day and the village all but empty. Desperate, he ran along the track that led to Wæcling Strete, toward someone who might be able to help them.

The clown steps out of the phone box and passes a Chinese quack. Here, signs in the window promise that herbs can fix his impotence, his addiction, his psoriasis and his eczema. In a back room, a quiet man from Chongqing mixes Arctium lappa with lophatherum gracile and mentha arvensis, cutting pills and distilling tinctures like they did in the old days. Remedies older than even the clown who has never had recourse to medication, whose bones have neither aged nor decayed, who has neither addictions nor chronic conditions. He was never infertile and might have sired an entire city with his progeny had he wished, but the memory of his own child would have dissipated; the unknown, unnamed infant who consumed his thoughts even at the last hour of his earthy life.

Chatter in the halls of heaven. A visitor who was far from welcome, yet who by the grace of God was ushered into the golden throne room. Here, he was granted an audience with the Almighty. Two saints had fled their calling and the Devil rubbed his hands in glee at how he might further ruin them. God pondered. Knowing all, he had seen the coenobites fleeing the garden by the Cunebourne, watched them build a life together in the village of Willesden, knew the love which they had for one another, and he in turn loved them.

"What is your wish, Ba'alzebub?" he asked.

The Devil professed that he could make the swineherd a bitter shell of man, a man who would forsake God and who would travel as if on rails to the eternal furnace.

"He is a good man," said the Almighty.

"We are all good until bad overtakes us. I shall prove that this wretched monastic has faith as thin as milk skin."

"What will you win?" God asked.

"The woman too."

"How long do you need?"

"A time," came the answer, "but he will turn."

God considered his children. The woman, he knew, remained dear to him. The swineherd wavered and Satan knew this. Where there was doubt, there was opportunity. Time could work for both of them.

"You have a thousand years," God told the Devil who, inclined to optimism by the perpetual heavenly chorus, felt victorious. A millennium to crush any vestige of faith in a man whose twin lights would soon be guilt and grief.

"Everything he has is in your power; you are his judge." God said to the Devil. "If he repents, they both shall live, only do not let him die before the final day."

"His body will live," smiled the Devil, "but his spirit shall be wormwood long before he meets his grave."

At this, the Devil bowed and took his leave. An angel approached the throne.

"How is Paradise, Dismas?" the Almighty asked.

"It is only my first day," the angel answered, "but I pray it never ends," his words dissipating in the rising and falling chorus that washed around him; only the nail marks in his hands and feet telling of his earthly life.

Leila. Not Godwyn, Leila. Wulfstan gone and the child refusing to crawl free and gasp its first lungful of air. Her strength spent. Just her now, alone in the hut as the fire's heat cooled with every minute her husband was away. Leila she was born, and Leila she would die. A brief window of joy had been hers. She had learned who she was, who perhaps she was born to be. A woman desired for reasons beyond power and lust. Loved. A worker who enjoyed the exertion; the weaving, washing and drawing of milk. Godwyn had rescued her and she had put her heart into being a nun, praying the divine office day in, day out for a king who still lived, whose son still fought the English cause against the Danes and who might yet prevail; and for whom she still prayed. For all the hardships of life by the brook, she would have been long dead, a battered heap of bone and hair in a Lundenwic gutter. The charity of Albric, the grace of God and the love of the Benedictine had rescued her. She no longer felt the baby and as she floated into unconsciousness, she prayed that her husband would come back with someone who could help her. Her breaths slowed and eyes that had long been closed began to dream. A presence in the room. Warming. Breath in her ear. Her eyes opened to radiant light and she heard woman's voice.

"Leila."

She wept. The voice was gentle, a kindness she knew she didn't deserve.

"Leila."

Her sobs increased as she saw the filth of her life arranged before her. Rutting in the alleyways and inns of the city, not all of which had been unpleasant, nor all of it for money. The triumph she had felt when Thorhild left the Abbey. The shrine she abandoned by the Cunebourne stream. Her passion for a Benedictine greater than her devotion to God.

"Leila," the voice spoke again. "You are dying and your child is dying. Death is coming. Hell or heaven, as the Almighty chooses."

"Hell it is," she thought, Satan's minions making the fire hotter as the seconds counted down.

"Die now, or you and the babe may sleep a thousand years."

She heard the words "a thousand years." She heard "sleep." Hell was hers, she knew it, either now or when she woke. In her delirium, neither hell now nor in ten centuries seemed more terrible, so why not leap into the molten sea and be done with it? She just needed it to end. Why wake in a millennium to find the one who she loved and cherished long dead? He had gone to fetch help and would be back. He was coming for them, of that she was certain. But if he found her dead, what inconsolable grief would be his? She could not put him through such pain. If he found her asleep, he would have hope that she might wake. Vain hope was better than none at all. Sleeping, he would lie with her and warm her; he would love her and grow old next to her.

"It is sleep I choose", she told the virgin, and so she slept.

Arrangements made, the clown crosses back to the east side of the road where a giant Halal Food Centre dominates the block between Netherwood Street and the Brondesbury railway bridge. Inside, Ameena Haran has bumped into her friend Nicole Okoro who she knows from the tenants' association at Webheath. Okoro wanting her to come to church tomorrow, Easter Sunday. Divorced from Saleem and a disappointment to her parents back in Jakarta, Haran still wears her hijab. She didn't go to the mosque for prayers yesterday; most of her friends aren't Muslim, most aren't even religious. Okoro who attends a Pentecostal church in West Hampstead has been handing out tracts all morning, and feels called to rescue her neighbour from the satanic morass of her own religious code. Haran is her drug and she's high on her, needing the fix that a conversion gives her. Okoro has all the words; like a sales rep reading from a cheat sheet in a mobile phone store, she knows what to say, how to push. As they stare at candy bars, Nicole preaches.

"Remember what we talked about? Let the fire burn in your heart."

Haran nods.

"Sure," and she reaches for a mint Aero.

"You're not listening to me."

"I am."

"What are you doing tomorrow morning?" Okoro asks. More a reprimand than a question. Haran doesn't have plans; she lives alone and doesn't want to commit.

"I'm not sure yet."

"What could be more important?"

Haran unwilling to tell Okoro that she hasn't been to the gym for three weeks.

"I'm serious Ameena. I know it sounds tough, but if your house was on fire, I'd want to get you out of that house. Hell is real, man."

Haran weak. Caving. Not wanting to upset her neighbour. She agrees to come. She could sit at the back and slip out early. Or feign a migraine.

"Let's get a coffee beforehand and we can go through some of John's Gospel."

Haran's heart sinking. She forces a smile as bright as she can muster and continues shopping, half of her Sunday now written off because she's a coward and Nicole Okoro is a bully.

The clown can think of a few things that might not be his fault, and many that are. A thousand years of misdemeanour. Everything that stemmed from abandoning Godwyn was most definitely his fault. He had been a blithe spirit, breaking rules wantonly. Sometimes he had been reckless, but always with forethought. He had agency in everything beyond his incessant toing and froing, but where he was not governed by the curse, he chose. So what was not his fault? He looks back towards the bridges. Barnes has gone, no doubt on some other righteous errand. It. He squeezes a mango outside the grocer's. He left his calling. Maybe it was that. He despoiled Godwyn. Perhaps it was that. But not his failure to return. No, he would despise the absolver for being so spineless and so forgiving. He takes a bite of the fruit. A voice from inside the shop:

"You buying that boss?"

The clown takes out a silver shilling from his pocket.

"Heads or tails?"

A man in a blue thobe looks at the coin.

"Tails."

The clown flips the coin high and catches it on the back of his hand with a slap.

"Tails it is!"

He hands the man a fifty pound note that he won't be needing and the shopkeeper roll s his eyes, holding it up to the light to check the watermark. While he disappears to

345

fetch change, the clown takes one more bite then looks over at a bin outside a newsagent's on the west side of the street.

"Eight ball corner pocket" he shouts, and lobs the mango overarm towards the goal. The fruit slams through the slot so hard that the bin shakes. He'll miss shopping.

Five days after the equinox, on the twenty sixth day of March in the year 1016, Athelred Dunheld and his cousins rode south along the Wæcling Strete in the hope of helping Ironside's army fend off the Danes. It was a noble skirmish for the three young men, and their status would place them with the officers, away from the heat of battle. Governed by duty rather than zeal and a desire to see bloodshed, Dunheld's father and the rest of his militia remained in Hendon, travelling to the city a day or so later. As the cousins neared the lane that turns towards Willesden, a peasant raced onto the main path and stopped when he saw them. Dunheld recognised the man instantly, though his clothes differed.

"It's the monk!" he cried. Their blood already up in anticipation of fighting Cnut and his hordes, revenge and serendipity had provided the men with a taster. As the hapless swineherd begged for help, Dunheld lashed him with whipcord and set upon him without mercy.

The clown looks around him at the traffic, the low rent shops and the broken people and sees no God nor any redemption, not for him nor any of these wasters. Maybe it was that first encounter with Godwyn that was not his fault. The fight that rescued her? He had enabled Godwyn to give up her vigil by the quiet waters of the Cunebourne stream. Allowed the city to encroach on what had once been holy ground. If he was innocent, that would mean that it was preordained; that God planned it as well as the penance which he served for a millennium. No, that would make God a cunt. He shook his head. God was many things but not that. He had simply given up on him, just as the swineherd appeared to have given up on his wife and child. You reap what you sow. Quid pro quo. But if God was not punishing him, who was? And if so, whose job was it to forgive?

Over on the west side of the street. Norris and Mishvelidze have moved on; Denzil Brown leans against the pillar box, chewing on the thighbone of a factory farmed Rhode Island Red. Between the chicken shop and a chemist, a dental surgery offers sunbeds and beauty treatments; a nondescript sign and information stickers littering the window. Laser hair removal and dental implants. Somehow it survives; if the clown knew anything about business, he would shit gold. He worked with his hands and always had. He scratched letters onto vellum with a goose quill, swilled out pig pens, tensed a bow and now performs sleight of hand that gulls goonfaced citizens into belief in magic. And he's never taken a single day of leave, not that anyone was counting. He pushes the door to the chemist and strides up to the counter where Emma Gadd has just placed a make-up brush, some chewing gum and a pack of Durex Thin Feel condoms 'for extra sensitivity' on the counter, Gadd paying with the gift card she received for her sixteenth birthday. Annabel Allen next to her, the two forming a human shield around their covert purchase. Being tall, the clown can see over their heads and places a handful of coins on the counter. One day of charity won't kill him.

"I'll get these."

The girls giggling. The man behind the counter looking over his glasses at the green haired white faced man.

"And these."

The clown adds a box of 'Pleasure me' ribbed and dotted prophylactics to the pile.

"What are you going to do with them mate," asks Annabel Allen, "make balloon animals?"

The clown snorts, then laughs. Face paint cracks around his eyes and he roars. Anabel Allen now self-conscious.

"Alright mate, it wasn't that funny, calm down."

The clown still laughing. Allen grinning too.

"Your mascara's running. Shit you're a hot fucking mess." The clown bent double with his hands on his knees. "Fuck's sake. You look after yourself."

Allen and Gadd gathering their swag, Allen calling over sweetly as they exit:

"Cheers for the johnnies."

Slowly, the clown recovers his poise and walks back out into the street.

Later as the sun began to set, three women from the village hurried to the swineherd's cottage. On returning from Hampstead, they had been told that Edith was struggling with her child, and one of them, a woman named Edrys had helped birth many children. On entering the hut, they saw no one; the charcoal barely glowed and both the swineherd and his wife had gone. The women ran to the river and searched the woods nearby. How could Edith have travelled in the midst of labour? And where was Athelwold? With no sign of violence or struggle, the disappearance remained a mystery. A story spread that the couple had been taken by wolves, or a dragon. None knew where they had come from, and began questioning whether the swineherd might have been an incubus; a demon in the shape of a man who impregnated Edith and spirited her away to his hellish underworld. So convinced were they of this that, months later, when one of the men saw Wulfstan on the road, terror rendered him unable to speak for a fortnight.

Death is everywhere. On the east side of the street, Sameera Raflique waits at the lights, broken. Abdul to whom she was married at seventeen, now buried; his messages still on her voicemail, the dent of his backside on the seat of the leather armchair, dirt from his hands still on the cracked bar of soap in the back bathroom. The knowledge that she will never hear him ask her if she'd like tea, the click of his key in the lock, talking over the TV, his laugh. All is emptiness. A blank flatline where once they had a future. Each day a joyless rerun of the day before; every moment one she wants to share with him when he gets home. Raflique had no idea it was possible to feel so sad. She wishes it had been her, then thanks God that it wasn't, that he wouldn't be left feeling how she does now. The children miss him, but not like she does. They don't know him like she does; they don't understand why he's not coming back. Death and five-year-olds. They're sad because she cries all the time. Today they're at Topsy Turvy in Brent Cross with Marcia's children. Two hours where she can run basic errands and not be mummy; where she can be Sameera, sad Sameera, indulging her grief, mourning her beautiful Abdul alone. The clown wonders what the woman might have lost. For the briefest of moments as she crosses the wide A5 and passes him on her way to the station, he feels kindred. He is her and she him. It never gets better, he wants to tell her. It hurts forever.

After slaying the swineherd, Athelstan Dunheld and his cousins arrived in a Lundenwic readying itself for siege, and found lodgings in the city. In April, the old king died and Edmund Ironside crowned king by those loyal to the succession. The king's council, the Witan, chose Cnut, and while the undead swineherd walked aimlessly north and south along Wæcling Strete, Ironside rode into Wessex to gather an army. With no king to defend it, the Danes besieged Lundenwic but Wessex was loyal. With its men behind him, Ironside broke Cnut's siege wall, beating the Vikings into submission at Otford and chasing the Danish army into the Kent flatlands. Sensing the turn of tides, Eadric Streona gave allegiance once again to Ironside, but fled at Assundon when the English were finally defeated. In October 1016, the Witan negotiated peace, handing Mercia and the north to the Danes and Wessex to Edmund Ironside. A month later, death came calling for the son of Æthelred Unred. Some say it was a Danish arrow, others poison, others that blackguards hid beneath the royal privy and drove a sword through the king's arse crack. With Ironside dead, Cnut was declared king of all England.

Upstairs in Globe House, a new build that that climbs four stories above the North London Line railway, Ion Williams stares out of the window of his one bedroomed flat. A halfway house that that overlooks the tracks. Halfway to where? It's not like he can go anywhere, Williams stuck in the limbo of the system. Even if they prove he did nothing wrong, there's no coming back. The shit sticks. Wife gone, his son now in New Zealand, as far away as he could fly from the horror back home. Fifty seven in a week and only his sister Carol sticking by him. An appeal in November. They reckon the boys must have collaborated. As a teacher – ex teacher – he could have told them that. When two pieces of homework came back the same, you knew one of them was copying. Five years, of which he's already served two and a half. Ion Williams, painted as a monster by the tabloid press, papers more interested in story than truth, innocent but forever contaminated. Just across the bridge is Brondesbury Station. A yellow and white Richmond train approaches from the east; people going somewhere. Willesden Junction connects with trains to Euston. From there you can travel to Birmingham and Glasgow; follow the West Coast Mainline to all points north. Jump on the Northern or Victoria to Kings Cross St Pancras and a Eurostar will take you to Paris, Brussels or Bruges. From here, the great railway networks of Europe fan out like a peacock's tail. The Trans Strait railway leaps across the Bosphorus to Asia. A ferry links Algeciras to Tangier and on to the ends of the earth. Not him though. Ion Williams tagged and going nowhere. Hanged by the testimony of two young men fifteen years after an event that never happened. And whatever compensation he gets once he's exonerated can never buy back his innocence. No smoke without fire. Mr Williams the nonce. If he's guilty, he deserves it. If he's pardoned, they'll say he got away with it. The stain. Williams watches the chap with the green hair and army boots pass by beneath him. Boy never seems to go anywhere either. A Stratford train approaches from the west. Then again, nor do the trains. East and west, always back to the beginning. Tangiers. That could work. Teach English and live like a king.

Tired of people and train watching, Williams grabs yesterday's *Evening Standard* and settles at the kitchen table. A footballer jailed for having sex with a schoolgirl. Hope the poor bugger's guilty, he thinks; that way he knows he's getting what he deserves. Williams' empathy broken. His trust gone. The child might be a victim, or she might be a destroyer of lives. Hating himself for having these thoughts, he keeps reading.

Down on the street, an ambulance screams past, the second in under an hour. The clown won't be needing one; for him it's too late. The movie is over and what has been sown is about to be reaped. That roughneck Galilean fisherman may have turned things around, but not him. Three times the man denied knowing the Son of God, hiding in an upper room as the Messiah was nailed to the timbers. Only when the resurrected Christ appeared, when the disciple saw him face to face, only then did he see; and now the basilica in Rome, the greatest and grandest church in Christendom bears his name. Too late is never too late, unless of course it's too late. The clock has to stop eventually.

The clown pauses at a rack or papers outside the newsagent's near the station. Plenty for the homesick Irish; the rootless bedsit navigators and the ones who made it, retiring in their big houses on the leafy lanes of Cricklewood and Dollis Hill. *The Nationalist*, *The Tipperary Star* and *The Munster Express*. *The Anglo Celt* and *The Limerick Leader*. Beneath these, folded so that only their mastheads are visible, *The Corkman* and *The Kilkenny People*, *The Clare Champion* and *The Connaught Telegraph*. A mix of gothic lettering and oblique fonts in reds, greens and blues. *The Roscommon Herald*, *The Enniskillen Echo*, *The Catholic Universe* and *The Westmeath Examiner*. Proud flagbearers for the thirty two counties and all major cities of Eire and Ulster; this shop one of their many northwest London embassies. *The Longford Leader*, *The Meath Chronicle* and *The Westmeath Independent*; *The Drogheda Independent* and *The Waterford News and Star*. So much news from such a small island. The clown had never really noticed the names but on this, his last day, he takes time to drink everything in. *The Leinster Express*, *The Midland Tribune* and *The Wicklow People*. *The Leitrim Observer* and *The Mayo News*. Magazines too. *Ireland's Own* with Derek

Ryan. He picks up *Ireland's Eye*: "1916 Commemoration a positive development for our nation." Everyone has to be from somewhere, he thinks, and we all have our stories. He doesn't care for the Irish. He was here long before they staggered to their bedsits from the boat train, these streets as far as a man could walk from Euston with two cases. Day labourers claiming County Kilburn as their own. This is Middlesex, home of the Middle Saxons, these Fenians a blot that only landed in the middle of the last century and bled into this one. Spade wielding grunts, forgotten by Ireland and never truly welcomed here; men toiling on construction sites for cash in hand to spend on cheap beers in windowless bars. A cheeseburger, a fight on the way home then blacking out on mattresses soaked in piss by the morning. The good life. They can all fuck off his land unless they're buying, in which case he'll have a pint of Carling and a whisky chaser.

Three men walked steadily south along the unswerving road through ancient woods. This was Leofstan's first journey in over five years; his commitment to perpetual prayer binding him fast to the monastery. The abbot did not walk without fear; these woods were far from safe. Wolves he knew, but the young scribe, Wulfstan had been lost somewhere on this road and the search party sent to bring him home had failed. A solemn mass had been sung in the abbey church for the monk who had been with them since he was a boy, whose codex remained unfinished and whose bones lay somewhere, possibly still unburied. Osfrith was among the travelling party; Caelstan too and the men were making for the King's Stone where, surrounded by jarls as skalds spun verses that would endure the centuries, the Danish prince Cnut was to be crowned king of the English.

It was early January of the year 1017, and cold. Recent snow had turned to slush making the going arduous, dampness underfoot adding to the discomfort. Stark black branches grasped at a blank sky and the men's breath quivered in front of their faces. As they neared the clearing known as Little Stanmore, a farm worker came their way, his hood up, his walk mechanical, his pack light. All three nodded a greeting and Osfrith blessed the man who looked down, uttered not a word and passed on, despite there being no one else on the road. The man's feet splashed in puddles and snow as if neither were of any concern to him. The monks glanced at one another and back at the traveller who neither turned nor slowed. The man had a demeanour which unnerved them; a vacancy and indifference, as if his footfalls were not his own. Leofstan shivered and this time, it was not the cold. He prayed for protection from dark spirits that still haunted the ancient woods. Later, as they broke bread in the abbey at Westminster, they spoke of what they had seen. None believed in ghosts, but the fellow who they had met on the road unsettled them.

"It was if he had been dispossessed of his soul," Caelstan said, and the others nodded, brooding on what they had seen.

Renate Pichl drives her yellow Jaguar XK10 under the monolithic grey London Overground bridge towards the city, past the green haired man staring at a rack of newspapers, past the flats where Ion Williams has just clicked his kettle on, past grieving Sameera Raflique. In the passenger seat, Pichl's friend Barbara Hirschenhauser; the women heading to the West End to spend Pichl's money. Or her father's. Hirschenhauser going along for the ride because she likes Pichl, and there will be a nice meal in Selfridges or Liberty which she won't have to pay for. At the same time, she feels disgust at herself, at the shameless opulence of her friend, her gaudy, compulsive acquisition of goods for which she has no need. They are off to get Pichl high, and it doesn't matter if that drug is a Fendi bag or Balenciaga shoes. Pichl once bought a wall of wool from a store in the Cotswolds; a woman who couldn't knit and never once tried to learn.

"Where does she put it all"? Hirschenhauser wonders. Pichl whose father aborted foetuses before it was legal, helping women fix inconvenience or horror in a brightly lit room above a bookmaker's in Harrow; a door with no sign through which entry was only allowed to the right people with the right money. The fat butcher left his daughter everything, and Pichl has never worked, only shopped, their lunches paid for in the blood of a thousand unborn children. It leaves a taste, Hirschenhauser thinks, consoling herself that she's simply being a good friend, sitting quietly in the heated leather passenger seat as Pichl regales her of the new three piece suite she has on order from John Lewis to replace the one she bought two years ago. They pass a group of people bending over a body outside Nando's, Pichl still quacking about the aquamarine two seater and the new bed linen she plans to buy from Harvey Nicholls as Hirschenhauser strains to see a grey-haired man collapsed on the pavement.

These were the wildwoods beyond the village, where any wanderer was free to gather what fuel he could. The forest's timbers were needed for homes, carts and hand tools and the woods were carefully farmed. Coppicers would cut a tree close to ground level, encouraging a plenitude of new shoots to grow from the stump. Fed by giant roots embedded deep in the clay and watered by abundant rains, flexible poles were ready for harvest within five years. Should sturdier timber be needed, longer intervals were taken. Here, where an Afghan grocer sells imported fruit and vegetables, and meat farmed and slaughtered in Leicestershire, men and women cared for woods that built London, and fed the boars on which they feasted. Not that he's nostalgic. He refuses to be. Since he broke it, it is and was and ever shall be broken, and like a bored youth who has kicked over a municipal litter bin and left the trash to scatter in the wind, he will simply walk away.

"Beni bloody Hana. It had to be."

The clown watches Andrew Saxby walk out of the station and turn left under the bridge towards Kilburn tube, throwing a quick "Sorry mate" to Karim Suj wrapped in a blue sleeping bag on flattened cardboard, hand upturned and a voice so quiet in the din that no one hears. Saxby on his phone.

"Beni. Bloody. Hana."

He's meeting the gang from Jackstar Poker, designers, coders and editors, a backstage crew for the website. All of them with a side hustle back then, and plenty more since. White Barry the drummer, who remained White Barry years after Black Barry left. Gene the Tory councillor. Marvin the gamer, as in proper Warhammer stuff, a man with a working knowledge of Cicero, Catullus and Lucretius from a year studying Classics at Kings. Big Andy, because when you hit fifteen stone, most other Andys are going to be smaller, and in a website back room there is no shortage of Andrews. Big Andy Saxby, bracing himself for the tourist hell of Covent Carden at Easter, but despite concerns aired robustly on the email thread, it can't be changed. Jubilee to Green Park, Piccadilly to Long Acre. A few pints in the Lamb and Flag, then food at Benihana. A nice way to kill a quiet Saturday. Saxby went on a date there once, a twenty-year-old Japanese girl who he met on a train. She had a giant bag of laundry and he offered to help her when she got out at Brondesbury

Park, not that it was even his stop, but she was cute and it was worth a punt. Saxby helping her carry the bag home, arranging to meet in Soho the following weekend. A loud Irish chain pub on Wardour Street – he let her choose - and when they played a song that took him back to when he was twenty, which he properly loved, she'd never heard of it. Talked through it. They walked arm in arm to Benihana, Big Andy glad to have a slim, beautiful girl at his side. Table chatter about her brothers and sisters, still all children; her mother, barely older than him; her coursework at Westminster Uni. Small things. She hated gambling on principle. He paid and at the night's end, waved her off the tube with a promise to call which he promised himself he never would. Beni bloody Hana. As Saxby continues to chat to Marvin, the clown stoops to hand Karim Suj a fifty pound note. The man with grey stubble and a black beanie takes the money in fingerless gloves and stares at it, as if Elizabeth herself might speak to him from the paper. His eyes dart up at the clown,

"Shukriya. Shukriya".

The swineherd hacked at pond ice with a heavy stone until it splintered and he could scoop water in cupped hands and drink. The keenness chilled his chest but slaked his thirst and he climbed the bank onto the path and continued walking. Yesterday, it had snowed, making his journey to Westminster a tortuous one, adding further discomfort to the vacuity of his mission. Now, the carpet that had been ankle deep had largely melted, and though it still drenched and froze his feet, he could see the rocks and potholes which tricked and tripped him while there was snow. He was just north of Little Stanmore when he saw them. The unmistakable girth of Leofstan, the short steps of Osfrith, the tall nodding form of Caelstan. Three saints passing a sinner, unrepentant as he had already been judged; the virtuous living and the wretched, weak undead. The swineherd had long since put his monk's robes away; they dishonoured those who still professed a faith. Instead, he wore a rough peasant's shirt and stockings, leather boots and a sheepskin cloak thrown over his shoulders for warmth. Today he had pulled the cloak over his head to keep out the worst of the cold and if they weren't looking for him, they would not have recognised him. He had much and nothing to tell them but what would it help if they knew? His soul was lost and could no longer be prayed for, and so he lay outside their sphere of influence. Had he been able to tell the men the truth, they might have sympathised, but for him, pity was worse than judgement. The conviction that he had betrayed and disappointed these kind men who had looked after him and raised him was overwhelming. He felt shame and the only solace in seeing them was that they looked well, Leofstan especially. The swineherd kept his head down and ignored their greeting.

The bar just past the bridge on the east side of the street is doing a roaring trade. A young blonde woman at a table outside is shouting a story to her friends which anyone across the street can hear. Beyza Çelik rolls towards the bridge on her mobility scooter, looking over at the drunk woman as she shrieks again. Not that the blonde cares; she has an Aperol in her hand and is set in for the afternoon. Outside the beauty salon next to the bar, a London plane tree in its spring wardrobe shows off clusters of pink blooms on every bough. A lone herald of spring where there once there were millions, and none of them planes. He learned which trees to lop limbs from for firewood. Not elm as it gave too little heat. Not birch as the smoke stung the eyes. Ash you could burn when green, but best of all was oak. No oaks line these roads. No woods save in the names. St. Johns Wood and Cricklewood. Borehamwood, Scratchwood and Wealdstone. The pink flowers making this dim corner of northwest London almost picturesque, and to tread on its fallen petals feels like sacrilege.

So many places to drink at this end of the High Road, and time for a few more before the drop. The clown crosses to the Ironworks, too recent a pub to have much of a story. An Irish bar when it opened, and always a bit of life to the place. A bunch of fiddlers or a guitar band seem like a good way to see this out. He walks down the stairs and the room is already sweating. On stage, a group of girls sing one of the old songs. The Irish are a mawkish bunch, he thinks, always sad at what they have lost, though to be fair, they've suffered more than most. He admires the spirit that does not die in absentia, and the unquantifiable love which the Irishman has for his sodden lump of land to the west; a fondness which grows the longer he is away. Perhaps it's this love that has made so many people crowd into a small pub off a fume choked street on the first Saturday of spring, all the sadder to be here and not there, eyes filling with tears as three colleens sing *The Fields of Athenry*. The girls finish to furious applause and step back as a young boy no older than twelve years old appears on the stage. The clown can barely see through the shoulders of the people in front of him, and moves to the bar where he orders a Beamish from a skinny man with thin tattooed arms and a ring in his nose. The boy on stage remains poised and silent for a few moments, composing himself. He wears a black shirt and green tie and the clown expects him to sing but instead, he begins stamping his boots in rhythm as the girls behind join in, their feet the drums. The boy's shoulders remain square, his head upright while shoes that the clown can hear but not see move in a frenzy.

"Go wee man!" screams a woman from the back of the bar and the clown pours the thick black milk down his throat. As feet stomp and stamp, he thinks back to those first days after Dunheld ran him through, how little he knew, how little he had lived. And now, he has seen centuries. He is older than trees; a man who walked these roads before Chaucer's pilgrims set off for Canterbury, before the Confessor built his great church at Westminster. He was older than the Conquest. He has met the battle weary from Agincourt and Crecy, Trafalgar and Waterloo. He predates the independence of France and the Americas, and has seen the fall and rise of every empire from Byzantium to Islamic State. He needs a piss and the gents in the Ironworks are close enough to the road to not bounce him back with his bladder still full. At the trough, a large man with a beard and a hurling jersey looks over.

"What's your story, big cunt?"

The clown grins.

"Roaming throughout the earth, and going back and forth on it."

"Turn a man's hair green, that could!" he grins. Then as the clown leaves, "Have a good Easter."

Back in the bar, the lad has finished his dance and some long haired teenagers are wiring up their guitars. But the clown has people to see, and still a little more time.

It was around the time of the coronation that a man named Edgar rode his horse south from Hendon along Wæcling Strete. He told no one of his journey and covered his head in a hood so none might recognise him. He did not stop until he had passed through the city gate at Wæclingacaester, tethering his horse at the entrance to the abbey. Genuflecting, he knocked on the wooden door. A bolt was slid away and a young Benedictine ushered him in. Leofstan was summoned and sat looking gravely as the nephew of the Middlesex ealdorman related events which had happened close to where the Cunebourne stream flows under the road that passes through Lundenwic to Canterbury. By now, Athelstan Dunheld was dead, a Viking axe chopping his leg off at the thigh as he fled Assundon, the wound as untreatable as it was painful. Edgar needed to confess; he had witnessed a killing on the road of a man who he believed had once been a monk - possibly a brother from the abbey of St. Alban. As the visitor described the dead peasant, Leofstan nodded. The monk had prevented the son of Odred Dunheld from despoiling a hermit girl who lived by the river, and had attacked him savagely. When they met again, the monk was dressed as a peasant and Dunheld had killed him in revenge. The death had lived with Edgar and troubled him. The peasant seemed desperate and in need; his wife was struggling to give birth, yet instead of helping him, they had slain him. Leofstan summoned Osfrith who recognised Edgar as one of the three men who he, Caelstan and Ealdred had met on the road to Westminster. Answers, finally but with them, more questions. The peasant met the description of the man who had so unnerved Leofstan and the others on the road near Little Stanmore. How had they seen their dead brother months after he was supposed to have been killed? And what had become of the hermit? Was she the woman caught in the pains of labour?

"A man is a book containing many stories," Leofstan said. "Perhaps we only read a single page, and from the one, to our detriment, write the others in our minds."

They offered Edgar the sacrament of confession which he took, but the man they had seen on their way to the coronation troubled Leofstan, and though it was summertime and the heat so strong that the stones of the church were warm to the touch, his skin prickled and the hairs of his forearms stood on end.

The clown climbs the stairs of the bar back to daylight and crosses the road again. He might as well go out on a full belly and here are two chicken shops next to one another. A last meal, albeit a cheap one. It's not like he has an appetite. He walks into the closest one and orders a factory farmed halal chicken burger and pale, limp fries. Mercy Nwokone and her ten year old son William also wait for food, and the clown settles on a high stool near the window. Taking a deck of cards from his pocket, he shuffles them in a high arc, releasing them like a flock of starlings, the thin rectangles falling back into his hands. William Nwokone is mesmerised; Tihad Hammami behind the counter is watching too. The clown fans out the cards with their faces to the boy.

"Pick one."

Nkowone nods and touches the two of clubs.

"Ladies and gentlemen. The two of clubs."

The clown shows the two theatrically to the others, then buries it in the pack. Throwing the cards up, he catches them with a clap of his hands, holding then out to the boy again.

"Find your card."

Nwokone scanning the pack for the two of clubs, but it isn't there. The clown now pointing at Hammami.

"Take off your hat."

The Tunisian obeying, and there on his head, the errant two. Mercy Nkowone laughing, William Nwokone wide eyed and unable to speak, Hammami dumbly inspecting his hat.

"How did you do that?" the boy asks.

"I've had a lot of time," comes the answer.

"Variety box and large fries?"

Hammami's colleague Izmet Pasha appears from the kitchen and hands Mercy Nkowone her food.

Never once did the swineherd give up hope of seeing his wife. In those early years, he scanned each face daily, watching the gait of any woman on the road ahead of him to see if it might be her. He craved information, waiting as long as the curse would allow him at the entrance to the lane that led to Willesden. But nothing. Each time his journey passed the bridge he slowed, taking in serene air that she once breathed, as if her exhalations had sanctified it. Yet she never came. In those days, people walked through fields and these tracks became the first roads. Few used the old Roman way as none needed to travel into the city. His journeys in those early centuries were lonely ones, especially so in the years immediately after the curse. Years passed before he spotted a face he knew; Alfred, crossing the path with a heavy sack. The man stared at him, horrorstruck.

"What news of Godwyn?" the swineherd stammered. The churl dropped his load, turned and ran as spilled turnips rolled along the compacted mud. He had no idea of what a ghoul he had become, why the man recoiled from him, or what had become of his wife and her unborn child. An entire threescore years and ten passed in the vain hope that he would recognise Godwyn's face or the shape she made against the light, but by the time the calendar turned to 1100, he ceased looking. She was dead. Buried in a grave he could never visit nor throw wildflowers on. It was over, and he now with over nine hundred years left of a life with nothing to live for. Damned already, he could do his worst and be his worst, for there are no prizes for virtue where he is going. All he had ever loved and would ever love he had lost and he stepped mechanically and alone into the new century.

The clown pushes the door to the North London Tavern. Stacey Valentine pulls a pint and recognises the clown's shape and the flash of green hair out of the corner of her eye, even though he's not been inside for over a year.

"Hello stranger,"

"Last orders," he says, wipes snot from his nose with his sleeve and sits on a stool. The men being served move away slightly, not wanting to engage with this weirdo.

"You off?" Valentine asks.

She must be fifty or thereabouts. Still a looker. Heavy eye makeup and a nose ring. He nods.

"Well, this one'd better be on the house."

Valentine pours the clown a pint of Kronenbourg and he grabs it, her hand still on the glass.

"Wait there," she says, winking.

Taking a metal optic, she draws off a double measure of Bells and places it next to the pint. A kind touch. He sculls a third of the beer as she watches.

"Steady on there, big fella!" Then, "Going anywhere fun?"

He snorts.

"You're a nice girl Stacey."

She looks away, embarrassed at the unexpected compliment. He drinks again, a smaller mouthful.

"I'm having a party. You should come. Bring people."

"No, but where are you going after that?"

He thinks for a few moments. A grin cracks his face paint.

"Fucked if I know."

"You been crying?" she asks. The kohl has smeared into the white.

"Laughing, actually."

"Shame you got to go then. Not many laughs round here these days."

Valentine heading off to serve another customer as the clown watches. He knows her life story, how she lives with a tiler called Derek who stepped in after Maurice left her with two children and ten grand of debt in her name. He likes that she's never asked why he doesn't age, almost as if she hasn't noticed. Maybe she still sees them as forever nineteen or twenty. Perhaps that was her happy place, but forever twenty three is torture. A thousand years on planet Earth and nothing to show for it. And this is his leaving do; a pint of weak lager, a shot of cheap whisky and a girl who tried to blow him in 1987. At least it's free. Stacy Valentine comes back to chat again.

"So, where's the party?"

"Follow the smell," the clown grins, gulping the rest of his pint and knocking back the whisky. "And as a dead man falling, down I fell."

He slips off the stool, straightens up and grins at her.

"You always were a mad bugger," she says. "Take care of yourself."

With spirits fuelling him, the clown exits the tavern and stands at the crossroads facing east. Half a millennium earlier, this whole strip was owned by the Gilbert family. A farm and a few scattered cottages that changed little until machines came. By then, the burgeoning city was greedy for land. Two railways ripped through the pasture and in place of hayfields, the British Land Company laid down slums; fetid tenements and a Baptist chapel to save any wretched soul for whom Station Road was the terminus. Now it's called Iverson Road, a gloomy run of workshops huddled under railway arches, the chapel gone for thirty years and anodyne flats raised up in its place. Behind him, Cavendish Road heads west past the pub towards Willesden, leafy and tree lined, another road he has never walked nor ever will. He crosses the junction to a Tesco Metro supermarket on the corner, above which a modern block of flats rises five storeys. Another new build faces it on the eastern side of the A5, both offering their residents balconies, like this was Venice or Amsterdam, and the apartments looked down on gondolas or the pleasure boats on the Herengracht.

Donnie Campbell sits with his back against the glass wall of the supermarket, fucked. A fleece-lined camouflage jacket and a cream-coloured blanket keeping him warm while he sleeps off the litre of Diamond White cider which he necked like it was 7Up. Next to him, Candice Bryant shouts incoherently. Black puffer coat with fur trim around the hood, pink beanie and a hard face; the stub of a cigarette poking through her fingers. The poor you will always have with you. Bryant not shouting at the clown, or Masters, or the old Iranian man waiting at the crossing, but answering voices in her head. What a shitshow. Ranjit Singh in tan car coat, black jeans and immaculate white turban walks into the shop next to the supermarket, yet another wholesaler of household wares whose mops and plastic panniers adorn the pavement like a low grade souk. The man is better than this, the clown thinks. Move on; keep journeying north, it gets better eventually. Travel that way and you will see the great Benedictine House revealed to Offa in a dream. Or turn south for Nash's triumphal arch and the magnificent shrine of the Confessor at Westminster. Maybe Singh owns the shop. Maybe his wife asked him to pick up a cheap can opener on his way home. A plane roars overhead but still cannot drown out Candice Bryant's rage.

Crossing back to the east side, the clown walks into the salon next to the new apartments. He's the only customer and sits in a chair facing a mirror. The girl knows the drill; clean off the old paint, re-colour the hair and reapply the face. She keeps a pot of white especially for him, and a black lipstick for which he is the only taker. The clown settles in to the chair as anodyne dance music plays quietly behind him. A cold swab of cotton wool draws paint and grime from his face and in the mirror, skin tones re-emerge. Caucasian. An Anglo Saxon male, no dark lips nor kohl around the grey eyes; a face as clean shaven as when he fled his hut to fetch help a millennium ago. The clown peers at his reflection, at the bloom of youth in his cheeks, the hair that used to be dull brown and which is now green and gelled into spikes. The girl shows him a palette of greens but today, his last day, he chooses brown, as close to the colour he remembers, and one he has not seen himself in for over six centuries. Leave this mess how he came in, he thinks; a purification. The girl leads him to another chair where he reclines, his neck cupped by the dip in the basin, the bite of the water slightly too hot but bearable, rinsing away tobacco, exhaust and soot as she soaps his scalp with firm fingers. She knows that if she says nothing, asks nothing, her tip will be bigger. The clown enjoys her attentive fingers on his scalp, an artist; not like the crackheads he pays for sex; prideless, joyless addicts who writhe and grind, minds on their next fix, saying what they think he wants to hear. Disgust, pity and ecstasy; what a cocktail. Here he feels tenderness akin to the old times when he lay his head on a woman's lap as a fire flickered, and she stroked his hair and told him stories of a nun called Thorhild.

Beneath the church at Willesden, in a crypt belonging to a family who no one remembers and which has long been sealed, a woman sleeps on a bed of goose down wrapped in crimson velvet. Her head rests on a satin pillow, her child asleep inside her. It was here the virgin brought her. None saw the slab placed above her tomb nor even knew of the vault beneath their feet. In the last century, a rug was laid on the slab, hiding it completely. In an alcove above the woman's bed, an ebony likeness of the Madonna cradles her own child. Believing the statue too precious to be left on display, a priest had replaced it with a copy soon after the church's dedication, hiding the original in the crypt. Lightless, noiseless apart from the softest inhalation and exhalation, the virgin watched over the sleeper and the child who rests inside her, and time passed.

Dye stings the roots of the clown's hair and ammonia strips membranes from his nose, making his eyes water. The girl brushes in colour, dabbing at his scalp in silence. He wishes it would hurt more; pain blessing but never fully absolving him. She takes the jar of paint in readiness to apply the clown's face, but he stops her. Not today. Once the hair has been rinsed and dried, she shows him his reflection. This is the man he has been hiding from, and how he'll take his final curtain. He hands the girl four fifties and walks back out onto the street, suddenly invisible, a tall brown haired young man in a long coat and boots, walking past the cafes, barbershops and Asian supermarkets that litter the stretch of High Road between the bridges.

In his extreme old age, Osfrith made one final pilgrimage to Westminster. A great gathering took place on Thorney Island as the Confessor dedicated the cornerstone of his new church on the site of the Benedictine monastery. Progress from Wæclingacaester was slow as the monk was beyond venerable, and was now considered ancient. White haired, his eyesight failing and his tonsure barely in need of shaving, Osfrith formed one of a party of seven monks who travelled south from the abbey of St. Alban. The old man sat astride a young donkey, his bones so light that the beast must have thought a child was riding her. Rain set in soon after they departed the city gates, and the monks wrapped themselves in goatskin capes, the road a mud ooze closing over their sandals. As they left Radlett, they passed a peasant travelling north. Decades earlier, a man who shared the same lack of purpose, the same gait, the same nonchalance to rain and the road beneath his feet had passed Osfrith's troupe, though all the men who had accompanied him back then were in their graves. Ever since Edgar's confession years earlier, the idea had troubled the old monk, and often when he could not sleep, he attempted to piece the puzzle together. How had their brother Wulfstan attacked Athelstan Dunheld and not returned? What life had he led, and where? This was the same man, he was certain, yet he had not aged a day. How could it be? Despite his frailty, Osfrith reached out a bony arm, and pointed, his words spoken but lacking any voice. None of his companions knew what their frail brother intended, and looked at the wanderer whose eyes turned to the old monk for a fleeting moment as they passed. But had they watched the man's face as he strode north, they would have seen tears fall and keep falling. Osfrith too wept. His grief was inconsolable. Worse than any wolf or any bandit, darkness had taken their brother, and when they reached the Knight's Bridge and rested for the night, he was still weeping.

On the clown walks to his vanishing point, into his own unknown. Was not the Viking Erikson afraid of sailing over the edge of the world, yet flew west on favourable winds regardless? Did not Magellan steer into the uncharted void, the blank space on the globe where conjecture and terror threw up serpents and kraken in a giant southern ocean? For him, there would be no return. No glorious homecoming, the earth was flat and it had its edge, a final frontier just ahead of him at the next crossroads. Here began the abyss into which his own ship would soon fall. Not for him the triumph of the navigator d'Elcano who hauled the carrack Vittoria home to Sanlucar de Barrameda after three years at sea. Nineteen men from a manifest of two hundred and seventy, dining first on rats, then leather and at the last, sawdust, just to bring their precious payload of cloves, nutmeg and cinnamon home. No, he would step off the earth and into an immortality of his own making.

Next to the salon, crests of blossoms shore up against the door of a bridal shop. The promise of a fairy tale; a month's salary on a dress worn once, the besotted throwing banknotes like confetti on a party that lasts a day. A shop for those whose story begins just as his ends a thousand years after it already ended, a never-ending lap of dishonour, a daily walk of shame. Who knew happy and ever after could be so separate? Or that the death that would part them would be another thirty lifetimes in which to grieve? The clown hoiks up a bolus and breathes in the cool afternoon air. No wedding for him today, but one hell of a funeral.

A blast of noise. The ghost of the great organist in the Gaumont State strikes up a funeral march, Bach's Toccata and Fugue in D minor. In Westminster Abbey, A man seats himself at the Grand Harrison & Harrison organ, stretches out his arms and he too hits the keys. A, G, A, trilling through G, F, E, D, C sharp and back to the D; his left hand playing the same notes an octave lower. Beneath the four thousand five hundred pipes of the great organ at St. Albans cathedral, a woman's hands flutter over keys. A, G and A an octave lower. E, F, C sharp, D. The clown crosses to the west side of the High Road where a gust of wind shakes delicate petals from a cherry tree onto the epaulets of his coat. More fuel for the fire. Past a newsagent's, past a pizza restaurant and a discount homeware's, past a hair salon and a café to another Tesco, bookending a block where a row of elegant town houses once faced the road. Before that, a timber yard occupied ground that had once been the landscaped park of Mapesbury house. Until the woods were cleared and the manor built, it was forest, and here, where a Shell garage dispenses petrol and comestibles beneath two bridges, there was a pit where men burned charcoal. Fire then and fire now. Fingers race across the keys, notes catching up with themselves. The clown walks across the garage forecourt and into the Spar supermarket in the shadow of the elevated railway. A gallon should do. He grabs a five litre red plastic petrol can and waits behind Sheila Shaughnessy who has filled up her 1998 Fiat Uno and also wants to buy a lottery ticket. A human roadblock. What an epitaph; it might as well be his own. One of the last human interactions on his thousand year journey; Shaughnessy also paying for a wad of scratch cards, just in case her lucky numbers aren't lucky, and scratching them at the counter. The clown emits a low hiss. The Indian cashier looks over Shaughnessy's shoulder.

"Yes mate?"

The clown pays for the can and five litres of Shell V-Power Unleaded 99 and pays with coins. Taking a fifty pound note from his pocket, he stuffs it in Sheila Shaughnessy's bag.

"It's a win already," he grins, and walks out into what's left of his Saturday. In the forecourt a woman in her mid-thirties wearing a short white skirt and a fur trimmed jacket hovers by pump number six, no car to fill up.

"Patti?"

She looks up, and then at his petrol can.

"Run out of gas?"

The clown reaches into his pocket and hands her a fifty.

"Thanks for coming."

Patti looks for his car.

"Where we going sweetheart? You can pay me after."

What he thought he wanted, he didn't. He has the end in sight and the time for last meals, last orders and last goodbyes is over. He realises he shouldn't have called her.

"Sorry to bring you out here," he says. "Plans changed. I just needed a friendly voice."

Patti looks at the fifty.

"A friendly voice?"

The money binds them. For as long as it has bought her, she is his. An army of one, someone on his side in case no one else bothers to show. Even if not actively cheering him on, at least she is here with him. Gunning for him. Patti OK-ing but not understanding.

"There's ten more of these if you promise not to stop me."

"Stop you from what?"

The clown pulls out a wad of notes.

"And if you don't ask questions."

"Well," she says cheerfully, pocketing the money in her coat as he walks off with his can towards the road. "Someone's got money to burn."

Either side of him as the clown walks beneath the wide single arch of the railway bridge, the walls are covered with murals. Blues, greens and browns, blurred and faded like a tattoo. Two young people sit in a glade reading a book; a cockerel; a young woman running towards a glass and steel mountain made from London skyscrapers condensed into a single gigantic pleasuredome. The murals have been graffitied over and never cleaned, projecting their own gloom to the late March afternoon. The clown continues towards the road, not caring that traffic is still moving steadily north and south. He will be gone soon. A red 189 bus sails past on its way to Oxford Circus, oblivious. A looming menace, the clown unscrews the cap, holds the can above his head and pours. The cold feels like an anointing. He sloshes the rest on the floor around his feet and tosses the container. Cars stop and Dennis Ribiero sounds the horn of his 2011 BMW 3 Series. The clown looks over at him and speaks with the zeal of a Victorian preacher.

"Your children who follow you in later generations. Those foreigners who come from distant lands will see the calamities that have fallen on the land, the diseases with which the Lord has afflicted it."

Nine months of joy and a millennium of self-loathing; lifetime after lifetime wracked with hate, rage and the uncontrollable desire for it to end. As Sainsburys truck prepares for the slow ascent of Shoot up Hill, the clown walks over to the driver's window of a 16 bus heading to Victoria.

"The whole land will be a burning waste of salt and sulphur — nothing planted, nothing sprouting, no vegetation growing on it. It will be like the destruction of Sodom and Gomorrah, Admah and Zeboyim, which the Lord overthrew in fierce anger."

He turns to face the traffic that has begun backing up on Maygrove Road, a side street that funnels out onto the High Road opposite the station.

"All the nations will ask: 'Why has the Lord done this to this land? Why this fierce, burning anger?' And the answer will be: 'It is because the Benedictine abandoned the calling of the Lord, the God of his ancestors, the covenant he made with him when he was still a child.'"

The clown walks across the yellow box junction where Christchurch Avenue to the west and Maygrove to the east meet the main north-south drag. Above him, a train races towards Uxbridge. To the north, a third bridge across the High Road is emblazoned with the words Metropolitan Railway, picked out in the maroon livery of the tube line.

"He took with him God's daughter from the banks of the Cunebourne Stream. And so the Lord's anger burned against this land, so that he brought on it all the curses written in his book. In furious anger and in great wrath, the Lord uprooted them and thrust them into another land."

The abbey at Westminster fills with the resonant tones of the Toccata, the organist working the pedals as well as his fingers, notes caressing the ornate tomb of the Confessor himself. Twenty miles north, the piece floats around the golden shrine of Alban as hands work masterfully across four keyboards. In the long demolished St. Paul's church on Kilburn Square, the ghost of Bonavia-Hunt throws his shoulders back, his head jerking as chords bounce off every stone. This is the clown's triumphal entry into the ever after, and he wants it on his own terms. The petrol warms him and his jeremiad over, he feels in his pocket for the matches.

A man lies unconscious on the pavement outside Nando's, plastic Tesco carrier bag flapping against his arm. Radika Modi who called 999 explaining how she saw the man collapse as two paramedics clear his airways and check for a pulse. Nothing. Modi telling them that she does not know him, but he spoke to her as he lay dying. Clearly, like it was a message.

"The eleventh hour has an eleventh hour," he told her. "That hour has a fifty ninth minute. The fifty ninth minute has a fifty ninth second. It is what you do in that second." The man gripped her hand, and was gone. One of the paramedics searches his clothes for a wallet and finds a library card. Kenneth Barnes. They dial in the information, place the body on a gurney covered in a red blanket and slide it into the back of the ambulance.

The clown takes one last look back into the horror but where before, there had been a steady two way flow of traffic passing in and out of the city, a crowd of people has gathered, pulled in by urban bush telegraph. A hundred of them, and more arriving by the minute, angling for the best view. Joining Patti are Raina Bechara, Carla Taha and the sulking Fatima. Nicolay Vidinov and the idiot Krastev. The borrower, Gbeho with banknotes in his pocket and the jacket gone. Rosalie Moraes carries a toaster that will fail to toast and Angie Boyle stares at Nina Kherkova from the vintage clothing store, wondering what would induce a woman to paint her hair blue. Ahmed Khan stands intoxicatingly close to Luca Bras Santi and his spider tattoo, and crooked May Wesley who has floated here on tramadol tap taps her crutch to the front. All of them here to watch the clown burn. O'Dwyer's boy ogles Anne Marie Bennemeier who is filming everything on her phone, oblivious to the eyes boring into her chest. In no hurry to return to Ruby Chen, John Gregg jostles for space with the DJ, Balthazar Vikkonnen and Archie Hatton who has had his lunch is now curious as to what the fuss is about. The crowd grows as people pour off buses and abandon cars. Here are the evangelists, Ashrif and Leoh, still arguing, and the singers from Kilburn Square who launch into an a cappella rendition of *Amazing Grace*.

"I come Grimalkin, paddock calls."

Harriet Gray, shopping cart filled with apples, head jerking left and right, unable to see beyond the musculature of Radovan Blaus, oblivious to the old woman behind him. Leonard Chester with a cookbook for his mother breathes the stench of stale cigarettes from John Mulligan's shoulder, the man form Antrim still waiting to be paid. Having successfully eluded the constant surveillance of his wife, Daksha Joshi talks at Kaitlyn Eastwood who is on another break, trying to find space where Joshi won't follow. On the edge of the crowd, Doreen Brown pushes her invalid son, Rudy and tries to find a way past Wasim Ali, his shift from McDonalds over but grease still in his hair, and the soles of his shoes slippery with fat. Like an audience waiting for a performance, they have gathered and keep gathering, crowds on the High Road north and south, crowds on the petrol station forecourt, crowds on Maygrove Road and Cavendish Road. The gambler, Tony Wu stands with Miriam Yahya who clutches not only a phone, but a tablet and an in-car router which she was browbeaten into buying by Ali Iqbal. Ryan, Tom and Viv Capewell stick together, not yet torn apart, Viv peering between the heads of Angeline Tousson and Mark Cadfield, arm in arm like the lovers they will never be. Viv asking if London is always this busy. The eleventh hour has an eleventh hour. Nolan Finnegan wishes he'd gone for a piss before he and Michael Whelan left the Coopers, traffic now at a standstill in every direction. No sound of horns, not even an engine. Everyone has climbed out of their cars to afford themselves a better view, and buses have emptied. There may be five hundred people now, and behind the clown, the traffic climbs Shoot Up Hill and into Cricklewood, more spectators arriving by the minute. The Red woman screams in Yoruba at Yamilé Haroun who takes pictures to show her sister in Hamburg and the clown takes a match form the box

Louche Fraser Stockman, squeezes up against Wedgy, Charlie and Ralph who have interrupted their game to join in the carry on, Stockman scanning the crowd for Thai girls. Behind them, some council workers in hi visibility jackets and three men who have pulled themselves away temporarily from the races in William Hill. Most shops in Kilburn have closed for business as there is no one to buy or eat or bet. Only Donnie Campbell remains dead to the world, dreaming of his mother crying, or a woman, he has no idea who, but he's been a disappointment to her. The eleventh hour has a fifty ninth minute. Shouts as Vasselis Diligiannis urges Kristina to push through the crowd, swearing at drunken Tommy McHenry to do one useful thing in his life and get out of his way. A crowd attracts a crowd and the clown has one, as far as the eye can see now, easily a thousand strong. Ion Williams, tag on his ankle stands side by side with Sameera Raflique, still weeping. He hands her a clean, white tissue which she takes, apologising.

"I don't know what's happening," says Alice Gould.

"No one does," Denzil Brown tells her as Malcolm Grey ushers his elderly neighbour Berenice Whalley through the sea of people, asking if they have chairs at the front. The fifty ninth minute has a fifty ninth second. Ameena Haran has freed herself from Nicole Okoro and, high on cheap booze, Candice Bryant is haranguing those around her, among them Stacey Valentine. Ranjit Singh presses a finger to his mouth which calms Bryant. Bharti Athinareyanan wants to know why everyone has stopped and Bianca Yidefonso letting her seventh call of the day from Emily Savage go to voicemail to talk to her. Sophie Simmonds carries Rosie while her errant spouse hoists Zach onto his shoulders so that he can tell them what's he can see.

"A man in a long coat. I think he's holding a match," the boy shouts. Salim and Yasmin Ormazd stand quietly, their meal finished, lost in the crowd, trying to make their way home, still not talking but her hand in his as drinkers from The Old Bell to the Ironworks pour into the road, some still carrying their glasses. Farah Alam has brought Hakan, Nihat and Birsen, and Carl Johnson holds his Staffie, Stella on his shoulder to stop her getting crushed.

Doreen Brown and her crippled son have reached the front where they stand with Patti and May Wesley. Between them, a small brown body wriggles; Hussein Hassan, cleaned up and in fresh clothes, breathless at the exertion taken to reach the front of the crowd. Around the clown a circle has been left clear. He looks around at the people who have come to watch his grand finale. There is Sheila Shaughnessy with her scratch cards next to Mehmet Güvenç who, fresh from delivering divorce to Angelica Falk, was filling up at the Shell garage when a man stepped into the road and stopped traffic. In the shadows under the bridges hovers a figure more spirit than blood and bone, a ragged, black-clad gespenst with hollow eyes and sidelocks and a sorrow that Sheila Shaughnessy feels she could reach out and touch. With bony fingers, the man scrambles up the brick pier of the bridge to assure himself a better view. Cartaphilus, still wandering, still ruing his outburst at the condemned Christ, still just a few seconds into his own eternity, now ringside for the exorcism of another accursed soul.

The clown strikes the match.

A woman screams, not the ranting of a maniac but a shrill, prolonged shout of pain. People turn from the clown to see what is happening.

"She's having a baby!"

The voice of Mercy Nwokone. The fifty ninth second. The ambulance carrying the corpse of Ken Barnes presses slowly into the rear of the human sea which parts slowly to allow it to pass. Chuck Konzauer knocks on the driver's window and space clears around a ragdoll body in a white shift dress lying on the blacktop, a small, slim mixed race girl with her belly swollen. As deft hands administer fentanyl and comforting voices offer support, the clown looks up at the commotion, the flame burning down the stick. Attempts to get the woman's name fail; either she cannot understand or cannot hear.

As the woman's body convulses, she screams a name.

"Wulfstan!"

The match drops and the infinitesimal scuff it makes as it lands is audible a millisecond before the clown roars and flames consume spilled gasoline with voracious hunger. Engulfed, he runs, tears streaming down his face, hissing as they meet the flames. People stepping away in fear and a medic throwing a blanket over him, pulling him to the ground, smothering the fire as the clown claws towards the prone body on the road. How did she know his name? He gets to his knees as burnt and blistered flesh regenerates before the astonished eyes. He stares at the woman.

"Who are you?"

But all she can do is scream with delirium as her body expels a child from her womb into the hands of a waiting paramedic. And then he sees it, nestling in the dip above her sternum, rising and falling with her breaths, a wolfstone threaded with a leather thong.

"Godwyn!"

He falls on her, her face warm against his. She grasps his head with her hands. Tears continue to fall. Deep in the shrivelled sarcophagus of his heart, dry wood buds and blooms.

In the halls of heaven, commotion. The Devil bursts angrily into the throne room whence he has been summoned.

"It is time," says the Almighty. "The sleeper awakes."

The millennium clock strikes and on the street beneath the bridge, the Virgin appears, radiant, bending over the woman who cradles her newborn with an expression of rapt love.

"Life or a thousand years?" she asks her.

A new question. Life, human life with all its filth, pain and immeasurable joy, or ten centuries in which to outlive and continue outliving.

"I choose to live."

The Virgin looks over to the clown. He feels like he is a child again back at the abbey, that everything will be taken care of, and her presence warms him.

"Do you believe, pilgrim?"

In the heavenly chamber, the Devil bites the knuckle of his forefinger and paces up and down the hall.

The Virgin's words falling like balm, sanctifying him at his journey's end. The fifty ninth second is past, the hour is nigh. Death and the fire should be his. So why the question?

In the great abbey of St. Albans, Easter Saturday tourists are struck by the energy of the organist, her hands weaving the counterpoint of the Tocata into the melody. Westminster Abbey resounding to the complex harmonies and rhythms as a man dwarfed by metal flues pulls stops, pumps pedals and introduces new voices that intertwine with the song. Bonavia-Hunt's ghost rising to the stretto, adding melody on melody, variations that sing out across the ugliness of Kilburn Square, echoing against the walls of the seventeen storey tower of dreams and the now empty market. Glory! All is glory!

The Devil curses God for his trickery, for sending an angel, and God reminds the ancient serpent that a man makes his own choices, and that he has sent many men many angels, with only scant reward. The clown takes the child in his hands. A boy. He stares at the wriggling infant with disbelief and joy. He had had a thousand years to make amends, to bless this place with kindness. Yet he treated every day with the same contempt as the day he was cursed. He had spat and sneered his way through centuries, a benighted spirit killing time, a leech that takes, adding nothing, a tick, a scab.

"A clever trick, Ba'alzebub," says God to the Devil. "Make a man feel punished and unforgiven by me, and he has no need of redemption. He can only live out his days in the despair of the damned. But I didn't curse him, did I? It is the Benedictine who punishes himself. It is the Benedictine who has never forgiven the Benedictine.

"Do you judge me, God of Heaven?" asks the Devil. "Devil is as Devil does. My tricks shall win this wager."

Redemption, even as he teetered on the edge of the abyss. The woman looks up at him.

"Þū brōhte help!" You brought help.

It's not your fault. It was never his. None of it. He loved Godwyn from the first and kept loving her. Dying, he loved her, and in the centuries that followed, it was love for her that gave his thoughts shape. She had kissed him by choice, fled the glade by choice, conceived their child by choice. Whatever was done had been done together. And as she slept, she knew he would return, and here he was. He wept as he cradled his tiny, sallow skinned child. It was the curse, not God that had condemned him. He had done nothing wrong.

"I believe," he tells the virgin. Speaking the words solidifies them, etching them onto the granite runestone of his heart.

"Life, or a thousand years."

"Life." he tells her. "I choose life!" and he laughs, an uninhibited shout of joy that expands his lungs, a heartfelt hallelujah so spontaneous and true that a demon hovering on the edge of the crowd howls as he is sucked back into the eternal void, and the Devil strides out of the throne room, slamming the golden doors behind him.

"How long was I asleep?" Godwyn asks in the old tongue. Above the shriek of a Jubilee Line train pulling away towards West Hampstead, a baby cries.

Printed in Great Britain
by Amazon

59773617R00215